# THE WOMAN FROM HEARTBREAK HOUSE

*Can she ever find happiness?*

The Great War is over and Kate O'Connor is ready to welcome back Eliot with open arms – but her husband is a changed man. Kate has become used to her independence, and to running the shoe factory, so Eliot's return creates tensions, particularly with Kate's son, Callum. It tears Kate apart to see such strife between the two men she loves most, and her sister-in-law Lucy seems determined to stir up the animosity in order to benefit her own son. When tragedy strikes, Kate cannot imagine just how much trouble Lucy's ambition can cause...

# THE WOMAN FROM HEARTBREAK HOUSE

# The Woman From Heartbreak House

*by*

Freda Lightfoot

**Magna Large Print Books**
Long Preston, North Yorkshire,
BD23 4ND, England.

British Library Cataloguing in Publication Data.

Lightfoot, Freda
    The woman from Heartbreak House.

    A catalogue record of this book is
    available from the British Library

    ISBN   0-7505-2480-4

First published in Great Britain 2005 by Hodder & Stoughton
A division of Hodder Headline

Published in Large Print 2006 by arrangement with
Hodder & Stoughton Ltd.

Magna Large Print is an imprint of Library Magna Books Ltd.

Printed and bound in Great Britain by
T.J. (International) Ltd., Cornwall, PL28 8RW

# 1919

# 1

The woman ran through the gathering crowds on to the station platform, the wind ruffling her red hair, slapping it across her face as she struggled to pin her hat in place. People stepped out of her way with a smile, seeing how flustered she was. She was not the first to appear thus on this particular morning, except that this woman seemed different from most, her slender body erect with pride, her bearing one of dignity and grace despite her anxiety.

She was regarding the train that stood puffing quietly at the platform with a mixture of outrage and defiance, as if it had no right to be there, and yet there was pain too, an agony in those soft grey eyes which made people turn away and pretend to concern themselves with the cloudy skies or a brown paper bag being blown along by the chill spring breeze.

The woman grabbed a porter. 'Is this the London train?'

'It was last time I looked.'

'When did it arrive?'

'Five minutes ago, six mebbe. The twelve-ten, running on time.'

Five minutes. Time enough for him to realise that she wasn't there waiting for him, as she had promised. Time for him to wander off looking for her, perhaps? Kate glanced about her, growing ever more frantic as the crowd thinned a little and people began to move away. Where could he be? What if he hadn't even been on the train at all? Oh, my darling, let nothing happen now to prevent our glorious reunion.

The men looking on couldn't help wishing it were them she had rushed to see with such anxiety in her lovely face, while the women envied her sense of style, and that natural beauty which meant she could still look stunning, even with no hat and her hair blowing everywhere.

She finally got the offending article in place, although the women tut-tutted when they saw that she did not possess a hat pin with which to anchor it. Consequently, mere seconds later it was knocked awry as a young soldier rushed past to gather his sweetheart tight in his arms, and they heard her cry out with despair.

Would her soldier come?

Kate Tyson stopped running and smoothed down her coat. Giving up on the hat, she tidied the rebellious red curls as best she could, pinning the mass of them back with a comb and a few hair grips, tucking a stray strand behind each ear.

Her two-piece was of blue linen with semi-raglan sleeves and a high buttoned collar. The shoes, of course, were of the finest kid leather with the latest and fashionably high Louis heels. Most of all he would notice the shoes, and hopefully her trim ankles. Kate had spent hours getting ready, so wanting to look her best.

If only Flora hadn't kicked up such a fuss at

breakfast time or Aunt Vera hadn't launched into one of her interminable lectures, she would have been on time. Now here she was, despite all her best efforts, arriving late on a draughty station platform, heart beating like a drum, sick with nerves and shaking in every limb.

Where was he? Where was he?

He would think she'd forgotten, that she hadn't come.

There wasn't even a band playing in welcome. So different from the day on which she'd first seen Eliot off to war, four long years ago. On that day there'd been a mood of celebration, certainly high optimism. The town band had played, the Mayor and his good lady handing out gifts and parcels of food to the new recruits taking the King's shilling. Almost as if the war were nothing more than a game which would soon be won and they would all be back home with their loved ones by Christmas.

But the war had dragged on and on, and too many of those bright, handsome young men never would return.

On the day he'd joined up, Kate and Eliot had been very much at odds, not having spoken to each other for some years. Yet her love for him, even then, had over-ridden all their differences and she'd been unable to resist coming to see him off.

That had been the day when she had told Eliot that Flora, her darling daughter, was indeed his, and later he'd come home on leave to make Kate his wife. Oh, she'd kicked up quite a fuss over that, had denied she needed him, but she couldn't ever deny her love for him and so they had married, a joyous day with all their friends present and Flora as bridesmaid.

Now Flora was a precocious ten year old and had thrown one of her tantrums at not being allowed to accompany her mother to the station, but Kate had been adamant. Her first meeting with Eliot after so long a separation must be private. They needed to be alone.

Bad enough that they must return to a house full of gossiping servants, not to mention his two aunts who, dear as they were, could be extremely intrusive.

And there was so much to tell him, so many details she had kept from him while he was serving King and country. Facts about the business that would now need to be revealed with great tact and care. Quite how that would be achieved, Kate had no real idea, frowning with new anxiety at the thought.

He knew that Kate's older child, Callum, was safely home again, of course, but she'd never quite explained how that had come about, deciding it was something best told in person rather than a letter. She would simply have to play it by ear, make her judgements according to his reaction to the changes that had taken place in his absence.

Kate felt a small nub of worry in the pit of her stomach when she thought of the reunion between man and boy. Eliot had always loved him as his own, but how would Callum react?

The crowds were moving away, families holding their loved one close, children carried high in their father's arms, some of them crying, not recognising this stranger who had burst into their lives.

Heart beating a little faster, Kate clenched her gloved hands tight. What would she say to her husband? Would they feel like strangers or reunited lovers? How would it feel to have him hold her again?

She momentarily closed her eyes on a rush of memory, remembering the glorious pressure of his body against hers, the warm touch of his hand, the roughness of his chin when he took her in a compelling kiss. Would she be shy like a young bride, or eager and passionate? To her shame, Kate rather thought it would be the latter.

'Step back, miss, if you please.'

All such concerns were wiped from her mind as the station porter waved his green flag, doors slammed, a whistle blew, and the next instant the train let out a great sigh and belch of steam, then slowly began to move out of the station. It was leaving, and still she hadn't found him. Kate was running alongside it, checking every window. Could Eliot still be on board, fallen asleep perhaps, or leaving again because she hadn't been here to meet him? No, no, he would never do that, surely. And then the train was gone, the platform was quite empty and she was alone.

Kate sat in the parlour at Tyson Lodge and rocked herself in misery as tears flowed unchecked down her cheeks. Lunch was over, the appetites of the two aunts, at least, not spoiled by anxiety as they had devoured several slices of bread and butter, boiled ham and tomatoes, and still he had not come. Kate had been quite unable to eat a thing. But then, this was not at all how she had planned things.

'Where is he? Why didn't he wait? Admittedly the train arrived five or six minutes before I did, but where could he have disappeared to in that short time? He can't have been on the train. Do you think he hasn't come at all? Oh, I can't bear the thought of something going wrong now, at this late stage.'

Aunt Vera frowned at Kate over her spectacles. 'Stop fretting, child. What could possibly go wrong? He probably missed that train and will be on the next. He is safe and well, be thankful for that. Our darling Eliot has survived the war and will soon be home in the bosom of his family where he belongs.'

'Do you think so?' Fresh hope began to glow inside Kate, masking her irritation that as a young matron of thirty-two she should still be addressed as if she were indeed a child. Typical of Vera's stern view of life, except that she was right in a way. Kate had been fretting for days.

But then, she'd wanted everything to be perfect for Eliot's homecoming.

Kate had been up since dawn making things ready, helping Mrs Petty their cook-housekeeper prepare food for a celebration like no other. In the last week Tyson Lodge had been turned inside out, every room scrubbed and polished and dusted, carpets beaten, vases filled with fresh flowers, everything in Eliot's study arranged just as he liked it with his favourite pen in its holder, a brand new blotter on the leather-topped desk, and the latest balance sheets from the factory waiting for him to peruse at his leisure.

Kate herself had occupied this room for much of the war and a part of her wondered how it would feel to relinquish it after all this time, to give up her managerial role at Tysons Shoes and return all decision-making to the factory's owner. Even the small business of making army boots she herself had started, successful though it undoubtedly was, had been swallowed up by Tysons during the war years, the two merged into one since that had been the best way to deal with things.

She still had a few little plans for the business buzzing at the back of her mind. Well, not so little, as a matter of fact. One in particular that she'd been toying with for some time.

Oh, but if he didn't approve, she'd give it up, and gladly. She really wouldn't object to being totally free from all responsibility. Kate could then devote her time simply to being a wife and making Eliot happy. She ached to hold him in her arms again, to love him.

Besides, she would not be alone in this change of circumstance. Since the Great War had ended, those women fortunate enough to have their menfolk returned to them – women who had worked not only in Tysons' Kendal shoe factory but had kept the local transport running, farmed the land, produced the weapons and equipment to keep their men at the front, all working at tasks women had never before tackled – must now learn to take a back seat, to be content once more with being wives and mothers.

Not that Kate had ever enjoyed such privilege in the past. Living as a young widow in Poor House Lane with a starving child to care for, she'd been grateful when Eliot Tyson and his first wife, Amelia, had offered to adopt her son Callum, even more so when they'd suggested that she should stay with him as his nursemaid.

But it had been bitter-sweet to be so close to him and no longer be recognised as his mother, and nothing had quite turned out as it should.

Later, her world had collapsed, everything turned upside-down when her small son had vanished. For most of Callum's childhood she hadn't even known whether he was alive or dead. Kate blanked out thoughts of those long painful years, as she always did. She really had no wish to remind herself of the agonies of those times.

Dragging her mind back from the past she focused instead upon the present and the question Aunt Vera was asking.

'Does she know? Is Lucy aware that Eliot arrives home today?'

'I wouldn't know.'

'Someone, one of her friends perhaps, might have mentioned it.'

'Oh, indeed,' agreed Aunt Cissie, ever her sister's echo. 'You must be prepared for her to call, Kate.'

Vera continued, 'Sooner or later, she will want to see him. He is her brother-in-law after all. If nothing else, she will wish to ensure that her allowance will continue, and may then give her version of – of events. Have you considered that?'

'I've no wish to consider Lucy today, Aunt.'

'Of course not, but I felt I should mention it –

16

warn you. She is so jealous of you, she will want to put her case. How will you cope when she does call?'

Cissie's eyes grew round with sympathy. 'Oh, my dear, yes. How will you cope?'

'I shall not receive her. Why should I?'

'Have you told Eliot yet about what she did – or rather what we believe she did? What she is alleged to have done?'

Still that faint doubt, despite everything they'd palpably suffered at Lucy Tyson's hands.

Before Kate had time to frame an answer, if indeed there was one to give, the house echoed with the rattle and clang of the front door bell.

Kate was on her feet in a second. 'There he is! He's here, I know it.'

She was running through the hall, anxious to reach the door before Ida or Mrs Petty. The bell was impatiently ringing a second time even as she flung the door open and, like a miracle, there he stood, his lovely, handsome face wreathed in smiles. Kate stepped forward, ready to fling herself into her husband's arms, and then she saw that he was not alone.

'Look who I found waiting for me at the station,' Eliot said. 'Lucy. Just as well since I must have missed you. Couldn't spot you anywhere.'

# 2

She had let him down. The reunion Kate had dreamed of for so long had all gone terribly wrong. Far more wrong than even Eliot appreciated. It was true that the minute they were alone, in their bedroom, he eagerly took her in his arms and kissed her with all the passion, all the love, she could wish for. Desire flared in her, as hot and strong as ever, but the hurt was there too, like a burr beneath the skin.

'Where did you go? Why didn't you wait?' she demanded, between kisses.

'More to the point, where were you, my darling? Did you forget I was arriving home today?'

He pulled her close and when she could catch her breath again, Kate pushed him gently away to frown at him with mock severity. 'How could I forget when I've been longing for this day for weeks ... months? What a thing to say! Haven't we been up since dawn getting ready? Mrs Petty has been cooking and baking for days. I do hope you're hungry?'

'Not terribly. Lucy insisted on buying me lunch.'

Kate's heart sank even further, if that were possible, then rallied quickly on a spurt of anger. 'And you let her, knowing we were all waiting for you at home?'

Eliot laughed, and the dark eyebrows lifted in

that mildly scolding way of his, the kind of look which firmly reminded her that he was the master here and could do as he pleased. For an instant Kate forgot that she was his beloved wife and felt as if she were still that struggling girl from Poor House Lane.

'I didn't know any such thing. The train came in and you, my dear wife, were not on the platform. Lucy explained how you'd been held up and...'

'She *what?*'

'Don't look so guilty, Kate. I forgive you.'

''Tis not guilt I feel, 'tis fury at her lies! Didn't I miss you by no more than a few minutes? The porter told me the train had only just arrived.'

Her soft Irish brogue surfaced as it did when Kate was annoyed and he smiled, enjoying this show of temper as he always had. She'd slipped from his embrace and her stance now was one of pride and obstinate defiance, which he knew well. 'Let me look at you, Kate. Dear heaven, I swear you are lovelier than ever, despite the storm brewing in those lovely grey eyes of yours.'

'And haven't I every right to be cross, with you wandering off for no reason at all?'

He chuckled, drawing her to him so he could savour the scent of her: lemon verbena shampoo, the tang of soap, and that special something which was uniquely Kate. 'I remember you looking every bit as truculent and defiant the very first day I saw you, when you were ready to take me to task for allowing my foreman to sack your rapscallion of a brother. I swear I was overawed by your beauty even then: by the set of that small

19

square chin, the way your nostrils flared with temper, those lovely eyebrows winging defiantly upwards. Ready to take on the world and do battle. I swear you made me tremble.'

'I did no such thing.' She could feel herself softening beneath his charm, the tug of a smile at the corners of her mouth.

'No need to make excuses, my darling. I know how hard you have worked, how overwhelming it must have been for you, taking care of everything. You are safely relieved of all that worry now. I am home again, so what does it matter if you were too busy to come and collect me?'

'Sure and it matters to me. I'll not have Lucy say what isn't true. I didn't forget and I wasn't at all *too busy!* She's just looking for any excuse to stir up trouble between us.'

'Nonsense! Why would she do such a thing? Lucy was only being kind.'

'She was not being kind, she...' But the look in Eliot's eye silenced her, made her bite her lip and not embark on her tale, not just now, not like this. Hadn't he only this very minute arrived home, and here they were quarrelling already? And if Lucy's actions had caused their quarrel, then hadn't she succeeded in her malice? Kate gave a small choking sob and fell into his arms. 'This isn't how I planned it. I so desperately wanted our reunion to be perfect, to be joyous.'

He stroked a damp tendril of hair from her hot cheek. 'And it is, my love. It is. I'm here, aren't I? We're together at last.'

She lifted her face for his kiss. Oh, why hadn't she told him the whole story from the start? It had seemed impossible at the time, cruel almost, to bother him with domestic issues while he was away fighting a war, when he might be killed at any minute and not in a position to do anything about the problems at home.

Now that dreadful woman threatened to rob Kate of happiness yet again.

And Eliot looked so desperately tired. His sensitive mouth seemed to have thinned with deep grooves marking each corner. The hawk-like nose was even more pronounced and the once fine bone structure more drawn, skin yellowed and pale. Was it any wonder after what he'd been through? He was thinner, and looked much older than the day he'd gone off to war. Kate had noticed that he moved with a stiffness to his gait, favouring one leg. She'd made no comment upon this, hoping he would tell her of the injury that had caused it when he was good and ready. His hands might be calloused and scarred but they touched her cheek with the same tenderness as before, the velvet brown eyes resting on her with love, and Kate was well content.

'There is so much we need to talk about, so much I have to tell you.'

'And I you. That I love you still. That we have all the time in the world now, my darling, to be together. Don't be cross with me for not waiting. Or with Lucy for booking us lunch at the County. I believed that you'd encountered some problem at the works. And it was a very hasty luncheon, I didn't even pause to partake of a dessert, or coffee, though Lucy urged me to have one or the other. Then she drove me swiftly home

21

in her fine motor, her latest acquisition no doubt. Apparently business is booming, which is good to hear. But never mind all of that now. I will gladly forgive you everything, if only you'll let me kiss you again, and again, and again.'

He began to suit actions to his words and how could she remain cross when he was kissing her face, her eyes, her throat, unbuttoning the high neck of her jacket, seeking the tender warmth of her breasts?

'Let me warm myself on your radiance. Kate, I have missed you so.'

Kate bit back the bitter disappointment, dampened her anger over Lucy's lies and machinations, and allowed herself to be swept away by a different sort or storm altogether.

Later, as they lay naked together in the big wide bed, content and happy, Eliot softly stroking her hair, she told him everything. The day Callum had apparently vanished off the face of the earth; one moment playing on the lawns, the next gone from their lives, would live forever in both their hearts. And they each suffered from the guilty knowledge that at the precise moment of his disappearance, they were paying him no attention at all but rather engaged in one of their spats.

If passion characterised their love affair, it had also blighted it in other ways. They had always disagreed on all manner of topics, not least politics and the manner in which Eliot ran the business.

But then Kate had never been the kind of woman to surrender her independence, or subjugate her own opinion to any man's. On the day that Callum disappeared she'd been standing her corner for the sake of a friend, Millie, who was being badly abused by Ned Swainson, Eliot's crooked foreman. Kate's antipathy to the man had a long history dating from the time he'd tried it on with her, and sacked her brother. Knowing this, Eliot had been inclined to believe that she was exaggerating in her account of his foreman's vicious behaviour. This had enraged Kate, and during the heated argument that followed, her son apparently wandered out of the garden and disappeared.

Following the terrible discovery that Callum had vanished, without anyone seeing him go, Kate had almost lost her reason. She'd searched for her son for years, her heart breaking from her need to find him.

Now she was able to reveal exactly what had taken place; the whole sorry story. Kate gently and calmly explained to Eliot that Lucy, his sister-in-law, was the one responsible. She'd taken revenge over the suicide of her wastrel husband, Charlie, blaming Eliot entirely for his untimely death because he'd adopted Kate's son, a child from Poor House Lane, thereby disinheriting his own family as a result. And she'd done it in the most cruel way: by abducting the boy.

'She muddied his smart new clothes and slapped him, labelled him with a new name, Allan, like enough to his own to confuse a distressed five year old child. Then she took him to the Union Workhouse on Kendal Green, and from there he was moved to the Brocklebank's farm out on the Langdales. The couple were not kindly disposed towards him, since he was but an orphan farm boy, in their eyes. Callum suffered badly at their hands.'

Eliot listened to all of this with increasing horror. 'I find this hard to believe. Absolutely incredible!'

'Nevertheless it is true.'

'How can you be certain? Has she confessed?'

'Of course not. I learned of it from Callum himself. All those years I spent searching for him, and on one occasion, unbeknown to me, I came so close to finding him. He was apparently helping Mrs Brocklebank on Kendal market and while I was busy buying from another stall, Flora began to chat with him, offered him some of her barley sugar. I scolded her for talking to strangers. But I didn't know! I didn't know it was Callum. I saw a woman berating a young boy as we moved away, but I didn't get a clear view of him. Oh, if only I had.'

'Kate, my darling, how a dreadful for you.'

'It tears me apart to think of it even now, to have been so close and not to have realised. Imagine what he had to endure: made to live in the barn with the animals, fed on scraps from their table, forced to work all hours and be shown not an ounce of love or pity. How can I live with that knowledge? It fills me with pain, with unendurable guilt.'

Eliot put his arms about her and held her tight as she quietly wept. 'We will not think any more of this matter right now. We will simply be glad that our boy is returned to us. I cannot wait to meet him, so don't you think, my darling, that it is time we rose and faced the world?'

She lifted her face to his one more time, still wet with tears, and he was so moved by the sight of her that he must love her all over again.

He ran a bath, peeled off his clothes and climbed in with her. There were angry purple scars on his right leg and he lowered himself into the water with care, but since he made no remark upon them, neither did she. He soaped her back, her breasts, teasing and tickling her. Kate wriggled forward to sit astride his lap, arching her back in sheer ecstasy as she rode him, but then remembered the injured leg.

'Oh, I must take care, I don't want to hurt you.'

'Don't worry, you aren't, and I need you so badly, Kate.'

'Is that all right?'

'It is bliss.'

Yet insufficient for his urgent needs so he lifted her bodily from the rapidly cooling water, laid her down on the bathroom rug and took her with the kind of force that left them both gasping.

It was late-afternoon when they finally emerged into the sitting room where the family were assembled, Kate quite flushed about the cheeks, Eliot looking remarkably pleased with himself.

The aunts were seated side by side on the sofa, for once not in their customary black but dressed in their best navy-blue chenille, to celebrate the occasion. Flora looked remarkably demure in a new white organza dress, though was sitting on the edge of her seat as if it were a huge effort for her to remain still.

25

With some relief, Kate noted that Lucy had at least shown the good sense not to enter the house, for all she'd clearly been anxious to see Eliot on his first day home. But then she hadn't been allowed to set foot in Tyson Lodge since the day Kate had turned her out of the family home and had publicly humiliated her before the servants.

However, as Aunt Vera had warned, Lucy might well attempt to return now, hell-bent on trouble, making Kate regret the mercy she'd shown on that fateful day by not reporting her sister-in-law to the police for abducting a child.

Not that she would allow Lucy to spoil this red-letter day for one moment longer. This was the day Kate had dreamed of for so long. Even as Eliot kissed each aunt on the cheek and hugged and kissed his daughter, remarking on how much she'd grown and how pretty she was, making Flora giggle with pleasure, his gaze was rivetted upon Callum, his adopted son and Kate's own first-born.

Kate's heart swelled with pride just to look at Callum.

Wasn't he a fine young man? He was tall for his sixteen years, well-made and strong and, in her eyes at least, remarkably handsome. The unruly thatch of hair was less fiery than her own, but its redness marked him as her son. His eyes were an enchanting blue-grey, slightly narrowed in that brooding way he had, and the mouth still tremulous and sulky as a child's. He reminded her very much of her own brother Dermot, which she hoped and prayed didn't bode ill.

He was leaning against one corner of the mantelpiece, seeming to indicate that he was on the fringes of this little group, this family, and really wished to play no part in it. She itched to tell him to take his hands out of his pockets and greet his father with better manners, but she held her tongue. This wasn't the moment for maternal nagging.

Eliot strode right over to him and grasped him by the shoulders, giving him a hearty hug and several paternal slaps on the back. 'Callum, I can't tell you how it warms my heart to see you, son! What good fortune that we are both returned home again, safe and well.'

There was a short silence during which Callum did indeed pull his hands from his pockets and stand erect, but only to move away from Eliot. When he spoke, his voice was soft, a chilling whisper. 'I am not your son, and never will be.'

# 3

Only Kate was privy to the flash of hurt that crossed her husband's face. 'Callum, don't say such a thing!' she chided him. 'Of course you are his son. Didn't Eliot and Amelia, your late mama, adopt you as a baby?'

Callum kept his gaze steady on Eliot for a full half-minute before redirecting it to Kate. 'You always told me, Mother, that *my* father drowned in the River Kent during a flood.'

'Well, to be sure that is so, but...'

'And having lived most of me life on a remote farm in the Langdales as little more than an unpaid slave, why would I see this man as me dad? I don't know him. He's nobbut a stranger to me. Some bit of paper dun't turn a person into a father.'

Kate was horrified. She heard the aunts give a collective gasp and even Flora's excited chatter was stilled. This reunion seemed destined to go wrong. 'Callum, that's a terrible thing to say. Take it back now, this minute.'

'No, no, the boy has a point,' Eliot conceded. 'He's right. Being accepted as a parent is more than just a legal process. Sadly, due to circumstances beyond our control, we have indeed turned into strangers. But it was not always so and I hope to rectify the situation, with effect from now. I am certainly eager to do my part. I hope you feel the same, son?'

'Me name's Callum.'

Another short silence during which Kate could tell Eliot was struggling to quell a burst of irritation. 'Very well, as I say, I've taken your point. I trust we can at least be friends?' He held out his hand and only when it became obvious that Callum was not about to take it, did he let it fall again to his side. Eliot quickly adopted a brisk manner. 'Right, time to sample this feast which Mrs Petty and her stalwart band have taken such trouble to prepare. Shall we go through to the dining room?'

Flora bounced to his side. 'May I go in with you, Papa?'

'Most certainly, my sweet. I shall take great pleasure in escorting so charming a daughter.' And he proffered his arm for the giggling child to take.

Smiling with relief, Kate turned to Callum, expecting him to do the same for her, but he simply strode past her, his stubborn chin held high, and she was forced to enter the dining room alone.

Nothing was ever easy with Callum. From the day she'd found him standing on the doorstep two years ago, his attitude had been steadfastly obstructive. Kate was disappointed, although she tried to make allowances. But it was immensely frustrating at times.

At fourteen he'd been at that awkward stage of adolescent self-consciousness where he could see nobody's point of view but his own. He'd felt betrayed, neglected, abandoned by his own mother, seeing himself as someone nobody cared for. And Kate didn't blame him for feeling that way.

She'd agreed to let him be adopted by Eliot Tyson and his wife when he'd been barely fifteen months old because she'd feared her child might otherwise die of one of the myriad diseases easily contracted in Poor House Lane, if starvation didn't get him first. She'd had no choice. Nor had she been so proud as not to see the advantages it would bring him. This way her Callum would grow up a gentleman with a good education and fine manners.

Except things hadn't turned out that way at all.

As a result of Lucy's abduction of him Callum had been brought up as a farm-hand. Since his return home, Kate was desperate to make up to him for all that he had lost.

She'd provided him with security in terms of an apprenticeship at Tysons' factory, had done what she could to improve his education. She'd also tactfully attempted to teach him good manners: how to say 'please' and 'thank you', and to use a knife and fork properly. She'd striven to dampen down the Westmorland accent he'd acquired on the farm, so that he wouldn't feel quite so awkward in company. Was it a crime for her to want her son to enjoy the finer things of life?

Oh, but even if she never succeeded in rubbing off the rough corners, didn't she love the bones of him? Nothing else mattered but that he was home safe and well, with her. He was her boy. Although she couldn't help wishing that it had never happened. If only he hadn't gone missing that day, how different life would have been.

*If only* ... two words that had haunted her for years.

If only she'd taken better care of him, paid more attention to her own child and less to the problems of others. If only she hadn't left him making daisy chains on the lawn while she ran after Eliot simply to win yet another argument.

If only she hadn't assumed, when she'd realised he was gone, that Eliot had taken him.

If only she'd searched harder ... ignoring the fact that she'd been obsessed with searching for him, had tirelessly scoured the town for weeks, months, years in the end, making herself ill in the

30

process. If she'd seen a child in the street who bore the vaguest resemblance to him, Kate's heart would race and she'd follow him until, realising her error, she would quietly weep.

Worst of all, if only she'd recognised him that day at the market, had remonstrated with the farmer's wife when she'd seen her berating the boy, instead of thinking it was none of her business.

If only she could turn back the clock and make everything come right.

If only!

But she could do none of these things. She could only accept how things were now and learn to live with them. Her heart sang with joy to have Eliot home. Yet seeing her husband attempt to embrace his adopted son, whom he'd loved as his own, and be so rebuffed, filled Kate with sorrow and a deep foreboding.

Kate took the first opportunity to suggest to Callum that he must be patient. 'Time will gradually resolve this sense of strangeness between the two of you. Eliot does care about you, very much.'

The boy said nothing, merely stared at her in sulky silence as he so often did.

He might be difficult, yet he was her son and she loved him. 'I ask only that you think how strange this must all be for Eliot too, after all he has been through these last years. Give him a chance to settle.'

'And what about me? What about what I've been through?'

'I know, m'cushla. I understand. Trust me, it

31

will all work out in the end. We need to allow ourselves time to get to know each other again, that's all.'

'I dun't want to get to know Lucy again, thanks all t'same.'

'No, no, of course you don't, me darlin'. 'Tis unthinkable!'

And there was another *if only*. If only Kate had called the constabulary when she'd learned of her sister-in-law's despicable crime. Instead Kate had turned her out of the house, thinking that would be shame enough for her snobbish sister-in-law. She hadn't felt it was her place to call in the police. The aunts would have hated a family scandal, and Eliot wasn't around to make the decision for her.

Where Lucy had lived since then, Kate neither knew nor greatly cared, though from snippets of conversation she'd overheard between the aunts, she rather thought Lucy was now occupying their old home in Heversham. Whatever she'd been doing, wherever she'd been these last two years, now she was back, interfering in all their lives as she so loved to do.

Kate could only hope that Lucy no longer had vengeance on her mind.

Now she smiled at Callum. 'I won't ask anything of you that is unreasonable, but I'm trusting you to be man enough to forget the past, to put it behind you and make a fresh start. All right?'

The boy said nothing, merely put his hands in his pockets and slunk away.

'I've had a word with him, so I have,' Kate

informed Eliot. 'Give him a little time and he'll come round. Isn't he feeling just a bit shy and awkward?'

'He was downright rude, Kate. He shouldn't be allowed to get away with such ill manners.'

'No, no, but he's that sorry. He'll be fine, you'll see. You both need time, to be sure, these things can't be rushed.'

Kate insisted that Eliot rest and recuperate, that he do nothing, that even the business be left to its own devices for a while until he felt fully recovered and ready to take up the reins again.

'And how will it survive meanwhile, may I ask?'

'Toby will look after it, though I'll pop in each morning for an hour or two, while you are sleeping.'

'Toby?'

'Toby Lynch, my foreman, if you remember? Since our two businesses merged, he's been vital to the smooth running of the entire company. I simply couldn't manage without him. He was instrumental in helping me deal with the unions just a year or two back: making a new agreement for a fifty-hour week and one week's paid holiday a year. Oh, and that we pay time and a half for overtime.'

'Whose side is he on?'

Kate laughed. 'Ours, of course. A happy work-force makes for full production. With the war over, there's general concern that there might be a slump, now that orders for army boots have dried up. We do need to talk about the factory, Eliot, but not yet. First you must rest and get properly fit and well.'

Kate was already turning over plans in her mind for how to counteract this downturn. She was keen to concentrate on the women's market, to produce more stylish shoes, as well as keeping up with the usual riding boots, working boots and classic gentlemen's lines.

Once Eliot was fully recovered from his trauma, she would enjoy discussing these ideas with him. Perhaps a part of her hoped that she wouldn't be entirely put out to grass. She still felt that she had much to contribute, that they could work together as a good team.

Kate enjoyed looking after her husband, fussing over him endlessly, bringing him cushions and cups of tea, and insisting Mrs Petty make all his favourite dishes. She bought him a walking stick too, which he absolutely refused to use.

'I can walk perfectly well.'

'Indeed you cannot! Don't be stubborn, Eliot, I can see how that leg pains you. The stick will help until you get your strength back.'

She put it in the rack by the front door but he never used it and when she remonstrated with him again, telling him he was hobbling like an old man and shouldn't be so damned proud, Eliot snapped at her that he was not an invalid.

And indeed he certainly didn't act like one. He had survived in one piece, at least, was still reasonably young and fit, and evidently still virile.

They were like young lovers again, hardly able to keep apart, constantly touching, sharing secret smiles, casting sidelong glances of agony at each other as the clock on the mantelpiece ticked slowly by, aching to sneak off to bed early but not daring to do so.

Once alone, clothes would be discarded with alacrity, buttons snapped, ribbons torn in their anxiety to touch flesh to flesh. Sometimes Eliot couldn't even wait for her to undress, or to reach the great bed they shared, pulling her into his arms the moment the bedroom door closed, pushing up her skirts and consuming her with his mouth, his body, his great need of her. He would take her up against the door, making it bang and rattle and the brass handle prod her back as he thrust into her. Whatever the servants would think, Kate dare not imagine.

But what better way to deal with the nightmares which seemed to haunt him night after night?

Afterwards they would lie entwined in the big soft bed, sated, replete until morning, and then on waking he would pull her to him while she was still half asleep and wake her with fresh loving. Kate would open herself to him gladly, take him within her. Simply to feel the warm weight of his body upon hers was utter bliss. And when the moment of climax came, she'd throw back her arms, gripping the bed-head in her ecstasy, wrap her legs about his waist as if she were a wanton and move with him in an instinctive rhythm, needing to give him all of her love and more. Afterwards, she would weep softly in his arms, overcome by emotion, quite unable to move or think.

# 4

Eliot wasn't certain whether he was awake or asleep, alive or dead. The dream was so real but then so was the pain, which meant he must still be alive, mustn't it? He'd been thinking of the boy, of his first encounter with his adopted son after all these years, wondering why he didn't feel more disappointed by his rejection, or any rush of thwarted parental love. Did he have any emotion left in him at all, or had it all run dry?

None of this seemed real. Nothing. Not this house, not his family or the business, not even Kate at times. Oh, yes, Kate must surely be a dream, a sweet and lovely mirage. Otherwise, where had she come from? How could she be here?

He was lying in the straw, smelling the unmistakable stink of pigs, mingled with the scent of his own blood, and cordite, wondering where he was and if he really was alive.

Everything had happened so quickly. They'd stopped to rest by an old church, foolishly thinking it might be a safe spot, but destruction had come on them right out of the blue, out of the blue heavens in fact, dropping like hell-fire on earth, blasting open a crater big enough to lose half an army in, or so it seemed. Certainly more than half of Eliot's men.

'Get down, keep your heads down!' He remembered that much, shouting to them, warning them. He must have done, because everybody did go down, some of them never to come up again.

What was left of his troop must have brought him here, probably because the sty had seemed the warmest, safest place to spend the night. He wasn't sure that the ripe odour didn't outweigh these benefits, but beggars couldn't be choosers. They'd slept in barns, cow sheds, beneath hedges, any place they could lay their heads.

And wherever he was, in some make-shift billet or his dugout, his rabbit hole as he called it, he would dream of Kate's lovely face. He'd conjure it into his mind and feast on it, until the pain of thinking about her became too great to bear.

The pain in his leg was worse. It felt as if some wild animal had sunk its fangs into it and was gnawing it off. He could see the festering sore, view it with a curious detachment, aware that the loss of blood was already great and that it showed no sign of stopping. He couldn't allow this to happen. He had to get up and take care of his men. Yet something was pressing him down. He couldn't move, was beginning to feel oddly detached and light-headed, the hole where a long shard of bone poked through seeming to grow larger by the second. Someone had ripped open his trouser leg, or had the shell done that?

There was a tourniquet of sorts; bandages stuffed into the hole. Neither seemed to be very effective as the wound was a mess of black and scarlet, of mud and blood, covered with flies half the time. Had he severed an artery? Was this how death felt: this aching tiredness, this desperate, dark chill?

'Where's the bleeding cavalry when you need it?' The voice came out of the darkness, from someone huddled shivering beside him. It was a good question.

'What a place to end yer days,' said another, 'in a sodding pig sty.'

'Aye, but at least we have a roof over our heads. They'll find us soon.'

'Pigs might fly,' came the droll response to this piece of optimism.

'If tha does see any flying pigs, mate, it'll be me, beggaring off up to heaven,' said another.

'Well, we're at least handy for a few bacon butties.'

Eliot had often noticed that the men were at their most flippant and jovial when their backs were against the wall, as now. They'd even named their gun pit Sandbag Villa, situated in Whizz-Bang Lane. Their sense of humour, black though it may be, helped to sustain them. He felt nothing but sympathy and admiration for the fortitude and courage of his men. They were filled with optimism, quite certain they would be the victors in the end. Morale was high, and it was partly his job, of course, to keep it that way.

He wished he felt half their courage, one fraction of their faith in the future. Instead he felt certain he was failing them. For some reason he was filled with fear, a cold crawling terror stealing away the last of his strength. He knew he mustn't fall asleep, that would be fatal. Somehow he must struggle to keep his eyes open, his mind centred.

He had to get them out of here but they were

still being heavily shelled, pinned down, unable to move, trapped like flies under a jar.

A great weight was pressing down on him. Was it the enemy? Were they being attacked again? Eliot tried to push the sensation away, to rise and fight back, shouting at his men to *'Move, move, move!'* He woke on a scream, with Kate ashen-faced beside him.

If life with Callum was difficult, Eliot proved to present greater problems for Kate. But then how could she expect him simply to settle back into domestic bliss after such a terrible war?

He seemed to find it difficult to concentrate, and showed not the slightest interest in the factory, or in his painting which had once so absorbed him. He would either sit in morose silence for hour upon hour or else be frenetically dashing about, insisting she leave whatever she was doing and they go out for a ride, or a walk, or to visit old friends. At once, this minute. He couldn't seem to keep still for a moment, even though, more often than not, his actions showed no real sense of purpose.

She tried to get him interested in his beloved garden, but he seemed to have lost all his old passion for that too.

'Do you remember planting these trees, saying how they would be here for our son, long after we were dust?'

Eliot gazed upon them as if they meant nothing at all to him.

Even the rose garden, where he'd loved to walk and kiss her under the arbour, didn't inspire him now. Where once he had known the name of every rose and never could pass one by without snipping off a dead head or drawing in the scent of its glory, now he seemed oblivious to their charms.

Kate had employed a young lad to assist Eliot in what she hoped would be a rejuvenation of both himself and his precious garden, but whenever Tom asked Eliot what he wanted him to do, her husband would mumble something then walk away in the middle of a sentence. It was all very worrying.

Kate couldn't begin to imagine what he had been through, what horrors he'd seen.

When he woke from one of his regular nightmares she would stroke his head, the tight hardness of his belly, and he would turn to her, taking her fiercely as if to banish the devils that haunted him.

He never spoke of the horrors, though she begged him to do so, hoping it might help to purge his mind in some way. He spoke only of practical matters, of their routine. And if he felt the need to talk, she would hold him in her arms, keep silent and listen, as now.

'We worked in groups of three – one to stand guard, one to clean up the trench while the third took a nap. We maybe got one hour's sleep out of three. Standing on the fire-step was the worst, watching and waiting, seeing nothing but the occasional flare, hearing only the odd explosion. It was the most boring job in the world, taxing the nerves to the limits, for if you let down your guard for a moment, it could be your last. You needed to be quick to spot whatever the enemy was throwing at you, so you could make a speedy evacuation of the trench if necessary. Besides which, falling asleep on duty was a crime for which a soldier could be shot.'

'Jesus, Mary and Joseph, *shot?* Simply for falling asleep?'

'War isn't a game, Kate. Men could die as a result of such negligence.'

Not that Eliot would allow that to happen to any of his own men. He'd been tough, but always made certain that those under his command were suitably camouflaged from aerial observation as German planes came over, often just when they were about to go to the battery to eat so that their dinners would be cold and unpalatable by the time the raid was over.

'Will Callum ever forgive me for losing him?' he asked.

'You didn't lose him, he was stolen. It wasn't our fault. He will see that in the end. He's just a boy. Give him time. He doesn't understand.'

'I had boys under my command. Almost as young as Callum is now, far too young to be facing what they were forced to endure, day after day. Yet they did their duty, usually without complaint. Will he ever accept me as a father, Kate, will he?'

'I'm sure he will, if we're patient.'

'Who was that boy we were talking to this morning?'

'That was Tom, the new gardener.'

'Why isn't he in the army?'

'The war is over, Eliot. Tom has been spared from joining up.'

41

'I prefer Askew. When is Askew coming back? He isn't retired is he? He said he never would retire, loved the garden too much.'

'Askew is dead, my darling. You remember he died right at the beginning of the war?'

'Did he? I forget. Could we have salmon for tea today? I love salmon.'

This was how his conversations went, darting from one subject to the next with neither rhyme nor reason.

He drew her closer to him, a slight smile curving his mouth into a softer line. 'Mealtimes were the only thing we had to look forward to, apart from the delivery of the post when I'd look for your letters. For breakfast we'd get an ounce of cold ham with maybe three-quarters of a cup of lukewarm tea. A bit of bread if we were lucky. Otherwise there were biscuits. Hard and tasteless though they might be, they were still welcome, particularly with a little cheese, even if it had probably gone mouldy. And we got any amount of jam. I'm quite sure that the war was won on jam butties and bully beef.'

And he laughed then, as if it were all some sort of joke, and Kate laughed with him. It was either that, or cry.

One of their favourite walks that summer was over Scout Scar, a soft Lakeland breeze taking the heat out of the beautiful June days. Rock roses grew in the crevices amongst the limestone and Kate could detect the sweet scents of lily-of-the-valley, saxifrage and columbine.

On this particular afternoon Eliot laid her

gently down in the long grass between the juniper bushes, making love to her as if she were a maid and he a mere boy. Crazy with love, oblivious of their middle-class, middle-aged, respectable station in life, they giggled at their daring, dozed and kissed, then loved again.

The auld grey town of Kendal was spread out in the valley below them, their town, their kingdom, and they felt as free as the clean Lakeland air buffeting their naked bodies, free to enjoy life and the glorious prospect of a brand new tomorrow.

'Have you thought about the future?' she asked, when she could draw breath. 'I have so many ideas I'd like to share with you, when you're ready.'

He smiled at her fondly, caressing the silk of her skin, her wayward, abundant hair. 'You wouldn't be my Kate, if you didn't have something to say on the subject.'

'It might make you feel better to start thinking about the future, stop you looking back into the past quite so much. Might even help to prevent the nightmares if you had something new and positive to think about, and plan for.'

'I will, I will. When the time is right, I shall at least agree to listen.'

But she couldn't wait for some unforeseen time in the future. Kate was bursting with impatience, needing to talk about it now, wanting to hasten his recovery and believing work was the answer, as it had been for her when at her lowest. 'I thought I might like to open a shop.'

'A shop?' Eliot looked startled, laughed, as if

she had said something amusing. 'What sort of shop, dearest?'

'A shoe shop, of course, what else? Don't you think that would be a grand idea? It would be stocked exclusively with Tysons' shoes, naturally. I would specialise in ladies' shoes, at least to begin with, and children's perhaps. Different styles and fittings. Lots to choose from. It would be bright and clean and very fashionable. A place a lady could feel comfortable in, not one of these dull, dusty shops nobody wants to go into.'

Her husband lay back with a sigh and closed his eyes, was silent for so long that Kate began to wonder if he had fallen asleep. In that moment, while she waited impatiently for his response, she realised how desperately important it was to her for him to agree, for Eliot to be as excited by the idea as she was. But perhaps she shouldn't have mentioned it quite yet. Perhaps that had been a mistake. It was too soon. She should have waited a while longer.

He sat up suddenly and looked about him, rubbing his eyes as if he really had been asleep. 'Time we were going, I expect. Mrs Petty will shoot us if we are late for lunch.' He got to his feet, holding out his hand to help her up. But Kate hesitated, had to persist. She simply couldn't keep quiet.

'And the shop?'

'What?'

'The shoe shop. Do you think it's a good idea?'

Frowning slightly, he looked bemused for a moment and then his brow cleared and he laughed again. 'Oh, that. I've told you, not yet, my darling. I can't put my mind to business matters just yet.'

'But we must do something, now that we no longer have the orders for army boots.'

'Later, my dear. Much, much later. Stop worrying about it. Right now I simply want to look at you, to know that I exist, that I'm free to enjoy you, enjoy life.'

And enjoy her he did. Eliot took her whenever and wherever he wished. In the stables when he was harnessing the horses ready to ride out in the carriage and young Tom could have walked in at any moment. On the kitchen table one night when she went down to get herself a glass of milk; in the summer house over afternoon tea; another time in the rose garden. And when the aunts came innocently upon them, Kate was mightily flustered to be found with her hair like a bird's nest, her bodice unfastened and the familiar tell-tale flush upon her apple cheeks. Not that the two maiden ladies gave any indication that they had noticed her disarray, they were far too well-mannered.

For all her concern over her husband's health, those first weeks of his homecoming were idyllic, so very precious.

So it came as a shock to Kate when, one morning some weeks later, their citadel of happiness came tumbling down.

# 5

From the moment of his safe return, Kate had been at pains to include Callum in absolutely every part of her life. He had missed out on so much through his childhood years, on all the opportunities she had wanted for him, but Kate was determined that his future at least would be secure and bright. Anxious for him to have a trade at his fingertips, she'd apprenticed him to one of Tysons' most skilled shoemakers, and he was doing well. Callum was methodical and painstaking, his fingers agile and supple, his strong shoulders able to bear the physically demanding job.

While living and working outdoors on the farm in the Langdales for most of his youth, he'd had little or no education and one day had confessed to his mother that he could not read. Kate had vowed to teach him, assuring him that it wasn't too late to learn. Callum was sensitive on the subject, feeling deep shame over this inadequacy on his part, and the lessons were carried out behind closed doors in the study, in private, never openly referred to in front of the family.

He had proved to be bright and intelligent, and even though he came to book learning relatively late in life, was making good progress. But finding books simple enough for him to read while still being suitable for a sixteen-year-old boy was well nigh impossible. Kate had settled on classic adventure tales for him, which he loved: *Arabian Nights, The Tales of King Arthur* perhaps, or *Around the World in Eighty Days.* These interludes of reading aloud became their favourite time of the day as it gave each the chance to get to know the other a little better. Every evening after Kate had watched and corrected as her son painstakingly spelled out words or did a few sums to practise his arithmetic, she would then read a little from a favourite book, Callum following the words along with her.

They were thus engaged one evening when Eliot walked in upon them. Kate had believed him to be taking a nap before dinner, and was startled by the sudden interruption. Callum leaped to his feet, his cheeks growing scarlet as if he were guilty of some crime.

Eliot frowned, then marching over, picked up the book and gave a snort of derision. 'What's this? *Robinson Crusoe?* Good Lord, not still needing your mother to read to you, boy, before you go to bed? Do you suck a dummy too?'

Kate, appalled by his insensitivity, was on her feet in a second, her hand reaching out to snatch the book from his grasp. 'Eliot! That is dreadfully unkind. Cannot mother and son enjoy a few quiet moments together? Isn't this the only chance we get to be together in a busy day?'

That too was a mistake. Her husband glowered. 'If you are implying that I'm not pulling my weight, then perhaps you're right. It clearly is time I did some useful work. As should this boy of yours, by the looks of it, if he still clings to his mother's apron strings. My boys didn't have stories read to them at bedtime – they lay listening to whizz-bangs, thinking they might have their heads blown off at any minute.'

'That's hardly my fault, sir,' Callum said, his face now white as parchment.

'Indeed not, but your freedom to read these pretty yarns is largely due to their sacrifice. Think on that.'

Without another word, the boy walked from the room.

Kate ran after him. 'Callum, don't go!' But he paid no attention and she knew instinctively, in that moment, that he would never come near the study for lessons again. It felt as if all her hard work to make up to her son for the years of neglect had been thrown back in her face. She was furious.

The moment the door closed she turned on Eliot. 'Why did you have to be so damned high-handed? Can't you see I'm trying to help him, to give him some of the education he missed? And you march in here like some commanding officer inspecting his troops and bark orders at him. How dare you! Do you not realise the courage it took for him to admit to me that he couldn't read, and wasn't he doing grand?'

Eliot was taken aback by her vehement attack and had the grace to look a little sheepish. 'I meant no harm. I didn't think ... didn't realise.'

'Then you *should* think. You should consider other people occasionally. Callum may not have suffered the war as your "boys" did, but nor has he enjoyed a stable, safe childhood with loving parents and a good education. Doesn't he at least deserve some of that now? Thanks to your vindictive sister-in-law, he was denied the opportunity.'

Quite unexpectedly, Eliot dismissed her comment with a casual shake of the head, 'I'm sorry, Kate, but I can give no credence to this tale of Callum's so-called abduction.'

She looked at him in astonishment. 'Are you saying that I'm making it all up, that I'm lying? Or perhaps that Callum is?' Kate appreciated that Eliot was deeply hurt by the boy's obstructive attitude, but not this. Not for one moment had she expected him to disbelieve her.

'I'm saying that a resentful adolescent is not a reliable source of evidence. Maybe he's always been lazy, didn't want to learn, and is now taking advantage of your soft heart, your sense of maternal guilt, to wheedle his way back in and have an easy life.'

'*What?* It hasn't been at all easy for him living here. And isn't the boy desperate to learn, thirsty for knowledge and information? He's making good progress. Or at least he was, until you barged in playing the sergeant-major.'

Eliot ignored her, unused to having his will challenged, his mind for once entirely focused on his argument. 'Was anyone else witness to this heinous act Lucy purportedly carried out?'

'Of course not, how could there be any witness? She did it in secret, cleverly covering up her tracks, but she most definitely *did* do it. She abducted my child!'

'Our child. You will keep forgetting the small matter of the adoption.'

49

'Don't split hairs, Eliot. Lucy *stole* him.'

'And you know this for certain because Callum says so?'

Kate was stunned by his disbelieving attitude. 'Yes, I do. 'Tis so. 'Tis the truth!'

He patted her shoulder, as if she were some foolish little woman who needed things explaining properly. 'I can well understand my darling how upset you must have been when he told this tale, but I ask you to consider what proof do you actually have? None. Only the word of a mixed-up boy who feels a natural resentment against the parents who allowed him to wander off and get lost. Any child would in the circumstances. In consequence, he has been allowed to stand as judge and jury against his own aunt. No wonder Lucy feels a deep resentment over being cast out from the family and her home.'

'*Lucy* feels resentment? She told you that, did she?'

'She did, over lunch at the County, the day of my return, She is at a loss to understand your behaviour. Her feelings have been deeply hurt, her life well-nigh ruined.'

'*Her* life has been ruined!' Kate felt her knees go all weak and wobbly, a sick feeling lodge itself in her stomach. She longed to sink into a chair but somehow remained standing rigid before him, determined to prove her case. 'And what about my feelings? And Callum's life? Who ruined that? *Lucy!*'

'So you say. Or rather, so Callum says.'

'And you'd take her word against mine?'

'I might well take her word against a vindictive

adolescent's. The matter needs to be carefully investigated before I can properly decide.'

'Investigated?'

Instinctively Kate had known that Eliot would see no wrong in his sister-in-law, or that he would forgive her if he did. Didn't he always see the best in people? He was far too soft-hearted for his own good. He'd been exactly the same over that conniving foreman, Swainson. He was the most incredibly stubborn, obstinately fair-minded man.

Concern about his reaction had been behind her decision not to call in the police the day she'd discovered the truth, knowing that Eliot would do anything, believe anything, rather than disturb the smooth running of his life, or face a family scandal.

Yet he *must* face the truth. She couldn't have him implying that her son was a liar.

'What about Flora, is she a liar too? The day Callum returned home, Lucy had promised to pick her up from school, but Flora says that her aunt wasn't there waiting for her as she usually was. Lucy arrived late and scolded Flora because she wasn't standing by the school gate. The child was going frantic, so she was, looking everywhere for her aunt. Then, Flora says, Lucy seemed to lose control and began to beat her about the head, slapped and punched her and left her for dead up an alley. Sure and Flora might well have died had not Callum found her and brought her home, black with bruises and covered in mud. Lucy had done that to her.'

'Did she say so? Did Lucy admit to having

beaten the child?'

'No, of course she didn't!'

'Did Flora say her aunt had done this heinous thing?'

'Yes, I'm telling you, so I am. She did.'

'And Flora came home with Callum? Quite out of the blue, our long-lost son turned up at this opportune moment?'

Kate hesitated fractionally before answering this question, her temper cooling a little. 'Y-yes, Callum found her lying unconscious in the alleyway.'

'What a remarkable coincidence.'

'Not so. Callum was attending Kendal market that day with Mrs Brocklebank, and sneaked off to walk by the river. He recognised this house and knocked on the door. Apparently Ida caught a glimpse of him when she was in the hall, though she hadn't the first idea who he was. Lucy sent him packing, which she would do, of course. She'd recognised him instantly, and no doubt took out her fury on Flora.'

'How do you know Callum wasn't the perpetrator of this crime, that *he* wasn't the one to beat up Flora?'

'Utter rubbish! He doesn't have it in him to beat anyone up. He's a very gentle boy.'

'You are his mother, you'd be bound to think so.'

'And why would he do such a thing?'

'Out of jealousy because Flora was still at home being petted and loved, and he, the outsider, was lost and forgotten.'

Kate could feel all the blood draining from her

face, from every limb, despite her heart pumping like a mad thing. 'That's not true. Callum adores Flora. To be sure he'd never hurt her, and they met once before remember, at the market.'

'When he learned who she was, and started to plan his revenge.'

'No, that's not the way of it at all. Flora told me it wasn't the first time Lucy had hurt her.'

'She'd be bound to say that, wouldn't she?' Eliot scoffed.

'Why would she? Why would she protect Callum? Flora was systematically abused over a long period, and I was too damned busy with the factory and with me own army boots business even to notice. How do you think that makes me feel?'

'Perhaps it was merely Flora's way of getting your attention?'

Kate stared at him, speechless for a long moment, quite unable to believe they were even having this argument. 'If you don't believe me, why don't you ask her?'

'I certainly will ask her. We'll get this matter cleared up once and for all, see what Flora and Callum have to say for themselves. But Lucy too should be allowed the chance to speak up on her own behalf. That is only fair and just.'

'For goodness' sake, Eliot, you're talking as if you were about to hold a court martial. These are your children we are speaking of here.'

'Nevertheless, we will conduct this investigation with all due propriety, honour and integrity. Lucy must be given the opportunity to put her case.'

# 6

Eliot chose to conduct the investigation with everyone present, as if they were young soldiers being called to account in front of their commanding officer. Callum and Flora looking distinctly nervous; the aunts sat huddled close together against the tapestry cushions, their faces mirroring their bemusement and dismay.

Today they wore their usual black. Cissie had removed her dog-scented cardigan in honour of the occasion. Vera still wore a fichu of lace at her throat, though it had been considered outmoded even before the war. Aunt Vera's short cropped hair was more of a muddy grey these days than the rich brown it used to be, if every bit as neat and tidy. Cissie, sadly, had never been tidy in her life.

It was all unspeakably awful. Kate strongly protested against it, hating the notion of seeing her children put under such close scrutiny before an audience, let alone the very idea of having to entertain Lucy in her own front parlour. She told Eliot as much.

'This is not the right way to tackle such a sensitive issue. Please, speak to each child alone first. In complete privacy.'

'We must not only be fair, but be seen to be fair.'

'This is not a court martial, Eliot.'

54

'I am aware of that. Nonetheless, justice must be seen to be done.'

'These are our children, not some of your men. This isn't the war.'

In some ways Eliot had almost enjoyed the war, relishing the company of his men. And then a bomb had destroyed most of the little church in which they were hiding, burying so many of them in stone and soil. He could remember seeing the ground pitted with holes. He was in one of them, grinding sand between his teeth, desperately fighting for air as he clawed his way to the surface. Some of the men were running, their cries of fear vying with the scream of heavy shelling all around. He'd got up to run with them but found he couldn't.

Yet he'd been thankful still to have his leg, for all he knew that it was broken. Had it not been for the quick thinking of his sergeant, who'd dragged him away from the strafing, the rest of him would have been riddled with bullets too.

He would never forget the horror of that moment. Dead men lying all around like rag dolls, one young face staring right at him, eyes wide open, sightless.

Moments before they'd been joking together, the boy planning how he would propose to his girlfriend, how many sons they might have. Now there was no response from the would-be bridegroom. Another soldier had risen on one knee, as if he'd just been about to get up and leave, but hadn't quite made it.

They buried them later, all of those fine young men. Eliot remembered propping himself against a tree, grating out a few words from some prayer or other through a dry throat, choking with the dust and ash of death, of destruction.

But one had run away, had deserted. He'd been brought back, of course, and dealt with as all cowards are. Put in front of a firing squad. Eliot himself had given the order with not a scrap of pity in his heart. How could there be?

He turned to Kate, trying to make her understand. 'You may have heard their side of the story, but I have not. I need to hear it from their own lips before I can judge its credibility. Whether they are heroes or lying cowards. And it is long past time to allow Lucy also to put her case.'

'Heroes or...? Eliot, I...'

'Enough. Ask Lucy to come in, Aunt Vera, if you please.'

And so she came, flouncing into the house from which she'd been banned with a smile of pure triumph on her beautiful face, violet eyes sparkling as if she'd already won a victory. As indeed she had, simply by being invited over the threshold.

Kate was forced ruefully to admit that her sister-in-law still looked marvellous despite her more matronly appearance these days, her plump breasts straining against the burgundy silk of her gown which was a work of art in itself with all its draped layers, tucks, pleats and folds. The colour set off the glossy jet of her hair, swept up beneath the silliest of hats which bore the tallest possible feather. Even her parasol was much frilled and beribboned. Not for Lucy the current fashion for simplicity and clean lines, although how she found

56

the money to be so elegantly gowned and so immaculately coiffured, Kate could not imagine.

Ever since she'd been widowed when her husband Charles had taken his own life because of insurmountable debts, she'd been supported by his brother Eliot and Tysons Shoes. Kate herself had been responsible for ensuring Lucy's very generous allowance was punctiliously paid each and every month while Eliot was away at war. It was meant to permit her to live in comfort, covering necessities such as rent, food and general living expenses. But it surely did not run to the kind of elegant clothes Lucy chose to wear, nor to keeping the French maid she insisted on having.

Kate didn't care to think what debts her sister-in-law had already acquired, or who would be responsible for paying them off.

She said nothing now as Lucy settled herself in the wing-backed chair set between the two sofas. She was almost purring with self-satisfaction, smiling at everyone around her with the kind of serenity that spoke of supreme confidence in her own feminine ability to manipulate a situation to her advantage. Lucy certainly did not give the impression of a woman shamed, a woman with something to fear. Kate felt chilled to the bone just watching her.

'This is so lovely, being home again,' she simpered. 'Though I'm not quite sure what the occasion is, or why I've been summoned.'

Kate bit back the comment which sprang instantly to her lips, that Tyson Lodge was no longer Lucy's home. But how could she say such a thing now that the master himself had returned and was the one who'd invited Lucy here? Kate glanced up into Eliot's face, carefully shuttered and inscrutable, and then across at her son.

Callum had adopted his favourite position, propped against the mantelpiece. Flora was seated on the corner of the sofa nearest to him, her fingers nervously pleating the fabric of her frock.

Neither so much as glanced in Lucy's direction and Kate's heart went out to them both. Something inside her seemed to swell with outrage at seeing her own children so cowed, so swamped in misery.

Eliot cleared his throat, looking very much the commanding officer about to issue a damning indictment upon his troops. But his eyes, Kate noticed, did not appear to be entirely focused, as if his thoughts were elsewhere.

They were indeed fixed somewhere in the past. He'd seen such dreadful things: limbs blown off, holes punched into his men. When would the sick feeling leave his belly? When did one grow accustomed to senseless slaughter? He doubted one ever did.

No wonder his boys had sometimes lost heart, but cowards had to be winkled out and dealt with. There was no room in a war for lead-swingers and liars, for those incapable of taking responsibility for their own actions, their own failures.

He had always taken his own responsibilities seriously, very seriously indeed, for the sake of the well-being and safety of the entire company. And, as it was in the army, so it would be in civilian life. The same standards must apply.

'We'll deal with Callum last. Flora, come here,

my child.'

Without having planned to do so, Kate found she was on her feet. 'This outrage has gone on long enough! Sure and you cannot expect my children to speak freely while Lucy is present. It's intolerable. An abomination. Utterly unfair, so it is.'

Eliot came and put a hand on her shoulder and gently pushed her back down in her seat. 'Maternal hysteria will assist no one, Kate. Let us all remain calm, shall we? I'm sure this whole business is no more than a trivial misunderstanding which can easily be cleared up.'

'Trivial misunderstanding? I don't believe what I'm hearing, why, I...'

'Kate, please. Do attempt to remain calm in front of the children.'

And Kate was forced to subside, as if she were the guilty party.

Flora was staring up at her father in startled dismay. She had Kate's fair complexion, lightly freckled, but Eliot's gloriously dark, chestnut brown eyes to match her dark brown, wavy hair. From the moment of her birth, the fuzz of dark curls and intelligent dark eyes had undeniably marked her out as a Tyson. No milk-sop baby blue for her. A pert chin and snub nose now showed her as a beauty in the making for all her schoolgirl, leggy awkwardness. Flora got up from her seat and stepped forward in answer to his summons and stood before Eliot, her gaze fixed on the toes of her shiny buttoned shoes.

'Tell me truthfully, Flora. Did your aunt here,

59

who apparently cared for you while your mother was working hard running both businesses because. I was away at the war, ever do anything deliberately to hurt you? Come, you can speak freely. Tell me the truth.'

Flora cast a quick, sideways glance across at her mother and Kate was up again in a flash, aching to rush to her side. Only the condemning light in Eliot's eyes and Aunt Vera's hand on her elbow persuaded her to sit down again. Nevertheless, she persisted in making her point. 'How can she speak the truth with Lucy sitting there?'

'Please do not interrupt again, Kate, or I will have to ask you to leave the room. This tribunal – er – investigation must be conducted fairly and properly.'

He could still hear the sounds of gunfire and bombing popping and cracking in his head, the sound of men screaming for their mothers. He could name every shell. Besides the whizz-bangs, so-called for obvious reasons, there were sling bombs; hand grenades; trench mortars – the most deadly of all; even oil cans filled with high explosives and any rubbish the enemy could pack into them. The entire area had been pitted with dugouts linked together by the infamous trenches, running with water and infested with vermin, so that your feet rotted where you stood, assuming the rats didn't gnaw your toes off first.

This house, this genteel life his womenfolk had led in it while he was away dealing with all of that, even Callum's bare existence in the farm in the Langdales, was paradise by comparison.

'Flora has nothing to fear. I am her papa and

will take good care of her. I am a man of honour and integrity, and expect any child of mine to be likewise. It is required of every Tyson, bred in us from birth.'

Kate felt herself shrink, knowing she came from no such grand family, that honour was something she and Dermot had never even considered, survival being everything to them.

'Now speak up, child. Has your aunt Lucy ever lifted a finger to hurt you? No, no, do not look at your mama, look at me. Tell me truly. Has she?'

Flora heard the rustle of her aunt's dress, could smell the over-powering perfume she wore which brought back so many painful childhood memories: nightmares even. Of being pinched on her tummy and smacked very hard on her bottom, of being made to march backwards and forwards with her arms raised, of being left out in the rain, forced to eat eggs which she hated and made her ill.

She'd tried once to explain her misery to Kate but her mother either hadn't understood or didn't believe her, telling her to be a brave little soldier, that they all had to do their bit. Adults never believed a word you said. Only Callum had ever truly understood, but then he had good reason.

The silence seemed to go on interminably, and then it was broken. By Lucy herself.

'Of course she will say that I smacked her. All children need discipline from time to time, and she was subject to the most dreadful tantrums. Kate spoiled her, you see, out of guilt for leaving the child to her own devices while she took on

61

your role, Eliot. Understandable perhaps, for the situation was extremely difficult, as you will appreciate.'

She sounded so reasonable, so calm. Kate could feel herself start to shake, itched to run to Flora and gather her darling child in her arms, but Eliot's hand was once again firmly pressing down upon her shoulder.

'I appreciate how difficult it must have been for you, Lucy. Indeed, we all suffered in our various ways, some more than others. Well now, Flora. Is this true? Did you have tantrums? Answer me now.'

Tears were rolling down Flora's cheeks. It was as if she were back there in her room and Aunt Lucy was telling her to get dressed, or undressed, or make up her bed, and the buttons wouldn't work in her small chubby fingers, or the sheets kept slipping off the bed, and every time she failed to obey an instruction, a ringing slap would strike her. The same words she heard so often then seemed to echo in her mind now.

*'You are so very naughty, no wonder your mammy neglects you and doesn't love you any more. You are going to have to learn better manners, or nobody will love you ever again.'*

Flora whimpered even now at the memory. 'No,' she mumbled, her voice barely above a whisper.

'What did you say, child?' Eliot persisted. 'Speak up so that we can all hear you.'

'No. She didn't touch me.'

'There you are,' said Lucy with great satisfaction. 'Didn't I tell you!'

# 7

The remainder of the investigation seemed very much a foregone conclusion. Callum was treated to a similar grilling to Flora, called upon to explain himself and present evidence of his claim against his aunt. Of course, the poor boy had none, other than a young child's sketchy recollections.

Lucy wept a good deal, sighing and dabbing at her eyes with a lace-trimmed handkerchief, throwing agonised looks at Eliot in an overt plea for sympathy. It was, Kate had to admit, a skilled and polished performance.

'So you have no real evidence. Neither the Brocklebanks nor the Union Workhouse can name the person who brought you to them that day?'

'No,' Callum mumbled.

'It could quite easily have been some right-thinking person who found you, a small boy of five at the time, wandering alone in the streets.'

'It was Lucy.'

'You *think* it was Lucy, but you have no real proof that it was. Isn't that correct?'

Silence.

'It could very easily have been another lady, who was simply trying to be kind.'

Callum's face was tight with anger. 'It were her.'

'You were known throughout that period as Allan?'

'Aye.'

'But if Lucy herself had taken you, why would she give the wrong name?'

'To cover her tracks. And she beat me, just as she did Flora.'

'We have already heard from Flora herself that Lucy never touched her. I put it to you that you told Flora to accuse her aunt of causing the bruises that day, to deflect the real blame from yourself.'

'That's not true!'

'Tell me, boy, why exactly did your aunt abduct you and apparently put you in the Union workhouse? For what purpose? What did she have to gain by such a cruel act?'

At this point, Kate felt unable to keep quiet any longer. 'I think I can explain. She did it out of revenge. Callum had usurped the place of her own children in your affections, robbed them of their inheritance as she saw it.'

For a second Eliot appeared discomfited and confused, a frown creasing his brow as he attempted to sift through the fog of his memory. Had he disinherited Lucy's children? He really didn't think so. But when had he last adjusted his will? Was it after Callum went missing, or before? It was all so long ago he couldn't remember. So much had happened since.

His leg was throbbing from standing on it for so long this morning and he longed to sit down and relax. He'd take a glass or two of whisky perhaps with his lunch, to numb the pain.

Pain. It was a small price to pay for his life.

The Medical Corps must have come to stretcher him out, risking their own lives in the process, for he'd found himself in a hospital ward. At least, he'd thought that's what it was. It turned out to be a clearing station for the wounded, little more than a huge tent, eerily dark and as close to hell as you could get without actually going there.

He brought himself back to the present with a jerk and glared at the boy in front of him, for a moment struggling to put a name to him, to remind himself of the object of this enquiry.

Ah, yes, lies and possible cowardice. The boy was blaming Lucy for his own childish foolishness, and naturally Kate was supporting him, looking for any motive Lucy might have, however unlikely. This was beginning to sound more and more like a tale in a penny dreadful.

The odour of death had been everywhere, that sickly sweet stink of rotting flesh, not quite disguised with an overlay of carbolic soap. There were sobs and moans and sounds of crying all around him; the injured being carried back and forth on stretchers, some with red tags on their feet, labelling them as not worth trying to save.

'Eliot?'

Kate's voice was coming through the mists of memory. Eliot mentally shook himself. He focused upon her lovely face with difficulty.

'I might have disapproved of Lucy's predilection for over-spending but I've always made a point of providing for her and her children ever since my brother died. And she was well aware that I would continue to do so, although obviously the factory would go to Callum, my adopted son, in the fullness of time. Lucy was aware of that too. Were you not, sister-in-law?'

'Of course, who else?' Lucy replied, with saccharine sweetness.

Eliot rubbed his leg, tried to ease it into a more comfortable position.

They'd needed to operate on it right away, to save it. Just before he began, the doctor had told him that he'd run out of anaesthetic. The agony of those long, pain-wracked hours on the operating table would be carved forever in Eliot's mind, although it probably didn't take anything like that long. He was one of dozens dealt with that day.

'Isn't the truth of the matter, Callum, that it was all some sort of silly prank, childish naughtiness that went wrong? You ran away because no one was paying you any attention that day, and in the way of all children who get lost, you blamed us, your parents, for losing you, and worse, for not finding you.'

'No.'

'Now you've latched on to Lucy here as a convenient scapegoat, because if she had carried out this heinous crime, we again would have to share some part of the blame because we never noticed her involvement. In fact, you'd rather anyone took the blame for those missing years than yourself. You are simply a cowardly boy, an adolescent filled with resentment, isn't that the truth of it?'

'*No!*' Callum almost shouted his reply this time.

By some stroke of good fortune, or medical skill, Eliot had managed to avoid infection and lived to tell the tale. But he would never forget the screams of those who didn't survive, the blinded men begging for water, the horrific burns, the missing limbs and the disfigurement of his comrades. No room in that tent for cowards. This boy didn't know how lucky he was to have escaped all of that.

Eliot had made up his mind.

Lucy was exonerated and was to be allowed to move back into Tyson Lodge.

Flora hid away in her room, refusing absolutely to come downstairs and welcome her aunt, no matter how much Eliot might exhort her to do so. Callum too was noticeable by his absence.

The little girl was distraught, sobbing that her darling papa did not believe a word she'd said. Kate cuddled and reassured her, trying to explain how her papa was not quite himself; that later, when he'd had time to consider the matter more closely, he would surely change his mind.

He certainly would if Kate had anything to do with it.

Not for one moment would she risk allowing that woman anywhere near her children in future. 'He'll come round to believing you, sweetie, I promise.'

'But it'll be too late then, won't it, Mammy? Lucy will already be here.' Flora's big brown eyes gazed at her in deep distress and Kate's heart clenched. How was she going to fully protect her child?

'Sure and she'll not lay a finger on you, not with Daddy and Mammy both here. She wouldn't dare. You're quite safe, my angel, don't you fret. Now why don't we put some rags in your hair, then you'll have ringlets in the morning? Make you look even prettier, shall we, my darling?'

But Flora shook her head, not in the mood to be pacified by such blandishments. It took some time, and at least two stories being read to her from her favourite *Hans Christian Andersen Storybook*, before Flora settled for the night.

Concerned that the outcome of this uncalled-for investigation would only make Callum's resentment against his father worse, Kate hurried along to her son's room. Finding it empty, she frantically searched the entire house and gardens, finally locating him in the summer house at the furthest end beyond the rose garden. It was the sound of sobbing which alerted her, some moments before she reached him. Kate hung back, hoping it would cease, not wishing to embarrass her proud, sixteen-year-old boy.

When the sound had eased to quiet sniffles, she called out his name. 'Callum, is that you? Are you there, m'darlin'?' By the time she reached him, he appeared quite composed, his dignity intact.

Kate put her arms about her son and hugged him tight. 'Wasn't that the most dreadful thing? You mustn't blame your papa too much, m'cushla. Hasn't he had a worse time in the army than we'll ever know or appreciate? I'll talk to him, so I will. Make him understand.'

'He never will.' Callum carefully extricated

himself from her embrace, embarrassed by this display of affection.

'He will so, given time. Not everything can be solved in the blink of an eye, not in this world. We need patience to be sure. Won't Lucy condemn herself, given time? No, no, don't look alarmed, I don't mean I'll let her harm either one of you, ever again. I mean, simply by her own difficult, selfish behaviour. Won't he soon remember how very mean and manipulative she can be? We only have to watch and wait, and he'll soon come to see the truth, mark my words. Now will ye walk yer mam back to the house and I'll make us both a mug of hot cocoa?'

'I'm not a child, Mother, to be mollified by such treats.'

Kate looked at her over-serious son with deep love reflected in her gaze. 'Don't I know it? And wasn't I robbed of all those precious years, just as you were robbed of your childhood? We can never get that time back but we must make sure that the future remains bright. We must make very sure of that.'

Kate couldn't bear even to consider how such a decision might affect Callum and Flora. From now on, for the rest of her life perhaps, she would have to be vigilant in protecting them.

Lucy came the very next morning, rolling up in her new motor which was piled high with her personal treasures, pictures, vases, *objets d'art* and a fine set of Moroccan leather luggage, not forgetting the French maid, just as if she owned the place.

69

Mrs Petty, the cook-housekeeper, was heard to remark to Ida that it was as if they'd been struck by a hurricane, and the entire household had got caught up in the blast.

'I've niver stopped since first light. That one could make a donkey run.'

Ida, who had never risen much beyond skivvy in all the twenty years she'd worked at Tyson Lodge, nodded in agreement that she likewise hadn't sat down all day either. Even so, she scurried about the kitchen, tidying things away, slicing bread, pork and pickle for Mrs Petty's late lunch, pouring boiling water into a bowl with a measure of cold, well laced with mustard which Mrs Petty swore was a sure cure for her bunions.

'Hurry up, Ida, me poor feet are fair killing me. By heck, but we've seen it all in this house. Such comings and goings we've had.' With a deep sigh of relief she sank her feet into the near-scalding water, tucking up her skirts to reveal a pair of fat knees encased in pale pink Directoire knickers.

'From the day Kate O'Connor arrived in her mucky boots and handed over that starving brat of hers for adoption, everything has been out of kilter in this household. And poor Madam, poor sweet Amelia, dying like that, thinking she was having a child of her own at last, when really she was suffering from a terrible tumour! Since her death we've had the abduction, the aunts descending upon us like a pair of meddling old crows, an illegitimate daughter, and the shock of the master marrying the nursemaid, our lovely Kate as she now is: the girl from Poor House Lane as she then was. Lord save us, what a pantomime!'

'Don't forget the war an' all,' said Ida, wanting to add her own two pennyworth to this litany of disaster.

'Yer right, lass. Even the bleeding Hun had to stick his oar in. What we've suffered! Hurry up with that cuppa, I'm fair clemmed. And I'll have a piece of that shortbread an' all.'

'Right, Mrs Petty. And a slice of the fruit loaf to go with it?'

'Aye, just to keep it company, why not? Lunch and tea all rolled into one. And what next, I ask you? Where will it all end up? In tears, mark my words.'

Having finally satisfied the demands of her superior, Ida settled herself at the table with her own stacked plate. The good food she'd always enjoyed at Tyson Lodge had fattened her up, and she was no longer the skinny wench she'd been when taken in as a girl by the first Mrs Tyson, picked from the workhouse out of charity. And hadn't that been a red letter day! Ida had never stopped counting her blessings since, even if there'd been far too much work for her to do since Fanny the housemaid had upped and gone to work for Kate, the new Mrs Tyson, making army boots. Fanny was married now and expecting her third, while Ida herself was still here in this kitchen, waiting on everyone hand, foot and finger, in particular Mrs Petty's feet, or saving her legs from walking up and down stairs.

Still, all in all, Ida really felt very content. And she and Mrs Petty did enjoy a good moan together about *them upstairs*. Made life more entertaining, like.

Ida took a huge bite of her fruit loaf and began to talk, spitting a few crumbs as she did so. 'Madam Lucy wanted to know why Mr Tyson hadn't got round to having a second bathroom installed, and sez how a hip bath is *so Victorian! Oi really do hexpect to 'ave hot water at the turn of a tap, Eliot dear.'* Ida attempted to put on a posh voice, mimicking Lucy with wicked accuracy and Mrs Petty gave a merry chortle, making her several chins shake and producing a loud burp from her over-stuffed stomach.

'Eeh, lass, you'll be the death of me with your intimations. But don't talk with your mouth full, it's rude. If I've told you once... Well, I do hope *you* told her that we've better things to do in this house than run up and down stairs with jugs of hot water for the likes of her?'

Ida, who would never dream of saying such a thing to a lady, even one she didn't like, and had simply bobbed a curtsy and scurried away, agreed that she had said exactly that.

'Quite right too. We'll make that madam rue the day she ever set foot in this house again, let alone made the young master out to be a liar. And we have our ways and means, don't we, Ida?'

'Yes, Mrs Petty.'

'Indeed we do. Indeed we do.'

# 8

This decision drove a wedge between Eliot and Kate. No more frolicking in the bath or tumbling in the hay. She lay on her side of the bed in frozen silence, and he on his.

She tried to be understanding, to reason with herself that he had only been trying to be fair. Kate rather thought he'd chosen to believe Lucy rather than Callum because he was already wracked with guilt over his brother Charles's suicide. Eliot had no wish to make a bad situation even worse. Far easier to sweep the matter under the carpet, in true Tyson fashion, and dismiss past events as an unfortunate childish prank gone wrong.

And on top of all that guilt, Kate was well aware that her husband must still be suffering from the trauma of his war years, so how could she condemn the action he'd taken? He simply wasn't up to making a sound judgement. His soft heart, his great desire for peace and a quiet life, would be bound to affect him, particularly in the light of Callum's continued resentment.

She would have to work on that particular problem, somehow persuade her son to accept the situation, and Eliot as his father. He must learn to put the past behind him.

And she must also work on Eliot. Kate still felt strongly that he'd made a bad mistake and felt

73

duty bound, for the sake of her beloved children, to make him understand that. After a few nights of obstinate silence, and days spent circling each other, avoiding the topic, the situation became unendurable and Kate could bear it no longer. She had to speak.

'You didn't believe him.'

'I've no wish to discuss the matter. The case is closed.'

'It is not a case. This is my son, *our* son, we are talking about here, and you absolutely refuse to believe him.'

'Callum failed to prove his case.'

'But he should be innocent until proven guilty, not the reverse. You made him out to be a liar, and Flora too.'

'They are children, perhaps not properly understanding the consequences of their sulks and petty actions. You've spoiled them, though who can blame you, in the circumstances?'

''T'was not pettiness, and how can you spoil children by loving them? I believe what they say. Had you seen Flora that day...'

'That's enough, Kate. The subject is closed. I've heard all sides of the argument and made my decision. Like it or not, Lucy is family. I'm surprised you didn't inform me of this situation years ago, when it all first blew up.'

'I thought you had enough to worry about, with the war an' all, and then your injuries. How could I?'

He looked at her properly then, recognising the sincerity in her soft grey eyes, and remained thoughtful for some moments. 'I can see you

74

might think that. Perhaps you were right, my dear. We will say no more on that score, but now I am home again and the matter has been dealt with, settled once and for all.'

He seemed so cold, so distant. Fear gripped her heart. She couldn't stand to lose him. It didn't bear thinking about. Perhaps she shouldn't push the matter too hard, not at first. It was too soon. She'd need to soften him up slowly, little by little.

Kate wriggled closer to her husband and tentatively stroked his arm. 'And are we still friends? You've been so indifferent towards me these last few days.'

He turned to her then with something of his old eagerness. 'Of course we are still friends. Don't I love you with all my heart? You are my beloved wife and I adore you. Our children will survive and grow out of their sulks and their adolescent moods. Trust me. It's a storm in a teacup. And you and Lucy will learn to get along. Give it a month or two and you'll be like sisters, as Lucy told me you once were.'

'Lucy said we were like *sisters?*'

'She did, both doing your bit for the war effort. So doesn't that prove that I'm right?'

The urge to say that Lucy had barely lifted a finger to justify her existence during the war, demanding to be waited on by Kate as if she were still a servant and not her new sister-in-law, that she was the one who *lied*, was almost overwhelming. Yet Kate hesitated. Where was the point in arguing further? Lucy had won, for now at least.

Besides, any further discussion was halted as Eliot began to kiss her, peeling her nightgown from her shoulders, and Kate was so relieved, so delighted that all was well between them again, that further protests and argument were set aside. There would be time enough later, when Eliot was feeling more himself.

Everywhere that Kate went she seemed to hear Lucy's strident voice calling out for Ida, or Mrs Petty, to bring her a tray of tea to the parlour, hot water to her room, a pill for a headache, or to sponge and press a gown. And if they didn't immediately answer her call, she would throw a veritable tantrum and shriek at the top of her voice, demanding to know if there was anyone in the house at all.

*'Is anyone listening to me!'*

Not if I can help it, Kate would think, making a point of hurrying out of sight as quickly as possible. Lucy was frequently in a foul mood because she didn't believe she was receiving the kind of attention she deserved.

'If she *had* got what she deserved, she certainly wouldn't be living like a queen in this house,' Mrs Petty tartly remarked on more than one occasion. Kate always pretended that she hadn't heard.

The French maid had lasted no more than a few days, departing in a huff because she was not allowed to take her meals with the family and thought it beneath her to eat in the kitchen. Not that Kate blamed the poor girl entirely. Mrs Petty was not particularly welcoming, and didn't Kate know how that felt? She had somehow survived her own baptism of fire, which hadn't been easy, involving being sent to Coventry for a number of weeks when she'd first arrived in Mrs Petty's kitchen. But she'd won the cook round in the end.

This poor girl had been less fortunate. There'd been something of a scene the very first day she arrived with Mrs Petty making rather rude remarks about frogs, and Ida doing a good deal of giggling behind her hand over the fancy frocks and furbelows the French maid insisted on wearing. But Ida's laughter had soon turned to sulks when she realised that Madame Celeste, as she liked to be called, expected to be waited on as much as her mistress.

'Nay, I'll not do it. I'll not. 'Oo does she think she is? I told her, ma'am, I did. I'm not paid to wait on the likes of her,' Ida informed Kate, outrage sharp in her voice.

Kate hid a smile. 'I rather think the master would say that you are paid to do whatever he tells you to, and this girl is employed by him and requires feeding.'

'Aye, fair enough,' agreed Mrs Petty, weighing in on Ida's behalf. 'But that doesn't mean she can't fetch her own hot water or clean her own shoes, do it?'

'Er, no,' Kate conceded. 'Perhaps not. But I'd be obliged if you would at least try to get along, for all our sakes. 'Tisn't going to be easy getting used to the changes around here.'

She hadn't needed to spell it out that she meant getting used to having Lucy around, and a chastened Mrs Petty and Ida both promised to do their level best.

Evidently their best wasn't good enough as the girl left by the end of the first week. The rather superior French maid had made too many demands and, sadly, her fate had been sealed from the start as Mrs Petty did not suffer fools gladly. When Celeste began to criticise her cooking, something previously unheard of, and had insisted that her lamb be cooked rare, not till it was falling off the bone as Mrs Petty liked to do it, she'd been presented with a plateful that was almost raw and stone cold. Celeste had duly taken offence and left.

Lucy was not pleased, and even less so when Eliot refused to replace her, very sensibly pointing out that if Kate could manage without a personal maid, so could she.

It was July before Eliot casually remarked he was ready to return to work. The roses were almost in bloom and Kate had hoped that he would be content to wander in the garden and nurture them into full flower, but it was not to be.

'First thing on Monday morning I intend to go into the office. I am well on the road to recovery, for all my knee still pains me occasionally. It's well past time I got my nose back to the grindstone and took my proper place in charge of Tysons Shoes ... or Tysons Industries as it has now become. You can stay in bed and spoil yourself for a change, my darling.'

'I'd rather come in to the office as usual. I'm in the middle of several matters which require my attention. Customers are depending on me.'

Kate felt some guilt over the way she'd neglected

78

the business in these weeks since Eliot came home. She really should be working on the new designs for the line of ladies' shoes she was planning. Women were now demanding lighter shoes in more fashionable styles, and she and Toby were investigating ways of changing the method of manufacture in order to make this possible.

Toby Lynch had first started working for Kate when she was out on the road, selling her army boots. He was a wiry man in his mid-thirties, of medium height with a tousle of blonde hair and a cheery grin. He'd had plenty of experience in the shoe trade and Kate both liked and trusted him. Since he'd never once let her down, she'd had no hesitation in making him the new foreman of Tysons Industries after Swainson left.

Yet she hadn't missed going in once. Every morning she would slip in for an hour or two, if only to check on progress, to talk things through and reassure herself that all was well. Toby constantly told her to stop worrying and enjoy this precious time with her husband. But Eliot was right. It was time for him to get back to work. It might help him to start looking to the future instead of back into the past.

'I will come in with you. It will give me the chance to explain everything we currently have in hand, since it's your first day.'

'Absolutely not. I forbid it. I can manage perfectly well.'

'But...'

'I will hear no buts.'

Kate adopted her most coaxing tone, using the lilt of her accent and all her feminine whiles to beguile him. 'Will you stop yer blathering and let me do this? Haven't I said that we need to talk, and don't I still need to have a role? I'm not ready to be put out to grass yet awhile. We'd make a good team.'

'Of course we're a team, and your role is clear and straightforward. You are my wife. No, no, my darling, you have done enough. It is my turn to take care of everything now. You can safely leave everything to me from now on.'

Stubbornly, Kate persisted. 'I shall come in later in the morning, then. I haven't had the chance to properly explain my ideas, my plans for the future. I'll do it then, so I will, when you've had time to get yer bearings.'

Eliot laughed softly, as if humouring her, yet absolutely refused to shift his ground. 'We will discuss them later, over dinner one evening. I will be obeyed in this, Kate, I do not want you at the factory on this day, not on any account.'

And Kate was compelled to let her arguments subside, thinking that perhaps it was fair enough that he be allowed to proceed alone, on his very first day back. Toby would be there to show him the ropes, in any case. And Eliot was still the master after all, perhaps needing to prove that fact, to reassert his authority with the workforce after his long absence. There would be time enough later for discussions and plans.

Eliot left, as promised, shortly after seven but Kate couldn't stay in bed, not for another minute. She was too used to rising early and going into the office. She quickly dressed, took some breakfast, then went about her domestic duties, of which there were few since Mrs Petty ran the establishment with such efficiency.

Kate attempted not to think of Lucy triumphantly ensconced in her room upstairs, although she was acutely aware of her presence by the toing and froing of Ida with jugs of hot water and breakfast on a tray. She'd also seen evidence of clothes taken to be pressed and ironed, shoes polished.

Some new house rules would have to be applied. Lucy needed it pointing out to her that the war had affected the servant situation quite badly. Tyson Lodge no longer employed the number of staff it used to in its heyday. Young girls nowadays had far more interesting and remunerative jobs to go to, and a good thing too in Kate's humble opinion. Lucy must learn to fend for herself a little more. She could at least take breakfast downstairs.

Admittedly the installation of one or two more bathrooms might be a good idea. This was the modern age after all, and renovations and refurbishments had been sadly neglected for years because of the war. New bathrooms would save all that carrying of hot water. Kate made a mental note to speak to Eliot on the subject when the moment seemed right.

Callum went off to the factory at his usual time, and Flora to school. Kate saw them both off, tidied up their rooms for want of something to do, and then wondered what to tackle next.

Lucy still hadn't risen, for which Kate was secretly thankful. She really had no wish to see or speak to her.

But Kate was at a loss to know what to do with herself. She was bored, nervous of the long hours, the endless day stretching ahead of her. Never in all her life had she been in a situation where she had time on her hands, hours in which she didn't have the first idea what to do with herself. It felt strangely unsettling.

What on earth did people do when they had no need to work? Kate wasn't really the sort to be content with embroidery or take up charity work as Amelia had done, the first seeming too indolent and frivolous, and the second an affront to human dignity in her opinion.

By eleven o'clock Kate was back in Eliot's study, where she spent the rest of the morning gathering her thoughts and putting the relevant papers in order. It had occurred to her that she would have to move out of here now and so she must make an effort to clear away her things. But where to put them? Where could she work instead?

Kate began to search for an alternative space, her mind instantly fixing on the small room upstairs on the nursery landing, where she'd spent so much time with Callum when he was a baby. She went straight upstairs to check it out.

Here were the old mahogany drawers, some of them still stuffed with his baby clothes. The little sailor suit and Lord Fauntleroy outfit that Amelia had insisted on buying... Good heavens, these things should have been thrown out years ago.

Kate buried her face in them as she had used to

do so often when he was missing, drawing in the scent of her child to ease her aching heart. Now they smelled only of mothballs, but they held such precious memories how could she possibly discard them?

She wrapped the clothes in tissue paper, along with several other items such as his first baby shoes, Flora's ribbons and christening robe, and put them safely in a box on the top shelf of the old wardrobe.

She found a copy of *Doctor Barker's Advice to Mothers* and began to read it, chuckling softly to herself as memories flooded back. She recalled how she used to pore over these pages, desperately anxious to follow the rules her mistress had set, although more often than not following her own instincts instead.

And here was an ancient bottle of gripe water which reminded her of the Gregory Mixture and Godfrey's Cordial which Amelia had at first expected her to use.

She'd made a start on emptying the top cupboard when the door opened and Lucy herself strolled into the room.

'I thought it must be you in here. What are you doing, cleaning and tidying? Once a servant, always a servant.'

# 9

Kate silently ground her teeth together. 'I intend to take over this room as my office.'

'Ah, afraid of having your nose pushed out downstairs?'

'Not at all, but obviously Eliot must have his own study back. I shall move up here.'

Lucy snorted with derision. 'I should think it an ideal choice. Back in the place where you began; where you belong. Eliot is in charge once more, his control over the family restored. Your days of ruling the roost are over. Don't think you'll have any say now in the future running of the business, not now Eliot is back in the saddle.'

'Well, that's where you're wrong. He's more than willing to listen to my ideas. In fact, he's agreed for us to have a short meeting on future business developments this very evening, after dinner.' This was far from the truth but Kate couldn't bear to have Lucy lording it over her.

'Then as a major shareholder, I shall insist that I be present too.'

Kate was startled, mentally kicking herself for mentioning it when she'd hoped for a private meeting. 'The day-to-day running of the business doesn't concern shareholders.'

'Indeed it does.' Lucy took a step into the room and hissed at Kate through tight, narrowed lips, eyes slitted like those of a cat. 'Don't think you can sideline me, Kate O'Connor, because you can't! I'm back and I intend to stay, so don't try anything you might regret.'

'The name is Tyson. *Mrs* Tyson.'

Lucy put back her lovely head and laughed. 'Call yourself what you will, you're still the girl from Poor House Lane so far as I'm concerned. But as of today your power is seriously curtailed, your influence over Eliot and Tysons Industries on the wane. Mine is only just starting to rise. Attempt to push me out and I'll make you rue the day. Remember that I've slept with your precious husband once already, and can easily get into his bed again, any time I wish.'

Kate felt as if she'd been punched in the face. Such a possibility had never entered her head. Could it be true? Eliot had never seemed to be the type to wander. He'd been a loyal husband to Amelia, and to herself, Kate was certain of it. But then, there had been that difficult intervening period...

Circumstances, malicious gossip and the loss of Callum, of course, had come between them. Could it have happened then? Surely not. For all Eliot's sense of guilt, he'd had no real time for Lucy. Even so, a doubt had been sown, one Kate would do her best to quash. She certainly had no intention of questioning her husband on the subject because that was clearly what Lucy wanted, to cause dissent between them. 'Sure and you're a terrible liar. I don't believe a word of it.'

'Suit yourself.'

Her challenge hadn't quite brought about the effect Lucy had hoped for, but not for a moment

85

would she show her irritation. She'd tried only once to get into Eliot's bed and, much to her chagrin, he had repulsed her. Not that Kate knew that, and Lucy was more than ready to say whatever was necessary to gain control of this household and reinstate her own children in it. Her son Jack should be the one to run the company with Eliot, and take over when he died. It was his birthright.

Her three precious darlings, all away at boarding school, would soon be reaching the end of their school year. She'd made arrangements for them to spend the summer with various school friends, since she couldn't possibly have coped with all three of them at the tiny house in Heversham. It broke her heart, of course, and naturally she missed them, but really children were such hard work.

However, farming them out could now come to an end. There was ample space at Tyson Lodge, and with servants on hand to deal with all the day-to-day unpleasantness involved in caring for the young, they would not intrude too much upon her social life. And they would be delighted by this momentous change in their circumstances.

Young Georgie still had a number of years of education before him, being only fourteen. Darling, irrepressible Bunty should really be sent off to finishing school next year, if only Lucy could persuade Eliot to pay for it.

But Jack, a year older than his sister at eighteen, was already considering various possibilities for a future career. Not a natural scholar, there was little hope of his getting into university, and Lucy certainly had no wish for him to enter the services. She held high hopes that, come September, he could be found a place in the business.

What was in Eliot's will? she wondered. It occurred to her then in a sudden flash of intuition that he might not have got around to altering it since Callum returned home. He'd surely made a will before he joined up, as most right-thinking men did, or perhaps when he'd married Kate O'Connor, but so far as he was aware at that time, he no longer had a son. Callum was missing, presumed gone for good, in which case the business would naturally go to his next of kin, to his nephews and niece. And he surely hadn't had any opportunity or thought to change it since, being still away at war.

So until he went to see the family solicitor, should some unforeseen and unfortunate accident happen to Callum, her own children would indeed be the ones to inherit. Who else was there to follow Eliot into the business?

Lucy spared no thought for Kate. So far as Lucy was concerned, she didn't feature in the picture at all. She must now step down from her self-appointed role as head of the family business and be satisfied with simply being a wife and doing as she was told, for a change. Hadn't Lucy herself made a point of emphasising this fact to Eliot? Only, more diplomatically, of course.

As for Flora, she was merely a silly little girl who would no doubt grow up into a silly young woman. Her father might leave her some shares, but never full control. Indeed, the future looked bright, very bright indeed. Although fate may need a helping hand to turn things in the right direction...

Lucy had a sudden urge to be alone, to think through the full implications of this revelatory idea.

As she turned to go, Kate scrambled up from her knees and hurried after her. Grasping the other woman's arm, she jerked her to a halt. 'If it's war you're after, you'll not find me frightened of a fight. I never have been. I'm Eliot's wife and the mistress of this house, not you. I'm the one who will partner him through life, and in business, not you.'

'We'll see about that. We will indeed.'

'And don't you ever try to hurt my children, or you'll be sorry, so help me God.'

Lucy walked away, laughing as if Kate had made some sort of joke.

Mrs Petty enjoyed nothing so much as to prepare dinner for the family. She'd little truck with fancy food and the kind of fashionable dinner parties that the first Mrs Tyson had loved to give, but roast beef and Yorkshire, substantial soups and hearty, rib-sticking puddings, were her speciality. There was no one in all of Westmorland, in her own humble opinion, who could make a better gingerbread and rum butter. And her Herdwick lamb would melt in the mouth, it was that tender; that French madam had had absolutely no notion of how to judge a good meal.

Today she was preparing individual cottage pies, one for each member of the family, with an extra large one for the master.

Ida thought this strange, considering it a break with tradition and something of a nuisance since it presented her with more washing up. 'Why are we doing separate pies, Mrs Petty? Wouldn't it be easier to mek one big un?'

'Aye, it would, but I have me reasons. Ask no questions and you'll be told no lies.'

Intrigued, Ida's head was suddenly filled with questions she longed to ask as she watched Mrs P mince and cook the beef in a big round pot, adding the onions and tomatoes Ida herself had chopped, together with a few precious herbs; and then prepare a separate, smaller pan, also of minced beef with far fewer vegetables and not even a pinch of pepper.

Frowning, Ida peered into the pan. 'Ooh, this meat's all greasy and full of fat and gristle. What is the butcher thinking of to sell us such rubbish? Shall I chuck it away?'

'No, Ida, you will do no such thing. *That's* for Madam Lucy's pie.'

Ida's eyes grew round with fright. 'Ooh! That's wicked. She'll notice and blame me.'

Mrs Petty briskly wiped her hands on her apron, the swagger of her plump shoulders loudly proclaiming that she didn't care.

Ida recognised the gesture and quickly added for good measure, 'I'm the one what has to serve her, remember? She'll be furious and make me tek it away. I know she will.'

'She wouldn't dare make a fuss, not yet, not till she feels a bit more secure like. But I'll have a spare one lined up, just in case.'

'Not one of ours?'

'No, Ida, indeed not one of ours. And we shall have some of the very best beef in ours. Folk generally get what they deserve in life, or so I've discovered.'

Dinner, as might be expected, was an uncomfortable affair which passed largely in silence. Lucy took the place she was offered, to Eliot's left, and rarely glanced across at Kate, seated to his right, beyond a venomous glance of triumph as she settled herself at table.

The entire family was present except for Flora, who had been excused as she was still considered to be too young for adult dinner parties. Callum, however, had been bullied into attending, and sat stiffly beside his mother.

The first course, one of Mrs Petty's filling country vegetable soups, was eaten in silence, Ida seeming particularly nervous as she served at table, Kate noticed. Her hands were positively shaking as she put out the individual cottage pies.

'How splendid!' Eliot remarked. 'I get my very own, and much larger than yours, ladies. What is there for afters, Ida? Spotted dick, I hope?'

'Jam roly-poly and custard, sir.'

'Even better.' And everyone smiled at Eliot, humouring his pleasure at the prospect of good food.

Kate had made a private resolve to behave as normally as possible. She turned to Eliot with a brilliant, heart-stopping smile, her blue-grey eyes twinkling with happiness. 'How did your first day go, me darlin'? Not too painful, I hope?'

90

'It was most – illuminating.'

'Did Toby fill you in on the state of trade and the policies we've been following?'

'He answered a few of my questions, as did many other people I spoke to. I doubt I shall have any trouble in settling back into the routine.'

'Of course you won't.'

'I hope your own day was pleasant, and much less stressful.'

'Er – yes, to be sure.' How could she explain that she'd been bored to tears, that her thoughts for the entire day had been fully occupied with devising a way to get back to work?

Even at the height of his powers, Eliot had never been a natural businessman, much preferring to spend his time tending his garden or painting beautiful pictures, at which he was most skilled. Kate still hoped that he would accept a business partnership between them, with herself remaining actively involved in the day-to-day running of the firm, so that he would have the time to pursue the pleasures he so enjoyed. She meant to talk this through with him, the moment she got the chance.

She cleared her throat. 'Perhaps, after dinner, we could have that meeting concerning future plans for the business? If you remember, Eliot, we discussed it this morning.'

He laid down his knife and fork with a gentle sigh. 'I hope we will be allowed to enjoy our food first, without any further discussion about business matters or your precious plans, my dear?' His smile was kind but his voice firm, and Kate hastened to agree.

'Of course, of course. There will be plenty of time later, at the meeting, for all of that.'

Pleased with Eliot's obvious irritation, Lucy said, 'What a workhorse you are, *sister dear*,' and hid a small smile of satisfaction while quietly pushing aside her own pie, half-eaten. If she were in charge of this household, she wouldn't allow such food to be given to the dogs.

The aunts were the only ones to speak after that, remarking politely upon the weather, the charity visits they'd carried out that morning, and the content of the vicar's last sermon. Vera, ever a stickler for propriety and a stalwart of the local church, would obey Eliot to the letter, and dear Cissie, the more mischievous and soft-hearted of the two, would never dream of disagreeing with her.

The two maiden ladies, having led a sheltered life, cared for in their youth by their father, then their brother George who had started Tysons Shoes, and finally by his son, their nephew Eliot, did not believe it their place to question any decision he might make. In their opinion men must be deferred to in all things as they were the ones with the intelligence to make all the essential decisions in life, the ones who ruled the world, as certainly Eliot ruled their own small portion of it.

Even so, Vera rather hoped that they too would be invited into the meeting, yet not for a moment would she say as much.

Once the pudding dishes had been cleared away and coffee served, Kate tried again. 'Shall we repair to the study now, to have our meeting?'

Her heart sank just a fraction as Eliot glanced

across at her with a startled expression in his eyes, almost as if he'd forgotten the subject had ever been mentioned.

Aware of Lucy's smirk of satisfaction, Kate ploughed on, smiling all the while to soften the force of her words, trying to still the disquiet that was eating into her soul over her husband's emotional state. Hadn't he only just returned from the war? Wasn't he bound to be a bit confused from time to time? He was settling, was he not, and would improve still further with time, love and patience. The trouble was that decisions about the business couldn't afford to wait. Something had to be done to protect its future now.

'Now that you feel well enough to face work again, I think it important you be put fully in the picture. I would welcome the opportunity to put forward the ideas I have in mind to help make the business more sound.'

His mouth twisted slightly at the corners, as if her earnestness amused him. 'If you insist, though it seemed sound enough to me. However, I can see I shall get no peace until you do.'

'I don't *insist*, Eliot, I simply think it might be useful.' Oh, and it would be so lovely, she wanted to add, to have a few private moments alone with her husband while she did so: to escape Lucy's eagle eye and the aunts' condescending disapproval.

She was to be disappointed in this. Even as she rose, cup and saucer in hand, Lucy did likewise.

'As shareholders, I believe the three of us should also be present at any board meeting. We too need to be kept fully in the picture. Don't you agree, Eliot?'

Vera was scrambling to her feet, delighted this suggestion had been made without her having to make it. 'Indeed, what a splendid idea. I should be most interested to hear your plans too, Kate dear.'

'And I,' Cissie put in, in case anyone should forget that she was there.

Eliot sighed with resignation. 'I can see I am being bullied from all sides, whether I like it or not. Very well, Lucy, Aunts, if you think you won't be too bored.'

'Of course I shan't be bored,' said Lucy. 'Not in the slightest.'

# 10

The meeting was not a success. Kate explained all about her dreams for developing a ladies' fashion line using a new process by which the outer soles were cemented instead of being stitched or welted on. Eliot was not impressed, claiming she was suggesting that Tysons produce lightweight rubbish.

'The shoes will be lightweight, yes, but certainly not rubbish. Not in the least. Tysons will continue to be known for its quality footwear. But the latest fashions demand that women show off their ankles, and they want pretty, delicate shoes to give the appearance of pretty, delicate feet. It is simple vanity, yes, but we must pander to it if we are to make progress in the post-war era. Toby has come up with a way of inserting a soft rubber pad under the insole, which supports the instep.

'We must also provide shoes in different widths and fittings. Not all women have the same shape of foot, even if they are the same size. We should accommodate that fact. And we must advertise.'

'*Advertise?* Tysons have never needed to stoop so low in the past. Why should we start now?' Eliot asked, in a tone which set advertising on a par with opening a brothel.

'Advertising is going to become increasingly important as firms compete for business through what could be a nasty post-war slump.'

'*The Times* is saying quite the opposite, predicting the boom will last.'

'Excellent. I hope they are right. However, we must make sure that we are a part of it if it does, and can survive if it doesn't.'

Eliot made a sound something like 'Harrumph!' He was beginning to feel like an outsider, a stranger in his own company, in his own home almost. Nothing was quite the same in Kendal, or England for that matter. Women were working and yet skilled men were in short supply since so many had been killed. Prices were soaring. Station porters were earning three pounds a week, while officers and gentlemen were walking the streets with no job to go to at all.

Lloyd George's government seemed hell-bent on bringing in all manner of legislation to control the railways, roads, canals and docks, working hours and wages, even intending to meddle in land with an iniquitous new tax. They'd be nationalising all of industry before long, the way they were going on.

Even his own wife was lecturing him.

Eliot almost longed for the regular routine of parade and drill, of giving his men their orders which they obediently carried out. Simple. Much easier than all this politics, the constant discussion of boom or bust, this confusion of choices and worrying need for decisions.

He wanted things to continue exactly as they had before the war, when Swainson ran things for him without bothering him about trifles. Instead of which he had this Toby Lynch character knocking on his door every five minutes, wanting a decision on this, that, or the other. Eliot longed for a placid backwater, for peace!

Kate was saying, 'We must create eye-catching posters and let everyone know what wonderful shoes Tysons produce. That we offer style and fashion, show how much trouble we take to provide the correct fitting. Ladies must be able to buy our shoes with confidence.'

Lucy said, 'My word, you seem to have this well thought out, all carefully planned even before dear Eliot has had the chance to settle in.'

Eliot frowned, clearly not liking the inference behind her remark.

Kate simply ignored her. 'It will be good for Kendal, and good for the men newly returned from the trenches to know that they have a long and secure future with the firm. Don't you see, Eliot, that this is the way forward? The war is over, now we must make shoes for a new peace.'

But he didn't see. Or at least, if he did, he wasn't admitting as much.

Lucy's remark had hit home and Kate could tell that he hated the fact that she had come up with the idea first, before him. He was even jealous of Toby Lynch for having solved some of the manufacturing problems in order to produce this lighter footwear.

'I will think about your suggestions,' he said, rather portentously. 'And make my decision when I am good and ready. I thank you for minding the factory for me, Kate. You've done a splendid job, but I am the master, don't forget, and I won't allow Tysons to become the kind of factory which produces slip-shod work.'

'Hear, hear,' echoed Lucy, who wouldn't have known a well-made shoe from a bad, caring only for the look of the thing.

Kate sighed, trying to smile and appear unconcerned. My goodness, but he'd grown proud and obstinate. It was one thing to refuse to use a walking stick when he was clearly in pain, quite another to risk the livelihood of their entire workforce. However, she wasn't yet ready to admit defeat, although persuading her husband to agree to her plan wasn't going to be nearly as straightforward as she'd hoped.

After the meeting, Lucy waylaid Eliot and took the opportunity to put in a word for Jack. 'He has completed his education and will soon be seeking a situation. I trust there will be ... I mean, I rather hoped that he might...' Lucy was appalled by her own dithering. What on earth was the matter with her? Could it have something to do with the bland expression of disinterest on Eliot's face, which gave the impression that he wasn't even properly listening to her? She straightened her spine. 'What I am trying to say, Eliot, is that I assume there will be a place for him at Tysons? He is family, after all. Your own brother's eldest son.'

'I am aware of who he is.'

'And then there is darling Bunty, who really must be properly finished.'

'Must she indeed?' He raised one dark eyebrow in that way he had when something amused him.

He might give every impression of taking life seriously, which he deemed appropriate where his own offspring were concerned, but when it came to his nephews and niece, it was a different matter. They were apparently to be viewed as some sort of joke. Lucy made up her mind to say so, but then Kate chose that moment to walk through the hall and he half turned away to follow her.

'Eliot?' Lucy grabbed him by the arm to remind him that he still hadn't answered her question. 'I was asking about Jack. He *is* to join the management team in September, isn't he? I would like to reassure him that his future is settled.'

'Lucy dear, I confess I haven't given a single thought to your son's future. That is for you, and for him, to decide. Nothing to do with me. Now, if you will excuse me? I believe this meeting is closed.'

And he walked away, following that trollop up the stairs while Lucy was left fuming in the hall, and in full view of that dreadful servant girl, Ida.

'Don't you have a bed to go to?' Lucy snapped.

'I were just locking up. Would there be anything more you'd be wanting, ma'am?' It was past eleven and Ida was dropping on her feet; would be most thankful to get to her bed, if ever she got the chance.

'Bring a small cup of hot milk to my room. Quickly, girl! I haven't all night.' Then she stuck her chin in the air and marched upstairs.

Ida returned to the kitchen, heated some milk, spat very gently into it, stirred it well, and took it upstairs to Lucy with all haste, as she had been bidden.

From that day on, Eliot didn't miss a day at the factory. He would rise at seven, enjoy an excellent breakfast, and sharp at eight would arrive in his office, having walked along the river path for the short distance between the two places. Kate would sit with him while he ate, watch him leave, but never once did he ask her to accompany him. On the contrary, he still obstinately refused to allow her to come into the factory at all.

'You have done your duty,' he would say, whenever she suggested it, or risked asking if he'd made up his mind yet about her proposed new line of ladies' shoes. 'And now I must do mine. I will keep you informed as to what I decide.'

'I should hope so, Eliot, since I own a part of the business too,' she gently reminded him. 'I believe I should have a say over what happens to my own section of the company, at least. Now that my workers can no longer make army boots, we must find other orders, other ways forward.'

It was the wrong thing to say.

'They are no longer *your* workers, Kate, and Tysons Shoes is safe in my hands, as it always has

99

been. You own a mere ten per cent, and since you are my wife and our lives and individual businesses completely merged, you can trust me to make the right decisions, as I did in the past.'

Kate was equally obstinate. 'I don't think so, Eliot. It isn't about trust, do you see, and things are no longer as they used to be in the past. We should be equal partners. The war, and the development of my own business, changed everything. I must insist upon being involved in any decision about the direction the company might take in the future.'

He was clearly irritated by her persistence. 'There are a great many women making demands they have no right to make. I didn't see any of them at the front when the going got tough.'

'Really? I believe there were some nurses pretty near to it,' Kate patiently remarked. 'Many of us were not at the front, I'll admit, although we kept you men well supplied with boots and armaments so that you could do your job properly, which means we have indeed earned the right for our voices to be heard. Now stop being so stubborn, Eliot, and agree that the world has changed.'

But he would not.

Kate was forced to resort to subterfuge, as women throughout time had found it necessary to do in order to achieve their goal. Two or three times a week she would wait until he was gone, then later in the morning she would sneak into the factory when she knew Eliot would be occupied. She was careful not to be seen by anyone, but it was not easy.

She would have a quiet meeting with Toby

behind closed doors, perhaps going on afterwards to visit the odd customer. She would love to have examined progress in the new design department that she'd set up but daren't take the risk. They'd be bound to mention to Eliot that she'd been in.

And Kate really had no wish to offend or embarrass him by an open confrontation despite being desperate to remain involved. She kept hoping that she would eventually win him round by quiet persuasion, but he remained adamant that her role was now that of his wife and help-mate, and nothing more, a situation she found hard to accept.

She even shocked herself by resenting the fact that Eliot had reclaimed use of his own study, for all she'd anticipated his doing so. There was her little hideaway upstairs of course, the old nursery, which she'd fitted out as a small office. But whenever she went up there to work, she was aware of Lucy's laughter and constant derision.

'Yes, go back to the nursery where you belong. Shall we have your meals sent up, as we used to? What would you like? Toast soldiers and jam? Rice pudding?'

It was hateful, and when she'd closed the door on Lucy's taunts, Kate found that she had little to occupy her, even there. She felt she was losing touch, being shut out of her own business.

Toby did his best to keep her informed on the days she didn't go in, sending her little notes, telling her of meetings held and decisions made without her presence or knowledge, offering to call round and explain things properly to her. Kate always refused to allow him to come to the house. The last thing she needed was to be caught holding clandestine discussions in the summer house with the foreman, thereby providing ammunition for Lucy to inform on her to Eliot, or maliciously accuse her of being involved in some sort of affair.

She tried a different tactic. 'Could I come and work in the design room, mebbe? I'm so bored at home, Eliot, with not enough to do. Could I not at least have the opportunity to express my ideas in some other way? I swear I'll not interfere in the decision-making process, or the actual running of the factory.'

'I will consider it, my dear, but knowing you as I do, I suspect this is merely a new means of trying to get your own way.' He kissed her as he said this, which quite took the sting out of his words, although of course he was absolutely correct.

'How could you ever keep your delightful nose out of what I was doing? You would expect every one of your designs to be chosen, the work implemented forthwith, decisions made of which you approve. I cannot allow that, Kate.

'Apart from the fact that you are my wife and I wish to take care of you, keep you safe at home, we do not see eye to eye on the future of the company. Tysons Shoes has an image to maintain, a quality and standard which is not in keeping with your feminine nonsense of pretty-pretty lightweight rubbish. So do stop fretting and relax. If you have too much time on your hands, take up gardening. I always found it very therapeutic.'

And then something happened which changed everything.

# 11

They were sitting in the summer house on a lovely August evening, the sun setting over Castle Hill, tingeing grey clouds with pink and gold in a cobalt blue sky, the river a slick of silver in the fading light. Kate had finally made the decision to give him her news. She'd kept the information to herself for several weeks, needing time to grow accustomed to the idea.

Of course she was thrilled, but at the same time stunned, knowing it would mean she must finally put her ambitions on hold.

Toby had told her recently that new orders were thin on the ground, that if something didn't happen soon he would be forced to lay men off. Eliot resisted all offers of help and it worried and frightened her. What would happen if there was a slump and the company went under? Kate had experienced poverty, had tasted its bitterness. She'd certainly no wish to return to Poor House Lane.

She'd tried to advise from the wings, as it were, making suggestions and comments which generally were not welcomed. Eliot seemed to view her interest as a threat, yet Kate felt sure Tysons was losing its way, not replacing the orders for army boots with anything new.

Her darling husband had never been the most diligent or gifted of businessmen, somehow lacking vision and flair, although he'd always done his best and generally managed to rise to a challenge. But he couldn't even seem to do that nowadays.

Despite a long and difficult summer in which he'd eased himself gently back into work, he still became easily confused, and his periods of depression were lifting only slightly.

Perhaps her present condition might make him realise that she wasn't attempting to usurp his role after all, that she had another which gave her equal fulfilment.

Even so, Kate had no intention of giving up her interest in the business entirely. Her private meetings with Toby remained a regular part of her life, and could surely continue, for she was in no way incapacitated. She still lived in hope of finding some non-confrontational way of persuading her husband round to her way of thinking. Her patience and skill had been exemplary, if she said so herself.

The thought brought a smile to her face. Maybe pride in new fatherhood would do the trick.

'You know that although I would love to be back at the factory, fully involved as I used to be, because I love to work...'

Eliot interrupted her with a heavy sigh. 'We've been through all of this Kate, *ad nauseam*. I believe the subject is closed.'

'I know, I know, and *you* know that it doesn't make the slightest difference to our life together, not one bit. I'm more than happy simply to be your wife and the mother of your children, and haven't I accepted that these last months?' This wasn't strictly true, as they were both well aware, but Kate was doing her utmost to appear content with her new status.

Eliot said, 'I'm glad to hear it. Other women have been happy to step down, now that their husbands are returned to them.' The grooves etched beside the corners of his mouth, Kate noticed, seemed deeper than ever, with no hint of a smile as he looked at her, ready to fend off further argument. His leg still pained him badly, and he still obstinately refused to use his stick.

'It was just that I felt I had so much to offer, and so little to do here that Mrs Petty can't do a thousand times better.' Wanting to bring a smile to lift the corners of that dejected mouth, Kate continued, 'But then, when did I ever have the chance to learn to be a housekeeper in Poor House Lane? We couldn't keep ourselves clean there, let alone the stinking hole in which we lived. Didn't Amelia despair of me ever learning civilised ways, even in the nursery?'

'I'd rather you didn't speak of Poor House Lane,' Eliot said, rather stuffily.

'Why not, 'tis the simple truth? That's where I lived, and bore Callum.'

'And now you are free of it, so we need never refer to it again, if you don't mind.'

'Oh, don't be such an old stuffed shirt! Is it ashamed of me you are? And here's me trying to tell you summat exciting. I'm saying, I dearly *would* love to be involved in finding and creating designs for new lines, but I can't after all. If I started work, sure I'd have to leave in no time.'

He looked at her, startled, his face frozen with shock. 'Leave? You're leaving me?'

'Jesus, Mary and Joseph, I never meant that I'm leaving you, you daft eejit! Why would I do that? Not while I've breath in me body. That's not what I meant at all. Only I'm going to have other things to occupy me over the next few months, something far more important to do with me time. The next year or so, I'd say.'

'And what that might be?'

'Can't ye guess?'

He looked into her dancing eyes and felt his whole body grow still. 'You're not!'

Kate dissolved into a fit of giggles. 'To be sure I am.'

'Oh, my darling, I don't believe it. You're...' Eliot was so delighted, so beside himself with happiness, he dare hardly say the words.

Understanding perfectly, Kate said it for him. 'Aye, you can say it, 'cos it's true. I'm pregnant. All them shenanigans we've been up to lately has had the expected result. It seems I'm not quite over the hill at thirty-two. Young enough anyways to make you a da again. Now will you give me a kiss, you old grumpy, and then smile a bit more, just to please me?'

Lucy was completely absorbed in watching Callum. She noted what time he rose in the mornings, how long he took over breakfast, even what he ate, generally bread and dripping, proving he was a common farm-hand still.

She would covertly watch as he pulled on his jacket, picked up his knapsack with his lunch box inside and headed off to the factory every morning sharp at seven, just as he was doing now.

Not that she rose this early every morning, but it was worth getting up on the odd occasion in order to observe what he did, what his habits were. One never knew when information, knowledge of any kind, might come in handy.

She'd certainly once made good use of the fact that his stupid sister found eggs abhorrent. Those kind of tactics would not serve for a grown boy, nearly a young man, naturally. Nor could she simply spirit him away to the workhouse this time. She would need to be much more subtle, far cleverer. But then, she *was* clever. And this time she must make it permanent. Lucy could not risk being discovered again trying to harm him, or her pleas of innocence would sound very thin, very thin indeed.

She might well have got away with her crime the first time around had Callum not returned to Kendal market, his curiosity stirred by meeting Flora, that hint of red in her dark brown hair betraying her Irish ancestry, and her pale, freckled face so like the remembered image of his mother's.

The unreliable memories of a young boy had brought Lucy shame and exile, near poverty and humiliation, living upon the charity of friends. Finally, when even they had grown tired of her, she'd been compelled to endure a miserable existence in the aunts' fusty old-fashioned house in Heversham. It stank of dogs and mothballs, with not a flicker of sunlight filtering through the leaded windows because of all the overgrown trees and shrubs in the tiny garden. Lucy had deliberately put up with that inconvenience, choosing to guard her privacy from prying eyes rather than bask in light and sunshine.

Oh, but she'd resented her exile. She most certainly had. She had a lot of ground to make up.

Later in the day, she would take out her brand new Austin 20, so distinctive and high-class, and drive it around town for a little while, calling on one or two of the few friends she still had left, for afternoon tea and a gossip.

When she'd grown weary of hearing Adeline Cross list the great accomplishments of her children, or Felicity Goodchild proclaiming how splendidly her husband was doing, Lucy would climb back into her motor and drive herself home again. Except that she would make a slight detour. She always judged the time precisely, so that she reached the factory at the exact moment Callum would be leaving.

Not that she ever offered him a lift. She would park up a side street and watch as he walked or cycled up Aynam Road with his chums. Five-thirty, without fail, every day.

Evenings seemed to be fully occupied, with Callum rarely spending one at home. On Mondays and Thursdays he attended a class at the Allen Technical College, something to do with bookkeeping. On Tuesdays he went up to Kendal Green for a game of football with his mates, and sometimes he would go to the swimming baths in Allhallows Lane.

On Fridays he always called at the library to change his book before going out for a beer to one of the less salubrious establishments in town, certainly in Lucy's opinion, who preferred the County or possibly the White Lion which were most commodious and comfortable.

She'd followed him only once or twice, simply to ascertain that he drank at what were known locally as Jerry shops, typical of his low-brow tastes. His favourite was either the Rifle Man's Arms or the Odd Fellows' Arms. He didn't seem to be a heavy drinker, which was unfortunate, and generally left well before closing time, being home by nine-thirty. Young Callum was becoming a most sober, right-minded citizen, and quite the scholar, or so he imagined, which made her task more difficult.

What she would do with all this information, Lucy hadn't quite made up her mind. But, by God, she meant to do something.

'You called me a stuffed shirt.'

Kate giggled, snuggling close against her husband beneath the sheets, twining her legs about his. They'd wasted no time in getting to bed that night, longing to be alone and revel in their joyous news. Eliot had been nervous at first, fearful of hurting her, but Kate had reassured him and they'd made love with such tenderness that afterwards she'd wept in his arms. 'And so ye are a stuffed shirt, so self-righteous and pompous these days. The fault of the army, not yours. Don't you need to learn how to relax and stop worrying so much? The war is over and the world is not going to blow up in yer face, nor crash and bang in your head any more. You're free, m'darlin'. Free as a bird.'

'To love you, and give you more children.'

'And isn't that the truth of it.'

'I didn't want you to have to work.'

'Sure, and of course I don't *have* to work, I just want to, and where's the wrong in that, will ye tell me? You were happy enough for me to run the company single-handed throughout the war, so what's changed? I'm still the same person, still as capable, still as argumentative and infuriating.'

He laughed. 'You can say that again.'

She smiled softly at him, loving him so much it hurt. This small miracle seemed to have brought them close again, and Kate couldn't have been happier. 'Will you at least give me a chance? Maybe I could do a bit of work at home, if you'd let me? And then when the babby is born and I'm on me feet again, we could get a nursemaid so I could come in to the factory. Not every day, mind, just two or three mornings a week, mebbe. How would that be?'

'I'll think about it.'

'You promise me?'

'I've said I will think about, haven't I? A man's word is his bond.' Eliot's voice was grave but his eyes were laughing at her, twinkling merrily.

'Well then, because I'm only a simple woman, I shall need you to seal your promise with a kiss.'

'I have no problem with that.' And he pulled her close to smooth his hand over her breasts, the ripening curve of her belly, and kiss her deeply and passionately.

'Will we tell them soon, tomorrow mebbe?'

'Must we?'

'Callum and Flora will need time to get used to the idea that their mammy is still capable of making love, let alone having more children. And the aunts'll want to start knitting. You know how they are. Getting ready for the babby will keep them happily occupied for hours on end. And sure as hell is hot, I certainly can't knit.'

'Kate!'

'Well, isn't that the truth? Remember when Amelia tried to teach me? More holes than knitting there was.' And they both laughed fondly at the memory then fell silent as they recalled how that was during her last illness, a sad and poignant time.

'Do you miss her still?' Kate tentatively asked, and Eliot looked at her for a long moment, unspeaking, then gathered her lovely elfin face between his two hands.

'I loved Amelia, as you well know, but I love you too. I love you more than life itself, if that doesn't sound too trite. I'm a very lucky man to have had so much love in my life.'

Kate's piece of news came like a bolt from the blue to others also.

'You're pregnant? Good God!'

'Yes, I was rather stunned too, but so pleased.'

Eliot put an arm about his wife and hugged her to his side. 'We both are. Isn't it wonderful news, Lucy?'

'Absolutely marvellous,' she agreed, struggling to disguise the sour edge to her tone. It felt as if shards of ice were stabbing her insides. Another child! It was unendurable. Where was the point now in incapacitating Callum when another boy could well replace him in a matter of months? The woman bred like a rabbit. Who knew how many more brats she might have before she was done?

Lucy was silently fuming. She'd been considering calling upon Swainson, the foreman who had once worked for the firm and been dismissed for taking advantage of the women. She'd thought he might assist her by breaking the boy's legs. She'd been so looking forward to seeing this workhouse brat confined to a wheelchair, which would not only have put an end to any hope of his running the factory, but also to his swimming and his football, as well as his nights out at the beer shops. It would have made his life an utter misery which was exactly what he deserved. Serve him right for not having stayed where she'd put him.

But something, she wasn't sure what, had held her back. Now she knew that wouldn't achieve her ends at all, not with another child on the way.

Then what was the answer? Should some desperately unfortunate accident happen to Kate herself, thereby disposing of the expected infant? But that would still leave Callum as heir, and Eliot in charge.

Flora, of course, was of no consequence, and could easily be controlled. So far, Lucy had exercised that power merely by a look, delighting in making the child shiver with fear. But she was willing to go further, if she felt it necessary. She was willing to go to any lengths.

But first she needed to think through all the

implications of this new development, to plan carefully. Nothing must be rushed.

She continued with her normal routine, her mind a turmoil of emotion as she strove to find a solution to her dilemma. Young Georgie had plenty of time on his side, but Jack and Bunty would be home by September, and Lucy was determined to have something worthwhile to offer them by then.

She continued with her afternoon vigils and a day or two later was parked in her usual spot, hidden up a side street some distance from the factory but with a good view of Aynam Road, along which Callum must walk. He was late today and she was growing tired of waiting. Lucy had almost decided to give up, in view of the changed circumstances. Where was the point? She must devise some other plan. The anger and resentment she felt towards the whole lot of them festered deep inside of her.

Kate O'Connor had no right to so much happiness, to lord it over her as the mistress of Tyson Lodge, let alone be constantly nagging Eliot to allow her to help run the factory as well. The woman had grown above herself and needed bringing down a peg or two, back where she belonged, in the gutter.

Neither did Eliot have any right to disinherit his own brother's children for the sake of a poorhouse brat. It was intolerable. Lucy would never forgive him for that, not for as long as she lived. If he'd left the boy to rot in Poor House Lane, her darling husband Charles might still have been alive today, she thought, conveniently forgetting that Charles's suicide had been caused by debt which she herself had helped him to accumulate.

And then she saw Eliot come out of the factory and start to walk up Aynam Road, more of a hobble in fact, favouring his injured leg as he always did. When he reached the corner of Nether Bridge, he would cross the road and call in the corner shop for his evening paper.

And suddenly the answer came to her. Neat and simple.

The engine was ticking over nicely, and it took no time at all to slip it into gear, hit the accelerator and surge forward, the power of the engine exciting her. There was even time to catch the startled expression in Eliot's eyes as he focussed upon her at the moment of impact, and then his body was flying upwards, right over the top of the car.

# 12

Lucy didn't wait to find out where or how it landed, she pressed her foot to the floor on the accelerator, skidded left over Nether Bridge, left again, and was soon racing away from town, quite certain that no one would have had the chance to take the number of her car.

There'd been some old dear standing on her doorstep but Lucy was quite certain she wouldn't have been near enough to identify the driver.

She found that she was gasping for breath, her nerves a jangle of excitement and terror. Oh, but she had never enjoyed herself so much in all of her life! Seeing a policeman come into view ahead, she slowed the car down to the correct fifteen miles an hour. She mustn't get too carried away. It was vital that she remain free from all suspicion.

Lucy made a wide detour of the town as quickly as she possibly could without drawing attention to herself, and miraculously was back home with the Austin parked in the garage within ten minutes. She slipped quietly in through a side door, calling for Ida to bring her a tray of tea to the parlour at once, as if she'd been there all along. Most satisfactory.

The doorbell rang. No sound permeated up the wide stairs to indicate that Ida was rushing to answer it, and Kate correctly surmised that she was engaged in some task for Lucy. She seemed to be constantly answering to her beck and call these days. Mrs Petty could well be out in the garden, collecting vegetables for dinner, or else gossiping with young Tom in the afternoon sunshine. Kate glanced at the clock. It was early yet, not quite five. With a sigh, she set down the pile of books she'd been sorting, wiped the dust from her hands on her apron, and hurried downstairs.

It was the local constable who was patiently waiting for her, and even before he spoke, the look on his face told her everything. She felt, in that moment, as if time stood still, yet the chimes of the grandfather clock in the hall sounded louder than ever, and a chill descended upon her, despite the August heat.

'I'm that sorry, Mrs Tyson. Happen it would be best if you sat down.'

'Oh, dear God ... Callum?'

'No, ma'am, don't fret none about your boy. It's – well, fact of the matter is...' This was the one part of his job that the constable hated the most. 'Is there anyone else in the house, ma'am? Can I call someone for you?'

'Please, get on with it. What's happened?'

'Well, the car didn't even stop, d'you see. It was all very quick. The master wouldn't even have known what had hit him. He were just walking across Aynam Road, limping like, one witness said. War injury, I dare say. He should have used a stick. Too proud, no doubt. Anyway, the motor car swung round the corner and ploughed straight into him. Like I say, didn't even stop, the villain, went shooting off out of town at the speed of light. We're trying to find out the make and registration number but all we know so far is that it was black, which doesn't help us much at all, does it? I mean, what else would it have been? Poor man didn't stand a chance. Blinded by the lowness of the sun to see proper, I expect. I can't tell you how sorry I am, ma'am. Never was a nicer bloke, and him just back from the front. Missed all them German bullets and bombs, only to cop it in his own town.'

The constable seemed to be asking and answering his own questions. Which was just as well since Kate was quite incapable of doing so. She'd passed out on Ida's clean doorstep.

The funeral took place early the following week at Kendal Parish Church where the vicar gave a lengthy eulogy on what a very fine gentleman Mr Eliot Tyson had been; how well thought of he was in the town, by townsfolk and factory workers alike; how brave he'd been in volunteering for active service; and how tragic it was that, having survived the war, he had not managed to survive the peace.

The respect and high esteem in which he'd been held were only too evident in a church that was packed to the door. Hymns were sung, prayers chanted and psalms read, before he was laid to rest in the parish churchyard.

Not that Kate was aware of any of this. She had been rushed to the County hospital where she'd lost her baby and had since lain in a stupor, unaware of anything going on around her.

All of which suited Lucy perfectly.

The reading of the will, some three weeks after Eliot's death, delayed out of respect for Kate's condition, was the first day she felt able to rise from her bed and come downstairs. She would not have achieved even this had it not been for dear Aunt Cissie's help and quiet persistence.

'I shall help to get you washed and dressed, dear girl, but it is essential that you are present. You must hear what is being said.'

And when Kate turned away with a groan, complaining that she didn't care what the will said, she simply wanted to be left alone, Cissie became surprisingly firm.

'You must get up, you really must. Lucy will be there, with all her children. They have arrived in force, don't you know? Jack, Bunty and even young George, dragooned into action to prove they are "family"; that they care. How would poor Callum and Flora feel if you weren't there beside them? Or are you going to throw in the towel and allow Lucy to take over?'

If anything was calculated to galvanise her into action, it was the thought of Lucy taking charge.

Kate submitted herself to Cissie's ministrations. A bath was drawn for her, her face and hands washed like a child's, her back scrubbed and her hair shampooed. The fresh lemon verbena scent of it made her cry, remembering how much Eliot had loved it. Then she was tenderly dried and dressed in the frock she generally wore for other people's funerals, had never intended to wear again for one of her own. It all seemed unreal, as if she were one step removed from everything, standing behind a pane of frosted glass, not quite able to see or hear what was going on beyond it.

With her face wax pale and her hair neatly tied back, Kate walked slowly downstairs, supported by Cissie every step of the way, to take her place in Eliot's study. Every day throughout the war she had occupied that room without a second thought. Now she hesitated at the door, summoning her strength before she was able to face the prospect of entering.

'Be brave, dear girl, you are not alone. Vera and I will be right there beside you, as always,' Cissie said, patting her hand.

Kate felt a rush of warm gratitude. 'Thank you.' She wanted to say so much more, about how she appreciated the support the aunts had given her so often in the past, despite their initial disapproval of her, but knew that she couldn't, not without starting the tears all over again.

Vera opened the door and the two maiden ladies helped Kate to a seat right in the centre of the circle of chairs set before Eliot's desk. The leather seat was cracked and she could feel the horse-hair stuffing pricking the back of her legs, but didn't ask for a better one or shift her position. The discomfort would serve to keep her mind on what was going on.

It seemed wrong to Kate that a stranger, Mr Jeffries the family solicitor, should be seated at Eliot's desk. She wanted to shout at him to go away, to tell him that her husband would not approve of his presence here. The aroma of Eliot's after-dinner cigars still lingered in the air, an acrid, stale odour that brought a rush of fresh tears to Kate's eyes. Would she ever get through this ordeal?

Kate was aware of Lucy and her three children, of Mrs Petty and Ida and the two aunts, all watching her with varying degrees of sympathy and concern. She must look what she was, a vulnerable young woman grieving for a beloved husband; a woman who'd just lost a precious child and had suddenly aged by ten years or more.

She also noticed that Callum was not present.

A small warm hand slid into hers. 'Are you all right, Mammy? Aunt Cissie said you were ill and that I was not to disturb you.'

'Flora, me darlin', how good it is to see you. Sure and Mammy's on the mend now. Can't you see?'

'Shall we proceed?' This from Lucy who, as Cissie quite rightly stated, had clearly put herself in charge. But then she'd no doubt organised the entire funeral since Kate had been incapable.

The solicitor cleared his throat, declared that this was Eliot Tyson's last will and testimony, and began to read.

Most of it went right over Kate's head. She was quite incapable of concentrating. She felt so restless and desperately tired. Even sitting in a chair took every ounce of her willpower. All she wanted to do was to put her head under the bed-clothes, go to sleep and never wake up. Except that was a wicked thought. What would happen to her children then? She mustn't even think such a thing.

Mr Jeffries seemed to be explaining how a small portion of the business already belonged entirely to Kate, and that Eliot's will concerned only the ninety per cent of Tysons that he owned. She lost track of his comments after that, as it all became far too convoluted and complicated.

She did hear that there were small legacies for Mrs Petty and even Ida which pleased her as it would secure their future at least. She heard the names of Lucy's children mentioned, though in what connection she couldn't have said. The outcome must have pleased Lucy for she gave a satisfied little grunt at one point, visibly relaxing as she cocked a look of pure triumph in Kate's direction.

When it was done and the document folded

away, Lucy rose gracefully and personally thanked the solicitor, shaking his hand before sweeping out of the room, nose in the air, her children following close behind without a second glance at Kate.

The main body of the complicated document had to be explained to Kate all over again afterwards, over a nice cup of tea which Mrs Petty brought to the small parlour.

The will had apparently been written at the time of their marriage, shortly after Eliot had joined up. He'd therefore made no direct provision for Callum, since the boy had still been missing at the time. The only mention of him was in the instruction: *'In the event of my adopted son Callum being found I trust my wife Katherine to make due provision for him out of her share of my estate as my sister-in-law Lucy must do likewise for her own children.'*

Apparently this had met with Lucy's approval.

Mr Jeffries went on to explain how the house and Eliot's personal effects and disposable funds were left to her in entirety. Now he paused, making sure that he had her full attention before continuing.

Following one or two charitable bequests and a codicil added later to set up a trust fund for Flora, the business known as Tysons Shoe Industries *'...shall be divided equally between my wife Katherine and my sister-in-law Lucy Tyson widow of my brother Charles. I trust that as the sisters they have now become they will feel able to work together to maintain the high standards of Tysons Shoe Industries. I leave my company safe in their hands.'*

# 13

Callum felt as if he was burning up inside with hatred and resentment. This wasn't how it was meant to be. Finding his mother had been the answer to his prayers, and even though things hadn't always gone smoothly between them, at least they were getting to know each other. And he'd been so grateful to get away from the Brocklebanks and that dreadful farm.

It crossed his mind that Mrs Brocklebank must have wondered what had happened to him, where he'd run off to on that market day. Not that he really cared what she thought. He was free. He had found his mother again. That was all that mattered.

Kate was kind and loving, and he liked her helping him with his reading. He'd been enjoying those lessons, that peaceful time together, at least until Eliot Tyson had poked his nose in. He hadn't been near the study since, of course. He'd not be held up as a laughing stock, not by anyone.

Accepting Eliot Tyson as his father had been one step too far, too much to ask. Callum was ashamed to say that he felt no great sorrow over his death, except for the grief it was causing Kate. Not only had she lost her husband, but the child she was carrying too.

Callum felt sorry for her. She rarely left her

room these days and he would often hear her sobbing late into the night. Sometimes he wondered whether he should go in and comfort her, and once had almost done so when she sounded well-nigh hysterical, but then Mrs Petty had come bustling along.

'I'll see to the poor bairn. I'll give her one of my potions,' she'd said, indicating the brown bottle in her hand. Mrs P was the nearest thing to a witch anyone could imagine.

Callum had left her to it, and while he was thankful to be free of the responsibility, not being entirely sure what he would have done if he'd gone in, he'd also felt a nudge of envy. It might be quite nice to be needed by your mother, for her to want you to sit beside her and know exactly what to do to help. But should Kate ever feel the need to have him by her, she had only to ask. So far, there'd been silence. Even the crying seemed to have stopped now.

Sometimes he offered to take in her breakfast or dinner on a tray. Generally she was lying in bed, oblivious of the fact that he was there. Until this morning when he'd discovered her sitting in a chair, staring blankly out of the window. He wondered if she'd been there all night.

'I've brought you breakfast,' he said, as he always did.

Rarely did she even respond, except on her better mornings. Sometimes she would smile a little, thank him or say that he was a good boy. Callum loved to see her smile. He ached to make her happy again.

This morning Kate had startled him by saying:

'Would we have been happier, do you think, Callum, if we'd stayed in Poor House Lane? Millie did, and she survived, along with most of her brood.'

'I don't know, Mam.' He liked calling her that, and did it more and more. It was much less formal, more personal somehow, than Mother.

He was rewarded with another of her rare smiles, as if she liked it too, but there was still that faint crease between her brow as if she sought the answer to a puzzle. 'Did I do the right thing? That's what I keep asking myself. It was for you, I did it for you. I was so afraid you might catch something dreadful and die. I wanted the best for you. Do you hate me for that? I didn't mean to give you away, and nor did I, not entirely. I wouldn't have agreed to the adoption if they hadn't let me stay on as nursemaid. Well, that was my official title, but you and me know different. Wasn't I always your mammy?'

'Aye, Mam, you were.' Flora still called her Mammy, but Callum didn't. He was nearly a man after all.

'But then you vanished and my world fell apart. I went back to Poor House Lane. Did you know that?'

He was surprised. He hadn't known that.

'Now I've lost him. I've lost my Eliot. Why do I always lose those I love best? Is it a punishment for wanting too much out of life, for being greedy?' Her eyes filled with tears and Callum hurried forward to give her an awkward pat on her shoulder.

''Course it isn't a punishment. Anyroad, who from?'

'From the gods. They get jealous if we mere mortals are too happy, so they do.'

Callum made a scornful sound deep in his throat. 'You've been listening too much to Mrs P and her weird notions. The old witch is poisoning yer mind. You were poor, near starving, stands to reason you'd want to better yerself. Who wouldn't? And from all accounts, tha's med a grand job of the business. All the men say so.'

'Do they?' She perked up a little at that, but then seemed to collapse in on herself again. 'But how can I carry on? How can I go on without him?' And she put her face in her hands and sobbed.

Life had been difficult enough before, but now the situation was a thousand times worse. And it was all far too convenient. Why had they never found the car that had hit him? Why was it going so fast, and why didn't it stop? It all sounded a bit fishy to Callum.

What was worse, as a result of Eliot Tyson's death, bloody Lucy now owned nearly a half-share in the company. She was also flouncing about the house as if she owned that too, and with his mother having locked herself in her room, she might as well.

Kate was filled with a terrible restlessness. If she sat on her window seat for five minutes, she must then get up and go and sit on her chair by the fire, or lie on her bed for a while. She would pick up a book and try to read, or glance at the newspaper, but the things that were happening in the world – riots in Liverpool in response to a

125

police strike, with hundreds arrested, and talk of a rail strike soon – seemed unreal. Kate was too tired to care, and she wasn't going anywhere, so what did it matter if the trains weren't running?

Thoughts tumbled over themselves in her head. She kept asking herself why it had happened, replaying that day in her mind like a stuck gramophone record.

Had Eliot been thinking of her and the baby, was that why he was knocked down? Because he hadn't been paying proper attention to what he was doing.

What a dreadful thought. In that case it would all be her fault. The more rational part of her mind told her this was nonsense, but then the questions and the need to apportion blame would start up all over again.

'It's my fault that I lost the baby,' she told Flora, as the little girl sat stroking her hand. Flora was appalled.

'Don't say such a terrible thing, Mammy. It is not your fault. You were grieving for Daddy. You were sick. Aunt Vera said you might have died.' Her lovely chestnut eyes filled with tears. 'What would I have done then, if you had?'

'Aw, cherub, I'd never leave you, I swear it.' And she grasped Flora to her breast while the pair of them sobbed out their grief. Then Kate pulled out her hanky and scolded herself for giving in to her emotions, trying to smile, for the sake of her little girl.

'What would Daddy say if he could see us now? Sure and he'd be ashamed of us, so he would. I remember him telling me that I mustn't be defeated, or give in to self-pity, if the worst happened and he didn't come back from the war. Get up and get on with life, he said. Nobody guaranteed that we'd all have our three score years and ten, now did they?' But before ever the words were out of Kate's mouth, the tears were flowing again. They just wouldn't stop.

And when she wasn't crying, she felt sick, nauseous. Sometimes she would shake with cold, even as sweat slicked her skin. And she constantly relived those dreadful moments when Constable Brown gave her the news.

Worse than that, in her mind's eye she saw the car, mysterious and black, driving very fast. She saw Eliot's startled expression, transfixed and blinded by the sun glinting on its windscreen, eyes wide with terror. She heard the screech of brakes, the impact of a heavy body on steel, the sound of glass breaking. It seemed so real in her mind, almost as if she'd personally witnessed the event.

If she could only focus her mind on the sequence of events, on how the accident could have happened, yet it seemed impossible. One minute her mind was numb, the next racing, not a coherent thought in it, only a tumult of questions going round and round in her head.

Who had been driving that car? Why had the driver not bothered to stop? Who would be so cruel, so uncaring? Or was it simply fear that had made them drive on?

Most terrifying of all, she needed to know if Eliot had died instantly, or if he'd lain in the road, dying slowly, as he waited for help? Oh, it was all too awful to think about, too dreadful and confusing.

If only she had the answers to these questions, she might then be able to accept that he was dead, that he wasn't ever coming back to her.

How was she ever going to live without him?

And yet a part of her still expected the door to open and Eliot to come breezing in, sweep her up in his arms and tell her how much he loved her.

Sometimes one of the aunts would creep in: Vera with hot lemon, as if she had 'flu or a sore throat, Cissie with a chocolate drop or mint humbug, as if she were a dog needing a treat. They brought her cups of tea she couldn't drink, food she couldn't eat, their eyes full of pity.

The nights were the worst, long and silent and endless, her body aching from exhaustion as she sat and rocked herself in numb misery in the chair, Eliot's photograph clutched to her chest. Sometimes she would walk quietly down the stairs and out into the starry night, slip through the stillness of the garden, the heady scent of night-stocks filling her nostrils. Then she would sit in the summer house, not crying now but with a small smile on her face, remembering, finding some solace and peace at last in those blissful memories.

How she would miss him.

'How can I stay calm?' The high treble voice rang the entire length of the landing, right to the small room at the back of the house where Callum was sitting hunched on his bed with his fingers in his ears, trying not to listen to their row. 'Would you, if you'd just put your bare feet on a slimy toad?'

'It isn't slimy, and it's a frog not a toad,' Georgie shouted back, hooting with laughter.

'I don't care what it is, it shouldn't be in *my bed!*'

A fair enough point, Callum thought, pulling the pillow over his head.

As if having the woman who'd abducted him back in this house wasn't bad enough, he now had her children to contend with as well.

Georgie was forever up to some stupid schoolboy prank or other, like tying tin cans to the cat's tail or putting that frog in his sister's bed this evening. Callum could hear Bunty ... stupid name! ... still screaming like a banshee and running all over the landing. Heaven help Georgie when she finally catches up with him, Callum thought, without too much sympathy.

She'd barely glanced at him since arriving earlier in the week in time for the funeral, except to look at him down her nose when her mother introduced him ... if you could call Lucy's offhand remark an introduction: 'And this is the workhouse boy.'

Bunty had not responded, not even to say hello, but there'd been curiosity in her eyes, and, surprisingly, sympathy. He was sure of it.

Jack had snorted with laughter, but then he was a pompous, middle-class prat. Full of his own importance, he looked upon himself as the man of the family. Even the way he dressed, in cravats and three-piece suits worn with silk waistcoats, made him seem like a forty year old instead of a boy of eighteen. And he was so arrogant! Callum could hear him now lecturing his younger brother, scolding his sister, just as if she had encouraged Georgie to play this practical joke on her.

The door burst open and Bunty burst in, flinging herself next to him on the bed in a paroxysm of tears. 'You'll protect me, won't you, Callum? I *hate* to be teased! It's not fair, two against one.'

He gazed at her in utter astonishment while she turned upon him a pair of blue eyes puffy with crying in a round face that was crimson with fury. She was a plump girl with untidy mouse-brown hair. For once her mouth had lost its perpetual pout as she pursed her full lips tightly together in temper. Nobody could call her beautiful, yet there was something about Bunty which was appealing. Perhaps it was the sense of humanity so obviously missing in the rest of her family.

Callum glanced anxiously at the door, which she had quickly closed after her. 'I'm not sure I can do owt,' he said. He preferred to keep himself to himself and avoid becoming embroiled in their constant rows and upsets.

'Oh, but Georgie makes me so mad, I could kill him!'

'Don't say that.'

She looked up, startled, and then the fury in her eyes instantly died to be replaced with compassion. 'Oh, I didn't think. I'm so sorry. Do you miss your father terribly?'

'He weren't me father. At least, I didn't feel as if he were. I didn't really know him, you see, having been snatched and taken away to that farm when I were nobbut a nipper.'

She seemed to consider this for a moment.

'That must have been awful. I don't remember much about my father either. He died when I was quite young. Did you hate it there, at the farm?'

'Aye, I did. Not the farm so much as the people, the Brocklebanks. I quite liked the animals, they were my friends.' Callum could have kicked himself the minute the words were out of his mouth. Heaven help him, what would she think of a chap who had sheep for friends? But Bunty wasn't laughing. Quite the contrary, she seemed to be agreeing with him.

'I used to have a cat once called Tiddles.' She gave a half smile. 'I wasn't a particularly imaginative child. Anyway, it disappeared, and then I discovered that Georgie had swapped it for a jar of worms from a friend. I hated him for that. Tiddles was my friend. I never had many either, as a child. I was away at school, you know, and people there prefer you to be pretty or terribly clever or rich, and I was none of those things. And I couldn't – couldn't make things happen like Jack can, or make fun of everything as Georgie does. And I'm not beautiful like Mummy. I was always the odd one out. Do you see?'

They looked at each other in complete silence for a moment and then Callum solemnly nodded. 'Aye, I do. I can understand that.'

She was nibbling on her finger nails, as she so often did. 'I was the one always feeling awkward, trying not to listen when they called me names like "fatty", or "chubby-chops". I hate being called names and made to feel stupid.'

'The Brocklebanks never called me by a name at all. I was always "you" to them. "Hey you", they'd say, "go and fetch me t'shovel." Or, "Hey, you, go and feed t'sheep. *You* do this. *You* do that.""

She looked at him, round-eyed with sympathy. 'It must have been awful, having no family of your own and being bullied like that. Kate blames Mummy, doesn't she? No, you don't have to answer that. I suggest we don't talk about what our parents did, don't you agree? Then perhaps you and me could be friends. I'd like that very much. Would you?'

Callum looked at her in surprise. Even now that his life was a thousand times better, he still didn't have many friends, beyond Flora and his mam, of course, and what Bunty said did make sense. Living in the past did you no good at all. 'Aye,' he agreed, surprising himself with his fervour. 'That'd be grand.'

# 14

In the weeks following they became inseparable. Bunty, who hated her name with equal fervour, was keen to get away from her brothers at any and every opportunity. Callum taught her how to fish, either in the River Kent or else they'd walk down to Sedgwick, where it was quieter, and bring back some trout for Mrs P to cook for lunch.

Then one Saturday Lucy declared that she'd had enough of being gloomy and they should all go on a picnic. The aunts did not approve.

'The family is still in mourning, Lucy. It is not appropriate.'

'It's not fair to my darling children to be stuck inside on such a lovely day. I'm sure Eliot would not have objected to their having a little fun.'

'We shall not join in your *little bit of fun*,' said Vera, somewhat testily. 'Nor will dear Kate.'

'There wouldn't be room for all of us in any case, not even in that old carthorse of a tourer.'

Jack perked up. 'Why don't we take both cars, Mother? I could drive your Austin.'

'No, you could not!'

He laughed. 'I'm eighteen years old! I can drive, you know. Freddie Makepiece's father lets me drive his Mercedes whenever I go and stay.'

'More fool him.' But Callum noticed his aunt was very pink about the cheeks. Now why was that?

While Lucy hurried off to instruct Mrs Petty to pack a large hamper and blankets, he sneaked out of the back door and crept quickly round to the stables, now used as garages. There was the old Crossley tourer which Eliot had bought before the war, and beside it stood Lucy's Austin 20.

Checking that he was unobserved, Callum slipped inside the garage and began to examine the car. It was gloomy in the garage, and not easy to see, nevertheless he found what he was looking for. The right-hand wing had a dent in it, and one of the front lights was broken.

Lucy was using the telephone when he came back into the house, speaking rather quickly and breathlessly, but she put the receiver down as he

133

entered so he'd no idea who she was talking to. All he'd heard were the words, 'See to it.'

She turned to him with a falsely bright social smile, hands clasped tightly together. 'I shouldn't think you'll wish to come with us on the picnic, will you, boy?' He'd noticed that she never used his name. So, apparently, had Bunty. She heard her mother now as she came into the room.

'He's called Callum, and of course he wants to come, Mummy. Callum is teaching me how to fish.'

'Oh, very well. Don't keep us waiting, boy, if you must come. Hurry up, we shall be leaving very shortly.'

'Callum! His name is Callum.'

The thought of being out in the sun, tickling a few trout, was sorely tempting and Callum bit back a sense of guilt because his mother would be staying at home. Not that Kate objected to his going. Autumn was coming and the leaves were turning gold and crimson, falling in crisp heaps on to the spongy earth. There wouldn't be many good days left. She thought the outing would do him good.

'Have fun, my darling. Are ye not young and full of life? Take care of Flora, that's all I ask. She spends far too much time in this dull old sick room with her mammy.'

'Why don't you come too? The fresh air might bring some colour to your cheeks.'

For a brief instant Callum thought he saw a spark of something in her eyes, as if maybe she did want to start living again, after all. He leaned closer, saying on a note of eagerness, 'Have you not wondered who did it, Mam? Who would want rid of Eliot?'

He'd startled her, he could tell by the way her gaze suddenly fixed keenly on his. 'What makes you say that?'

Should he tell her about what he'd discovered in the old stables? No, not just yet. Where was the point in upsetting her further until he had more proof? But he could plant a seed of doubt in her mind. 'Don't you think it's all a bit too convenient, a bit peculiar it should happen just after you'd told everyone about the babby?'

'I – I don't know. I hadn't thought. It was just an accident...'

How had Callum become aware of her own crazy thoughts? She hadn't mentioned her concerns, had she?

'What car would *accidentally* be going at that speed? It demands a lot of effort, for one thing. Keeping your foot flat down on the pedal isn't easy. Cars don't go fast of their own accord.'

Kate was staring at him now with a mixture of fear and panic in her eyes. At least that was better than indifference, he thought. Callum was about to say more, to hint at his decision to make some sort of investigation, when the door opened and Lucy came in, carrying Mrs Petty's small brown bottle.

'Kate, really, what are you doing sitting by the window where you'll catch a draught? Come along, Callum shall help me get you back into bed, then I'll give you a sip of Mrs Petty's elixir and you'll sleep all afternoon like a baby. We shall bring you some lovely fish for your tea.'

And so Callum did as he was bid and left his mother, beguiled by the prospect of a day's fishing. But he remained troubled. Something wasn't right, and he'd recognised that fear in Kate's eyes too.

It was obvious from the start that he and Jack were not going to be soul-mates. The picnic was a disaster, Jack clearly irritated because Callum caught more fish, and because he and Bunty were giggling together, having a good time. He tried to butt in once or twice but Bunty told him to go away and stop pestering them.

'You can't be horrid to me one minute and then expect me to be nice to you the next.'

'Well, if you'd rather spend time with the peasant brat, so be it.'

'He isn't a brat, or a peasant.'

'He lived in a workhouse and was brought up on a farm. Sounds pretty peasant-like to me.'

'Oh, do shut up, Jack. Stop being rude.'

Jack was annoyed, and, as they were climbing into the boat, began to rock it, very badly, making the water slap against the sides and Bunty give a little squeal of fear. 'Go on, peasant, fall in why don't you and give us all a laugh?'

Callum managed to hold on but, unsurprisingly, Georgie started messing about and did fall in, getting himself soaked through, which annoyed his mother greatly as he would make the back seat of the motor all wet. Lucy insisted he strip off and spend the rest of the day in his swimming trunks while his clothes dried. Georgie happily obliged, not minding in the least.

Inevitably, Lucy spent most of the day basking in the sun with her eyes closed, and at lunchtime while she gorged herself on champagne and smoked salmon, Georgie and Jack set about building a camp fire and began cooking dampers out of flour and water, and burnt sausages.

'None for you, peasant, so don't even think of asking.'

'We don't want any,' Bunty stoutly declared. 'Come on, Callum, let's take our egg sandwiches and go and fish in peace.'

Which they did. Callum was beginning to quite like Bunty. She certainly knew how to stand her ground, refusing absolutely to be brow beaten by her two obnoxious brothers. And when he helped her to net a large brown trout, she flung her arms about his neck and kissed him. Her mouth tasted surprisingly pleasant, her breasts wobbling enticingly against his chest, and as she smiled cheekily at him, asking if he'd like another, he grinned shyly back and nodded. The second kiss was even nicer.

Kate had made sure she took only the smallest sip of Mrs Petty's elixir, and managed to spit at least some out the minute Lucy had left. She really must instruct Mrs P to stop giving it to her. Whatever it was, it drained the life from her. A small throb of pain beat in her temple. Ignoring it, she got out of bed, hoping she could fight off any sense of drowsiness as she needed to think, to examine Callum's comments about the accident, recognising that he'd been suffering the same sort of torment as herself. Asking the self-same questions.

Why would a car be travelling so fast? And why couldn't it be found? If only she could get her thoughts into some sort of order and work it all out. Could Callum be right in his suspicions? Could it have been deliberate? Who would do such a thing? Surely even Lucy wouldn't stoop so low?

Kate shook the thoughts away. What was happening to her? She must be growing fanciful, confused, wrong in her head to be imagining such wickedness. Lucy may have made mistakes in the past, and was certainly a difficult woman, but she'd surely learned her lesson, hadn't she? In any case, why would she kill Eliot? For the inheritance, of course. For money, and for power. But was she capable of being so callous, so brutal? Surely not. Most important of all, if Callum *was* correct, how could they prove it?

A part of Kate didn't want to worry about such problems. Her headache was growing worse and she longed simply to climb back into bed and think about Eliot.

She needed to remember every last detail about him: the way he would smile at her as if she were all that mattered in the world to him, the twist of his brow when they'd had one of their regular spats and disagreed over something. At least it was never over anything trivial.

A dozen times a day she would go to his wardrobe and bury her face in his shirts and jackets, breathing in the scent of him, causing a pain to build within her, a physical constriction robbing her of breath, of life almost. Yet it was worth the agony, if for a second she could bring the essence of him back.

Kate knew she should have gone with her children on their picnic today, but somehow she hadn't been able to bring herself to do so.

She recalled picnics by the lake with Eliot, sailing in a steam yacht, long romantic walks over quiet fells, and in the spring a visit to the nearby Lyth Valley to see the snow-white damson blossom was always a treat, it being such a wonderful sight to see. Every spring when the orchards came to life again a festival would be held, and much feasting and merriment take place. Damson day was special, a day to enjoy tasting the variety of food and drink made from the fruit: jams, chutneys, wine, and damson gin of course. There would be music and jugglers, Morris dancers perhaps, and lovers such as themselves would dance and kiss, Eliot telling her she was more lovely than all the blossom in the world.

How would she ever manage without him? Where was the point in going on? And yet she must. Did she really want Lucy to take over the business, which she almost certainly would try to do if Kate didn't watch out?

She couldn't just lie here falling deeper and deeper into depression. Kate crossed to her wardrobe, pulled out a skirt and sweater, began to dress herself with slow, clumsy fingers. The buttons seemed too big for their holes and it took an age to fasten them but finally she managed it.

Kate knew she had decisions to make about what she was going to do with all the empty years stretching ahead of her but her mind felt like soggy porridge, splinters of light stabbing her eyes so that she could hardly see. Splashing cold water on to her face helped a little. She dragged a comb through her hair, pushed her feet into a pair of shoes, the prospect of struggling with stockings too much of an effort to contemplate.

She needed to know what was happening to the business. Somehow it seemed vital that she find out now, without any further delay.

What had possessed Eliot to give his sister-in-law such a large share? What had he been thinking of? But in her heart Kate knew the reason. Lucy was family and Eliot was nothing if not a family man, someone who believed in loyalty and honour. His family were of vital importance to him, and he'd suffered to the end over the death of his brother, for all the two of them had never been close.

Had he suffered when the car struck him that fatal blow? Kate prayed there had been no time for him to think, or to face the prospect of his own death.

No one heard her go down the stairs. Mrs Petty and Ida were no doubt busy in the kitchen and everyone else was out, the aunts about their church business, the rest of the family on their picnic.

By the time she reached the garden gate, Kate was panting for breath. By the end of the road before ever she reached the bridge, she guessed that she wasn't going to make it. The walk to the factory was far more than she could cope with, and she certainly wasn't fit to drive. The exertion of getting this far had taken everything out of her. It was this damned elixir Lucy kept spooning into her. She wouldn't touch another drop.

A dizziness swept over her and then Kate was forced to sit down on a wall for a moment or two to wait until it passed. Perhaps if she sat here for a while the nausea would ease and she would be able to go on, but the headache seemed to be getting worse, pounding like a iron foundry now.

As luck would have it, at that very moment, like a pair of small sailing ships with sails flapping, the aunts hove into view. Umbrellas in hand and hats aloft, they were utterly shocked to find Kate sitting on a garden wall.

'What in heaven's name are you doing here, child?'

'You shouldn't even be out of bed so soon after losing the baby.'

They led her back to her room with much stern scolding, then ran about bringing hot water bottles, smelling salts and cups of camomile tea. When they finally left her in peace, Kate put her face in her hands and cried. Would she ever feel normal again?

Delayed by events, Jack started work on the fifteenth day of September instead of the first, as initially planned. His first week was spent largely in observing, which he considered to be boring and a complete waste of time, and he was then put to assist old Jem, a journeyman shoemaker. Jack protested loudly, making a great fuss and claiming to be no good with his hands, or to have any ambition to become a manual worker. His role should be in the office, he said, as he was to be one of the bosses. Toby Lynch insisted that the best way to learn the business was from the floor up, and when Lucy made a fuss at home she was not surprised to find that Kate backed him up.

'It's what Eliot would have expected,' Kate insisted, proud of herself for making a stand.

Jack sulked, of course, and was even more peevish as a result, but Lynch refused to back down and Lucy was helpless to make any changes without Kate's agreement.

Callum might have thought the whole squabble worthwhile, even hilarious, if it had inspired his mother to get back to work, but she still stayed mainly in her room, venturing out only occasionally to walk about the garden a little or sit in the summer house. The workers at the factory were growing increasingly restless at her continued absence.

Toby Lynch would ask Callum to his face when she might be returning and he could only shake his head and say that he didn't know. Apparently not satisfied with the answer, one day Toby called at the house and spoke to Lucy.

'I need to speak to Mrs Tyson. There are decisions to be made.'

'You can tell me. I shall make them for her.'

Toby hesitated. He knew the sister-in-law had been left a share of the factory, which troubled him deeply, and was also aware that she knew nothing about either shoes or business. 'I reckon I'll wait for Kate. I'm not surprised she's feeling low but if I could just have a word, I might be able to persuade her to get going again, to come into the office. The operatives are missing her. The place doesn't seem the same without her. Folk are asking after her.'

'She'll come when I think she's fit and ready,' answered Lucy, rather testily. 'I will not have her upset.' And smartly showed him out of the house.

Callum, listening to this from behind the door, was deeply troubled. It sounded almost as if Lucy cared deeply about Kate, and didn't want his mother to go back to the factory, which didn't make any sense at all.

# 15

At the very next opportunity, when Callum had brought up her breakfast tray and they were alone, Kate asked him the question that was bothering her the most. 'Have the police been round again? Have they found the car?'

Callum shook his head. 'They've called, but say it's a hopeless task. It could've been anyone. It's true that there are more and more cars around Kendal these days, although I wouldn't have thought all that many, at least not that are capable of going at a speed that can actually kill a man.'

'It takes very little to kill a man, Callum. Or so it seems.'

Callum told her then about what he'd found when he examined Lucy's car. Kate was appalled.

'Dent in the wing? Broken head-lamp? But why didn't the police spot that when they examined it?'

'Because they *haven't* examined it. Why should

they? Constable Brown did ask if she possessed a motor, but Lucy started weeping and wailing as if she were the grieving widow, not you, and he was thankful to escape the house before she started having full-scale hysterics. Since then, he's called once or twice, but only to say that there's nothing to report, and he never stays a minute longer than necessary.'

'But that isn't right, not right at all. Oh, dear, do you really think she might be involved, Callum? Surely even Lucy wouldn't stoop to ... to...'

'Murder? Why not, since she's not against abducting and molesting children? Will I call and tell the police constable about what I found, do you reckon?'

'Oh, dear, I don't know. I can't think!'

Yet Callum could see that as painful as the subject was, talking about it had rekindled some of that fighting spirit in his mother which was so much a part of her nature. There was a change in her. He could sense it. A good thing, surely.

'Toby Lynch has called too. Several times, in fact. He says they need you back at the factory, Mam. There are decisions to be made, and everyone there is worried about you.'

'Are they? Toby called here, you say?'

'Aye, to ask after you.'

'Sure and he's the kindest of men! Maybe I will go in next week, or even tomorrow. Mebbe it'd do me good. What do you think? Is it too soon?'

Callum was pleased. 'I think you should.'

And Kate did indeed get up at her usual early hour, and dressed for work, feeling very proud of herself at how much easier it was this time. She even managed to put on her stockings correctly. But when she went down to breakfast, Lucy was appalled by the very idea, and insisted she go straight back to bed.

'I thought I heard you getting up. What are you thinking of? You simply aren't up to it. Your health and your nerves are far too fragile.'

'I'm feeling much better, so I am. Mebbe doing something, getting back to work, will be good for me. Callum thinks so.'

'Callum is a stupid boy. What does he know about losing babies and grieving? And how can you think of yourself at a time like this? You're still in mourning. This is not the moment to be *doing deals* at the factory, with Eliot barely cold in his grave. Don't you care about him at all that you can so quickly recover? People will think you heartless.'

And Kate fled back to her room.

A day or two later, Callum called at the police station. The desk sergeant rubbed a hand over his chin and looked doubtful about his story. Confronting Lucy Tyson with suspicions that her motor car might have been involved in the accident evidently did not appeal to him.

'Are you sure about this, lad?'

'Yes, I'm sure. I saw it with me own eyes, just the other day. It had a dented wing and a broken headlamp.'

'That doesn't prove her car sustained this damage as a result of her running down Mr Tyson. She might just have hit a lamp post.'

'I know, but you must admit, it's suspicious?'

'We'll have to see about that. I'll happen have the constable call by for a brief chat and see if he can wangle a dekko at the car in question, without causing too much upset, like. I can see you're a lad what cares about his mam but this is a delicate matter. We have to tread carefully. Be sensitive to family feelings.'

Callum couldn't see what was so delicate about checking out a vehicle. Seemed like common sense to him, however, his own part in it certainly was very delicate indeed. 'You'll warn the constable not to mention that I was the one who told you?'

There was curiosity and speculation in the sergeant's gaze, yet he pursed his lips and gave a sharp nod. 'I'll tell him it's a routine check which should have been done before now. I'll claim it was my fault for not thinking of it earlier, only she's a bit of a tartar your aunt.'

One morning the constable paid a call, and, to Callum's great surprise, Lucy did not throw a tantrum when he tentatively asked if he might just take a look in the stables at the Austin. Quite the opposite, she led him there with a cherubic smile on her lips, which instantly aroused Callum's suspicions.

The Austin looked pristine, the wing smooth and shiny, the broken lamp replaced with a new one. The constable took off his helmet and scratched his head, then offered his deepest apologies for having bothered her and slunk away. He didn't even glance in Callum's direction, but Lucy did.

When the policeman had gone and they were alone in the stables, she turned to him with a sweet smile. 'I wonder what, or who, gave Constable Brown the notion that my car might be damaged? I really can't think, can you?'

Callum shook his head and made himself scarce.

Kate was not in the least surprised by their failure. 'It must have been Swainson. She'll have kept in touch with him, though I've heard nothing from the man in years. He could have fixed up the car for her, no questions asked.'

'You need to tell me more about this Swainson.'

'He's a bad lot. Trouble with a capital T. Greedy and resourceful. The kind of man who uses other people for his own ends. I persuaded Eliot to sack him from the job of foreman at Tysons, but it was hard. That's what we were quarrelling about when you were taken that day. I'm not sure I have the strength for another battle, not on me own. Look what happened when I thought of going into the factory. Lucy demolished me in seconds.'

'You aren't on yer own. You have me now.'

She smiled at him, stroked his cheek. "Course I do, and aren't I the lucky one? But Lucy is far cleverer than either of us have given her credit for.'

'Then we need to be cleverer. We need to fight her.'

Kate gave a wry smile. 'I'm not sure that's possible, not without a lot of agony. 'Tis certainly true that I underestimated her, or she wouldn't

147

have succeeded in keeping you away from me for so long, let alone stealing you in the first place. But this business – this is even worse. I can't bear to think of her doing that – deliberately – to my darling Eliot. Running him down... Oh, God! I hope you're wrong and she's innocent! I mean, we've no proof, have we?'

'We could find proof, somehow.' Callum realised that if they were ever going to succeed in proving what an evil, conniving woman Lucy was, he would need all his wits about him.

His mother had fallen silent and he wanted to bring the spark of battle back into her eyes, which had somehow been swamped once more by despair and misery. 'How? What can we do?'

'I don't know yet but I'll think of something.' Callum had a sudden idea. 'I could ask around, see if anyone saw anything. See if I can find any witnesses, someone who mebbe spotted Lucy's car before she struck.'

'Oh, Callum!' Kate shook her head. 'The police must have already done that. Leave it.' And she sank back into herself, staring unseeing out of the window, as if the discussion had exhausted her. Callum crept away. But she hadn't said that he mustn't do it, so his decision was made.

Lucy was in a fury. Just when she thought justice had been done for the death of her darling Charles, that interfering little busybody had to go and poke his nose in! He should have stayed in the Langdales and thank his lucky stars no worse fate had befallen him. He had no right to any Tyson money. It was hers, every bit of it. She wouldn't tolerate interference, she simply wouldn't. And Lucy could tell by the sly way Callum kept glancing at her that he remained suspicious.

The police had called again, asking more questions about what she was doing that day. And they'd promised to come back, once they'd made further enquiries. It was all extremely uncomfortable and not a little alarming, thanks to that brat.

She sent word to Swainson that she needed to speak to him, sending the note as she usually did via his weasel son, and one evening received an acknowledgement in return. Since she couldn't possibly be seen with him in a public place, they were to meet in a quiet country lane north of Kendal, close to the woods at Crook. Swainson would presumably ride there on his bicycle while Lucy took the Austin. A pretty enough spot in the daylight but eerily quiet after dark. She wasn't looking forward to the encounter.

Lucy parked her motor and sat waiting for him. Thank goodness for her precious motor! What freedom it gave her. But she needed more. She needed complete control of what should rightly have been left to Charles, and now belonged to their children. It was all Kate O'Connor's fault. If she'd never given up her son for adoption in the first place, her precious Eliot would still have been alive today.

A tap on the window made Lucy jump. Swainson got in beside her, just the smell of the man making her recoil, let alone the sight of his evil face, that twitching moustache above the yellow teeth, the mean little eyes that didn't quite move simultaneously to peer at her from beneath a thatch of dark, greasy hair. Ned Swainson was not the sort of person one would choose as a friend, though better that than have him as your enemy.

'What's up? More problems?'

He was nothing if not succinct.

'The police have been poking around, thanks to that dratted boy.'

'They won't find nowt. I fixed the car. The lad's asking a lot of questions an' all, from what I've heard.'

Lucy was even more alarmed. 'What sort of questions, of whom?'

'Calm down, don't get your knickers in a twist. It might be just a rumour. If not, I'll soon find out. I'm keeping a close eye on the situation.'

'See that you do. I thought I'd got rid of him. Now he's back and it won't do. It won't do at all. I don't want anything else to go wrong.'

He fell silent, clearly chewing this over, so close to her in the confines of the car that she felt tainted by the strong smell of tobacco emanating from him together with something else she couldn't quite put a name to, but far from pleasant. Lucy edged away. Yet as always he held a perverse fascination for her, and even now a twisted part of her mind wondered what he would be like as a lover.

'The lad wouldn't present much of a problem on his own. It's the pretty widow, she's the one we need to worry about. Want me to fix her an' all?'

There was a long pause before Lucy answered. 'No, I'm working on Kate. I think I can deal with that little problem myself. She's going nowhere until I'm good and ready.'

'Take care. We can't have too many bodies littered about the bloody place. The police really would get suspicious then.'

'Depends how it's done,' Lucy agreed with a calculating smile. 'There are ways.'

They sat in the car for another hour, discussing various ways and means, and then Swainson made to leave.

'There is one little task you could do for me...'

'What's that?'

When she told him, he began to laugh, a harsh, barking rumble coming from the depth of his tobacco-encrusted lungs. 'I shall enjoy that. Anyroad, whatever you decide in the end, just mek sure you don't implicate me. And I shall expect a sizeable reward for smoothing the path and helping you, preferably in the form of me old job back, but if that's not on, I wouldn't say no to a bit of hard cash instead.' He held out one grubby palm and Lucy stared at it, perplexed.

'Are you asking for money?'

'I have expenses, greasing other palms for one thing. Smooth paths come at a price.'

Irritated, Lucy dug in her purse and tossed a few coins at him. Still the palm remained outstretched, and with a grunt of annoyance she tossed in a few more. 'Don't push me too far. I'll not be bullied, not by anyone, not even you.'

'I don't reckon you're in any position to argue.' And on that disquieting note, he slipped quietly out of the car and disappeared into the night.

Lucy sat for a moment in the darkness, trembling with barely restrained anger. What had she started? The path she trod was a dangerous one, and she was not so stupid that she didn't understand Swainson could easily turn against her if he became dissatisfied with what she was offering. She needed more money, desperately.

Later that same week Kate was sitting in the summer house, her favourite place. These were a special feature of the town, gracing the long, narrow gardens of Edwardian dwellings and Georgian town houses alike. Many were made of the local limestone, although Eliot had chosen a pale green slate brought down from Coniston for his. It was an octagonal building with one arched window and a matching door, constructed on two floors; the lower one contained a tiny fireplace where Kate liked to light a fire in the cool of the evening and quietly read a book by lamplight. In the upper loft, open to the rafters, she and Eliot had spent many treasured moments alone. It soothed her to sit here and think of him.

Callum was right, though. She really should get back to work. The factory needed her. Toby needed her. He'd sent several cards and messages via Callum, but a part of Kate was afraid that if she became too involved in work she might forget Eliot, or lose touch with him in some way.

In an alcove by the side of the fireplace she kept a selection of his books, along with a box of matches and the oil lamp. As she pulled out the lamp, preparatory to lighting it on this cool

September evening, something heavy fell out of the alcove on to the floor. It made her jump.

'Oh, what was that?'

Alarmed, she quickly struck a match and what she saw made her blood run cold. It was a rat: large, black and hairy with huge yellow teeth.

# 16

It was most definitely dead, Kate was relieved to note, feeling proud of herself for not screaming, although she certainly shuddered, and even squealed a little.

But then this wasn't the first rat she'd encountered, which helped. The creatures had been two a penny in Poor House Lane. This one had surprised her because she'd never seen one at Tyson Lodge in all the time she'd lived here and wasn't expecting to, despite its close proximity to the river. Which no doubt was where this one had come from. Probably found itself trapped and had died. Of what? she wondered.

Frowning, Kate peered more closely and was surprised to note that it had something fastened around its neck. It seemed to be a label with writing on it. Bending down, she overcame her disgust of the creature, struck another match, lit the lamp and held it close so that she could read in the gloom. The writing was clear, written in black ink, and consisted of two words: *You next.*

'My dear, who would do such a thing?' Not unnaturally Aunt Vera was appalled, and was all for calling in the council to fumigate the place. Kate managed to stop her.

'Where would be the point? We live by the river. It flows right by the garden. They would say we are bound to get rats. It's not important, and Tom has already disposed of it. I didn't want Flora to find it.'

'Oh, my dear, no, of course not.'

She'd made no mention to Vera and Cissie of the label tied around the creature's neck, and had removed it before instructing Tom to toss the thing on the bonfire.

'What's wrong?' Lucy airily enquired, coming into the parlour to find the three of them in a huddle. They broke apart instantly.

'Nothing,' said Kate, rather too quickly, aware of surprised glances being exchanged between the two aunts. 'Just enjoying what me old daddy would have called a chin-wag. "Holy Mauther, Katherine girl," he'd say. "Have you nought better to do wi' yer day?" Kate laughed, rather louder than she should, though nobody else did.

'Well, if it's something funny, allow me to share the joke?'

'No, 'tisn't funny at all,' said Kate, still laughing. The last thing she wanted was to tell Lucy about the rat.

Because there was the possibility, of course there was, that Lucy was responsible. It was the sort of malicious act which would give her pleasure. But Kate needed proof before she started making accusations. And if indeed it was Lucy,

154

neither had Kate any wish to give her the satisfaction of seeing her discomfited by any such prank. 'It's just some person thinking I might have a typically female phobia about – about something, and I don't.' And now she laughed all the more.

Clearly the two aunts thought her reaction to the rat was extraordinary, bordering on hysteria, so Kate beat a hasty retreat. Lucy must have thought her quite demented, laughing so uproariously over nothing at all.

But however flippant she may wish to appear before them all, and even if she didn't have a phobia about rats, Kate was nevertheless deeply concerned. If someone was trying to scare her, they had succeeded. Dealing with a dead rat was one thing. Finding one with a label round its neck which amounted to a death threat was another matter altogether.

Who had put it there? That was the worry.

Was it Lucy, or could it be Swainson? Would he hold a grudge against her for all these years because she'd accused him of abusing the women workers and got him sacked? But that was before the war. Why choose this moment to seek his revenge?

Maybe because she was alone and vulnerable again.

And what should Kate do about it? If she told Callum, he'd go mad with rage, so he would. He'd be sure to link this to Eliot's death and ask even more questions, turn over yet more stones. There'd been a great deal of malicious gossip about her in the past. The last thing Kate wanted was for her son to hear a lot of nasty lies about his mother. No doubt it was one of the old guard stirring up trouble again for some daft reason.

Should she tell Toby? He would be quick to offer support, but for some reason Kate balked at involving her foreman in what surely was a personal matter and nothing at all to do with his role at the factory.

She'd just have to treat it as a harmless prank, and keep her wits about her.

'I have tummy ache, Mammy.'

'Aw, now, what has caused that, m'cushla? Did ye eat something that disagreed with you mebbe? Or are you trying to miss school today because it's a mental arithmetic test?'

'I like school, and I don't mind arithmetic. Oh, but it hurts!' Whereupon Flora suddenly retched and vomited all over Ida's clean floor.

She was sick many more times and Kate called the doctor who told her not to worry, that it was quite normal for children to pick up stomach infections at school.

'Plenty of fluids and rest, Mrs Tyson, and she'll be right as rain in the morning.'

But what if she isn't? Kate thought. It was odd that Flora, normally such a healthy child, should suddenly become sick so soon after her mother had found the rat. Had the creature spread some sort of infection? Should she mention it to the doctor? Kate decided against it, not really believing such a thing to be possible. This wasn't the Dark Ages, after all. Rats didn't bring the plague any more. It was a childhood complaint, nothing more, and she was behaving like an over-fussy mother.

Kate put Flora to bed, sat with her and soothed her with a cool, damp cloth till she fell asleep. Then she went to see Mrs Petty.

'Has Flora eaten any eggs, Mrs P, inadvertently I mean?'

'Bless me, no. I'm most careful about that, ever since we had that dreadful business years ago. I wouldn't ever hurt the little lamb.'

'No, no, I'm sure you wouldn't. And nobody else would have call to be near her food, would they?'

The two women gazed at each in contemplative silence for a long moment. Finally, Mrs Petty gave a cautious response. 'Not that I'm aware of, Mrs Tyson, but I'll keep better watch in future, you can be sure of that.'

'I'd be most grateful.'

Neither of them said a word more about what, or who, she'd be watching for, but Kate went away satisfied.

For three days Flora was sick but then she started to recover. On the fifth day she insisted on going back to school, although she was still pale and sickly-looking.

'I feel better now, Mammy. The sickness has gone away.'

''Course it has, me darling.' But Kate's worries had not. Not in the slightest.

From that day on she never knew a moment's peace of mind. If someone was out to hurt her, for whatever reason, she would deal with it. But if they were after her children too, then how

157

could she ever hope to protect them? They had to go out into the world: Flora to school, Callum to his work, to his classes and his sports clubs. She couldn't guard them every moment of their day. Who was it who wished to hurt them, and why? Surely it couldn't be Lucy. Hadn't she learned her lesson in the past? But if it was, and this was war, then who could Kate trust to help her?

When the second rat was found, in Kate's bathroom this time, the police were called. The aunts insisted upon it, and even Kate was unnerved by the rat's close proximity to her bedroom, and, more frightening still, to Flora's.

Constable Brown came within the hour wearing his usual bland, professional expression. 'Nah then, what have we here?'

Vera showed him the rat. 'Do not tell us, Constable, that it has come from the river because that much is obvious. But how did it get upstairs and into the bathroom?'

The constable eyed the creature with placid detachment. 'Oop the drainpipe, Miss Vera. Rats can be right nifty in drainpipes. But don't you worry about it, I know a chap who can sort this problem out for you. Put down poison like.'

Kate sat up, alarmed. 'Poison? No, no, I don't want any poison about the place.'

'There's no other way of getting rid of the nasty things, ma'am.'

'But my daughter has been sick recently, I don't want her to become ill again.'

Lucy said, 'For goodness' sake, Kate, you're becoming quite paranoid.'

'Nay, li'le lass'd go nowhere near t'place where this chap'd put his poison. She'll be quite safe.'

Aunt Vera frowned. 'You don't think Flora being sick has something to do with the other rat you found, do you, Kate?'

Lucy gave a little squeal of dismay. 'What other rat? Has there been more than one? Where? Oh, my goodness, we're infested!'

Kate felt trapped. 'Sure, and it was nothing. I just found it in the summer house, that's all.'

'Well, *you* may be quite blasé about finding rats in summer houses, coming as you do from Poor House Lane and the gutter, but *we* cannot take such a casual view.'

'Indeed, Miss Lucy is right. You should have reported it right away, ma'am,' the constable gently scolded, 'then summat could have been done. Rats is vermin, we don't want a plague of them spreading all over Goose Holme. They has to be seen to.'

'We did suggest reporting it, dear,' Cissie reminded her. 'But you insisted on hushing the matter up, which wasn't really sensible.'

'No need to be embarrassed,' said Constable Brown, quite kindly. 'Rats is common enough by the river like.'

'Yes, I know, but I didn't think it *was* an infestation. I believed someone had put it there deliberately, d'you see?' Oh goodness, now she'd done it. Kate hadn't meant to go that far.

'Deliberately?' The constable was all ears, wanting to know more. 'Why would you imagine such a thing?'

The decision to tell him about the label seemed

to have been made without conscious thought, and was probably for the best. Hushing things up, as Aunt Cissie said, was not really a sensible option, not now that Flora was involved. The constable listened, open-mouthed. When she was done, and it didn't take more than a few seconds for Kate to tell her tale, the silence in the room was palpable. Kate herself tried to ease the atmosphere, make light of the entire episode, already regretting her confession. She could almost feel Lucy's eyes boring into her. 'Someone was obviously playing a prank. Perhaps it was Georgie?'

'Georgie would never do such a thing.'

'Well, I don't know what it was, I really don't.'

Aunt Vera said, 'This puts an entirely different complexion on matters. You said nothing to us about any label, Kate, or any threats! Oh, my word, how dreadful!'

'Can I see it, this label?' the constable asked.

'I threw it away. Burnt it. The rat too.'

Lucy let out a quiet sigh. 'So you have absolutely no proof of this apparent threat upon your life.'

Kate saw her mistake at once. 'N-No, but then Flora was sick, and she never is. She's such a healthy child. Someone could have tampered with her food. That's why I don't want any poison around the place.'

The constable was aghast. This was a long way from a simple infestation by vermin. 'You imagine someone tried to poison your daughter? By heck, that's coming it a bit thick, if you don't mind me saying so, ma'am. Have you the proof to make such an accusation?'

Kate was almost in tears, heartily wishing she'd kept her mouth shut, or disposed of the second rat without telling a soul. She felt duty bound to explain, wishing Callum were present to support her. 'My husband was killed in an accident just a few months ago, or at least we think it was an accident, although you say you can't find the car and... Oh, I don't know.' She caught Lucy's eye again and felt herself shrivel inside.

But the constable had remembered the broken headlamp and the damaged wing on the Austin. 'I seem to recall being asked to investigate a suspicious motor on these very premises, but I found nowt. Nothing untoward at all. Did you call in the police on that occasion too?'

'No, of course I didn't.'

'Did you happen imagine you saw a damaged motor in the garage, or dreamed the label?'

'No!'

Lucy interrupted. 'I must apologise for my sister-in-law. She has not been herself since the death of her husband, as you can imagine. Quite out of her mind at times, with grief, I shouldn't wonder.'

Both of the aunts were nodding sagely.

'I can well believe it, ma'am, certainly I can. Terrible thing to lose a loved one, and in such a dreadful manner. It can quite knock you off yer perch like. Plays weird tricks with the mind, does mourning.'

'Quite, and children are often sick, are they not? Flora had a tummy upset, nothing more.'

Constable Brown conceded this with a sad shake of his head. 'Mine are allus ailing with

161

summat or other.' He turned to Kate with a sympathetic smile. 'I should put all this business out of yer mind, if I were you, ma'am. And I'll get that chap in to mek sure you get no more rats bothering you.'

Perversely, Kate now became desperate for him to believe that it really was deliberate. She wasn't going out of her mind, she said, these things did indeed happen. The constable was nodding agreeably but all the while edging away. 'Please don't listen to Lucy, she'd say anything. Didn't she once abduct me own child?'

Constable Brown's jaw dropped yet again. 'Abducted your child! What, little Flora?' First an alleged murder, then a death threat and poisoning, now an abduction. Whatever next? He was beginning to see that the sister-in-law might well have a point. This woman was deranged.

'No, Callum. It was a long time ago, when he was small. We did report it at the time, when he first went missing. We searched for years, but I didn't know then what had happened to him.'

'Oh, aye, I do remember summat about a child going missing in Kendal. Turned up though, didn't he? Went walkabout, I expect, and got himself lost, as children do.'

'No, no! He was abducted, I tell you.'

The constable kept his face entirely bland, his tone patient. 'And when you discovered that he'd been abducted and not got lost at all, did you report your findings to the police?'

A momentary hesitation. 'Well, no, I – I didn't think it would be appropriate.'

'Why was that exactly?'

162

Again Kate felt trapped, as if she'd led herself into a quagmire into which she was sinking fast. 'We decided it was best not to make a fuss. Wouldn't it have meant a dreadful scandal? And with Eliot away in the war, sure it would only have upset him. We thought we could handle it ourselves. Keep it in the family.'

'Keep it in the family? An abduction? I see.' The policeman was frowning at her, and Kate could tell that he didn't see at all, and who could blame him? 'So you decided against bringing proper charges. Was this, do you think, because you didn't have sufficient evidence? Since the lad had come to no harm, apparently.'

'None whatsoever,' interrupted Lucy. 'You really must take no heed of my sister-in-law's somewhat wild accusations. As I say, she's not quite herself at the moment. I believe finding the rat has upset her more than we appreciate, and right now she is badly in need of rest, if you wouldn't mind leaving.'

'Aye, I reckon that'd be for t'best.'

Kate tried again, her voice rising in pitch as she grew more desperate to make him believe her. 'But she hurt Flora too! Beat her and made her eat eggs and...'

'Aye, right. Eggs, well, yes. Nasty things, eggs. Don't care for them much meself.' He was backing away, anxiety to escape speeding his steps.

Kate could see it was hopeless. He didn't believe a word she said and Lucy was leading him out, showing him the door. Aunt Cissie was saying something about asking Mrs Petty to fetch Kate a nice, soothing cup of tea, and in no time

163

at all, she found herself hustled upstairs and put to bed, just as if she were an invalid and not a right-thinking woman at all.


# 17


Callum tried everything he could think of to lift his mother from the resulting depression into which she seemed to be sinking further and further with every day that passed. Her work at the factory had once been so important to her; now she was turning into an over-zealous mother, rarely allowing Flora out of her sight. Kate walked her to school, collected her again on the dot of four, spent every hour she possibly could with her, even fussing over what she ate, insisting on tasting everything herself first. She wouldn't even allow her to go to the bathroom alone, all of which Flora found utterly demeaning and restricting.

'Will you tell Mammy to stop worrying about me, Callum? I'm better now. And I'm too big to be so mollycoddled.'

'I know you are, pet. It's just that Mam has not been herself lately. I'll talk to her.' He said nothing to Flora about the saga of the rats, which he considered unsuitable information for a child, but he was deeply concerned about the whole episode.

The matter had apparently developed into a ding-dong row between Lucy and the aunts, though what exactly had been said on the subject, he couldn't be entirely sure. He only had Mrs Petty's garbled version of events but Lucy seemed to think they'd deliberately kept it a secret from her.

She wasn't the only one to be annoyed by being kept out of the picture. Callum had felt sick to his stomach when he'd learned what had happened, and tackled his mother on the subject.

'Why didn't you tell me about the rat, not to mention this dratted label? Where is it?'

'I burnt it, like I told the constable. I couldn't bear having it in the house. It made me feel all funny inside.'

'That was a stupid thing to do. Haven't we been seeking proof that someone is trying to hurt you? Now you find some and throw it away.'

'But it was probably nothing more than a...'

'Don't call it a prank, not again.' Mother and son came closer to falling out in that moment than they ever had before.

'Lucy thinks I'm suffering from paranoia.'

'I'm not surprised. You've just supplied her with the evidence.' Callum's heart sank as he saw the tears start to flow and silently run down her cheeks. His mother was the bravest woman he knew, not the sort to cry unless she was deeply troubled. He put his arms about her. 'Don't cry, Mam, I'll sort it. And at least you don't have to worry about our Flora. She's as lively as a cricket.'

It was Flora herself who came up with the solution.

'Mammy, Aunt Vera says a change of air would do you so much good. A blast of fresh air cures the blues, she says.'

Kate managed a smile. 'And where does Vera reckon I should seek this magical cure?'

Flora screwed up her snub nose. 'She suggested Harrogate, but I'd like to go somewhere more exciting, like Torquay or Blackpool. Sea air is so much better for you, don't you think, Mammy?'

'I'm sure it is, m'darlin, but I'm not really in the mood for a holiday. Wouldn't I rather stay in me own home?'

Flora considered this with all seriousness. 'Callum and me could come with you, to look after you.'

'Callum and *I*. And what about school?'

'I could ask for a week off. You could send a note. I just want you to be happy again, Mammy. And it might be fun, just the three of us. We'd be very good, wouldn't we, Callum? And I can't remember the last time I made sand pies or went paddling. It must be a whole *year* because we didn't go *anywhere* exciting at all this summer.'

And that was what did it. Kate actually laughed out loud at this remark, then planted a kiss on her daughter's brow. 'Sure and we can't have that, now can we? A whole year and no sand pies. And you're absolutely right, m'darlin'. We've not done anything exciting at all this summer. Goodness me, what a shocking thing. I'm neglecting me own children, so I am.'

If she couldn't stir herself for her own sake, she would do it for her children, and where safer than away at the seaside? Wouldn't it do darling Flora good too?

Callum damped down a burst of jealousy that

166

it was Flora who had succeeded in bringing this smile to her mother's face, and not him. But he was glad that something had raised Kate from the abyss, because the aunts were right. A change of air would do her the world of good.

But he declined to join them. 'We're rushed off our feet at work. I'll keep an eye on things here, Mam.'

She understood instantly what he was saying, nodded and then kissed his cheek. 'Yer a grand lad. A fine boy anyone would be proud to call son. Don't I love the bones of ye?'

He smiled, warming to her love as he always did. If he'd missed out on years of her loving as a child, she'd certainly made up for it since. He grinned. 'Besides, I don't have a bucket and spade.'

'We could always buy you one,' Kate teased.

They took the train to Scarborough in the end, with the intention of staying for a week, the two aunts insisting on accompanying them, just in case Kate should suffer a relapse.

On the second morning following Kate's departure, Callum came down to breakfast dressed in his old working clothes, as usual, but Jack was in a smart suit and tie.

Callum glanced at him in surprise. 'By heck, tha'll not be much good in t'workshop dressed up like a dog's dinner.'

'Dog's dinner? Is that some quaint local phrase? I don't intend to be in the workshop, or the finishing room, or any of those other dreadful places where the dirty work is done. I shall be in

167

the office from now on.'

'Of course he won't be in the workshop. I've given new instructions. After all, once darling Jack is twenty-one, he will be taking his rightful position as head of the company.' Lucy had apparently decided, without reference to anyone, that her son would work in the office in future, alongside Toby Lynch, and learn all there was to know about running the business. She sat smiling proudly at him, ready to see him off.

Callum wondered what his own mother would have to say about this plan when she learned of it. It would hurt her badly to see Jack strutting about, making it clear he meant to take Eliot's place.

'And don't think I'll be seen coming in with you any more, because I won't. Over my dead body! You and I won't be mixing in future, not at the factory and even less here at home. I shall be one of the bosses, while you ... you're nothing but scum,' Jack taunted.

'Bugger off then, see if I bloody care! But tha still needs to know how to mek shoes fost, afore tha can start telling men such as Billy Braithwaite and Jack Milburn right way to do their job. You need to understand leather inside out.' Somehow Callum's accent always became more broad as Jack's became more refined.

Lucy gave a trill of laughter. 'Don't be ridiculous! We pay other people to understand the actual process. Dear me, what nonsense you do talk, and very badly too, if I may say so. Perhaps we should send you for elocution lessons as well as back to school.'

Jack piled his plate high with bacon and scrambled eggs, tucking in with gusto. 'Not my problem. That's for the peasants, for the likes of you and your kind, the sort who come from the wrong side of the blanket and have to work for their living.'

Callum jumped to his feet, sending the jam pot and the sugar bowl flying in his fury. 'Right, that's it. I've had enough of your nasty insinuations. Take that back or I'll mek you live to regret it.'

Jack simply laughed. 'Look at him. What a sorry mess. Doesn't even have any table manners.'

Lucy said, 'Pray sit down, boy. I won't have your workhouse fisticuffs here.'

'Then tell your blasted son to stop insulting my mam. I were born in wedlock, all right and proper, as he knows only too well. My dad – my real dad – was drowned in the river.'

Now Jack was on his feet, glaring across the table at Callum, as if he'd like to drag him over it and punch him one. 'Exactly. You're not a Tyson, you're an infiltrator into this family, and you'll get none of the Tyson wealth, not if I've any say.'

'Aye, but you don't have any, do you? Tysons Shoes belongs to my mam. Don't forget that.'

'Sit down, both of you. You too, Jack.'

While Callum remained on his feet, fists clenched, Jack smoothed down his lapels, shook out his napkin and returned to his seat, a scornful sneer on his handsome face. 'Fortunately that is no longer the case. My mother owns half the business now.'

'Indeed I do,' said Lucy softly, as she calmly reached for a slice of toast and began to spread it

169

with marmalade.

'Not quite half. Mam still owns the majority share and is in overall control.'

Lucy looked clearly irritated to be so reminded. 'As things stand at the moment, but situations can change very quickly.'

'Indeed they can,' Jack said, nodding in agreement with his mother. 'Who knows what is round the corner? And with my superior intelligence and good breeding, you haven't a chance of outflanking me. I can outshine your gutter manners and lack of education any day of the week. I doubt you can even read. Make no mistake, I'll have you out of this factory in no time, once I'm fully in charge.'

'Quite right too, darling.'

Callum very nearly lunged for him again, but managed to control himself just in time. Instead, he had to be content with one last parting shot.

'Don't ever underestimate my mother. She may be a bit down right at this minute, but she'll bounce back, mark my words. She'll return to her desk, and when she does, she'll not be alone. She has friends, and she has me. Remember that!' Then he left the room without even finishing his own breakfast, despite having a long, hard day's work ahead of him.

Callum hunched his shoulders and went off to meet his mates, as he usually did. Maybe he was wasting his time staying on at the factory, and he should make a break for it right now. It was certainly true that he wasn't interested in owning the place. All he wanted was to feel that he belonged, to be a part of a family, and if Lucy hadn't turned up like a bad penny, he might well have managed that in the end. He might even have come to accept Eliot. A part of him was sorry that he'd never got the chance.

Later that day, he saw Jack being escorted round the factory by Toby Lynch, heard the foreman describing the various processes to him, explaining what was going on in each room. All about the men who cut the leather for the uppers, and another thirty or so who cut the soles. In the closing room well over a hundred girls formed the uppers which were later attached to the soles in the finishing room. Last of all, the boot or shoe was burnished, buffered and polished, then sent to the packing room where they were sized and paired off, the shoes put into plain white boxes and the boots strung up and packed in cartons ready for dispatch to the shops.

At one point Jack actually stood by Callum's bench, picked up a boot, and, turning it over, made a great show of examining it. 'And if a shoe-maker doesn't come up to scratch, he presumably gets sacked, since standards at Tysons are so important?'

Toby half glanced at Callum, then tried to edge Jack away before replying.

'Well? I asked you a question.'

Toby looked uncomfortable, holding out his hand for the boot, but Jack held on to it. 'That has ever been the case, aye. Standards have always been high at Tysons.'

'Quite so.' Jack dropped the boot back on the bench, casting a glance of malicious triumph at

171

Callum, though he'd found nothing wrong with it. 'So what happens if someone doesn't fit in, if they're a trouble-maker?'

The resentment clearly bubbling beneath the surface between these two young men was such that Toby Lynch sought to deflect Jack by changing the subject. 'During the war this factory was like a mad house. Hundreds of pairs of boots were being shipped out daily. Now it's quiet as a graveyard, by comparison. Kate has plans to change all of that, but they haven't yet been put into effect.'

'She might never do so now,' Jack said, again casting a scathing look at Callum, who was keeping his head down as he laboured, wary of upsetting the foreman.

Toby looked at him askance. 'Nay, nothing'll get the better of our Kate. She'll come round. She'll learn to live with her loss, as we all must. Then she'll be back in here telling us all what to do, which will be grand. We all look forward to that day.'

Jack scowled and muttered something under his breath before suggesting that he had seen all he needed to in here, thank you very much, and was ready to move on. Just as if he were the bloody King come to inspect the troops, Callum thought, boiling with rage.

Despite Callum's resolve to keep his head down and himself out of trouble, even if he did have no wish to own the blasted factory, having Jack lord it over him was galling to say the least. Not only that but he was spending money like water, going

172

out on the town with his 'chums' night after night.

'Anyone'd think we were med of brass,' Callum grumbled, but only to himself.

He made up his mind to continue with his investigation, to start asking a few questions. He was of the opinion that folk might agree to talk to him when they'd avoid getting involved with the police.

He knocked on several doors on and around Aynam Road and the factory, spent hours trudging up and down streets, and finally struck lucky.

He found an old woman who was more than willing to talk, in return for a bit of company from such a nice young man. Her name was Edith and she was quite lonely because her daughter had moved away when her husband got work on the canal. She fed Callum seed cake and tea while she told her tale. She well remembered seeing a black motor car lurking up her back street. Edith claimed it was because it was often there, round about the same time each day, just when the factory workers were heading home.

'I remember saying to my friend Maggie, "It's up to no good, posh car like that up our street. Don't make no sense."'

Unfortunately, she'd never plucked up the courage to go near enough to look inside, so could give no description of the driver.

He begged her to tell her story to the constable, for the sake of his mother, and after some persuasion, and because she'd heard nothing but good about the second Mrs Tyson, Edith agreed.

Delighted by his success Callum dashed off at

173

once to the police station, not noticing when a shadowy figure slipped into the small terraced house only a moment or two after he'd left it.

The next day, when Constable Brown finally found the time to accompany Callum to hear the old woman's story at first hand, they found the house shuttered and closed, with no sign of her. Neighbours believed old Edith might have gone to live with her daughter in Lancaster, but nobody could be quite sure. Even her friend Maggie was at a loss to know where she might be.

'She niver towd me where she were going.'

The constable was not pleased, accusing Callum of wasting police time.

Callum urged Maggie to think back, to remember what Edith had said about the car, asking if she could remember anything about it herself. But the woman simply pursed her lips, shook her head and said she knew nowt about owt, which was plainly her final word on the subject.

Undeterred, Callum carried on knocking on doors, asking questions, pestering and hectoring, unwilling to admit defeat. He was well liked by his fellow workers as a quiet but steady lad, yet they'd become strangely reticent of a sudden: as if struck deaf, blind and dumb. His good luck had come to an end. Nobody would talk to him after Edith's disappearance. He found only closed doors.

# 18

Constable Brown returned to Tyson Lodge a day or two later to explain to the late Mr Tyson's widow how even this interesting lead had turned into a dead end. Unfortunately, she wasn't available and he addressed his words to Lucy instead.

'A new *lead*, you say? To what exactly? I believed the matter to be closed.' Her finely drawn eyebrows lifted in cold enquiry. 'I'm afraid that you've been sent on a wild goose chase. But then, my dear sister-in-law has not been herself lately, as you've already seen, and we cannot blame the boy for trying to protect her.'

'Only right for a lad to look after his mother.' The constable eased his collar, clearly not enjoying this mission. A waste of time, in his humble opinion, but his sergeant had insisted he investigate the matter, not wishing it to appear as if the police were failing in their duty. 'The plain fact is, I've nothing further to report. We can find neither sight nor sound of old Edith, though if we knew exactly where her daughter lived that might help, but the son-in-law no longer works for the canal company and the entire family seems to have done a moonlight flit.'

'You never can rely on such people,' Lucy agreed sympathetically.

'I thought it would be best if I came and told Mrs Tyson herself, personally like, as I promised the lad we'd report the result of our enquiries.'

Lucy offered him one of her practised smiles. 'I'm afraid she isn't here. She's in Scarborough, resting. Is it urgent? Would you like me to telephone her, or write a note?'

'No, no, please don't bother her. The poor lady has had a hard time of it, I reckon. Just tell her, when she gets back, that so far as we can make out, there's nowt more we can do. We'll have to consider the case closed, though we'll keep our ear to the ground and if we hear owt of interest, we'll pursue it, naturally.'

Lucy saw him out, slammed the door shut after him then swore very loudly. This was not what she'd expected or planned, not at all. And she certainly knew who to blame.

Swainson was not sympathetic. 'I got rid of the old woman for you, warning poor old Edith it was in her best interests to make tracks. I sorted your car, got the police off yer back, even left the rats, exactly like you said. If you're wanting me to do owt else, like sort out that workhouse brat, for instance, it'll cost you.'

'I've paid you plenty already, more than enough.' Lucy was shocked, already beginning to regret the quantities of notes she'd slipped his way. 'I'm not made of money, don't think I am.'

'Are you not? Could've fooled me. And you wouldn't want me shooting me mouth off to the police, telling 'em all I know, now would you? 'Course, a handsome woman like yourself could find some other way to settle the debt, I dare say, if you set your mind to it.'

'What are you implying?' Lucy gave a little shudder, although a part of her brain registered that he thought her handsome and she was woman enough to feel flattered. She did so love to be admired, even by an odd fish like Swainson. He was a man, after all, with quite a reputation with the female sex, so he must have some charms.

On this occasion they had met in the lee of Scout Scar by the old race track. Little interest had been shown in racing since before the war but today a trotting race was being held, the neat little carriages already lining up for the first race. There were several booths selling sweets and treats, the usual beer tent and even a little merry-go-round for the children. Lucy had come with Jack and Bunty for a pleasant afternoon out but had slipped away quietly to meet Swainson while her son placed his bets.

No one could see them, tucked out of sight behind a copse of sycamore that leaned into the wind on this breezy western fellside that separated the vale of Kentdale from the Lyth Valley. At least, she sincerely hoped not.

He'd taken off his flat cap as he studied her, rolled it in his lean, weathered hands for a moment and then tucked it into his back trouser pocket.

Lucy arched her brows at him, thinking that perhaps a little flirting might soften him. 'You clearly know how to flatter a woman, but nothing I have could possibly be of interest to any man. I'm merely an old widow-woman.'

He edged closer and she could smell the beer on his breath. It was strangely intoxicating. Even the way he didn't quite look squarely at her fascinated Lucy. He'd at least shaved this morning since there was no sign of stubble on his chin, save for the moustache above the thin line of his mouth, and she wondered how it would feel pressed against her own.

'Not so old that you don't get a bit frustrated like, with no man around.'

Something like excitement jolted inside her, low and deep in her belly. Lucy knew she should express outrage at his effrontery, push him away and go back to her son and daughter.

But he'd rested one hand on the trunk of the tree behind her head and was leaning closer. 'I certainly feel the lack of a good woman at times. There must be a way that old acquaintances, such as ourselves, can reach some sort of under-standing.'

For all it was a chill autumn day he wore no jacket, only a checked waistcoat, shirt sleeves rolled up to reveal arms that were well-muscled and strong. Surprisingly, the fact that he wasn't in the least bit good-looking did not disturb her as much as she'd expected. Lucy was both repelled and fascinated by him, and deeply curious. But then, it had been a long time since she'd been this close to a man. Something fluttered in her throat and she tried to clear it, then offered him a cool smile before asking in low, husky tones, 'What exactly did you have in mind?'

He showed her, with vigour and authority. Pushing her against the rough tree trunk, he yanked up her skirts, unfastened his flies, and lifting her against him, thrust hard into her. Lucy didn't cry out or protest. She grasped tight hold of his shoulders, steadying herself as she flung back her head and lost herself in sensation. There were no kisses, no soft words, nothing to distract her from raw pleasure, but then she always had enjoyed sex, and the fact that they were within strolling distance of her own son and daughter at the trotting track gave an extra fillip to the thrill.

When he was done, they each adjusted their clothing, agreed a date to meet again, as one might arrange a business meeting, and then Lucy walked away first, head held high, well satisfied. A useful encounter, she decided, and really quite titillating. And so much cheaper than parting with hard cash.

Over dinner that evening, when Jack had counted his winnings, crowing over his good fortune, Lucy informed Callum of the constable's visit.

She cast him a sideways, quizzical look, watching for his reaction. Lucy vividly recalled her discussion with Swainson only a few hours earlier, before they'd got involved in other matters, and wondered what it would cost her to be rid of this brat completely. No, not quite yet. Too soon. One thing at a time. 'Apparently a witness came forward and then vanished. The constable didn't say how the police came by the information. Do you know anything of it, Callum?'

His face a mask of innocence, Callum said that he knew nothing at all.

Lucy considered his reply thoughtfully before shrugging her elegant shoulders. 'In any case, this lead, if that's what it was, has proved as fruitless as all the rest. The case, they assure me, is now closed.'

Not if I can help it, Callum thought, surprising himself by the rush of anger which tightened his chest. He felt more caring of his adopted father in death than ever he had in life, but then he'd never been given a chance to get to know him properly, because of this woman.

Callum realised, however, that his failure to find the proof he needed was about to rebound upon him. He knew, without a shadow of a doubt, that Lucy suspected him of meddling, and that his life was about to become a great deal less comfortable.

He was absolutely right, and her very next words confirmed it.

'I'm sorry to have to say this, Callum, but I think it would be best, while your mother is away at least, if you were to eat in the kitchen. Jack finds it difficult sharing meals with you and then working at opposite ends of the spectrum, as it were, in the factory. And you must admit, it is never a comfortable experience for anyone. I simply won't have a repetition of that fracas we had the other morning.'

'Eat in the kitchen? Why should I? I'm not a bloody servant!'

'My dear boy, you certainly sound like one.'

Bunty, equally appalled, attempted to defend him. 'You can't do that, Mama. You can't ask Callum to eat *in the kitchen*, it wouldn't be right!'

Lucy ignored her. 'If you would but mind your language and your manners, I may reconsider. Until then, I would prefer it if you dined elsewhere. I must confess that, personally, I find your presence at our table – well, I hate to use the word but it is the only one appropriate – deeply offensive.'

'Mam won't stand for it.' The decision left Callum more angry on Kate's behalf than his own. He didn't care where he ate. He already felt himself to be an outsider in this household, and would be glad to escape the constant bickering with Jack, having him watch every move he made, picking fault over the slightest mistake, like using the wrong knife or dropping his napkin on the floor. But this house had been left entirely to Kate, and, as her son, he too had rights. Who were these people to make him feel unwelcome? Callum also felt certain that Eliot Tyson, who had adopted him when all was said and done and therefore must have cared for him once, would be ashamed to have a son of his eat with the servants. It didn't seem right.

Yet did it really matter?

Eliot had not named him as heir. He'd left his money and possessions to the two women, taking it for granted that his missing child never would come home again, so why should Callum care? Why did he waste so much time worrying about the man when he was dead?

Because the one person who would surely be hurt by this piece of malice, was his mother.

Callum tried again to make this point. 'You'd never try this on if me mam were here.'

'But she isn't, is she?' Lucy sweetly reminded him.

'I could write and tell her. Anyroad, she'll be home soon.'

'Do as you please,' she told him, clearly un-moved. 'Your mother will do as I tell her, and so will you. As for you, Bunty, if you wish to have your year in Switzerland, and be finished, then keep your nose out of what doesn't concern you.'

'But I don't *want* a year in Switzerland, or any-where else for that matter. I've told you a thou-sand times, Mother, I don't care about *being finished*, as you call it.'

'Oh, yes, you will care, miss. You will go to Switzerland, I do assure you, and quite soon. I'll not be shown up in society by any daughter of mine, and if you don't go out into society, how will you ever find a husband?'

Callum was reduced to watching with pity in his blue-grey eyes as Lucy turned her attention to berating Bunty instead.

Mrs Petty was equally affronted when she heard the news. 'By heck, that's a fine kettle of fish. The cheeky madam! Never you mind, lad, you'll do aw reet wi' us in t'kitchen. And you'll allus get the choicest meat at our table.'

'You mean, we don't get the choicest cuts in the dining room?'

Mrs Petty adopted a puzzled expression. 'I don't know what it is about meat, lad, but when I has to cook it for that madam, as opposed to your lovely mam, it never quite turns out as it should. Funny that!'

Callum snorted with suppressed laughter. He liked Mrs Petty, he really did. '*She's* talking about wanting to hold dinner parties,' he warned her. 'So the meat might have to behave then.'

'Dinner parties?' Mrs Petty looked aghast. 'Nay, not with the master so recently buried? He'll turn in his grave.'

'Spin, I shouldn't wonder, with all I've heard she's got planned,' Callum agreed. 'But then, he only has himself to blame for leaving her such a large share in the business.'

Mrs Petty clicked her tongue in disapproval. 'I can't imagine what he was thinking of to do such a daft thing. Not like him at all. But then he allus was too soft where family was concerned. I know he felt guilty over his brother, but why would he cut you out? Don't make no sense.'

'Well, I was missing when he made the will, and he wasn't expecting to die so soon, was he?'

'Even so.'

'There's nothing wrong with the will, Mrs P. He left the decision over who was ultimately to inherit to Mam and Lucy to sort out between them, so it's bound to be Jack since he's a Tyson and I'm the infiltrator, the outsider.' Callum didn't even know why he was defending Eliot. What did it matter who inherited?

Mrs Petty shook her head. 'Nay, the master loved you as his own. Broke his heart when you vanished. Eeh, lad, if he'd known when he wrote it that you were still alive and kicking and might come home one day, he'd never've left things in that unsatisfactory way. He niver got the chance to change it, what with the war. You must stand yer ground, don't let 'em shove you out. You has yer rights too, workhouse kid or not. Just like our Ida here. Ida, have you peeled those spuds yet, or are you day dreaming as usual?'

183

# 19

Within days of Kate's departure, Lucy brought in decorators and had them start on the refurbishment of the drawing room. She threw out the shabby old sofas, rugs and curtains, had them strip the Victorian flock wallpaper from the walls and burn off the old brown paint, just as if she were the mistress of Tyson Lodge and Eliot's widow.

'Did you ask Mam if she minded, if it were all right to chuck her husband's stuff away?' Callum wanted to know, horrified by Lucy's autocratic manner, which seemed to be growing worse by the minute.

'Your darling mama is well aware that Tyson Lodge needs updating. Goodness, I don't even have my own bathroom as the house possesses only one. Don't worry, I shall have everything tidy and shipshape by the time she comes home. The dear lady will be delighted to have been spared the bother.'

A note had duly been dispatched to Scarborough to urge the aunts and Kate to stay for a second week, or preferably three, as a bathroom leak had been detected and much-needed repairs and refurbishments were in hand.

Lucy brought in plumbers, electricians and carpenters, and set about installing a second bathroom in the single bedroom which adjoined her own. Also a cloakroom on the ground floor, and another, smaller bathroom at the back of the house, for the aunts to share. She didn't trouble about the servants, considering facilities for them to be an unnecessary expense.

Mrs Petty made a private note of this decision too. It would not be forgotten.

Lucy drew up plans, agonised over colour schemes, purchased curtain fabric and found a woman willing to drop whatever she'd been doing and make them up within a week. She visited every furniture store in town, and also in Carlisle and Lancaster, purchasing new chandeliers and lamps, sofas and pretty little tables, and an elegant dining-room table and eight chairs.

'Exactly the right number for a dinner party, and really, I'm utterly ashamed to invite anyone to sit on those battered old balloon-backed monstrosities. Absolutely ancient! Came in when Victoria was a girl, I'm sure. Art Deco is the coming thing now. We must move on and be modern. These improvements should have been made years ago. Matters will take a turn for the better now that I am back. Mark my words, standards will be raised.'

'And a good thing too, Mama,' agreed her sycophantic son Jack.

Callum watched events unfold in gloomy silence, simmering with resentment on his mother's behalf. He wished he could write to Kate and urge her to come home, warn her that this woman was taking over her house. But how could he? She had to be allowed time to heal, to make a full recovery so that she could better

185

stand up to her sister-in-law. It would do no good at all to bring her home too soon only for her to sink back into depression.

But if Lucy did succeed in taking over the running of the house, as she clearly intended to do, and her son ultimately took control of Tysons Industries, Callum would be out of both home and job because not for one moment could he contemplate living and working under such circumstances. He'd have to go off some place and start a new life, join the Navy perhaps.

Only then he wouldn't ever see Bunty again, and he wouldn't like that one bit.

They'd taken to meeting in the summer house. That they were in love was beyond doubt. This was the main reason why Bunty had no wish to go to Switzerland, though neither had she any wish to be turned into a lady, if it meant ending up like her own mother. Nor did Callum wish her to go. He loved her exactly as she was, and certainly didn't want to risk losing her to some well-heeled dandy.

He told her so now as they cuddled up together, hidden from view in the upper loft. He kissed her soft lips, stroked her full breasts, held her close in his arms. ''Course, she might make you go. You're only seventeen, after all. And I'm not even quite that, though I soon will be. It's not as if we can get married or owt, not yet.'

'But you would marry me, wouldn't you, Callum, if we were old enough? If we were eighteen, for instance, we could elope across the border to Gretna Green.'

She could hear a wood pigeon cooing in the trees, smell the dampness of autumn in the air, the lingering scent of a garden bonfire.

'I don't know 'bout that.' Callum was nothing if not cautious, 'Your mam wouldn't approve. She intends to pick out a fine rich husband for you.'

'I don't think I could bear that.'

'Me neither.'

They looked at each other, appalled by the prospect.

'We'll have to run away then. It's the only way.'

'I can't, not just yet.'

Bunty pouted, which made her look temptingly seductive. 'Don't you love me at all, then?'

''Course I love you. I worship the ground you walk on. Only me mam needs me to stop on around here for a while longer, at least till I'm sure she's on the mend. Besides, I need to be content in me own mind that it's the right thing to do, that you love me enough. You're a lady, after all, and I'm – I'm a peasant, like yer brother says.'

'Oh, don't listen to Jack. What does he know about anything? I do love you enough, I do, I do! Kiss me again, Callum, and I'll show you how very much.' And he was happy to comply.

Their loving hadn't been entirely chaste. Sometimes he grew quite daring, unfastening the buttons of her frock and slipping his hand inside to caress her soft, plump breasts, as he was doing today. Bunty never made any sort of protest, as eager to taste the pleasures of the flesh as he.

Tonight they were more daring still, perhaps in

defiance of her mother's strictures. They'd sneaked out after dark for this blissful hour together, and Bunty didn't hesitate to help him remove her dress, followed by her chemise, so that she was dressed only in her cami-knickers, and soon not even those.

'You're so beautiful, Bunty, how could I not adore you?'

Callum felt that familiar tightening of his loins, then a breathless urgency that he'd never experienced before. He had to touch every part of her, explore the soft folds and secret delights of her enchanting body. He was fascinated by the bush between her legs, by the way her nipples sprang to the lightest caress, the way she moaned softly when he touched her in her most intimate places and lay back in open invitation. How could he resist, loving her as he did?

They lay together afterwards on the dusty floor, a patch of moonlight illuminating their nakedness for it had been short work for Callum to remove his own garments and claim her as his own. It had been the first time for both of them, but the whole delightful experience had seemed perfectly natural, and neither gave a single thought to the possibility of any consequences.

It was as they were creeping back through the garden, giggling as they stumbled over some tree roots since they had only a pale moon to guide them, that a voice rang out.

'What the hell have you been up to now, peasant?'

Callum was stunned and appalled to find their

way blocked by the tall, arrogant figure of Jack. His mouse-brown hair wasn't slicked down as it usually was, but spiky and rumpled, his tie loose and his collar undone. He'd clearly been drinking, and his foul mood all too evident.

Not answering his question, Callum turned to Bunty. 'Go to bed, don't you get involved in this.'

'But I am involved. Jack, this has nothing to do with you. Callum and I are – friends, and we're entitled to meet and – and talk, if we want to.'

Jack snorted. 'I bet that's not all you were doing! My God, I'll have you for this. First you go around asking questions, calling in the police and practically accusing my mother of causing that damned accident to your stupid father, now you're interfering with my sister. Take your filthy hands off her!' Jack lunged for Bunty, grabbing her arm and dragging her roughly to his side. 'As for you, you stupid little tart, we'll see what Mother has to say about this.'

Bunty's eyes grew wide with fright. 'No, no, you mustn't tell her, you mustn't say a word! I don't understand. What are you accusing Callum of? What was all that about the accident?'

'Shut up, and do as you're told.'

'You leave her alone, you bloody bully!'

'Or else what? What will you do? You don't belong here. You're not a genuine Tyson, not part of *my* family. You're a brainless, spineless brat! Eliot Tyson disinherited us because of you, workhouse bastard that you are. And he caused *my* father's suicide.'

'That's not my fault, even if it's true, which I

189

doubt. And who says you have any right to the business?'

'I have the right because I'm a Tyson, *and you're not*. If your father really was drowned in the river, then you should follow him to his watery grave. Or better still, maybe we should fix up another accident ... to your stupid mother this time.'

Callum flung out a fist and smashed it into Jack's sneering face. Blood spurted, making a satisfying mess all down his clean shirt front. Jack glanced down in surprise, flinging Bunty aside as he put one hand to his injured nose, cursing under his breath.

'You've ruined my best shirt, you turd!'

He flung out a wild punch, roughly aiming at Callum's nose, which he missed.

Callum couldn't help but laugh, seeing Jack nearly overbalance himself in his efforts to retaliate. It was a mistake. He'd been almost as surprised as Jack to find that his own blow had connected. He'd never had much opportunity for fighting, not on the farm in the quiet of the Langdales, although the farmer had knocked him about quite a bit.

Unfortunately, Jack had been taught the sport of pugilism at public school and his next punch did not miss. It landed full on Callum's jaw, sending him sprawling. Callum was back on his feet in a second, but, drunk or no, Jack was the better fighter, aiming blows with remarkable efficiency, demented with fury and fighting like a madman.

Not that Callum was simply going to grit his teeth and take the beating. He'd done enough of that over what seemed like a life-time. Instinct came into play, fuelled by all the pent-up frustration and rage battened down over years of abuse and neglect, and by the burning resentment he felt towards this man and his dratted mother.

He defended himself with gusto, if not particularly effectively, certainly doing his best to counter the punches, managing to dodge some of them and giving as good as he got to the rest. Blood flowed, teeth were broken, knuckles skinned and bruised, and all the while Bunty's screams overrode it all.

They might well have gone on until they'd actually killed each other, or one of them was at least knocked unconscious, had not Lucy's voice rung out across the garden.

'Who's there? What is going on? If you don't get off my land this minute I'll set the dogs on you.'

Since the dogs in question were Aunt Cissie's lazy hounds, Callum almost laughed out loud, except that Jack's knee chose that second to connect with his rib cage and, with all the wind knocked out of him, Callum crumpled and fell to the ground. He was vaguely aware of a tussle going on between Jack and Bunty as he dragged his sister away, but was in no position to protest or to help her. Callum knew when he was licked. He lay on the ground, quite unable to move. And if he didn't have a couple of broken ribs, it would be a miracle.

Lucy found him within seconds, and, sparing not a thought for the possibility of such injuries, dragged him to his feet then pushed and shoved him up the stairs to his room at the back of the house.

Flinging him on the bed, she bore down upon Callum in a flurry of rage, the like of which he'd never before seen in all his life. She stormed about the small room like a hurricane, picking up books and hurling them to the floor, sweeping a photograph of his mother right off his bedside table and smashing it to the ground.

Callum could do nothing. He lay curled on his bed, nursing his injuries while she wreaked her revenge.

Then Lucy turned her attention to him, spitting and hissing at him like a wild cat, berating him with the kind of unleashed fury he'd never before witnessed, not even in Mr Brocklebank, so that he actually feared for his life. One punch on his ribs, which could well be cracked, and she could easily puncture his lungs.

'If Jack has given you a pasting, you must have richly deserved it. Pity I came outside when I did. Next time I'll leave him to finish you off. Let this serve as a warning to you: keep your nose out of my affairs! No more questions asked, no further visits to Constable Brown. Do you understand what I'm saying? You may think you've beaten me ... getting back here, causing trouble at every turn ... but I'm not done with you yet, not by a long chalk.'

Callum spoke with difficulty, his lips so badly cut he could barely move them, and his mouth tasting rusty with blood. 'I'm not scared of you. There's no way you can hurt me more than you have already.'

She laughed then, throwing back her head and almost chortling with glee, as if welcoming the

192

challenge. 'Oh, yes, there is. The best way to hurt you, boy, is through your mother. And nothing would give me greater pleasure.'

Mrs Petty claimed never to have seen such injuries in all her born days, declaring her own simple skills with herbs and medicines to be quite inadequate to the task. But Callum wouldn't hear of her calling in a doctor.

'Too many questions. I'll be OK.'

'You will not, young man, not in your present condition.' She'd found him still in his room the next morning, having gone looking for him when he hadn't turned up for his breakfast in the kitchen, as arranged, or gone off to work at his usual time. 'So what happened? Walk into a door, did you?'

'Can't say.'

Mrs Petty snorted with disgust, not wishing to appear soft with the lad even though her heart went out to him, seeing him so badly injured. 'You mean, you won't say. Well, I only hope the other chap is worse. Lads will be lads, I suppose, when all's said and done. But we has to do summat about this mess.'

She sent Ida scurrying for hot water and the pair of them bathed and tended Callum's wounds, washed his face and bruised knuckles, then seeing how he winced, trying to protect his ribs, strapped him up with some strips of old sheeting. 'If tha's broken owt, it'll get more painful later, rather than less, so take a swig of this.'

Despite his protests, Mrs Petty forced down a spoonful of her famous elixir. 'You can have another spoonful when it gets bad. I'll leave it by your bed. Only one, mind. It's powerful stuff. What a commotion we're having today! Didn't you hear mother and daughter having a right set to earlier? I'll have to look sharp because I has to help pack Miss Bunty's luggage. She's off to her fancy finishing school.'

'What, now? Today?' Callum was shocked and struggled to sit up.

Mrs Petty pushed him gently down again. 'Left this morning, first thing. Her luggage is to be sent on.'

And so Callum was left alone with his loss; to his tears over losing Bunty without even having the opportunity to say goodbye, and to his worries over his mother. What would happen when Kate came home? Lucy's threat had been all too real. The battle lines were clearly drawn. She'd failed to rid herself of him thus far, but had practically admitted that she'd succeeded with Eliot. His mother might well be next. How could he possibly protect her?

# 20

Kate returned home a few days later, to what appeared to be utter pandemonium, viewing the scene before her in complete bewilderment. When she had left, the house had been perfectly calm and quiet. Now, a mere two weeks later, she seemed to be surrounded by mess and mayhem on all sides with dust, dirt and chaos everywhere, workmen occupying every room.

From what she could see through the open door of the drawing room, the plaster from the ceiling was all over the floor, and the sound of hammering coming from the dining room was deafening. Kate stood transfixed in the hall, staring about her as if she didn't know quite where she was. What could they be doing in there, and what would Eliot have said about all this mess in his lovely old house?

It was Aunt Vera who came to her senses first. As she spied Lucy running down the stairs to greet them, she set down her carpet bag with a thump and stoutly enquired what on earth was going on.

'Oh, dear, you've come home too soon,' was Lucy's swift response. 'You should have stayed on for a third week as I begged you to in my last letter, then I could have had everything looking quite lovely by the time you got back.'

Vera, who was unused to being challenged, tartly responded, 'All what looking lovely? This is much more than a burst pipe.'

'Which you led us to believe was the problem,' echoed Cissie, looking prim.

'I can only think you've suffered some sort of flood to cause such mayhem.'

Lucy gave a trill of false laughter. 'Dear me, no, nothing so dramatic. The river has behaved itself beautifully but I decided to go ahead and install a second bathroom. I really cannot endure Ida bringing up jugs of hot water every day. I never feel quite clean and the water is generally lukewarm by the time that ancient hip bath is full. I've also installed a bathroom for you, dear aunts.'

'For us? Oh, my dear,' Cissie declared.

Vera was not so easily mollified, although Cissie had quite perked up at the thought of a proper bathroom. 'And who is paying for all this, might I ask?'

Lucy smiled pityingly at her. 'I'm sure dear Eliot's estate can run to a few small improvements. It's long past time the house was brought out of the Victorian age, don't you think? We agreed upon that, did we not, Kate?'

'Did we?' Kate struggled to focus on the mass of detail Lucy was giving her, her voice rattling on about the hours she'd spent searching for the right curtain fabric, or paint, or wallpaper, as well as bullying people to come and get the work done quickly and spare Kate the trouble.

'I thought it would be an excellent opportunity to make a start while you were away, to save you the bother since you were so low. I know it looks bad at the moment, but at least you avoided the worst of the mess. Sadly, now that you have returned home a week earlier than expected, my lovely surprise has been ruined.' Lucy sighed melodramatically. 'But I'm quite certain that you'll love it, once the house is clean and tidy again, the new furnishings arrive and...'

'New furnishings? What new furnishings?'

When she was in Scarborough, walking along the sea front, Kate had thought herself well enough to return home and take up the reins at the factory again. Enjoying the stiff sea breezes, eating the excellent breakfasts provided by the landlady at their small hotel, she'd felt alive again, fit for anything.

But now, standing here in the midst of this chaos with Lucy pointing out all the deficiencies of her home, high-handedly making changes without consultation, Kate could feel her new-found confidence and courage beginning to slip away. 'I don't recall agreeing to new furnishings, or anything else for that matter.'

Lucy patted her hand in a condescending manner. 'Oh, dear, and I so hoped that the sea air would do you good. Have you no recollection of our little discussion before you left?'

'Discussion?' Kate began to feel even more confused.

'When we spoke of the need for a second bathroom, didn't we also decide to replace those dreadful old sofas, and that ancient dining-room suite? I felt certain that you would remember. We did agree that it must be done.

'Admittedly,' Lucy continued, 'we did not discuss redecoration, but I decided there was little point in bringing new furniture into a faded, shabby room, and so I called in the decorators to spruce the place up a bit first. Long overdue, I feel. My dear, it was filthy, and I'm sure you'll be pleased with the result when it is finished.'

It all sounded so reasonable that even the aunts were silenced.

But Kate still felt a glimmer of concern. Had there been a discussion about the house? If so, why couldn't she remember it? What was going on? She felt very much as if she were being manipulated, pandered to in some unidentifiable

197

way, yet could not work out the reasoning behind it.

Kate never quite knew where she was with Lucy, or what she was thinking. One minute she would be asking herself if her sister-in-law was capable of true evil, the next Lucy was being so sweet and helpful the idea was ludicrous. Where had her bite gone, her venom, which was almost preferable to this mincing affectation? Or was she genuinely trying to make herself useful?

Perhaps there had indeed been a discussion and Kate simply couldn't remember. Every time she thought she was feeling more herself, something would go wrong, and control over her own life would slip away from her again.

Lucy said, 'Do come along into the small parlour, which is relatively quiet and peaceful, and I'll have Mrs Petty bring us in some tea.' And she led the way, just as if she were indeed the mistress of Tyson Lodge, and not an interloper.

Kate was sitting in the garden beneath the grove of trees. She couldn't bear to go inside. The noise and the dust were too much. Here, in the quiet of a golden October afternoon amongst the trees which Eliot had planted, she could find sanctuary. She remembered that other morning in autumn so long ago when she'd discovered him planting a dozen young saplings. She'd been so young, so much in love, but she'd only been the nursemaid at that time, and he her employer.

'Haven't you enough trees already?' she'd teased him, meaning the gracious avenue of beeches which lined the drive, and the woodland copse of ash and rowan that stood behind the house, shielding Tyson Lodge from the terrace of fine houses beyond, and the high school from which each afternoon burst forth a chattering mass of giggling girls.

'One can never have enough trees,' he'd explained. 'We must plant for the next generation.'

'For Callum, you mean?'

'For Callum, and for his children, and for all future generations to come.'

Kate wiped a tear from her eye at the memory. Poor Eliot hadn't even been given the chance to make proper provision for this son he'd worshipped and thought lost. But perhaps the trees were his best legacy, certainly the most enduring.

And here her boy was, alive and well, walking towards her with a frown of concern on his handsome face. She thought that face paler than it should be, and more gaunt. Had he lost weight while she was away?

Kate called to him, 'Don't look so worried, aren't I just fine and dandy?'

Callum came to sit beside her on the bench and wasted no time over greetings. 'What do you intend to do about Lucy?'

'And hello to you too, m'darlin'.'

'What do you intend to do?'

Kate sighed. 'In what respect?'

'You must stop her from taking over.'

Kate tried to collect her thoughts but still they kept slipping back to Eliot, and she found that she was less concerned about the changes to the house than she'd at first thought. But then nothing really mattered, not any more. 'I was a bit put out at first, a bit disorientated, you might say. But the bathrooms are an excellent idea, so perhaps we really did have that discussion and Lucy means only to help.'

'Pigs might fly! She means to take over.'

'Oh, Callum, we can't let old feuds last forever. Let bygones be bygones, isn't that the best way?'

But he was having none of that. 'You have to do something. Are you going into the factory soon? Toby Lynch is itching to put those new plans for a line of ladies' shoes into operation. You just have to say the word. He was asking after you again today. He needs you there, the men need you.'

Kate smiled at him. 'I believe there are women working in the factory too,' she teased.

Callum gave her a sideways grin, 'I'm glad to see you've at least got some of your sense of humour back. It's good to have you home, Mam.'

'It's good to be home, m'cushla. Give yer mam a quick kiss while no one's looking. Flora smothers me in kisses all the time, but sure I'd like one from my boy too.'

Callum swiftly complied, although he did first check over his shoulder to make sure he was unobserved. But then he returned to the matter uppermost in his mind. 'I spoke to Constable Brown while you were away. He may call and see you, or he may have given up on the case, I'm not sure.'

He explained briefly about the missing witness and Kate tried to take in what he was telling her. 'They don't seem to have found poor old Edith yet. I think you were right about Swainson help-ing Lucy. My bet is that he scared the old woman off, her family too, and the whole lot of them have run away, which doesn't help our cause one little bit.'

Kate sighed, not really wishing to have the agony of the accident revived by the police all over again, though she didn't say so. She knew it had hit Callum hard, losing Eliot before he'd had the chance to see him as a father.

'I'd rather not think about all of that just now. I'd like just to sit here awhile, under Eliot's trees ... which are now your trees by the way, since he planted them for you and your children.'

Callum looked surprised. 'He planted them for me?'

'That's what he said. He believed trees were the best heritage in the world.'

Callum thought this a rather fanciful notion, pleasant though trees undoubtedly were, but he didn't say as much. His mother, he'd noticed, often had a way all her own of looking at things.

'Will I see you at dinner?' she asked as he got up to go.

Callum shook his head, his expression dead-pan and his Westmorland accent coming very much to the fore. 'I eat in t'kitchen these days, with t'other servants.'

For a long moment Kate couldn't quite take in what he'd said. 'I don't understand?'

'That was another of Lucy's decisions. Appar-ently it offends her sensibilities to have me sit at table with them, therefore she told me to eat in t'kitchen with Mrs Petty and Ida. Suits me fine, matter of fact.'

It did not suit Kate. Discretion being the better part of valour though, in view of all that she must face in the coming weeks. Somehow she had to find the courage to return to the factory despite the implied threat of that dead rat, with inevitable confrontations with Lucy. Therefore, Kate opted not to make too big a fuss. She approached the subject with laudable tact and diplomacy.

'I understand that Callum elected to eat in the kitchen with Mrs Petty while we were away. Isn't he the big eejit? Though perhaps it's just as well. His table manners are not what they might be. But then, he hasn't had things easy, and boys will be boys. He no doubt believes "please" and "thank you" to be only for bairns. I've made it clear that in future I shall expect him to be properly attired, with his best manners in place, and that he is to sit at table with the rest of us, as is only right and proper. He's not a child, after all, but the son of the house.'

This last was the nearest Kate dare go, in her current state of health, to reminding Lucy of Callum's position. It did not go unnoticed.

'My dear Kate, I sympathise entirely with your efforts to civilise the boy. What a trial sons can be for a woman alone. Jack too can sometimes be most obstinate, won't listen to a word I say. But then he knows exactly what he wants out of life, and means to get it. So like his father. Oh, dear, if only poor, darling Charles were here now to help raise his son as the gentleman he undoubtedly is.' Having successfully reminded Kate that she too was a widow, but that her own son had the breeding which Kate's clearly lacked, Lucy offered up the saddest, sweetest smile. 'What a trial life is for we women.'

Kate made no comment. If it was pity Lucy was after, she was knocking on the wrong door.

'The point is, I'm afraid, that Callum and Jack are constantly at loggerheads. Why, I even caught them fighting the other night. They would no doubt have torn each other to shreds had I not intervened. Did Callum not tell you? I felt compelled to take Jack to the hospital. He was in such a state, I feared his nose might be broken. Fortunately it was only badly bruised but that wild son of yours has no idea of his own strength. You should try and tame him or who knows what he might do next?'

Kate had grown increasingly bemused throughout this long complaint. Now she said, 'Callum said nothing to me of any fight.'

'He wouldn't wish to appear in the wrong, would he?' Lucy sweetly remarked.

'I thought he looked gaunt, and rather pale. So what did Jack do to him to provoke such a response?'

'Nothing, dear Kate, nothing at all. That is my point entirely. My son neither said nor did a single thing to warrant such an attack. It was entirely unprovoked. Rather you should ask your son the reason, for I'm sure I can think of none other than that he was making a nuisance of himself to my daughter. Just as well I sent Bunty away to Switzerland. I really can't have her contaminated by such loutish behaviour.'

'Sure and he'd never hurt a fly, certainly not Bunty. He adores her.'

'That is precisely what I'm afraid of.'

Kate became aware that her cheeks were burning. 'I'll speak to Callum.'

Lucy sighed. 'The matter has been dealt with. By me. Bring him back to the table by all means. He is your child, after all, the son of the house, as you say. I'm simply saying that we must watch him most carefully, make sure his jealousy of Jack doesn't get out of hand again. I'll not tolerate any more displays of peevishness on those grounds.'

'Jealousy of Jack? Peevishness, why...'

But Kate got no further since Lucy didn't stay long enough to hear her out. She swept away in her rustling taffeta gown, chin high and nose firmly in the air.

# 21

In the event, dinner that evening and in the days following passed without incident, Callum sat at table next to the aunts, in his best bib and tucker, and uttered not a word. Jack sat at one end of the table and Kate at the other. She tried not to see any significance in this new placement.

The workmen continued to come in sharp at eight every morning and Kate could find no fault with the work Lucy had ordered. And Lucy continued to exercise charm and good temper at every turn. It was all most unsettling, leaving

Kate feeling unneeded, almost superfluous to requirements, which did no good at all for her battered self-esteem.

Even on her first day back at the factory, she felt very much like a spare part. Almost the first thing Toby Lynch said after expressing his pleasure at seeing her again, was that she was not to worry as they were managing perfectly well without her.

'I'll go home again then, shall I, since I'm not wanted?'

'That's not what I meant, and you know it, Kate. What I'm saying is that the workers have pulled out all the stops to carry on as normal, knowing you weren't yourself and needed to rely on their support at this difficult time.'

Kate looked abashed. 'Tell them I appreciate it. I'll tell them myself, soon as I can face them. Callum says you called at the house asking after me. Thanks for that too.'

'I was needing a word when I had a problem on one occasion so called at the house, but the other Mrs Tyson, Mrs Lucy, didn't seem to think you were up to it.'

Kate frowned. 'She never said. Mebbe it would've done me good to think of a problem other than me own.'

'That's what I thought.'

'It's true that I have been a bit down, got a bit too ... introspective.'

'Don't worry about it. We've coped fine.' Toby smiled, and it dawned on her then that he wasn't a bad-looking man, quite nice in fact, with that shock of fair hair and his cheery grin. His eyes, she noticed, were a deep grey, almost charcoal, and he had a gentle, quiet manner to him. She was lucky to have him here, looking after things for her, but it was long past time she got herself back into harness and took charge herself. She couldn't mourn forever, or risk losing what Eliot and she had built up over the years. Where was the sense in that? It wasn't what Eliot would have wanted.

As they talked, Toby made it plain that he was keen to set in motion the new line of ladies' shoes, that everything was in place and their sales figures were in desperate straits. 'Something has to be done, and fast,' he insisted. Kate agreed that they should get on with it.

'Can you do that, just tell me to get on with it, without consulting the other members of the board, or Mrs Lucy, now that she's your partner? Or should I set up a board meeting to discuss the matter, plus any other ideas we might come up with?'

Kate was stunned. She'd known, of course, that things would be different in future, that she wouldn't have quite the same freedom in running the factory as before. Eliot had left her in total control while he was at war but even the complexities of his will had not entirely sunk in. She hadn't really given the matter any proper thought. Now she considered Toby's words with all due seriousness.

'I expect you're right and a board meeting would be the proper course of action. You'd best send out the notices, Toby. Thank you.'

'I'll arrange it.'

'I'm aware that Jack has started work here. Which department is he in? Who have you apprenticed him to?'

Toby shook his head. 'Mrs Lucy made it clear that he was not to be trained as a shoemaker, after all. He was to be in the office, working in administration and management, is how she put it.'

Kate was silent for a moment, thinking this through. No wonder relations between the two boys were difficult, if Jack had effectively been set above Callum and was not to serve his time in the shoe trade as Eliot would have expected. Since Toby was clearly not prepared to comment further, she merely said, 'I see. Well, I shall look into it, see how he's shaping. And my son, is he behaving himself?'

Toby gave a wry smile. 'Seems anxious to get home most evenings, I was wondering if he had a girl?'

Kate raised an eyebrow, then smiled. 'Is that the way of it? Well, no wonder he's gone all caring and concerned, of a sudden. He must want my approval.' And they both chuckled, making the usual remarks about young love. Was there more to this tale about Bunty than she'd realised? Kate wondered, and sighed. Perhaps it was just as well she'd been packed off to finishing school. The last thing they needed right now, were more complications.

'And what about you, Kate? Will you find new love, d'you reckon, one day?'

Not even glancing at him, and therefore missing the eagerness with which he waited for

207

her reply, Kate brushed the question aside with the comment that it was far too soon even to contemplate such a thing.

'I'm sorry. 'Course it is. I spoke out of turn.'

'No, no, I don't mind your asking. Life goes on, as they say. It's just – too soon. Much too soon even to think of anyone else taking Eliot's place.'

After that they got down to business, going through the figures, dealing with the problems associated with keeping the new styles suitably lightweight. When she left the factory that day Kate was feeling much more herself, better than she had in an age. It hadn't been easy, going back, but she'd coped, and felt quite proud of her modest success.

Now all she had to do was deal with the board meeting.

It was a disaster. Not only was there Lucy to contend with, but also the aunts, and to Kate's surprise even Jack. She ventured to ask if this was strictly necessary and received the sharp retort from Lucy that it certainly was, since he may one day be taking over the company.

'I don't think that has been decided yet,' Kate very reasonably pointed out.

'There you are, doesn't that prove that I need him here, beside me? Need somebody on *my* side.'

'This isn't a question of sides. We're not about to go into battle.'

But on that point Kate was entirely wrong. They seemed to disagree at every turn. When she described the need for a new advertising campaign,

208

Lucy was adamant that they should not stoop so low. 'Didn't dear Eliot make his opinion on the subject abundantly clear, insisting that it would demean us?'

'It would also make us more competitive.'

'Eliot didn't see it that way, and I for one agree with him.'

Kate couldn't bear this woman telling her what Eliot would or would not have believed. What right had Lucy to voice his opinion? 'Sadly, my husband is no longer here to speak for himself, so I must learn to make decisions without him.'

'You cannot have things all your own way, Kate dear, since he gave me a say in the business too, in lieu of my darling Charles, and particularly since your judgement is somewhat warped, shall we say, at present.'

'Warped? What are you talking about? It's not in the least bit warped.'

'Perhaps warped is too strong a word, but certainly damaged. You aren't thinking clearly, anyone can see that.'

''Tis not so. Aren't I feeling much more meself? Getting back to work has done me a power of good, so it has. Toby was only saying so the other day, were you not, Toby?'

He nodded, his expression carefully non-committal as he watched the two women, but he was worried. The aunts seemed equally concerned, he could tell by the way they were fidgeting with their gloves, desperately trying to avoid eye contact. They were clearly embarrassed but they too must realise that Eliot Tyson had made a bad mistake, pandering to his own sense of guilt over his brother, by leaving matters in this unsatisfactory way. He'd effectively neutered Kate's power. She was going to have a struggle to maintain control, possibly even find herself with a real fight on her hands.

'Indeed, you are not at all yourself.' Lucy's voice was rising in pitch as she warmed to her argument. 'You're making wild accusations left, right and centre, even laying the blame on me for poor Eliot's death. Paranoia, I believe they call it. We are all trying to be patient with you, Kate. You've been overcome by grief over the loss of your husband, which no one can wonder at. I can understand, absolutely, what you are going through. Haven't I suffered a similar fate myself?' Lucy took out a lace-edged handkerchief and dabbed at her eyes.

Yes, Kate thought, and you may well have been genuinely fond of Charles, but you loved his pocket book more. And then, to her horror, realised that she'd actually spoken this thought out loud.

'How dare you say such a thing?' Lucy screamed, jumping up and knocking her chair to the floor with a great crash, making Vera start with alarm and bringing Cissie to the verge of tears.

Kate held her nerve, determined to remain calm while needing to make it plain that she was not the only one with flaws. She'd felt as if she was on the road to recovery. Now Lucy was pushing her back into that pit of dark despair. She could feel it closing in upon her, a cloying blackness that deadened all sound and took away all rational thought. She had to fight the feeling if she was to survive. 'I dare, because it is true. You continued piling up debts even after the poor man was dead, and Eliot paid them off.'

'Only by selling *my* beautiful mansion on Lake Windermere. I shall never forgive him for that, never!'

'He is dead, Lucy. You can no longer lay the blame for your own stupidity at Eliot's door, or at mine for that matter. And as to running the factory, I do know what I'm talking about. Better than you. Besides building up a business of me own, making army boots, I'm the one who kept this company going throughout the dark years of war, and will continue to do so.'

'So my wishes are to be ignored, are they?'

Toby hastily intervened, before matters came to blows. 'Ladies, ladies, let us remain calm, shall we? We still have a great deal of business to get through.'

Toby had replaced Lucy's chair, poured everyone a glass of water, tugged at his waistcoat, filled in with a few inconsequential facts and details, giving everyone time to calm down. Then he took the plunge with his own idea.

'I was thinking that, just because we can no longer make boots for the services, it's no reason to stop making them altogether. We obviously still manufacture men's working boots, but we could also branch out into boots for sport: for cricket, hockey and football. And of course climbing boots, which would sell well here in the Lake District.'

'What a splendid idea,' Lucy said, having smoothed down the pleated skirt of her new two-piece, adjusted her fox-fur hat and restored her composure. 'I have simply loads of friends involved in all manner of sporting activities, as well as climbing, of course. I could ask them to test them out for us. Wouldn't that be ripping fun? Some of them are quite influential and their word would count for a great deal.'

'It would certainly be a good way of getting free boots for your friends,' Kate remarked with unusual tartness.

Lucy smiled, as if she'd drawn blood and was pleased by the fact. 'At least it would be preferable to putting advertisements in common newspapers. You should be pleased that Toby, at least, is thinking clearly. One of us needs to.'

Toby said, 'Kate, what do you think?'

'I agree. The idea is a good one.' But as she jotted down a note on her pad, Kate wasn't quite quick enough off the mark. It was Lucy who called the meeting to a vote on the matter.

'And we'll vote on the advertising suggestion too. I'm sure, Aunts, you will agree with me that Tysons does not wish to become embroiled in anything so demeaning?'

Toby intervened yet again, gently pointing out that, as the largest shareholder and chairman of the meeting, Kate was the one who must call a vote. 'And we cannot take two at once. They must be done individually.'

'Oh, very well, but do get on with it, Kate, for goodness' sake. Really, you do seem to be losing your grip.'

An ominous silence fell over the table as embarrassment permeated the assembly, nobody quite knowing what to say.

Aware that the hand holding her pen had begun to shake, Kate set it down, swallowed carefully and called for a vote on Toby's suggestion to make boots for sport and for climbing, ploughing through an atmosphere which felt as thick as treacle. What was wrong with her? Why did Lucy have the ability to turn her to jelly?

The motion was unanimously accepted, as was hers concerning a new line of ladies' fashion shoes, and Kate was secretly pleased with herself. An achievement there, at least.

She lost the vote on advertising, and also one on an improved design for their shoe boxes because Lucy considered it to be an unnecessary expense, and the aunts, always fearful of spending money, agreed with her.

Kate decided against raising her idea for producing varied fittings for her proposed line of ladies' shoes, and more importantly for children's. She'd had enough for one day, felt utterly exhausted and emotionally drained by the whole performance. The subject would have to be addressed at some other time.

But if this was an example of how things were going to be from now on, running Tysons Shoes was going to become increasingly difficult, if not impossible.

Back at the house, over tea and scones, Vera tactfully attempted to point out to Lucy that perhaps she'd been rather hard on Kate at the meeting.

'The dear girl is doing her best under most trying circumstances. It can't be easy getting back to work after such a tragedy, learning to face a future without dear Eliot. They were very much in love, you know.'

Lucy did not wish to hear how much in love they were, or to be the object of criticism by the aunts. 'I know that Kate O'Connor has been nothing but a source of gossip and scandal ever since she first set foot in this house. She's inveigled her way into our lives, first disposing of Amelia, then getting herself pregnant by Eliot, and now the poor man has conveniently died, leaving her very comfortably off indeed.'

Vera was shocked. 'She did not *dispose of Amelia*, as you put it. Poor dear Amelia was sick with a tumour and Kate valiantly nursed her to the end. What are you suggesting? Surely you are not implying that Kate meant Eliot to die, that she in some way caused that accident? What nonsense! Quite impossible.'

'How can we be sure? The police never did find the car that hit him, so how can we ever know the truth?'

Cissie interrupted her. 'My dear, I can't believe you would imply ... in any case, the old Crossley could never be driven so fast. And I'm absolutely certain that Kate would never hurt darling Eliot, although others might consider it politic to do so.'

Even Vera was shocked that Cissie, of all people, should venture to express an opinion, particularly one loaded with such dark insinuation.

Lucy glared at her for several long seconds

214

before giving her most wintry smile. 'Whoever, or whatever, caused it, that accident was most unfortunate and we must learn to make the best of things. But I cannot allow Kate to rule the roost entirely. Eliot must have left me such a substantial share for a reason. Perhaps he didn't trust her either? Perhaps he too thought that her judgement was flawed? Or perhaps she threatened him in some way.'

'Oh, dear me, no. Surely not!' Vera reached into her bag for her *sal volatile*. The entire morning had been an immense strain for her. The arguments at the Church Council meetings were as nothing compared to this.

'She certainly had the most to gain from his death, and showed little eagerness to welcome him home. She wasn't even at the railway station to meet him. It was most fortunate I happened along when I did. Poor dear Eliot felt so abandoned.'

'She was held up by the children,' Cissie said, growing increasingly distressed by the direction this conversation was taking.

Lucy ignored her. 'After all, Callum is not Eliot's true son, and Kate herself is not, strictly speaking, even a member of the family.'

'Meaning because she married into it, as you did?' said Vera, in her most waspish tones. She hadn't particularly welcomed Kate O'Connor into Tyson Lodge, all those years ago, nor did she feel entirely comfortable with her now taking over what was, in effect, the family business. But neither was she terribly fond of Lucy, let alone the arrogant Jack.

Lucy was clearly irritated by the remark,

despite its evident truth. 'I'm speaking of the future, of who will take over in the fullness of time. It is imperative that the business remain in the family, with a genuine Tyson at the helm. Jack has a far greater right to it than that son of hers. Callum is nothing more than a workhouse child with not a scrap of breeding in him, as we all know.'

'Callum has the makings of a fine young man,' Cissie burst out, once again bringing startled eyes swivelling in her direction. 'I will not hear him so maligned. He is working hard at his books as well as at the shoemaking, going to night classes, doing all that he can to better himself. I admire him enormously.'

Vera nodded vigorously. 'Quite right. Well said, Cissie.'

Lucy leaned closer. 'It is not well said. Callum O'Connor must never be allowed to take over the management of Tysons Industries. *I will not allow it!*'

'I do not see how you could prevent it, should Kate choose to leave it to him,' Cissie valiantly responded. 'He is Eliot's adopted son, as you said yourself, and Eliot left Kate, his widow, with a majority share in the business.'

Lucy's eyes narrowed, her mouth curled in derision as the tone of her voice chilled to an icy contempt. 'If you two dear ladies wish to continue to live under this roof, *and* receive your regular monthly allowance from Tysons Industries, then you must learn to keep opinions of this nature to yourself. If you don't like the way I run things, you can always go and live in that musty old house of yours in Heversham. You could easily live out your last years in genteel poverty and isolation there. If that fails to appeal, then I'd advise you to acquire the art of tactful silence. It will do you no good at all to try my patience too far. Do I make myself clear?'

# 22

Kate had hoped that work would be good for her, and in a way it was. It stopped her from thinking, kept her mind fully occupied, yet it did nothing to banish that sick feeling from the pit of her stomach, or the pain that rushed in upon her when she woke each morning.

Responsibilities lay heavy on her shoulders. Prices had risen and the operatives would watch her with doubt and suspicion in their eyes, wondering if she could make it, if Tysons could survive in the new post-war world when the inevitable crash came.

Kate worked hard and tried not to worry, to concentrate on small things, on the routine she had planned that day, on her children. Flora was a delight, forever caring and so resilient, as children are. There had been no repetition of her sickness and she seemed to have accepted that Lucy would be staying. She coped by largely ignoring her, saying little when in her presence, and, to her immense relief, Lucy likewise ignored Flora.

This may have had something to do with a little spat which occurred between them that was really most entertaining. Wicked though it undoubtedly was, it quite cheered Kate up.

It had begun when Lucy told Flora one morning at breakfast that eggs were good for her.

'I don't like them.'

'You should eat them.'

'I know you once tried to make me eat them. I remember that very well, because you made me sick.'

'I never willingly made any child sick, or forced you to eat eggs.'

'Yes, you did. But you can't make me any more. My mummy is here now, to stop you doing nasty things.'

Lucy looked enraged and affronted by the accusation, as if she were a perfect innocent, or else had conveniently wiped from her mind all the horrid things she had done to Flora when she was small. 'You're a big girl now and should eat everything you're given. You're far too fussy.' And she spooned a large portion of scrambled egg on to the child's plate.

Flora looked at it in disgust. '*You* eat it,' she said, 'if you like it so much.' And picking up the plate, dumped the contents into her aunt's lap.

Lucy leaped to her feet, screeching with rage, yellow scrambled egg sliding down the front of her pleated linen skirt. 'Control that child, or I swear I won't be responsible for my actions!'

'It's your own fault, Lucy, for trying to bully her. Just leave her alone.' It was very naughty of Flora, and Kate did make an effort to scold her, but it was half-hearted. The child's face was such a picture of mischievous delight, glorying in this small revenge, that she didn't have the heart to be too cross.

From Flora's point of view, her show of retaliation had worked. Lucy left her alone after that.

Lucy was hot, bothered, and decidedly *dishabillé* by the time Swainson was done with her. He wasn't exactly the ardent type but he certainly was not lacking in either energy or imagination. Today he had chosen to take her on his grubby little kitchen table among the detritus of the scrappy meal they'd shared, knocking plates and mugs to the floor in the process while he ravished her like a common kitchen maid. So *deliciously sordid!* And it had happened without any warning. He'd suddenly leaped on her, right in the middle of a most serious conversation about how she was to oust Kate from the factory and replace her with Jack.

Lucy could see now how he'd used to ravage the women outworkers when he inspected the work they did for Tysons Shoes in their own homes. How extremely convenient. But then those women were cheap and of no account, not like herself who was never anything but in control. Or at least that was what Lucy told herself.

It was simply sex, which she enjoyed enormously. Where was the harm in that? She had always been a woman with appetites. She and Charles had played such games together once. So entertaining! Perhaps she could train Swainson in

219

some of them. Would he dress up for her? Let her spank him? She glanced sideways at his sour expression and had second thoughts on the matter. More likely he would turn on her and give *her* a good walloping. She must ever remember that he was not her gentle, darling Charles.

There were times when Lucy thought he was losing the thread of what this was all about. It was about her, not him; the re-establishing of power for herself. Money in her pocket, not his. Yet Swainson seemed much more concerned with his own neck.

'What do I get out of it?' he kept asking. 'When do I get me old job back?'

Having him back in the factory, swanking about his power over her, was not a part of Lucy's plan. But she had to keep him dangling. One never knew when he might be useful. 'Not yet. Be patient,' she would soothingly remark.

By way of compensation he would demand more and more money if asked to do this, or that, or whatever task she had planned for him. She'd tried to get him to stir up resentment amongst the men at the factory, but that hadn't worked. Loyalty to that woman was too strong in them. Surely only fed by pity.

Lucy had got him to offer bribes but Toby Lynch had come along at the crucial moment and that hadn't worked either, although Swainson had never given her the money back.

Jack wasn't on the board yet, and that must be Lucy's main objective. Co-opting him on to the odd board meeting wasn't enough. To achieve a secure position for him, that must be her next task.

Even the depth of Lucy's purse had its limits, so she would sigh and open her blouse, or her legs, whichever appealed most at the time, as it was far too expensive to keep giving the man money. And it really wasn't too bad. So long as she held her breath and didn't breathe in the rank odour of him, satisfaction could be provided for both parties.

This wasn't the first time Lucy had been to his house, a revolting little dung heap in a not particularly salubrious area of Kendal, out on fellside. She'd never agreed to grace his bed with her presence. That would have been one step too far. Heaven knows when he'd last washed his sheets, but she wasn't against a jolly little tumble, on the hearth rug, on the stairs, wherever they happened to be at the time. So long as her lovely ebony hair didn't touch any revolting, verminous pillow.

And at first she'd enjoyed it. Quite a lot, in fact. When he was pounding into her she found it helped her to vent her own pent-up anger and frustration with life, with her dratted sister-in-law and those venomous old aunts.

Yet Lucy had begun to think that really she should be finding someone more suitable to entertain her, more of her own class. She was growing bored with his uncouth manners and violent snorting at the moment of climax.

Now that the alterations on the house were practically finished, she ought to be extending her social life, as she'd always promised herself that she would. Once Jack's position was secure, Swainson would be superfluous, although how she would manage to dismiss him from her life and keep him quiet about the things he knew, was a problem she hadn't yet solved. And he might still prove useful to her, if things got tricky, so she must tread carefully.

Right now he was poking into her with his fingers and Lucy rolled her eyes. 'Yes, all right, one last go and then I really must be off, I have so much to do today.'

He wasn't even listening. He turned her over and took her again, pressing and thrusting against her just as if he were rolling pastry on the rough wooden table, making her squeal out loud with painful ecstasy. Perhaps she'd leave things as they were, for now.

If only Kate could resolve her own problems with her sister-in-law quite as easily as Flora seemed to have done. Every night when she came home from the factory, instead of her being able to relax, there was Lucy waiting for her, ordering her about, telling her what to do, saying when she might eat, criticising her clothes, her appearance, the waxy paleness of her face.

And night after night she filled the house with her noisy friends so that Kate would be forced to escape to her own room with the door shut fast, hoping for a bit of peace.

One night, after Kate had spent a blissful hour or two alone with Flora, reading to her daughter and playing games of Ludo and Snap, she opted for an early night as she felt bone weary after a hard day at the factory. She took a lovely hot bath, made herself a cup of hot cocoa in the small nursery kitchen next door, as she once used to do when Callum was small, then slipped thankfully between the sheets. She was just beginning to drift off when Lucy burst into her room, crashing back the door and switching on the light.

'Get out of bed this minute!'

Startled, Kate rubbed her eyes, struggling to wake up. 'What's going on? What's happened? Is it Flora?'

'Have you forgotten that we have the Blythes here for supper tonight? Didn't I specifically remind you about them only at breakfast this morning?'

'Did you? I – I don't recollect you saying anything about the Blythes, or supper.'

Lucy flung open the wardrobe door. 'That is half your problem. You can never remember a thing I tell you.'

'What time is it? It's nearly nine. Isn't it rather late for a dinner party? And I'm so tired, with an early start tomorrow. Can't you manage without me for once?'

'No, I cannot. They have already arrived and are enjoying aperitifs, wondering where the hell you are. Naturally that dreadful woman, your useless cook, is equally late with the meal, so there is still time for you to redeem yourself. Get up, get dressed and make yourself presentable. At once! Thomas Blythe is an influential man in this town, a town councillor as well as owning a chain of ladies' fashion shops in Manchester. You see, I do have the interests of the business at heart. Far more than you do, it seems. And at least I can remember what I'm supposed to be doing from one minute to the next.'

Throughout this diatribe Lucy snatched garments from the wardrobe, underwear from Kate's chest of drawers, shoes from the shelf and flung them on to the bed. 'Don't just sit there. Get up, I say!'

Kate had no alternative but to scramble out of bed, hastily dress and hurry downstairs to endure a long and difficult dinner. Not only were the Blythes present but also several of Lucy's more vociferous friends. Wearing as it was for her, Kate couldn't help feeling even sorrier for Mrs Petty and Ida, working so late.

Poor Ida looked fit to burst into tears when she very nearly dropped the soup tureen as she lifted it from the table, preparatory to taking it away. Only Thomas Blythe's swift intervention saved them from a catastrophe.

Lucy was furious, of course. 'I'll speak with you later, Ida. Tell Cook we are more than ready for the next course.'

Ida went off red-cheeked, only too aware that the simmering rage in Lucy's face would erupt like a volcano, the moment the guests had departed.

Kate felt awkward witnessing the girl's humiliation. Lucy was giving the strong impression that she was now mistress of Tyson Lodge and was in a position to order the servants about as she pleased. And Kate too, apparently.

There was something about her sister-in-law's abundant self-assurance, her assumption that she was entitled to take charge and make all the decisions, that chipped away at Kate's fragile ability to cope and undermined her own sense of confidence.

Lucy was currently presenting herself as indispensable, a favourite theme.

'Now that my dear brother-in-law isn't here to share the burden of running this house and the business, I do what I can to offer my support and take my share of the responsibility. As dear, darling Eliot would expect. Poor Kate certainly couldn't cope on her own. She doesn't have the background to understand the finer details of society, for one thing.'

Kate could ignore the snide remarks about herself, but Lucy's constant use of endearments whenever she referred to Eliot infuriated her, and she had to grit her teeth to prevent herself from rising to the bait.

On the few occasions when she had attempted to stand up to Lucy's domineering manner, her sister-in-law had wept into her handkerchief and claimed that she was only trying to help, which somehow made Kate appear ungrateful as well as incompetent.

Alternatively, she would gaze upon Kate with pitying eyes and offer to fetch Mrs Petty's elixir, or to call in the doctor. 'You still aren't well, I do understand that, otherwise why would you attack me in such a heartless manner? It has all been far too traumatic for you. Many of the soldiers returning from the front are being offered psychological help to overcome their traumas, their shell-shock and the like. Perhaps that's what you need too.'

Kate had been shocked by that suggestion.

'Don't be silly, of course I don't. I haven't fought in a war. I'm fine, so I am. Simply tired and a bit overworked.'

She could have added that Lucy herself might be extremely diligent when it came to criticism but strangely absent when real work needed to be done.

Generally, though, Kate opted for the remedy of silence. It was the only way she could truly escape the bite of Lucy's tongue. The only place where she could not be pursued. Kate could live perfectly well in her head for hours at a time, without anyone bothering her there at all. Except for Eliot, who lived in her head too, but she was content to have him there, where she could commune with him in private.

Mrs Petty had never seen the like in all her born days: dinner parties at least once a week and often twice. She was quite worn out with all the extra work. Half the time she didn't even know how many were coming as madam didn't trouble to send out invitations, proper stiff cards, as Amelia used to do. No such niceties these days, just a quick call on the telephone, mostly to men who were so in demand following the losses in the war that they either didn't turn up at all, because they'd got a better offer, or they brought a friend along too without any sort of warning or permission asked. It was all most vexing. Mrs Petty never knew whether she was feeding eight or fifteen.

Such was the case yesterday evening. One minute it was to be a quiet supper with only the

Blythes invited, and then suddenly it escalated into dinner for ten. Was it any wonder the meal had been late? And poor Ida was still smarting from her telling off.

'I thought she were going to sack me on the spot, Mrs P. What would I have done then, eh?'

'You'd have gone and got a proper job, lass, one that made you more brass and gave you less bother.'

What was even more shocking was that, more often than not, these affairs would go on for half the night, and the amount of alcohol consumed was astonishing. A vulgar display of impropriety, in Mrs Petty's humble opinion.

'I like a bit of a knees up meself,' she told Ida in all seriousness, 'but this takes the biscuit. All these gentlemen friends of hers, pissed as newts, if you'll pardon my French, often requiring a bed for the night because they've imbibed that much they can no longer stand.

'Which means more work for you and me, girl. Beds to change, sheets to wash, more breakfasts to cook, and so on and so forth. Bless my poor aching feet, there's no end to it! And on these wages? It's slave labour. I don't know about you, Ida, but I'm on me uppers. My bunions have bunions me feet are that bad. I might just tek it into me head to retire, and go and live with me sister Annie on the Fylde coast after all. She keeps on asking me. I would too, if it weren't for our Kate. But somebody has to keep an eye on that poor lass, so who better than us, eh, Ida? Who better than us?'

# 23

Kate began to doubt her own judgement. If she was forgetting discussions about house improvements, and dinner parties, what was happening to her? She went every day to the factory, trying to solve problems and answer queries, working herself to the point of exhaustion in the hope that she would sleep. But there were constant interruptions from Lucy. She would call in to the office unannounced, enquire what Kate was doing and question whatever decision she'd recently made, generally coming up with an alternative. She asked so many questions that it would feel like an interrogation, casting doubt on every decision Kate had made.

Once, when there was a selection of shoe samples on Kate's desk, Lucy picked one up and examined it with open contempt. 'Why have you chosen to manufacture this particular style? Quite dreadful. Outdated. I wouldn't be seen dead in a pair of shoes like this.'

'This is one of our standard lines, popular with the older customer, Lucy.'

'We must produce shoes for the bright young things, for the modern woman.'

'And so we will.' Kate indicated a selection of neat, stylish shoes, all light in weight, some with fashionably pointed toes and Louis heels, others single-barred pumps with a high-waisted heel and one tiny covered button. This was the most popular look for everyday. And then there were high-tongued, cutaway, crossover and T-strap styles. 'Shoes for dancing in and for walking in the park with your young man,' Kate smiled. 'And in a selection of colours: leaf brown, black or patent.'

'Very nice, dear, I dare say, but what we really need is something more exciting, more dashing. I've seen some fabulous harem slippers in rich brocades, satin, silk, and velvet with wonderful embroidery, or stitched all over with beads or rhinestones. Marvellous fun! And so Egyptian. Why cannot we make shoes like that?'

Kate sighed. 'Because it isn't the sort of shoe our customers would expect, not from Tysons. We aren't a Moroccan bazaar producing shoes for the Bohemian set. We are making stylish footwear for modern young women who wish to be smart: both practical and fashionable.'

'Sounds pretty stuffy to me. And Jack tells me that some of the leather cutters are refusing to work overtime.'

'That was because he ruffled their feathers by refusing to pay them the proper rate for the job.'

'Nonsense! These people earn far too much as it is. They should be thankful they have a job at all, when so many are unemployed. Goodness, some of them are hobbling into the factory on sticks and crutches, which must affect the level of their efficiency.'

Kate gritted her teeth yet managed to smile. 'And we are all grateful for the sacrifices they made fighting a war to keep us free, particularly if they continue to work despite their injuries.'

Even with right on her side, Kate felt worn out by the constant battling, by fighting every inch of the way. How much longer could she go on?

'You need more help, that is the root of the problem,' Lucy said, maintaining that her son's contributions were invaluable and essential. 'Put Jack on the board. He'll sort everything out.'

Kate disapproved strongly of Jack constantly interfering and poking his nose into matters which weren't his business, loudly voicing his opinions, of which he had many, despite not yet having completed any satisfactory training himself.

'I don't think so, Lucy. Thank you all the same for the suggestion.' And for once Kate went off feeling quite proud of herself.

Sadly her show of independence was dented when Jack's intervention did indeed prove to be useful on one occasion when a young woman in the finishing room wasn't doing her job properly. The girl had proved to be inefficient and lazy, not producing the kind of quality work Tysons was reputed for. She was also adept at stirring up trouble among the other girls and constantly bickering with her supervisor. Kate knew she should deal with the matter, nip the rebellion in the bud before it got out of hand, but the girl had lost her father during the war and Kate balked at firing her.

Jack had no such compunction. He sent her packing without even a warning.

Lucy stated this proved that Kate was losing

her nerve. Perhaps she was right.

The success of Tysons Shoes was based on the premise that they were a team, a family almost who worked together taking pride and interest in the product. Everyone in the factory believed in excellent workmanship and good shoemaking. No cutting corners or making do with shoddy, inferior materials. Respect for the customer, giving him, or her, the best value for money, was of paramount importance. Quality was their watchword. Yet here Kate was, slipping up and making mistakes within months of Eliot's death.

There were other mistakes too. She kept forgetting things, quite important things, which worried her so much it left her feeling constantly tired and depressed, and then she wouldn't sleep properly, which reduced her level of concentration even more. A vicious circle she couldn't seem to break out of. It was as if she'd never had the holiday at all. All the benefits of those few quiet weeks in Scarborough seemed like a distant memory.

She could have sworn that she'd given Jack the production schedule for the new lightweight line, with the target date for when she expected it to be in the shops. Kate felt certain she remembered telling him, 'See that Toby gets that today, the moment he comes back from lunch.'

But Toby had not received it. Consequently the work was not set in motion when it should have been and now the line would be late reaching the shops. Jack swore she'd never given him the file, and when she challenged him on the subject, he went to the filing cabinet and plucked it out.

'There you are. It's still here. You never even gave it to me.'

It was all most troubling. Had she truly forgotten to give it to him? If so, then why was she certain that she had? It would be easy to accuse Jack of negligence, except that he had proved the file had never left her cabinet. It was most worrying.

The result was that Kate began to question herself more and more. Her self-esteem, already low following Eliot's death and her miscarriage, plummeted still further and she began to lose faith in herself, couldn't be certain that her judgement was safe, that any decision she made was the right one.

'Don't worry. It's all part of grieving,' Toby consoled her. 'Perfectly normal and natural. It will pass with time.' If it hadn't been for Toby, Kate thought she might well have gone mad.

Now it was Kate's turn to suffer one of Aunt Vera's little pep talks. 'I know you and Lucy have not always seen eye to eye, dear, but I do believe she has turned over a new leaf. She does seem to be curbing her excessive spending, which was ever her major fault in the past.'

'And what about all these refurbishments? What about those? I doubt the money is coming out of Lucy's pocket.'

Vera looked a touch discomfited. 'True, but as you said yourself, the house did need modernising, and I must confess we've grown extremely fond of our new bathroom, have we not, Cissie?'

'Indeed we have,' Cissie agreed.

'The money came from the estate for those improvements, true. Only right and proper, don't you think?'

'From my inheritance, you mean?'

Again Vera averted her eyes. At times Kate was very nearly her old shrewd self. It was most pleasing and yet disconcerting. Why was she so inconsistent? 'Quite so.'

Cissie said, 'I'm sure Lucy is trying to mend her ways though. Why, she is even lecturing Mrs Petty on household thrift, would you believe?'

Kate could well believe it.

Mrs Petty had complained bitterly to her about how every part of the house had been refurbished and updated except for the kitchen. 'I still have to carry coal up from the cellar, or rather Ida does, and she's not as young as she used to be. But how else would we keep warm, cook all them meals, or get hot water, since we've no fancy gas geyser in my kitchen, nor any new-fangled gas cooker neither. I still have the range to black lead every week.'

She went on to supply an even longer list of deficiencies in her working conditions to which Kate ceased to listen, having far too many other pressing matters requiring her attention which somehow seemed more important. Yet she did promise Mrs Petty that she'd look into it, at least get her a new gas geyser for the hot water.

She'd done nothing about it so far because for some reason Kate felt it meant tackling Lucy on the subject first, almost as if she needed her sister-in-law's permission. What on earth was happening to her?

Vera was saying something along the lines of Lucy's simply trying to make herself useful. 'She has no desire to be a liability, which I can well empathise with since Cissie and I felt much the same when we first came to live here, for all the number of empty rooms and Eliot's generosity.'

Cissie nodded vigorously.

Kate said, 'Except that Lucy is on at me the whole time, correcting me, criticising, finding fault. It seems to be turning me to mush.'

Vera gave a polite cough. 'I suspect that is partly your own lack of faith in yourself. And with your background, who can blame you if you feel a little ... shall we say ... inferior? You're really a very capable woman, Kate, we are all aware of that. Surprisingly so considering your disadvantages. But you must remember that it is only a few months since the accident and you are still grieving for your loss, and the loss of your child.' She patted Kate's hand. 'Allow Lucy to help, dear. Don't feel you must fight her the whole time.'

'And pray for guidance,' added Cissie, grasping the hand Vera had just relinquished and giving it a little squeeze.

'Yes, Aunt Vera, Aunt Cissie, I will do my best,' Kate agreed, feeling suddenly very tired and quite unable to summon the energy to argue any further.

Lucy's social life was growing more hectic by the week, by the day even. Essential, in her view, if she was to find herself a new husband. It surely wasn't too late. She was still the right side of forty, although only just, so time was of the essence.

There'd been little hope during her two years of exile, but now, with a share in Tysons, she had a better chance of snaring someone. Not that she wanted a fortune hunter. Apart from any other consideration there was little actual wealth attached to her shareholding, only prospects of same for the future. And even that depended on Kate's competence, in which Lucy had little faith. She was banking on gaining complete control, hopefully through Jack, then things would be very different.

Not that she had any wish for dear Jack to wear himself out with the business. When he grew bored with it, she wanted to be in a position to sell, then her darling son could become the gentleman he deserved to be, and she could sit back and enjoy her reward.

In the meantime, what Lucy needed most was to marry wealth. Unfortunately, the stock of eligible men was low.

So many had been killed off in the war, so many ancient families gone to the wall. With no sons to inherit, stables empty, no servants to look after the estates properly, taxes rising and incomes falling, land and fine houses were being sold off to profiteering city types who moved in and aped their betters, pretending to be what they weren't.

Although being connected to a title and landed gentry would be fun, Lucy was not entirely against these Johnnie-Come-Latelys, so long as they were *very* rich. And she certainly had no wish to lumber herself with faded grandeur. Living in a draughty, ancient pile was not to her taste at all.

Nor was she quite of an age when she could guarantee to supply any future spouse with an heir, so she must choose with care.

Lucy rather saw her later years spent in becoming a hostess of note and fashion, one whose dinner parties must not be missed at any cost. Although short periods spent exploring the continent during the winter would not go amiss either.

She longed to be one of the new breed of hostess who possessed flair and élan. The kind who held the new-style cocktail parties, serving champagne with *crème de menthe*, White Ladies, and enough gin to sink a battleship, not to mention dinky titbits of food served with consummate imagination. She'd read all about it in *Vogue* magazine. All of which made Mrs Petty's culinary efforts look positively Victorian by comparison, but then the woman *was* Victorian.

Like it or not, the dragon must be brought to heel. Mrs Petty would do as she was told or suffer the consequences.

But Lucy had begun to despair of ever striking lucky in the marriage stakes.

Callum was missing Bunty badly. Not only was she his only real friend but he loved her devotedly, ached to hold her in his arms again. She was still at her finishing school in Switzerland and hating every minute, as she'd expected. They wrote letters of love and longing to each other, rarely missing a single week. In addition, Callum would keep her abreast of all the gossip and news back home, Bunty equally concerned about Kate, and appalled by her mother's apparent vendetta against her. The pair were united in their hope that one day they'd be free to be together, despite everything.

But Callum hadn't heard from her for a week or two now, which was slightly worrying. She'd complained of feeling unwell the last time she'd written, maybe she'd caught the 'flu or something. Switzerland must be pretty cold at this time of year. And then a letter came saying how much she was looking forward to seeing him at Christmas.

*'We need to talk. There's so much I need to tell you. I do wish we were old enough to marry. That would solve everything. Couldn't we elope, like Romeo and Juliet?'*

Callum smiled affectionately to himself as he read her eager words. She really must hate that school. Poor Bunty. He wrote back, gently reminding her that Romeo and Juliet's love story didn't exactly have a happy ending and he was very determined that theirs would.

'We'll marry just the minute we're old enough to please ourselves. Till then, my love, we must be patient.' But he finished with lots of words of love, saying how much he missed her and how he too was longing for Christmas to come so they could be together again.

As if she didn't have worries enough, Christmas to arrange for one thing over which Kate was making not the slightest effort, Lucy received a

237

most disturbing letter from the school, concerning Bunty. The headmistress was threatening to expel her for misbehaviour and wished Lucy to come and collect her at once.

She was flabbergasted. Bunty had always been an individual, fiercely independent sort of child, but it surely wasn't in her nature to cause mayhem and bring expulsion upon herself. What on earth could she have done? Smoked an illicit cigarette perhaps? Got a little squiffy with her friends, as young girls did from time to time? Whatever it was, it was obviously something the prissy headmistress disapproved of, silly woman.

Perfectly certain that she didn't have the time to take the boat train to Switzerland right now, Lucy sat down and wrote to the school, insisting that they at least keep her daughter until the end of term.

The response this time came from Bunty herself, by telephone. A frantic, desperate appeal for her mother to meet her at Liverpool Street station on Saturday as she was on her way home, via Harwich, and would do her best to explain then.

Lucy very nearly refused, in a fury that her wishes had been ignored. How dare the school dismiss her darling daughter! Such effrontery. What could the girl possibly have done to deserve such treatment? She was soon to learn.

A tearful Bunty sat in the station buffet weeping salt tears into her tea cup while she confessed to her mother that she was almost three months pregnant.

Lucy could actually feel the blood draining from her face, and then flooding back on a tide of fury. Had they not been in such a public place she might well have knocked her child to the ground, so livid was she.

'You've ruined everything, you stupid girl! Destroyed your future, your reputation, all my efforts in trying to make a lady out of you. You've turned yourself into a harlot. Who's the father? I'll kill him with my own bare hands.'

Faced with this prospect, Bunty very nearly refused to say, but then how could she and Callum ever marry if she didn't tell? 'He will marry me, Mama, there's no problem about that. We love each other, were intending to marry anyway.'

'We'll see about that. *Who is he?*'

The moment Callum's name was out of her mouth, Bunty recognised her mistake. If her mother's face had been pale before, it now bleached to a ghastly hue. 'Never,' she hissed. 'Never will you see that boy ever again, not while I live and breathe.'

Lucy wasted no time. She took her sobbing, seventeen-year-old daughter straight to a doctor she knew and before the afternoon was out, the 'problem' had been dealt with. Lucy then telephoned the headmistress of another school that dear Teddy had recommended, giving a garbled explanation for the reason things hadn't worked out very well for the girl in the previous establishment, and offering a large donation for the new school's inconvenience.

A couple of days later, Bunty was put back on the boat train and returned to Switzerland, although to a different school in a different town; rather like an unwanted parcel going the rounds. There would be no hasty marriage and certainly no baby, not even Christmas in her own home. She would spend it at the new school, which, as her mother explained, would allow her ample opportunity to consider the error of her ways.

'Callum will wait for me,' Bunty sobbed. 'I shall please myself what I do when I reach twenty-one. We'll get married then, see if we don't.'

'You will do no such thing. By then, my girl, I will have married you off to someone who can teach you the merits of decent behaviour. Until then, you will stay where I put you, in Switzerland.'

'I shall have to leave when I'm eighteen,' Bunty retaliated.

'No indeed, nineteen is the age agreed for you to be properly finished. After that, I had hoped to find a good family to take you under their wing, people of wealth and influence. I even dreamed of seeing you presented at Court. Now that may be impossible. We're in danger of having your chances utterly ruined unless you keep this matter absolutely quiet. Not a soul must know of it, do you understand? The headmistress of your new school certainly doesn't. If we're careful, we may still be able to salvage your reputation and find you a good husband.'

Bunty sobbed, 'I don't want a good husband. I want Callum.'

'There will be no further correspondence between the two of you. Ever!'

Try as she might to fight her cause, Bunty's

defiance was weakening. Always afraid of her mother's anger, and only too aware of how badly she herself had transgressed, she felt nervous of what Lucy might do next. It was soon made abundantly clear.

'You will do as I say in this. Not another word will be exchanged between you, not even by letter – not if you want Callum to keep his job at the factory, and to stay safe and well. Do I make myself clear? Stay away from him or you will regret it. I have means of getting my own way. Don't make me use them.'

# 24

As the New Year came in, Lucy put her daughter's problem firmly from her mind and set about her campaign of husband-hunting with renewed fervour. She had her hair shingled, went on a diet and desperately struggled to squeeze her plump bosom into the new, flattened lines; her legs, which she'd always thought rather good, were shamelessly on display with skirts worn at least three inches above her ankles. The fashion pages rumoured they might go shorter still!

She attended any number of weekend parties, desperately keeping the flame of hope burning. But even if Lucy were fortunate enough to catch the eye of a young man, the next morning at breakfast he could well start flirting with someone else, or have left early and gone off for the day with some silly young flapper. It was all most disconcerting and meant that she had to start again from scratch, chatting and flirting, striving to listen and be attentive, which was too often stupendously boring.

If I am going to be bored by some old buffer, she would say to herself, he'd better be rich and on his last legs, ripe for leaving me a large fortune. On the whole, though, she preferred younger men. So much more exciting in bed. Capturing a rich one would be her ideal.

Having satisfied herself that Tyson Lodge was now in order, and that her dinner parties, lunches and delightful little musical soirees had met with reasonable success, Lucy decided to expand her horizons. She began holding weekend affairs to which she invited all the right people, either Of Our Class, or else with sufficient funds to counteract the lack of good breeding.

She took up golf and archery, since they would bring her into the company of the right people, and gave instructions for the installation of a tennis court. If they chopped down a few trees in the garden there would just be sufficient room. Not that she mentioned this plan to Kate who would only make a fuss.

Lucy was intent on becoming known for her sophistication, for her fashion sense, her gramophone records, her bridge parties. She even bought a Pekinese dog which yapped all the time and drove Aunt Cissie's dogs wild, but she was a cute little thing, and so *modern*.

One evening she was walking in the garden when

a figure stepped out of the bushes, quite startling her. It was Swainson. 'You haven't been to see me for a while, so I thought I'd pop in.'

Lucy felt a surge of panic. 'But you mustn't. Don't ever come here again, understand? We mustn't be seen together. Far too dangerous.'

'Haven't you got something for me? Why the long silence?'

How could she tell him that matters were going along swimmingly, that she really didn't need him any more, or not at the moment anyway? 'Wait here, I'll fetch you some money.'

'I'll settle for a bit of the other.'

Lucy was irritated. 'Not now! I have dinner guests arriving at any moment. Wait in the summer house. I'll bring you something out later.'

He grabbed her arm as she turned to go, a fierce iron grip that seemed to cut off her circulation. 'See that you do. I'll be waiting.'

Back in the house she was distracted by the arrival of her guests, and by the time they'd all had drinks and were being served canapes, it had started to rain. Lucy certainly was not prepared to risk getting her hair wet or her gown spoiled simply in order to keep Ned Swainson happy. She'd deal with him another time.

Besides she had Teddy to amuse her now, and he was such a darling, very fast, and far too young for her, of course, but willing enough to take her to bed when she'd a mind, and his love making had so much more finesse than Swainson's.

'You'll stay over tonight, won't you, darling?' she would say, or merely give him a look or a

243

wink, and he'd be more than happy to oblige.

Weekend parties were *so* convenient, and he proved to be a vigorous lover although not necessarily the perfect candidate for a husband. His shoulders sloped and he slouched somewhat, but then he was dreadfully lazy. He smoked and drank a great deal, which wasn't particularly a problem because everyone else did, and Teddy certainly liked to follow every trend, but he was also undoubtedly shallow, selfish and utterly irresponsible.

'Lend me a fiver, sweetie,' he would say. 'I know of a sure bet on the three-thirty at Doncaster. I could put one on for you too. Just need to give a chum a ring on your dinky phone.'

And Lucy would make a great show of sighing and complaining, though not really minding at all as she peeled off a few notes, then let him kiss her all over by way of reward for her generosity. He did sometimes win and bring her more notes back, although not quite as often as she would have liked.

They enjoyed several weeks of the most entertaining high-jinks in her bedroom but then she found him in bed with Silky Shackleton. Too shaming for words, Silky being a good ten years older than Lucy herself.

'You prefer the older woman then?' Lucy snapped at him.

'Of course, dahling. Why do you think I sleep with you? Not a problem, is it?'

And there was the nub of it. Of course it was a problem. There were so many young girls around and so few young men that finding one interested in a woman about to turn forty wasn't easy. Lucy had no wish to be thought of as an 'elderly fruit'.

Besides which, those young men who had survived the war were utterly cynical and selfish, devoting their lives entirely to the pursuit of pleasure. Their starry-eyed idealism had been crushed out of them in the trenches and they had little patience now with stifling morals, pettyfogging rules or social niceties.

They wanted to have a good time and not think of tomorrow.

In a way their attitude took some of the fun out of what Lucy's own generation had called house parties. No more creeping along passages and landings; nor any necessity for secret assignations. You could simply make a straightforward arrangement with the man of your choice, and no one would bat an eyelid.

Teddy once told her, 'You know, it really wouldn't matter, old thing, if there were a fire drill, burglary or some such that got everyone up in the middle of the night, so long as it was a false alarm, you understand. No one would care a jot if they emerged from the wrong bedroom. I don't think Freddie Macintosh has slept with his wife in months.'

Teddy himself certainly couldn't be accused of being the faithful type.

Lucy put an end to their affair, naturally, refusing ever to sleep with him again after the Silky Shackleton betrayal. Well, perhaps just occasionally, if she was in the mood. And he did still have his uses. There was no one, simply no one, that Teddy didn't know, assuming he wasn't related to them, that is.

Only this morning, she'd casually risked a query of a most delicate nature. 'If one of your relatives were rather – below par, shall we say, Teddy, where would you send them for a little extra-special care? Somewhere discreet, naturally.'

Unlike most people, Teddy did not investigate her reasons for asking. He simply gave the matter a moment or two's consideration and then came up with a suggestion. Several, in fact, but one in particular appealed. Lucy resolved to discuss the matter later with Jack. She always valued her son's opinion, largely because it generally coincided with her own.

It all proved remarkably easy to arrange. Lucy did worry that perhaps she should have made her move sooner, since the stupid woman was showing obvious signs of recovery. Quite remarkable, really, when you thought about what she'd been through. Nevertheless, it was not quite too late. Nobody else had noticed how much better Kate seemed of late.

When Lucy suggested to her that she might care to accompany her to the next weekend party, Kate was admittedly taken by surprise. 'Why would you want me tagging along? I'm not seeking a husband, and I'll only cramp your style.'

I'm thinking of you, dear Kate. Can't you at least concede that I care about your welfare just a little? They're friends of Teddy's. Own a marvellous place in the country, apparently, right up in the borders of Scotland, so it will be a real treat.

Lots of fresh air and vigorous walking. You'll love that.'

'I couldn't leave the children, not for a whole weekend.'

'Callum is hardly a child and is rarely home in any case what with all his football and cricket, and evening classes. Darling Flora will be spoiled rotten by the aunts. Besides, she'll hardly notice you're gone before you'll be home again. It's only a Friday to Monday do. Oh, do come along, why ever not? A break would do you the world of good. I shall be off with the hunting and shooting brigade during the day myself, but you'll be perfectly free to be superbly lazy and idle, read a lovely book or explore the countryside, as you will.'

'I do like walking, it's true.' Strange as it might seem, Kate felt sorely tempted. Perhaps Lucy was right, a break would do her good.

Lucy gave a trill of laughter. 'I know what you're thinking. I can see it in your eyes. Won't we squabble the entire weekend? Surely not. We're mature, sensible women, and we really must try to get along. This is as good a way to start as any, don't you think? You're no good to Tysons Industries, nor to my investment in it, if you start being ill again, now are you? So, what do you say?'

Kate came to a decision and agreed that she would go, suddenly attracted by the idea of a trip to Scotland. She'd never been and had heard it was very beautiful. Eliot used to wax lyrical about its heather-clad hills and magical glens, promising to take her one day. Well, that couldn't happen now, but she could still go, walk on those hills and remember the happy times they'd enjoyed together. It really was time she started living again.

Toby agreed to stand in for her, pleased for her, quite certain that the fresh Scottish air would indeed do Kate a world of good.

'Don't think about the business at all, be sure that it will be safe in my hands.'

Kate smiled. 'I know it will. You are the one person I can trust implicitly. We came through the war together after all, did we not?'

'We certainly did.' He looked at her then for a long moment, saying nothing, not even smiling. 'Take care, Kate. Don't let Lucy take you over completely. I want to see the old Kate back, the one bristling with defiance for authority, with fire in her eyes and ambition sharp in her belly.'

Kate chuckled delightedly. 'Is that how you saw me?'

'Trouble is what you show on the outside, all that pride and courage, is not necessarily the real you, the part that lives on the inside. You need to protect that soft inner core a little better, Kate, in case someone destroys it.'

She gazed at him in all seriousness. 'What a strange thing to say. Who would want to do that?'

'Do you really need to ask?'

Kate shook her head. 'If you mean Lucy, she now has exactly what she's always wanted, almost a half-share in the business and the opportunity to run Tyson Lodge.' Kate sighed. 'I have to admit that she has made significant improvements to the house, which I'd neither the heart nor the time to achieve. You know I've never been the domestic sort, so let her organise it, I say.'

'Don't underestimate her. It's not just the house she wants to organise. She loves to manipulate people.'

A small shiver of doubt crawled down her spine and Kate frowned. Was Lucy attempting to manipulate her in some way? If so, how? In the house, yes, but Kate could live with that if it made for an easy life. And of course Lucy grumbled constantly about the need for more profits from the business, always wanting to do things her way even when she hadn't the first idea what she was talking about. Yet she seemed to have been losing interest in the battle recently, certainly on the business front, concentrating more on her own social life now that she had a fine home in which to display her hostess skills.

'At least her desperate search for a husband has kept her out of the office lately. And, you never know, she might find one and move out altogether.'

'The sooner the better. You too might find a new husband of your own one day.' And if she heard something more in that casual remark, read any hidden meaning between the lines, she pretended not to understand. Kate had other priorities at present. She did like Toby very much. He was a fine man with excellent qualities, entirely trustworthy, steady and reliable, completely unflappable and with a strength she could only admire. He'd been the best of friends to her, but fond as she was of him, she didn't feel ready to embark upon a new relationship. Finding herself again was far more important.

Kate said, 'Will I ask Lucy for the proper address and telephone number, then you can ring if there are any problems?'

Toby put his hands in his pockets and rocked back on his heels with laughter. 'I thought you said you trusted me implicitly? Now you're wanting me to telephone and give bulletins.'

Kate flushed. 'No, course I'm not.'

'Then get away with you and stop worrying. Have a lovely time.' He instinctively put out his hand, as if to stroke her cheek, then dropped it to his side again without touching her, his own face warm with embarrassment.

Kate smiled, suddenly overcome with a strange shyness. 'I will so. I'll dance some of them high-land jigs, and show off me skill with an Irish reel. You should see my feet fly!'

'There you are, you see, bubbling with anticipation. You sound better already. Now go. We can manage a few more days without you. Come back on Monday with the sun in your hair and a song in your heart, just like the old Kate. And take care,' he called, as she went off with a cheery wave. He did not move from the spot until she was quite out of sight.

'You don't mind my going?' Kate said to Callum, for the umpteenth time.

'No, Mam, I don't mind.'

'Have you heard from Bunty yet?'

He shook his head, his face darkening with concern. 'I haven't heard a word in weeks, nothing but a Christmas card. She still hasn't properly explained why she didn't come for Christmas. Has Lucy said anything to you?'

'Not a word, but when did she ever confide in me? Write again, I'm sure there's nothing to worry about. Probably busy doing exams, or some such.' Then, as she half turned away, a thought struck Kate. 'Do you put the letters in the post box yourself, or on the hall table for Ida to take?'

Callum looked surprised. 'On the hall table.'

'Ah. Then why not try posting them yourself? Just in case.' They grinned at each other conspiratorially. 'You *are* getting better,' Callum laughed. 'That was really quite sharp. Have a grand weekend.'

'So I will, me lovely, so I will.' And she kissed him soundly, despite his protests.

# 25

'You didn't say that it was a castle.'

The size and setting of the place astonished Kate. Tucked against the side of a mountain, the ridge of which extended like a crooked finger, pointing westward and ending in granite crags that looked for all the world like knuckles on a giant hand. This was a place where eagles must surely fly. Below, was a drop of several hundred feet to a wooded valley. The mansion itself was crenellated with the statutory pele-tower, great hall and two wings forming three sides of a court-yard. It was into this that Lucy drove her motor.

'To be truthful, I didn't know what to expect. Goodness, I'm tired. We really ought to employ a chauffeur.'

Kate laughed. 'We can't afford one. Anyway, I thought you liked driving.'

They had driven up in Lucy's Austin 20 piled high with far more luggage than Kate would ever have dreamed necessary for one weekend, until Lucy had explained the need for changing four or five times a day.

'One comes down for breakfast in one outfit, then changes into shooting, walking or whatever gear is appropriate for the sport of the day. Riding clothes are essential, naturally, and one's tennis racquet, golf clubs and such. One never knows when one might get a game in. There are clothes for afternoon tea, and of course one changes for dinner, and then there are lounging about clothes and going to bed clothes.' Here she chuckled seductively. 'Those are vitally important if one wishes to encourage the right sort of attention, although hopefully won't be worn all night long, so they can be more decorative than comfortable.'

'One would hope they are at least warm, though, considering the Scottish climate,' Kate said with a touch of dry humour.

Lucy glanced sharply at her and frowned, as if this evidence of the old Kate were not only un-expected but unwelcome.

Fortunately, at this point a manservant appeared who instantly began to heft luggage out of the vehicle and carry it into the house. He did not invite them to follow him yet it seemed the right thing to do, Kate carrying a small piece of hand luggage, Lucy nothing at all.

'Shall I carry yours for you?' Kate offered.

'Don't fuss. Leave everything for the servants to deal with. That's what they're for. The staff will unpack everything too, press out the creases and tidy it all away. That sort of thing.'

Kate was mortified. 'Oh, I do hope they don't! My clothes are so shabby and old, and I'm not sure I've brought any of the right things. This is a far grander house than I'd expected, or am used to. If they knew I was really nothing more than an Irish nursemaid from Poor House Lane, sure and they'd never let me over the threshold.'

She giggled, suddenly finding the whole notion of her humble self walking into this grand Scottish castle in the middle of nowhere very funny indeed.

Lucy did not seem to share her amusement, and, as she ushered Kate through the front door, gave a somewhat testy reply. 'You'll have no problems whatsoever, so long as you do as you're told. Simply follow what everyone else does, and try to relax. Elvira who runs ... who owns this little pile will take good care of you. Now let's get inside. I'm desperate for a lovely hot bath and a long sleep.'

Kate did not see Lucy again for the remainder of the afternoon, and assumed she must be resting. She herself made up her mind to take a walk in the woods surrounding the house and explore.

First she was shown to her room which was

rather small, Kate thought, considering the size of the property. The polished oak floor boards creaked loudly whenever she stepped on them, while most of the limited space was taken up by a cavernous wardrobe and a bulky Empire bed which looked comfortable enough, even if the quilts and covers did seem rather ancient. These items were all the room contained, save for a chest of drawers and a small sink over which was set a mirror on the wall behind, far too high to be of any use, with a rush-bottomed chair nearby.

The walls were plain whitewashed, the paintings hung on them of dour highland cattle, and a window looked out over the courtyard – green brocade curtains not quite reaching its sill. But a pale winter sun was streaming in, the snow lying crisp on the mountain tops, and Kate felt perfectly content. Getting away from Tyson Lodge had made her feel much more relaxed already.

And even though she would obviously meet up with Lucy again, at dinner and so forth, there would also be new people to meet and to talk to. The pair of them didn't need to socialise too much, which was a blessing. Besides, Kate really should express her gratitude for being included in this trip. She rather thought she was going to enjoy herself.

She was intrigued by the fact that her room was situated high in the eaves on the second floor of the tower, reached by a winding spiral staircase. The maid who'd helped her to unpack explained that the tower's purpose had been to hold back the English.

'To be sure, I've been trying to do that all me

life,' chuckled Kate.

The maid didn't laugh at her joke, seeming to find her good humour puzzling.

'What's your name? You must call me Kate.'

'I'm not supposed to tell you.'

'Why ever not?'

'It's against the rules. Too familiar. I'm to call you Mrs Tyson the whole time.'

'I see. And what do I call you?'

'My name is Winnie,' the girl answered, in a voice scarcely above a whisper, glancing back over her shoulder in case she should be overheard. Then in a louder tone, she briskly continued, 'We don't fight the English now. That was back in the fifteenth and sixteenth centuries. Unsettled times they were, hereabouts.'

'I do beg your pardon. Of course, they must have been. I didn't mean to be flippant.'

Seeing how upset Kate looked, the little maid offered up a shy smile, again dropping her voice to a whisper. 'Don't ye fret, I dunna care much aboot history neither. You can see a picture of old Lord Glenmurray, whose place this was back then, in the Great Hall.'

'Oh, I'll make sure to take a peek when I go down to dinner.'

The maid gave her a sideways look but said nothing further, concentrating on folding towels, smoothing back the bedcover, plumping pillows. Kate went to help her.

'You don't have to do this.'

'I don't mind. I like to be busy, and these sheets are lovely. All embroidered and pure Irish linen.'

'Aren't ye the lucky one? Could just as easily

have been darned and scratchy.'

Kate didn't believe that for a minute.

'You're lucky to be put in this room, I'd say. That doesna always happen either.'

'I'm sure there are many finer ones in this grand castle, not that I'm decrying this one, you understand. It'll do me a treat. Besides, I was only a last-minute addition to the party.'

'You seem happy to be here, anyway,' Winnie commented, thumping a pillow and seemingly reluctant to leave Kate on her own. 'That's good.'

'And why wouldn't I be happy? 'Tisn't every week I get invited to stay in such a grand place. A fine Scottish castle, no less.'

'It's not always the case. Folk aren't always pleased to be here.'

Kate smiled understandingly. 'I expect the Scottish climate is a little severe for some of your guests.'

'You could say that. Some certainly do feel the cold. Speaking of which, there's a hot water bottle on the top shelf of the wardrobe, and an extra blanket. The chamber pot is under the bed.'

Kate giggled. 'Thank you, but I'd rather use the bathroom. Is it down the hall?'

The woman half turned away and didn't seem to hear Kate's question.

'How many rooms does the castle have? What I really mean is, how many guests will be here for the weekend?'

Winnie put the hot water bottle back on the shelf and smoothed a hand over a black velvet dress hanging in the wardrobe. 'My, you've brought some lovely clothes. I hope you get the chance to wear them.'

'I'm reliably informed that I will. 'Tis sorry I am you've had so many boxes to unpack. Me sister-in-law insisted I bring half of what I own with me. Most of it is ancient but I did buy one or two new items, for the evenings, you understand. I'm not normally the elegant type, more likely to put on the nearest thing to hand.'

'Oh, but ye look so smart. I love that tweed costume ye wearing. Real elegant.'

Kate chuckled. 'Probably because I've not been too well lately, so I've lost weight.'

'Och, aye, we're used to that here, for sure.'

'Are you? You surprise me. I'd've thought all this outdoor hunting, shooting and fishing would kindle a hearty appetite in a body, not to mention long rambles over the heather, which I most certainly mean to take.'

'Och, you are funny, ma'am. Oops, sorry, didn't mean to be rude.'

'You weren't, Winnie. Not at all. I dare say it's because I'm Irish. People not used to me think I talk too much. Kissed the Blarney stone. Aw, but this surely is the ideal spot for relaxing and unwinding.' Kate rushed back to the window to study the view, ''Tis lovely, so it is. I'm itching to climb that ridge and touch the snow, mebbe throw a few snowballs.'

The little maid gave a snort of disapproval. 'It's cold. You don't need to touch snow to know that. And you don't want to go getting yourself all cold and wet, on top of everything else you have to deal with.'

Kate turned to her with a smile. 'What do I

have to deal with?'

'You'll be wanting to step out of that lovely costume now, I'm thinking,' Winnie said, evading the question. 'Shall I hang up the skirt and jacket so it doesna get creased? There's a robe hanging behind the door, see. Then you can have a wee lie down.'

'Why would I want to lie down when there's all that wild, beautiful countryside out there? I've been cooped up in a motor all morning so I shall stride out over the moors and dales, the hills and glens, or whatever you call them here. Work up a healthy appetite for me dinner, after which I shall be more than ready to be waited on hand, foot and finger for three delicious days of sheer indulgence. I expect the other guests will be arriving shortly, will they not?'

Winnie offered up a weak smile and made a hasty exit.

'Aw, blast,' muttered Kate to herself the minute the girl had vanished out of the door. 'Didn't I forget to ask her what time dinner was? Well, if I don't see anyone else to ask, I suppose I'll just have to assume it's seven o'clock and mebbe go down around six-thirty, just to be on the safe side.'

Kate still hadn't seen Lucy by early-evening.

She'd spent the afternoon enjoying a delightful walk in the grounds, meandering along stony paths that wound between lush azaleas and rhododendron bushes. She'd tramped through heather, though not quite high enough to reach either the ridge or the snow line, thrusting her way through bracken and prickly undergrowth until she reached a wire fence bordering a pine forest. Kate would dearly have loved to slip through to explore but there were notices everywhere, forbidding her to do so.

Only once had she seen a small group of people come out of the castle, but she'd been too high up the path then to shout down to them and ask about dinner.

She'd found a small, stone summer house where she'd sat for quite a while, thinking. Inevitably it reminded her of their own little summer house, and she started remembering Eliot, thinking of Callum and what a fine son he'd made, and of Flora and how her little girl was so quickly growing into a woman. How she would enjoy watching her grow up!

Kate even let her thoughts slip further back, remembering her old friend Millie and her husband Clem, who'd lost an arm in an accident and had never worked again. He had turned to drink, which had killed him in the end. The last she'd heard of Millie was that she'd married again and moved to Manchester with whatever was left of her brood, perhaps hoping for better prospects with her new husband.

Kate thought she must make an effort to go and visit her. It would be good to see Millie again, and talk of old times.

Thinking of Millie was a natural progression from remembering Eliot. Kate recalled with a smile the day he'd ventured into Poor House Lane, begging her to come back to the Lodge after Callum's disappearance. She'd refused, of course, stubborn as ever, despite his courage in broaching those rat-infested quarters. He'd come again too when she'd been in labour with Flora. Forever thinking of her. Always putting her first, always so caring.

How very fortunate she'd been in having his love. How tragic that the war had damaged him, left him bitter and disorientated. Kate understood why, that he couldn't rid his mind of all that suffering. Well, now he was free of it. The trials and tribulations of life were over for him, but he would continue to live in her heart. He would forever be loved.

Kate's eyes filled with tears, which even after all these long months since Eliot was killed were never far away whenever she thought of him, but this time she brushed them impatiently away, determined to be more positive. She had to try to stop weeping, must make every effort to fight against the desire to indulge herself in mournful thoughts which could so easily turn into self-pity and depression. She had to fight that at all costs, or she'd be back in the black pit all over again. Besides, she was here to enjoy herself and relax, an essential part of the healing process.

She found herself smiling now, remembering that if it hadn't been for Millie nagging and shaming her into confessing how she really felt about him, how much she loved him, Kate might never have agreed to marry Eliot at all.

Oh, and wasn't she glad that she had? Even if their time together hadn't lasted as long as they'd both hoped, they'd been happy as larks. No one could take those precious memories away from her. They'd helped to make her what she was, and would enable her to go on, for Eliot's sake.

Tired from her walk, Kate fell onto her bed and slept for hours. She woke late, dying for a cuppa, having slept right through afternoon tea. Her tummy rumbled with hunger.

The light was almost gone and Kate hurried to change and get ready. There was no time now to hunt along strange corridors for bathrooms, that treat would have to wait till morning, so she scrubbed herself quickly down with cold water.

She was excited, foolishly so. It was so long since she'd had the opportunity to dress up and meet new people. How silly of her to oversleep.

''T'was all that fresh air and sunshine after me long journey. And I've worked up quite an appetite too,' she said to herself, giving a happy little chuckle.

She'd chosen an ankle-length gown for her first evening, in black of course but brightened by touches of purple silk at the neck, sleeves and hem of the organza over-dress. It was multi-layered and flowed quite beautifully, feeling soft and delicate against her legs.

Kate could see nothing of herself in the small mirror high up on the wall without first climbing on to the rush-bottomed chair, which she now did. It offered her a glimpse of her middle part, around the waist, but little more, so she had no real idea of how she looked. Nevertheless, Kate felt perfectly elegant in her new gown. Her shoes were of her own design with a pointed toe, a bow trim and a beautifully shaped Louis heel. Perhaps she would be able to find the opportunity to point them out to the other guests and talk about her new line of elegant footwear.

Kate looked at her watch again. Twenty minutes to seven. She got up and wandered about the small room, wondering what time it would be polite to go down. Too soon and she'd be kicking her heels in the Great Hall, too late and she'd be embarrassed.

She fussed with the hem of her dress, hung a row of jet beads about her neck, put a dab of powder on her nose, a daring touch of rouge to her lips, adjusted the jewelled clip that pinned up her wild red hair. Then she drew in a deep breath for courage, picked up her bag and evening gloves, and was ready to venture forth.

Except that something was wrong. For the life of her she couldn't seem to open the door. It was locked fast.

# 26

Over the following weeks, Lucy didn't give Kate another thought. She'd returned from the weekend in Scotland, giving a harrowing explanation of how poor dear Kate had tried to harm herself and that it had been decided she should stay on for a while, till she was more herself. There were questions of course, much agonising and concern, tears from Flora and anger from Callum.

As the cold of winter began to bite, snow clung

to the Lakeland hills and ice formed on the River Kent. The entire household appeared to have sunk once more into gloomy mourning. Mrs Petty would frequently forget even to draw the curtains in the morning and Lucy would have to remonstrate with the stupid woman.

'Can I send Mammy a get well card?' Flora asked.

'Very well. Leave it on the hall table and I'll see that it is posted.'

Callum said, 'Let us have the address and we can post it ourselves. We aren't helpless.'

'Your mother is safely settled in a nursing home and not to be disturbed,' Lucy tartly informed him. 'Peace and seclusion are what she needs right now, not moans and groans from her children. You surely don't want her harming herself again, more effectively next time? It was a miracle she was found in time and that there was a doctor present.'

When Flora had gone off to bed to write her card, Callum asked, 'How did she harm herself?'

'I really don't think you want to know.'

'Yes, I do.'

'She slashed her wrists. There, do you feel any better for knowing that?'

Lucy cast him a challenging glare and Callum glared right back. After a long moment, it was Lucy who broke away. He really was a most difficult boy. Having settled the matter of Kate, to her own satisfaction at least, Lucy refused to answer any further questions and got on with enjoying her new freedom. She'd achieved her goal. She was now entirely in control, free to put

263

the next part of her plan into action.

With Kate gone, she could award herself the status and rewards in life that she richly deserved, and override Toby's obstructive attitude towards darling Jack.

True, there were still a few problems requiring her attention. Ned Swainson, for one. He seemed to see himself as a permanent fixture in her life. Not so, she told him.

'Our relationship is over. You've done what I asked, now you can safely leave the rest to me.'

'But you'd still like me to keep me mouth shut, I dare say,' he calmly reminded her, smoothing one hand along her thigh as they sat in her new motor. She'd got rid of the Austin 20, in case the police came prowling round again, and replaced it with a Daimler. A much classier car, and far more appropriate for her new status in the town as a local employer.

Lucy slapped the hand away. 'What good would it do you? No one would ever take your word against mine. They'd say you were simply being vindictive because you'd once been sacked by Tysons and never reinstated.'

'I could tell them different, say how you deliberately ran down your own brother-in-law with yer fancy motor car, say what you and I have got up to since. How would that look plastered all over the pages of the *Westmorland Gazette?*'

Lucy let out a trill of amused laughter. 'You could say nothing that anyone would believe. I'm a person of note in this town, I'll have you know. You are a nobody.'

Ned Swainson's face darkened, his mouth

twisting, mean little eyes flickering this way and that as his rapid thought processes sought a way to beat her at her own game. 'Then mebbe I should just go to the police. They'd listen. Oh, aye, the police would listen to me all right. They'd know the risk I took by talking to 'em, so they'd be bound to take note.'

'Don't be ridiculous! You wouldn't dare. You could end up behind bars yourself.'

'It might be worth the risk, if you were there alongside me. Anyroad, what've I done? Nowt by comparison. Mended yer car, left a rat or two lying about the place. You're the one with blood on yer hands, and they'd almost certainly start asking some awkward questions about that accident, and about where Kate Tyson is now. Why she's incarcerated in that Scottish castle or wherever you've locked her up, when there's not a damned thing wrong with her. They might well see how that will further your own greedy ambitions.'

Lucy ground her teeth in frustrated rage. 'And the price of your silence would be?'

He chuckled, low and maliciously. 'You know that as well as I do. Cash would be preferable, and plenty of it, but in the meantime I'll make do with payment in kind.'

Yet again Lucy felt compelled to comply with his demands, resignedly lifting her skirt, turning her face away with a grimace as he grunted and heaved against her. Yet she found herself responding to his demands, her excitement mounting along with his, gasping at the final thrust. Unsavoury he may be, but he rarely disappointed.

Later, washing the smell of him from her body

in her lovely new bathroom, she resolved to find a different solution. Ridding herself of Swainson and his greedy, mucky little paws, was turning into a priority. But how much would it take to keep him away permanently? And how to be sure he wouldn't come back, asking for more? The last thing Lucy had expected was to be caught in a web of blackmail.

Perhaps the answer was that if she couldn't afford to buy him off, then she must implicate him more fully in her scheme. His hands needed to be as bloody as her own.

Once more Lucy arranged to see him, and after handing over a fistful of notes, said, 'See to Callum for me. Teach him a lesson for interfering in what doesn't concern him.'

Swainson counted the money and pulled a face. 'This is but the first installment, I assume?'

'Rid me of that boy and you can have whatever your heart desires. He's no fighter. My own son trounced him so he won't put up much of a fight. Do with him as you will. He's all yours.'

Not a day went by when Kate didn't regret putting her trust in Lucy. Whatever had possessed her to imagine that her sister-in-law had invited her along for a weekend because she craved Kate's company, or cared a jot about the state of her health? What utter nonsense! She'd had quite a different purpose in mind altogether.

The shock of realising where she'd really been taken still overwhelmed Kate at times as if a mist had cleared and she'd suddenly caught a glimpse of a nightmare reality. Then, realising the awfulness of her plight, she'd start to shake with fear all over again.

Fortunately or unfortunately, depending on how she was feeling on any particular day, she was often quite incapable of too much thinking or contemplation of her lot, being too befuddled by the pills they gave her.

Sometimes, if she was clever, Kate managed to avoid taking these by holding them under her tongue or secreting them in the palm of her hand till she could dispose of them safely. But that only worked with the careless nurses, the ones who didn't ensure that she'd swallowed them by checking her mouth afterwards.

At least they made her sleep. Deep sleep, the patients were frequently and constantly informed, was the answer to all their problems. It was somehow supposed to allow the mind time to recover.

Patients in the castle were given morphine, bromide or laudanum, sometimes as much as twenty drops. Despite her efforts to stay alert, the longing for sleep became seductive. To Kate, as with many of the others, it represented a welcome escape from the fear and monotony of the days. It seemed best not to think too deeply about where you were, or why you were here. Or, worse, when or *if* you would ever get out.

There was little hope of escape. Some tried, but they didn't get very far. The nurses, or warders, whatever they were, were vigilant in keeping the patients secure.

Even on the days when Kate was still capable of rational thought, of viewing her life with some sort of cool detachment, where was the point?

She was trapped as securely behind locked doors as she had been on that very first night.

How naïve she'd been, how foolishly trusting. All dressed up and ready to attend a lovely dinner party yet unable to get out of her room. She'd hammered on that locked door until her knuckles were blood raw, and still no one had come.

She'd no recollection of getting a wink of sleep that night. It had all been so unbelievably awful that Kate hadn't properly been able to take it in, quite certain there'd simply been a mistake, that the door had become jammed or locked by accident.

Not until morning, when breakfast arrived in the form of a dish of porridge and a mug of weak tea, did she learn the terrible truth. It was brought not by Winnie, the talkative little maid, but a grim-faced woman with whiskers on her chin and her mouth set in a thin, tight line.

Kate had challenged her at once. 'Why have I been left all alone here, locked in this room and ignored all night? This is no way to treat your guests.'

'A guest, is that what you are? Well, that's one way of looking at it, I suppose.' The woman had thought this so amusing that she'd laughed uproariously as she'd plonked down the tray, and then taken great pleasure in telling Kate the unvarnished truth.

She was not here for a pleasant weekend party at all. This was a private asylum run by the formidable Miss Elvira Crombie.

'You're here because the magistrates, or mebbe your own kith and kin, consider it necessary for your own safety, and theirs too probably. Violent, are you? Many of our inmates are.'

'No, of course I'm not violent. Why do you call your guests inmates? What are you talking about?'

And so it had been explained to her, most carefully, how Lucy had made the arrangements, booking her in for as long as it might take to make her well again. And no matter how many times over the following weeks Kate might protest she was perfectly well, that there was really nothing at all wrong with her, nobody took a blind bit of notice.

There were many at the castle who were indeed mentally ill and in need of special care, though whether this was the right place for them to receive it, Kate couldn't say. She often heard shouts and blood-curdling screams, particularly at night. And obsessive banging as if someone were beating their head against a wall, or the endless rattling of a door as if some poor soul were attempting to escape. The noise that emanated from some of the closed doors was chilling, and there was a stink about the place: of urine, stale sweat and human excrement. Her new friend Peggy told her that many patients were left untended for hours on end and couldn't hold on so they'd do it in any old corner of their cell, then paint the walls with the stuff in their frustration. It made Kate shudder to imagine their suffering.

But she soon discovered that many of her fellow 'patients' were no more mad than she was. Rather they'd endured misfortune or tragedy in their lives, such as Peggy whose babies had died and she'd been blamed, or men like Arthur in the men's dormitory whose entire family had been wiped out in a fire, leaving him suffering from severe depression as a result.

On that first morning, the grim faced woman added one final warning. 'You've had it easy thus far, but think on, breakfast in bed won't happen every morning, so make the best of it. Soon the routine starts proper. Right from morning baths to evening prayers, you'll have to jump to it and do as you're told along with everyone else. You can look forward to joining the others in the dining room for your meals. Now that truly *is* Bedlam, in there. What a treat you have in store.'

The sarcasm in her tone made Kate shiver with foreboding. But before she could ask any more questions, the woman handed her a couple of pills and a glass of water. 'Take these. Sleep is the best way to restore equilibrium to the brain and resolve your mood disorders.'

'I don't have any mood disorders. What is it you're trying to give me? I won't take it.'

But she had taken it, there'd been no other choice. The medication had been forced down her throat, a second nurse being called to hold her down while the job was done. Then they'd both departed, still laughing, as if it were all a huge joke. The key had turned in the lock with a hollow click, a sound that made her sick to her stomach on that day and every day since.

Kate had no recollection of how long she'd slept in that first week, but when she'd finally woken she was no longer in the tiny room up in the eaves of the castle but a long bleak dormitory with only a locker to call her own. All her personal clothes and belongings had been taken away from her, and she'd not even a curtain for privacy.

That was when she'd met Peggy, sitting on the next bed, her round, sympathetic face and mothering ways a blessed relief after being starved of both company and food for so long.

'Eeh, at last, they've let you come round,' were her first words. 'I'm that glad to see you open yer eyes, chuck. Can you manage to sit up and tek a sip of this water? I'll help, come on, try.'

'Where am I? I think I've wet the bed. I stink.'

'Don't you fret about that. They're supposed to come and put you on the chamber pot every few hours, even when you're asleep, but they generally forget. Anyroad, it's nearly dawn. We'll be having our baths soon.'

'Oh, bliss!'

Kate longed to soak herself clean in lovely hot water, and wash her tangled hair. But then that was before she'd encountered the dreaded Elvira in person, or experienced the bathroom routine.

# 27

Swainson had a plan which he set about with gusto. Kate Tyson's lad was a regular at the Rifle Man's so it was no problem at all to call in there one evening and challenge him to a game of skittles. Swainson let him win, several games in fact, saw how the lad started to swagger and look pleased with himself after a pint or two. Swainson, however, kept his own consumption of alcohol to a minimum.

He casually suggested that the game might gain a little more edge to it if they had a small wager. Callum eagerly agreed. Hadn't this newcomer already proved how hopeless he was at the game? With youthful over-confidence, he believed his money to be perfectly safe.

Besides, he was desperately saving up. He still hadn't heard from Bunty and it was driving him mad with worry. Not for a moment did Callum believe she no longer loved him. He was convinced that her mother was in some way responsible for keeping them apart, and the only way round it was for him to go to Switzerland to see Bunty. Callum was desperately trying to raise sufficient money to buy himself a train ticket.

Again Swainson allowed him to win the next couple of matches, and each time as Callum won and Swainson lost, the wager went up. And then, as if by chance, Swainson won a game.

'Well, would you believe it? Mebbe I'm learning, or else it was beginner's luck.' He pocketed the five shillings, a fair sum, which had collected up with double or quits in wager after wager. 'Don't look so doleful, lad. I'm sure you can win it back. Let me get in another round. Cheer you up.'

Callum was in dire need of some cheering up. There seemed to be nothing but worries in his life right now, what with his mam and Bunty both in difficulties.

'You do want a chance to win it back?'

Callum did. His eyes were bleary, his gait unsteady, but he hated to lose.

Swainson won again. He won the next game, and the one after that. The more he won, the more desperate the lad became, obviously annoyed by his own failure. It really was quite amusing. Little by little Swainson took all his wages off him, and then, refusing an IOU, walked away.

Since he'd no money left to drink with, it wasn't long before Callum left the pub. All Swainson had to do was wait for him up one of the dark yards nearby. The poor sod never knew what hit him, and the lad put up a feeble defence. Swainson grabbed hold of him by the hair and shouted into his stupid face.

'Lay off asking questions about the accident. Understood? Got it? I hear yer bloody mother's gone mad as a bleedin' hatter and they've locked her up in a Scottish castle. Lay off, or happen you'll be joining her there.'

He punched Callum a few more times to make his point more forcibly, then left him sprawled in the muck, spewing the contents of his belly into the gutter.

Ned Swainson swaggered off well content, if aware that he hadn't exactly done as he'd been in-structed, that the lad would easily recover, poorer and wiser but still alive. But then Swainson had no intention of getting blood on his own hands. He wasn't daft. He would leave that dubious pleasure to Lucy.

He'd done enough to keep her dangling, which was really all that mattered so far as he was concerned. And she'd find it very difficult to shake him off because he meant to stick to her like glue, doing just enough to keep tabs on her, but not enough to incriminate himself too deeply. She might be glad of that, one day. Or she might be sorry she'd ever got him involved in the first place. Only time would tell.

Jack drew his mother's attention to Callum's injuries, making it clear that he was not responsible.

'It must be that low crowd he's got himself involved with down at the Rifle Man's. Showing his lack of breeding.'

Lucy said nothing but was thoughtful. So Swainson had carried out her orders, but only to the bare minimum. He'd let the lad live to fight another day, not even frightened him enough to make him run. The man was cleverer than she'd given him credit for, obviously taking great care not to implicate himself in anything too serious.

Would she ever be rid of Swainson, parasite that he undoubtedly was, or Kate's brat for that matter? The boy remained a thorn in Lucy's side, as he had been all his life. A solution must be found. But she must also ensure that it was one which did not throw suspicion upon herself.

For the moment Lucy was forced to put the matter out of her mind as other, far more pressing issues, claimed her attention. Not least the fact that she was growing seriously short of funds.

Money did have a habit of slipping through her fingers like water, as darling Charles used to say. But then it hadn't been her fault that his dratted family had kept them so short of funds, insisting they live almost in penury with only a handful of servants. And then poor Charles had died, robbing her even of that much dignity, all because Eliot absolutely refused to be responsible for his brother's debts.

It gave her enormous satisfaction now to be sitting in the sumptuous elegance of Eliot's study, enjoying the fruits of her brother-in-law's labours, sipping Eliot's Madeira wine, savouring a few chocolates bought with Eliot's money. Although it had not proved to be exactly a pleasant morning, spent poring over the household accounts which did not make easy reading. Lucy was not good at accounts, and making figures balance was quite beyond her. Vera could have done the job for her, or Toby perhaps, but that would have meant allowing them to pry into matters which didn't concern them.

She refilled her glass, to help her think.

The Americans might well be stuck with Prohibition but Lucy's wine cellar was stuffed to bursting. She thought of it as hers now, in view of the way things were. Eliot had always kept a good cellar but Lucy had replenished it, stocking up on gin and vermouth, Cointreau, sherry and rum. Teddy adored his whisky and cocktails were *de rigeur*.

Anyone who was anyone felt obliged to offer drinks before a dinner party these days, and all night long if the guests required it, so naturally it was essential to keep a good stock in the house. Lucy rather thought she might buy a cocktail cabinet from which to serve them, although what she really needed, of course, was a butler.

Fortunately the Bennet boys were always ready and willing to act as barmen for her. They'd once tried to instruct her in how to make a Manhattan – two-thirds rye whiskey, one third Italian vermouth with a dash of bitters. Then it had to be stirred and served with crushed ice, apparently. But that was only one drink, there were a dozen more to master.

'Darlings, too, too complicated! I'll leave it to you boys.'

'Don't fret, old fruit,' they told her, making Lucy wince at their choice of appellation. 'We'll see your guests want for nothing.'

She was quite certain their eagerness to help was due to their own fondness for the bottle. By morning she would generally find them both dead drunk under a table somewhere. They'd been like that ever since they'd miraculously survived the Somme together while losing most of their pals. All perfectly understandable, and great fun, but not quite the image she was trying to create.

Being at the cusp of fashion was all very well but her personal allowance didn't cover anything like the costs involved. Even the household budget didn't run to hiring butlers, bar attendants or outside caterers, and now with having to pay for Kate's care as well, ready money was growing ever harder to find. The sooner she rid herself of the encumbrance of her sister-in-law, the better.

Eventually, Lucy intended quietly to remove her from the private home and put her into Lancaster Moor or Prestwich, which would cost nothing at all, with the added advantage that, once incarcerated, her blessed sister-in-law would forever be lost in the system.

If Kate hadn't been queer in the head before she went into the castle, she surely must be by now. Elvira had practically guaranteed it.

Elvira Crombie turned out to be a dragon of the first water. A large woman with a voice that could stop a nurse in her tracks at fifty paces, she eschewed the overalls worn by her staff and dressed in garishly coloured, flowing gowns, arms and neck jangling with cheap jewellery, her grey-streaked black hair coiled in a thick plait around her head. Patients could hear her coming from miles away; the clinking and jingling of her beads, the heavy tread of her flat feet, bringing a ripple of fear as each wondered if they were to be her next victim.

She spent much of her time in her tiny parlour drinking gin, her temper depending on whether she had recently imbibed or was suffering the results of a hangover. Her nasty dark eyes with their blurred, slightly unfocused gaze would home in upon a patient and if she didn't care for what they were doing, or even how they looked, she would pounce with her malicious claws out and torment them to the point of tears.

On the morning Kate had finally been allowed into the bathroom following her long, induced sleep, her wild mass of red hair, admittedly not looking its best after several days of neglect, instantly became the focus of Elvira's attention.

'That'll have to go. We canna risk any vermin here.'

Kate was appalled. 'My hair is not verminous! I wash it three times a week.'

A snort of laughter. 'Nor can we afford the hot water for such vanity. Before you climb into that bath, we need to be rid of this mess.' Whereupon, she pulled a large pair of scissors from the pocket of her gown and ordered Kate to sit.

'I will not! Sure and you'll have to tie me down first.'

And that's what they did. Elvira called a nurse to assist her and the pair of them tied Kate to a chair with two leather straps and then she was shorn of her luxuriant mass of curls. When it was done she was ordered to strip off, then frog-marched to the bathroom. She was too shocked even to cry.

The bathroom was a cavernous place in which stood two rows of huge, claw-footed Victorian baths, a row of patients queuing, half-naked, awaiting their turn in them. When Kate took her place in the queue all the baths were already occupied, some by whimpering females, others grimly silent, some even still strapped in their strait-jackets.

Kate stood there in her thin nightgown and shuddered with cold and fear. Never in her life had she felt more deeply afraid. With the loss of her hair she felt she had lost a part of herself, her personality, her dignity, and was finally beginning to understand the true depth of her predicament.

She'd longed for a bath, had dreamed of this moment. But why was no steam rising from any of them, and why did the bathroom feel as cold as a butcher's shop?

She was soon to discover for herself. 'Holy mauther! 'Tis freezing cold,' she cried as they man-handled her into one, its water recently vacated by the previous occupant.

'Excellent for the circulation of blood to the brain,' Elvira informed her, eyes twinkling maliciously.

Kate instantly tried to climb out again but Elvira instructed a nurse to restrain her and Kate promptly found herself encased in a strait-jacket, her arms strapped tight across her chest, pressing painfully against her breasts, the strings tied to iron hooks on the wall behind.

And as if that wasn't bad enough, ice was then tipped into the water making her squeal in agony. 'That'll teach you to complain. Never know when you're well off, that's your trouble.'

Kate couldn't remember enduring anything so terrible in all her life. Even in Poor House Lane they'd managed to warm the bucket of water they drew from the well for their ablutions. And all around her, echoing eerily in the huge room, came the pitiful cries and screams of her fellow patients. Those who created the most fuss, or became demented with hysterics, were struck about the head with a wet towel and then marched off, dripping wet. Kate didn't care to think what fate awaited them.

She spotted Peggy nearby, and watched in silent horror as she was held underwater for what seemed like an eternity, relieved to see her come up spluttering. Moments later, as her friend passed by, wrapped in a thin towel, Peggy's one thought was for Kate. 'Don't make a sound. Say nowt. Grin and bear it, otherwise it'll get worse.'

'How can it get any worse than this?'

'There's a bath outside, in t'yard, and if you think it's bloody freezing in here, you want to try *that*.'

Kate bit down on her lip and gave barely a whimper when a second block of ice was dropped on her feet. Later, when she'd been released and taken back to the dormitory she was to share with the rest of the women patients, she rubbed herself dry as best she could, dressed in the thin grey gown provided, and then collapsed in tears on the bed.

Later, Kate learned that although Elvira seemed to have marked her out for particular attention, she largely allowed her nurses to do as they pleased with the patients, which was the reason for the abusive treatment they suffered. The staff were no doubt badly paid, worked long, tiring hours in difficult circumstances, and were not encouraged to treat the patients with any kindness or consideration.

There were one or two who did try to show a degree of humanity. One in particular, a small Irish nurse called Megan, took pity on Kate, perhaps since they shared a homeland, and would shorten the agony of the freezing cold baths to the minimum, and defend her if she noticed her being picked out for extra bullying.

When one of the other patients once flew at her, clawing and scratching at her face in a fever of dementia, it was Megan who saved her, managing to pull the crazy woman off before she quite gouged Kate's eyes out.

In general, though, Kate knew she was on her own, would survive this ordeal by her own will-power and strength, or not at all. Neither the other nurses, nor Elvira herself, would lift a finger to help. If some patients raved or became demented, little or no attempt was made to calm them. If they got entirely out of hand, nurses were free to inflict whatever punishment they considered necessary.

But then many of the methods of treatment felt like punishment. Emetics were popular, inducing vomiting and diarrhoea, and considered to be one of the major 'cures'. Apparently they were meant to draw poison from the blood and drain water from the brain. A clean bowel, they said, was imperative for sound mental health.

Kate couldn't see how it could possibly help, for all she admitted she had no knowledge of medical matters. What it really succeeded in doing was keeping them closely confined to quarters. Nobody wandered far if they thought they might be desperate to visit the lavatory every five minutes.

When Kate once complained of being thirsty and asked for a drink, they brought her vinegar and lemon, which gave her the runs for days.

She learned, one way or another, to keep her wits about her, to avoid taking the pills, to do as she was told and to keep her head down, aware that Elvira seemed to take a special interest in her; her beady black eyes constantly watching and observing. And if she stepped out of line by just the slightest degree, Elvira would take over from the nurses, as she had done in the bathroom.

Kate assumed this extra attention had something to do with the amount of money Lucy must be paying to keep her here. Had she paid above the odds to have Kate guarded more carefully?

As spring approached and the winter snows melted, there were moments, perhaps when a door was opened or they were allowed a precious half-hour out in the garden, when Kate would catch the sweet scent of heather that clothed the infinite vastness of the moors beyond, the sharp tang of the seemingly endless pine forest that surrounded the castle, and the freshness of a morning breeze. Her heart would ache then with the longing to be free, so badly that it physically hurt, making her feel sick with fear that she might never escape this dreadful place.

It made her all the more determined somehow to get word to Callum, tell him exactly where she was. The thought of spending years in this place, as Peggy had, didn't bear thinking about.

# 28

Lucy had reached the decision that her worsening financial state was all the fault of the company. Therefore, the company must rectify the problem. She called in to see Toby one morning, sweeping into his office unannounced to inform him that her allowance needed increasing, as did the household budget.

'Pray see to it at once.'

He rose from his chair, as manners decreed, but only to regard her with inscrutable calm, not even raising his eyebrows, quite unmoved by her temerity. 'I'm afraid that is not possible.'

'I beg your pardon! Are you questioning my authority?'

'Certainly not, but what you ask simply cannot be done, not without Kate's permission for one thing.'

Lucy's face began slowly to turn crimson with rage and her lip curled upward unpleasantly. 'Kate is scarcely in a position to give her permission for anything. She can barely remember her own name.'

'I'm sure she will recover soon and be back with us, quite her old self again. I intend everything to be in good order when she does return.'

'You have no say over what happens in this business! None at all. I've been granted a pittance to live on which, considering I own half of this company, is monstrous. I need twice as much again at least. Standards must be maintained and I really do not think that...'

'You don't quite own half, and it is hardly a pittance,' Toby gently pointed out.

'*Do not interrupt me when I am speaking!* How dare you? You will double my allowance at once.'

'Would you care to be seated so that we can discuss the matter further?'

'No, I would not!'

'Very well, as you wish.' Toby picked up the pen he'd set down when she burst in, and calmly returned to his desk to continue with his work.

'As I say, I'm afraid I cannot do as you ask.'

'Oh, yes, you can, and will. There is nothing to discuss. Just do it. At once.' Lucy whirled about and, clearly satisfied that she'd made her point, stuck her nose in the air and prepared to sail out of the door. She was stopped in her tracks by his next words.

'No, I'm sorry.'

'*What?*' Her scream of outrage was so loud Toby was quite sure that half the factory must have heard it. He took a deep breath and ploughed on. 'We need every penny we possess to develop the new line, buy in materials, maintain equipment and pay wages. The boom is over, trade is slack and recovery will not be swift. Even Kate is not taking any money out of the business at present.'

'Kate has no need of any since she's off her head, quite run mad. Nor will she ever need it again, the way she's going.'

Toby ground his teeth together, striving to hold on to his patience and to damp down his worries over Kate so that he could concentrate and prevent Lucy from damaging the business. 'That has yet to be determined. I'm sorry, but there's nothing I can do.'

'There is something *I* can do.' Lucy stepped forward and ripped the sheet of paper from his hand. 'What is it that so absorbs you? Figures ... balance sheets ... fairy tales? No doubt you are busily feathering your own nest while Kate is away.'

Toby's first instinct was to leap to his own defence, but he knew that would only be a

284

mistake. He wanted to ask if Lucy understood balance sheets, but where was the point? They both knew she hadn't the first idea what she was reading. Nevertheless, her gaze scanned the list of items, clearly seeking to find fault.

And then her eyes lit up. 'Look at the amount we spend on wages. Good gracious, a mammoth sum. This must be reduced at once.' Stabbing her finger against the offending item.

'Don't be ridiculous.'

'Excuse me?'

Realising he'd broached upon rudeness and was only an employee after all, Toby hastily apologised. 'I beg your pardon, Mrs Lucy. What I meant to say was, it is indeed a large sum but it's quite impossible to reduce wages any further. We need all our operatives. Besides, they're good workers and depend upon Tysons for their living. There are few other alternatives in town.'

Her expression was cold as flint, and just as hard. 'That is no concern of ours.' She slammed the accounts back on the desk. 'Choose the youngest and strongest. Keep the best, but the absolute minimum, mind, and make them work harder. Sack anyone who is old, slow, been off sick too much, or not pulling their weight as they should. And do it today, or I'll do it for you. And once you have cleared this place of parasites, the company can easily afford to increase my allowance.'

Despair cut deep into Kate's soul. If she hadn't been mad when she'd arrived in this God-for-saken hole, she certainly would be if she stayed in it much longer. Holding on to her sanity was her single, over-riding concern.

Keeping track of time was difficult enough, the endless days all running into each other, every day exactly the same as the one before. The cold baths every morning, the awful food, the hours of staring into space with nothing to occupy her, the restrictions and punishments, the bleakness of her surroundings, the pills that dulled her senses, all played their part in making her life a living hell.

But being deprived of visitors, of not ever being allowed to see her children, was the most mind-numbing torment of all. The pain of living without Callum and Flora tore her in half, and would surely destroy her in the end, if nothing else did.

Sometimes they would be allowed pencil and paper to write a letter home. Many of the patients had forgotten how to write, if they ever knew, but Kate would snatch the opportunity with gratitude and eagerness.

But then she'd be at a loss as to what to say. Anxious not to disturb Flora and yet keen to alert Callum to her predicament, she would chew on her pencil and dither, aware that the half-hour allotted for the task was rapidly ticking away.

Whether the letter ever reached a post box, let alone her children, Kate was doubtful. Once in those first few weeks following her arrival she'd been given a letter which they'd obviously written together, carefully choosing words meant to cheer her. It was falsely bright and optimistic, striving to reassure her that they were thinking of her each and every day. Flora said how much she loved her and was trying to be patient, longing to visit her mammy but willing to wait until she was feeling better. Callum's one concern, he said, was for her mental health.

Much of it made no sense to Kate, and bore little relation to the many letters she had sent them, as if they really had no idea what she was going through, or even where she was. There'd been nothing since. Though that didn't prove they weren't trying to write to her, and she certainly believed they were indeed thinking of her.

Kate was perfectly certain that her lovely children were doing their best and that someone, the dreaded Elvira perhaps, or Lucy herself, was blocking contact between them. Despite the bitter disappointment she felt, the ache of loneliness in her breast, Kate convinced herself that now Lucy was rid of her, there was little more hurt she could inflict. What more could she do? Callum would guard Flora, and Toby was minding the company.

Kate's one consolation was that whatever pain Lucy might inflict upon her, she couldn't steal from her the love of her children.

Toby did not do as Lucy had commanded. He did not order an increase in her allowance, and he did nothing about sacking any of the workers. The moment Lucy discovered this she again marched into the factory, demanded a full list of employees and struck off a dozen or so names with no thought or consideration whatsoever for their circumstances, or even if they were good workers.

Toby glanced at the list in horror. 'I've already told you, this can't be done. We need every man and woman on the pay roll. These are good people and once the orders start flowing in, they'll be needed, every one of them. We hope to be rushed off our feet soon.'

'But they are not rushed off their feet at present?'

'Not yet, but...'

'Then we can dispose of them. If and when we do need them, when we have these orders you keep promising me, we can take them on again.'

'But that might be too late. They may have moved on to another town and then we will have lost their skills forever. In any case, we owe a duty to the community to keep workers on when there is the hope of better times ahead.'

But Lucy was unrelenting. 'The community is of no concern to me. We have to see to our own livelihoods first, not theirs.'

'But that is exactly my point. The workers are the ones who provide us with...'

'Enough! If you do not do as I say, Mr Lynch, then your own services will no longer be required.'

Toby tried once more to protest, his voice growing heated, on the verge of forgetting quite who he was addressing. 'I don't care about myself, it is simply wrong to sack these men. You can't do it. You can't sack Jed Marshall, he's one of our best shoemakers.'

Lucy set down her pen with a sweet smile. 'Twenty men given their marching orders by five o'clock or I will put my own list into effect, and personally see that they are escorted off the premises. The choice is yours.'

At the door she paused, turning her elegantly coiffed head for one last parting shot. 'Oh, and don't worry about my allowance. I have already spoken to our accountant and put that into effect.'

'Then God help us all,' Toby murmured to himself, as she strode away.

He agonised over the list all afternoon, ticking a name here with his pencil, then rubbing it out again and ticking another. Eventually he had his twenty names. Some were almost ready for retirement anyway, though how they would manage without a regular wage coming in, he'd no idea. A couple of men had war pensions, albeit small ones, the rest were women who he hoped would at least have a husband to care for them. Trouble was, with so many men lost in the war, he couldn't even be sure of that.

It seemed bitterly cruel, and he hated himself as he handed out the letters.

'What's this, lad? A Christmas card come early?' they joked.

Toby shook his head. 'It's not my idea. It's Mrs Lucy's orders, not mine. I want you all to know that.'

There were expressions of shock, outrage, bitter complaint, of course there were, but he made it clear that he could do nothing. It was out of his hands.

He sincerely hoped this would be the end of it. If not, then he would be next, and who would Kate have on her side then, when she finally returned home from wherever Lucy had put her? He'd give his right arm to know exactly where that was.

By the end of March Toby was complaining to Lucy that there were insufficient funds in the company's business account to finance their outgoings. 'We seem to be spending far more than our income can justify.'

'Bad management,' Lucy replied, implying that the fault was entirely his. 'Who is responsible for winning orders?'

Reluctantly, Toby named the marketing manager and her response was predictable.

'Sack him.'

'But it isn't his fault. He is bringing in good orders now, I do assure you, and has made some excellent contacts. The problem lies elsewhere. Money is simply bleeding out of the account and...'

But Lucy wasn't listening. 'What we need is someone new and go-ahead in charge of sales. This idiot is clearly useless. I shall put Jack in charge.'

'But he has no experience of marketing.'

Lucy smiled. 'He has charm and charisma, which is far more important. Experience will soon follow. He'll have the lady shop assistants eating out of his hand in no time. You'll see.'

'But it's the shop managers and proprietors who give the orders, not the shop assistants,' Toby objected, desperate over losing yet another excellent employee. 'And the operatives will go on strike if we keep turning people off like this.'

'Don't be ridiculous. The operatives will do as they're told and be thankful it isn't them. I'm perfectly certain Jack will come back with a flood of orders within weeks. In the meantime, I'll speak to the bank manager. Our credit is good.'

Any further protests by Toby were ignored, nor was Lucy prepared either to look at the balance sheet or have it explained to her. The matter, so far as Lucy was concerned, was settled.

Her visit to the bank manager later that day went entirely according to plan. But then she'd known that it would. The man was a family friend, had been for years, and was more than ready to lend Tysons a substantial sum against the property they owned.

Lucy really didn't know why her sister-in-law was so against borrowing money, probably nervous of asking because she did not possess friends of this man's calibre. It took a woman with *savoir-faire* to run a business, not a little guttersnipe like Kate.

Before the month was out Lucy called an Extra-ordinary General Meeting and put Jack's name forward as a director. 'He has done well in sales and marketing so has earned his reward, don't you think?'

Unsurprisingly Toby resisted the motion, pointing out that decisions of this nature shouldn't be taken without all the company directors being present, meaning Kate; that a directorship was not normally handed out so easily, and the quantity of orders still fell far short of expectations. He fought hard, insisting Jack was too young, too inexperienced, had too much to learn.

'I've been left in charge of this factory, to watch over Kate's interest. I cannot sanction this move.'

Lucy scornfully reminded him that all the directors who were fit to vote were present and that he was only the manager, so had very little say at all.

The aunts concurred, the vote was taken and the motion carried with only Toby opposing it. Jack had been voted on to the board as a director, at last.

## AUTUMN 1920

# 29

House parties, in Mrs Petty's opinion, were a nightmare, probably because Madam Lucy never seemed to be satisfied. She would complain bitterly about the lack of a country house in which to hold them, and the consequent difficulties of finding 'a good shoot', or of not having access to the lake for sailing and fishing, or even a tennis court, all of which she'd apparently enjoyed at her old house in Windermere.

She'd even complained of the shallowness of the river, comparing it with the Avon, the Thames, and other grander rivers down south where a boat could apparently sail freely without holing itself on rocks.

It would come as no surprise to Mrs Petty if

Madam Lucy didn't order a lake to be dug, though happen that were a bit beyond even her skills, in the middle of Kendal. She'd already made a start on installing a tennis court, though what Mrs Tyson would say when she discovered that all those lovely new trees her husband so lovingly planted had been toppled, Mrs Petty didn't care to consider. Certainly young Callum had put up a valiant fight against their destruction.

Mrs Petty and Ida had heard every word of the raging argument which had lasted for hours, without moving an inch from their seats in the kitchen. It had rumbled on for days, right up until the moment the men with the saws moved in and the trees were taken down.

They hadn't seen the lad for days afterwards. And somehow he hadn't seemed himself since. He'd given up on his night classes and taken to imbibing a pint or two too many at the Rifle Man's or the Odd Fellows' Arms. It broke Mrs Petty's heart to see such a fine lad start to slip. But then he was also worried about his mam, which she didn't wonder at. She'd heard of some funny business in her time, but this took the biscuit.

'*Biscuits!* What did we do with those ratafias, Ida?'

'I put them on the trifle, Mrs P, like you said.'

'Thank heaven you did summat right, for once.'

'I does me best, Mrs P, even though I'm that wore out.'

'I know you do, lass, and yer not the only one to be knackered. Eeh, there's too much to think of, too much for the pair of us to cope with on us own. I'll have to tell her again. We need more help, but the miserable bugger won't give us any. Yet she must spend a small fortune on her frocks and fancy jewellery and folderols, not to mention a new fast car, I notice, and all the alterations she's done on this house, even a grand piano installed in the drawing room.'

'That's for them musical swarays,' Ida explained.

Mrs Petty sniffed loudly. She did not approve of all these goings-on, even the music wasn't fit to listen to.

'Hearken to that row.' Cocking her head to one side, she indicated the noise emanating from the front of the house where Lucy and a small côterie of her friends were apparently practising their repertoire, in preparation for the event that evening.

'Are they singing or crying?'

'Well might you ask, Ida. Like braying donkeys, or happen lunatics in bedlam would sound better.' Mrs Petty clapped her hand over her mouth. 'Eeh, I shouldn't say that. What am I thinking of?'

She paused in her labours, lemon grater abandoned, screwing her eyes tight shut for a moment as if in pain. 'Do you reckon she's getting any better, our lass? I do hope they let her have visitors soon. It don't seem right her being stuck in some Godforsaken wilderness with no friends or family near.'

'Mrs Lucy says that's the whole point of the place. It'll give her a better chance of recovery.'

'Well, I must say, I never reckoned our Kate as

294

the suicidal type, not even when she lost her beloved husband. She's been down afore ... we're witness to that, eh, Ida? ... and she's bounced back again.'

'Aye, she has.'

'Summat's wrong somewhere. Why would she suddenly tek it into her head to slit her wrists, and during a weekend away, in the home of a perfect stranger? Choose how, it don't seem right. And even if she did, why isn't she getting any better from all this expert care she's supposedly having? Months it's been now and not a word from her, not even a postcard. Eeh, I niver thought to hear meself say it, but I'm that worried about t'lass, I am really.'

They both stood for a moment in silent companionship, brows creased in worry.

Wiping her hands on a cloth, Mrs Petty drew out a large handkerchief and blew her nose very loudly, then reached for the kettle. 'Let's have a brew. I can't bear to think of her suffering. Eeh, I do hope she's on the mend.'

As Mrs Petty slid the kettle on to the hob and Ida fetched the shortbread biscuits, Kate was drinking cabbage soup with a spoon. Thin and watery, with precious little in it by way of vegetables, it was near tasteless but it staved off the worst of her hunger. Following this came a plate of what could only be described as 'slops', an unidentifiable mess largely made up from the leftovers of previous meals, grey flakes of what might be meat mixed in amongst the potatoes, turnips and barley. It was far removed from the crown of lamb that Mrs Petty was preparing for Lucy's guests that evening.

Kate picked at the mush with her spoon, pushing it about her plate, as always her appetite waning the instant food was put before her.

She couldn't remember the last time she'd eaten anything which had possessed any flavour or required much chewing, but then they weren't ever allowed knives, so where was the point in serving anything which required cutting? Her dreams were haunted by memories of succulent roast beef, of Mrs Petty's steak and kidney pie with its rich, flaky pastry.

There had been days when food had been denied her completely, because she'd transgressed against one of the unwritten rules, or 'misbehaved' in some way. More often than not kicked up a fuss because they wouldn't let her go home.

Kate knew that she should be grateful for the sustenance, that she really ought to eat every revolting scrap, considering there'd be nothing more until breakfast time, and not much even then. Lukewarm porridge, if she was lucky, which at least lined the stomach for an hour or so, otherwise bread and milk which always tasted revolting, the milk slightly sour and the bread soggy.

But she couldn't eat these slops. She really couldn't. Her stomach heaved at the thought.

Her friend Peggy, her only friend in this dreadful place, had told her that the meals were prepared by the patients, who were not above spitting in the food, or worse, if they had a grievance against the nurses. Which, of course, most of them did have.

A sharp tap on her shoulder brought Kate out of her reverie. 'Eat up, number 172, we won't have food wasted in this establishment, nor will we hang around all night, waiting for you. Time you lot were all tucked up in your warm and cosy beds.' The nurse cackled at her own joke, since warm and cosy were not epithets which could rightly be attached to the hard iron bedsteads they were obliged to sleep in. Nor was their night attire of the sort meant to withstand the sharp cold of a long Scottish night, the thought often reducing Kate to grim laughter as she recalled her conversation with Lucy on that subject.

'I'm not hungry, thank you.'

The woman nipped a fold of skin on Kate's neck between her fingers and thumb and pinched it hard. 'Eat, if you know what's good for you.'

Kate knew that it was important not to react. No matter if she was near passing out from the pain of the woman's tenacious grip, it did no good at all to object. She'd tried protesting, in those first weeks, when she'd still had the energy to feel outrage over her treatment.

On one occasion she'd asked for simple bread and cheese instead of the revolting slops. She'd been given it too, except that the bread had been mouldy and the cheese alive with maggots. She'd objected, naturally, refusing even to touch it.

Two hulking great nurses, although warders would be a better description, had borne down upon her, strapped her in a strait-jacket and tied her to her bed for thirty-six hours. During those long, dark hours, in which she'd wet herself like a baby, Kate had learned what it was to be truly afraid.

And she'd still had to eat the bread and cheese. The two warders had stood over her while she ate every scrap, mould, maggots, and all.

Now, generally speaking, she complied, following every order to the letter, eating whatever was put in front of her without complaint. Life was simpler that way, and a part of her clung on to the hope that compliance on her part would win her freedom in the end.

Peggy was much more volatile, and fiercely protective of her new friend. 'Here, lay off her,' she said now. 'Who would want to eat this pig-swill anyroad?' And turning her own plate upside down, she let the contents fall with a sickening plop on to the floor.

Three of Peggy's babies had died mysterious deaths, simply stopped breathing in their cot, and she'd been held responsible. She swore her innocence over the loss, but no one believed her. After five years at the castle, was it any wonder if she sometimes lost her reason? 'It's only fit for cockroaches,' she screamed now. 'Which is what you lot are, bloody cockroaches! So get down on yer hands and flamin' knees and *you* eat it, lick it all up, if it's so bleeding good!'

It was as if a switch had been flicked, or a gate opened. Pandemonium broke out as several of the other patients on nearby tables started throwing their food on to the floor too, stamping on it and screaming with laughter, calling the nurses cockroaches, rats, and other abusive names.

The rebellion spread like wildfire across the room. Spoons were hammered on tables, plates smashed to the floor, one woman even climbed on a table and began to strip off her clothes and dance. Warders rushed around beating patients about the head with wet towels in order to silence them, until eventually calm was restored once more and everyone was seated again, cowering and subdued.

Two warders bore down on Peggy, man-handled her into the all-too-familiar strait-jacket and marched her away.

Kate desperately tried to stop them. 'Don't do that! It's not her fault. I was the one who refused to eat the stuff, not Peggy.'

Even as she protested, she knew her pleas were useless.

'If you were the one who started this, 172, then let's see if a night or two in isolation will sharpen your appetite. I know a nice little padded cell just built for trouble-makers like you.'

After two cups of strong tea and several of Mrs Petty's homemade shortbread biscuits, Ida glanced up at the clock ticking loudly on the kitchen wall. 'Shall I start squeezing the lemons, Mrs P? For the lemon meringue.'

Mrs Petty came to with a jerk. 'Aye, lass, you do that. Squeeze every last bleedin' drop out of them and pretend it's that madam's blood, why don't you?'

The caterwauling from the front of the house seemed to have increased in volume as they got back to work, and the pair of them winced. 'I prefer a nice Strauss waltz meself, not this banging and jumping about, this Black Bottom and Charleston. Disgusting, if you ask me. What happened to dignity, that's what I'd like to know? Shaking yer nether regions at a chap. Immoral!'

Ida stifled a giggle. She rather liked jazz herself, and had often peeped in at the goings-on in the drawing room through a crack in the door to watch the dancing. It all looked exciting, really good fun. 'I see what you mean, Mrs P,' she politely agreed, remembering how old her friend was.

Mrs Petty was indeed feeling her age. She was worn out by the endless cooking, the arguments over menus, the complaints if something didn't turn out quite right.

'You'd think I'd nowt else to do in life but stuff mushrooms. What's wrong with a nice Irish stew, I told her, with plum pudding to follow? But no, that's only good enough for the likes of us. The peasants! Her fancy friends must have quails' eggs, turbot, pigeon pie, and pheasant stuffed with truffles. Followed, of course, by a most succulent array of peaches, plums, raspberries and strawberries, for all they're not in season half the time, and enough meringues, jellies, trifles, sorbets and tarts to make even a bishop sick, and they're known for rich living, they are. My fingers are worn to the bone wi' kneading and beating, stirring and whisking.

'And where does she find the money, that's what I want to know? Bread has gone up to one shilling and fourpence, would you believe? And milk is elevenpence a quart. I don't want to buy the blasted cow, I told the milkman. What a cheek! Where will we all end up, I ask meself?'

Ida sniffed sympathetically, having heard it all before. 'You should've seen the state of the blue bedroom last weekend. Vomit everywhere. Turned my stomach it did. I should be paid extra for cleaning it up, I should really.'

'We should both go on strike, lass, same as the miners. Twelve days they were out and succeeded in getting a bit of a pay rise. Happen we should try it.'

'Aye, but the miners aren't up against Madam Lucy, are they?'

'No, Ida, you're right there.' Mrs Petty let out a heavy sigh. 'In the meantime, beat me a dozen eggs, lass. *Modom* wants proper custard with the pear tart at her soirée this evening. I'll give her "proper custard", as if I'd make any other sort!'

'And there's to be another 'ouse party this weekend an' all,' Ida added, eyes wide with outrage. 'I heard her on t'telephone this morning, ringing up that Teddy bloke and various others of her friends. *"Dahling, do come. It'll be such fun!"*' Ida imitated, making Mrs Petty chortle with delight.

'Aye, and where does that madam sleep at these weekend dos of hers, that's what I'd like to know? Different chap every night, I'd say. She's certainly not where she should be come morning, I'll tell you that for nowt.'

'Yer right there, Mrs P,' agreed Ida. 'I never know where to take her breakfast tray.'

'Well, I know what I'd like to put in her

scrambled eggs, I'll tell you that for nowt. A few of my choice "mushrooms", carefully selected and finely chopped. That'd fettle her nicely, that would.'

Ida's eyes rounded with fright and her jaw fell open, revealing all the blackened stumps of her teeth. 'Nay, you'd not *poison* her!'

'There have been times when I've been sorely tempted to give her the same treatment she meted out to our little Flora with such callousness. Madam Lucy ain't no innocent. She's a wicked woman who deserves to be boiled in oil or flayed alive for the damage she's done to this family. And I hope I'm around to watch when she gets her comeuppance. By heck, but it'll end in tears. Mark my words, it'll all end in tears. Eeh, Kate love, come home quick. We need you.'

# 30

Callum had done everything he could think of to discover where his mother was being kept, and failed utterly. The most he'd learned was from that chap who'd diddled him and beaten him up, shouting summat about her being in a Scottish castle. So far as Callum was aware there were any number of the damn things, so how could he possibly find out which was the right one, even if he possessed the transport and the funds, to go and look?

He felt such a fool, such a complete failure.

Lucy was being obstinately reticent on the subject, admitting only that the castle was in the borders and insisting Kate still needed time to recover. The very idea that his mother, who had endured so much and always showed such fighting spirit, would suddenly take it into her head to end it all, was quite beyond his ken. Callum did not believe it.

Nor did Toby Lynch, and the pair of them would often discuss their concern over a pint or in snatched conversations at the factory.

Only this morning, as Callum had been eating his sandwiches in his dinner break down by the river, Toby had joined him. Even though he was Callum's boss, and strictly speaking they shouldn't fraternise, their shared concern over Kate had forged a bond between them. There were times, as now, when rank and status could be set aside and they would converse simply as friends.

To Callum it was a huge relief to find another man he could talk to and share his worries with. Toby was the solid, dependable type, not one to panic easily or allow himself to be put upon. It surprised Callum sometimes that Toby Lynch still found the time to enquire so often about Kate's health when he was more than fully occupied fighting daily battles at the factory, not only with the men, but with Lucy who seemed to think she was entirely in charge while his mam was away.

Toby said, 'The address must be somewhere among Mrs Lucy's belongings. Besides, don't you write to your mother regularly?'

As so often, there wasn't any preamble to

Toby's question. He spoke as if this were a mere continuation of an ongoing discussion, which it in effect was. Their shared concern over Kate's whereabouts and condition had scarcely been out of their minds since the weekend Lucy had returned alone from Scotland.

Callum agreed that they did indeed write, every week: 'Only we don't have the address. We give the sealed envelope, or postcard, to Lucy, and she addresses it. We don't even know if Mam gets the letters because we never hear a word in reply, not since that one and only letter we received back in January, shortly after she arrived. It's hard on Flora, she's missing her mammy. I've argued with Lucy on the subject, swallowed me pride and pleaded with her even, but she is absolutely adamant that she won't divulge it. Claims to be afraid I might go storming up there and drag Mam out long before her recovery is complete.'

Toby's face had grown dark with anger throughout Callum's explanation. 'Well, of course you would,' he snapped. 'If you didn't, *I* certainly would. I don't believe, any more than you do, this tale of Kate going off her head or attempting to slit her wrists. It simply isn't in her to do such a dreadful thing, not when you and Flora mean so much to her. However depressed she might be, however much she might be mourning Eliot, she would always put you first. She lives for you two. Lucy is lying.'

'But how to prove it? More important, how to get around her lies and discover the truth?'

Toby sucked in his breath. 'That is the problem, I will admit.' The pair of them were thoughtful for a long while, concentrating on eating their sandwiches, watching a pair of moorhens bobbing about in the river. Toby eventually said, 'So you don't fancy rooting through Lucy's things?'

Callum shrugged. 'I already have. Found nothing. She's far too clever to be so careless.'

'Even clever people, at least people like Lucy who arrogantly imagine themselves to be cleverer than everyone else, do make mistakes. They get over-confident and slip up. We simply have to be there when she does.'

Lucy was obliged to call again upon the bank manager, with funds growing ever more tight. Her friends were slowly getting the message that she was no longer such an easy touch, except for that dratted Swainson who was still leeching money out of her, coming round regular as clockwork every few weeks. A little bit here, a little bit there. It was costing a small fortune Lucy could ill afford just to keep his mouth shut, yet she couldn't ever seem to satisfy him. Anyone would think she was a bottomless pit of money, so she had less and less patience with Toby's cautious management of the business, or with the dividends it paid. What on earth was the man's problem? It was vital that Tysons Industries be restored to its former glory and generate sufficient money to fund her glamorous lifestyle.

This time it took more of her charm to win the bank manager round. He sat in his swivel chair, tapping his spectacles against his teeth whilst he listened, apparently unmoved by her tale of woe. 'Business not too good then? Seems to have been suffering from Kate's absence, wouldn't you say?' he pointedly remarked.

Lucy was incensed by this but did her best to disguise her wrath. 'My sister-in-law has, I'm afraid, badly neglected the business for some considerable time. I'm having a perfectly frightful struggle trying to keep things on an even keel as a result.'

'Hmm,' he said, looking far from convinced.

'You wouldn't see a poor widow woman struggle, would you, Norman?' Lucy purred, fluttering her eyelashes provocatively at him and angling her body so that he could see her figure to its best advantage. Darling Charles had always declared she had the finest breasts in Christendom.

The manager, happily married and with four daughters, cleared his throat and mildly enquired, 'What sort of sum were you thinking of?'

When Lucy told him, a small crease of concern appeared above the bridge of his nose and he put back his spectacles, as if he needed them to view her properly and help him to think. 'My word, that is a considerable sum, dear lady.'

Lucy gave a trilling, light-hearted little laugh. 'You surely aren't suggesting that Tysons' credit isn't good? We have substantial assets.'

There was a silence. 'Indeed you have but, correct me if I'm wrong, as I understand it, they belong to your sister-in-law. Is she in agreement with you over this loan? Have you spoken to her about it?'

Lucy briefly explained why this was impossible, dabbing her eyes with a lace handkerchief as she did so. 'It really is very sad, but the tragic loss of

306

her husband has quite turned Kate's mind.'

'I'm sorry to hear it. A finer lady never lived.'

Lucy smiled tightly, not really wishing to sit in the bank manager's office and hear him praise Kate. She rose gracefully to her feet, stretched out her hand. 'Thank you for listening to me, and for agreeing to help me through this sticky patch.'

The bank manager also rose but did not take her hand immediately. 'I don't believe I have agreed quite yet, certainly not to the sum you mention. I could see my way to allowing your overdraft to rise to half that amount. Beyond that you'll need to make savings of some sort within the factory.'

Lucy drew in a sharp breath of relief and managed a bravely devastating smile. 'I'm sure that can be arranged.'

'Perhaps you'd care to take coffee while I have the papers drawn up? I'll have my secretary attend you.' So saying, he led her from his office back into the reception area where Lucy was left kicking her heels until the secretary bustled in with a tray of coffee and Marie biscuits.

Later, when the papers were all signed, the manager took Lucy by the elbow and led her to the door. 'Remember what I said about reducing costs?'

'I already have the matter in hand. We were somewhat overstaffed and I've made stringent cuts.'

Again he frowned, his concern deepening. 'I've never considered Tysons Shoes to be particularly overstaffed, although it is certainly well supplied with skilled workers. I was meaning hidden costs

– insurance, postage and stationery, heating bills, advertising and making sure that you source your materials carefully with no overstocking of leather. All of that needs to be looked into carefully.'

'Of course, of course.' Having got most, if not all, of what she'd wanted, Lucy was anxious to leave.

'But curb your own expenditure a little too, dear lady. It was ever a weakness?' With a small bow he took his leave, while a shocked Lucy found herself to be in full view of his dratted secretary who had clearly heard every word but was vigorously pretending to be otherwise occupied.

There was one way, Lucy decided, that savings could be made, and that was to rid herself of the encumbrance of Kate. She wrote to Elvira the very next day to make an appointment to check on her sister-in-law's progress, tactfully suggesting that it might be time to make some decisions about Kate's long term future; that it was best not to let the matter drift on too long.

If she hurried, she would just be able to get the letter off before lunch.

Lucy poured herself her usual glass of Madeira before pulling out the latest bill from the asylum, which she'd secreted away in a leather folder tucked right at the back of the top drawer of Eliot's desk. She dashed off a cheque for the correct amount, shuddering at the cost, which only served to harden her resolve still further.

After that she swiftly penned her note and

sealed it with the cheque in an envelope, upon which she scribbled the address, copying it from the bill spread open on the desk just as the dinner gong sounded.

Smiling to herself Lucy slid the envelope into her pocket, tidied everything away and went off to lunch. She would pop the letter into the post box herself, just to be on the safe side. She had no wish for Ida, or any other curious onlooker, to take note of the Scottish address.

It was long past time for her generosity to cease, time to think of herself and her own children, to have the upstart moved somewhere safe and cheap, a place from which there was no return. Kate O'Connor's days were numbered.

The next house party Lucy had planned was to take as its theme 'The Harem'. She'd ordered a gorgeous, floaty, sari-type garment for herself in a beautiful peacock blue trimmed with gold braid. Her plan was for Teddy, dressed as the Viceroy of India, to escort her to the dining room at a slow walk, allowing all the guests ample opportunity to admire her in the gown. They would then follow on behind before singing the National Anthem and commencing the meal.

Lucy strongly approved of the Empire and colonialism. How else would those poor unfortunate souls who were not born British possibly survive?

Feeling herself duty bound to play the benefactress, in keeping with her theme, despite being short of ready money, Lucy had bought gifts for all her guests: cuff-links for the men, earbobs for the women. For the food, she intended to offer authentic Indian dishes, except that Mrs Petty was being even more difficult than usual.

'Curry? And what might that be when it's at home?'

Lucy explained it as best she knew how, even offering a few recipes she'd discovered in one of her *Ladies At Home* magazines. 'I would also like Bombay duck, Tandoori chicken, kebabs and meat balls, and lots of rice of course. Oh, and you'll need to buy ginger, cumin and turmeric powder and a dozen other spices in order to make them. Here they are, all listed, the recipes plainly set out. All you have to do is to follow them carefully. I'm sure even you can manage that.'

Mrs Petty read through a recipe for cashew rice, one for coconut chutney, others for devilled eggs and a bewildering variety of curry dishes, with increasing horror. 'You want me to grind and pound all these spices, assuming I can get me hands on such fancy stuff in Kendal? All this fuss and bother for one meal? Nay, and it'll be that hot and spicy, nobody'll like it. Why don't I make a nice hot pot? Always goes down a treat does my hot pot.'

'You'll cook exactly what I tell you to cook, or take two weeks' notice.'

Mrs Petty drew in a long breath, swelling her already generous figure to balloon-like proportions. 'Begging yer pardon, I'm not accustomed to being so dictated to. I'm a professional cook, used to finding me own receipts, if ye don't mind. The first Mrs Tyson always let me have a say in choosing the menus.'

Lucy was almost scarlet with rage by this time, a hot tide of fury bubbling within her. 'I am *not* the first Mrs Tyson, and certainly not the second, so don't start quoting me what your darling Kate allowed you to do either. I'm in charge now, and intend to remain so. We *will* have curry, samosas, and everything else on this list, *because I say so*. Is that clear?'

Mrs Petty allowed the silence to hang for quite some moments before giving her response in a voice barely above a hiss. 'Or I get me notice, is that the way of it?'

'That is very much the way of it. Take it or leave it.' Having resolved the matter to her own satisfaction, Lucy turned to leave, but was halted in her tracks by Mrs Petty's next words.

'Then I'll leave it, if it's all the same to you. I've had enough of being bullied and bandied about. I've worked for this family for forty year or more, and never been so treated. Ye can stick yer two weeks' notice! Have me pay packet ready by noon. I'm off to me sister Annie's on the Fylde coast. She's been begging me to go and help with her boarding house for years.' So saying, Mrs Petty untied her apron strings, shoved the stained garment into Lucy's shocked face, and marched out of the door.

'I've had an idea.' Toby caught up with Callum one afternoon as he pulled his bike out of the shed at the end of his shift. Grasping the boy by the elbow, he propelled him through the crowd of workers making their way home, to a place where

311

they could talk unobserved.

'Since Kate wasn't committed by the magistrates, presumably this private asylum has to be paid for?'

Callum gave a sarcastic grunt. 'I assume Mam is paying for her own incarceration, one way or another.'

'Be that as it may, there must be bills, accounts, invoices, some form of demand for payment, which will come regularly, perhaps every month. And on that bill there'll be an address.'

Callum's eyes lit up. 'Why didn't I think of that? But where would she keep it? Happen in Eliot's study. Lucy seems to have taken that over as her own. She calls it the library or summat equally daft. I'll have a look around, see what I can find.'

'Take care. Don't let her catch you snooping or she might move Kate somewhere else, and then we'd really be in trouble.'

'Aye, she's good at tricks of that sort.' Callum frowned, remembering how Lucy had done exactly the same to him as a child, moving him from the Union workhouse where she'd first put him, to Mr Brocklebank's farm in the Langdales where no one would ever think to look. Kate had told him how she'd thought of the workhouse eventually and gone there to look for him, only she'd been too late.

'Leave it to me. If there's a bill there with the address on, I'll find it.'

# 31

A new cook was hired at once for the weekend party, with strict instructions that she was on a month's trial and would only be given permanent employment if she suited.

Two new maids were also taken on, Ida having likewise handed in her notice and quit. She certainly had no intention of carrying on without her good friend. Unthinkable! Fortunately, Mrs Petty had made it clear she was more than welcome to join her in Blackpool.

'I reckon our Annie will be glad of another pair of hands, even though you do cost a fortune a feed.'

'I could try to eat less,' Ida promised, suddenly fearful she might be left behind.

'Huh, was that a pig flying by, or a pink elephant? Still, I expect we'll manage, as we always have.'

Callum and Flora were devastated to lose them both. It felt as if their last link with their mother had been severed. At least with Mrs P and Ida around, they'd felt that somebody cared about them. Now they felt bereft, abandoned, and not a little scared. Who would curb Lucy's excesses now? Who would check the food served to them? Who would give Flora a loving cuddle, or tend Callum's bruises, when dear old Mrs P had gone? She'd cleaned him up yet again, following

313

his dust-up in the pub after the skittle match, urging him with her usual banter to pick someone his own size next time.

'Or you could always join the Temperance League,' she suggested, with a sly wink. Callum had the grace to look shamefaced.

There'd been a tearful farewell, Mrs Petty promising to visit, although they all knew she would never be allowed to set foot in Tyson Lodge ever again.

'You two poppets will have to come and visit us, on the Fylde coast. Me and Annie will be right glad to see you any time. She's got this gradely boarding house in Blackpool. Twelve bedrooms it has, up by the north pier.'

'Oh, do you think we could?' Flora asked, desperate for some glimmer of hope in what seemed like a bleak future.

Callum mumbled, *'She'd* never let us go.'

'Don't you fret, love. We'll work summat out to get round madam. Our Annie is the wily sort and not easily defeated.'

After the pair had gone, marching off into a cold, misty October afternoon carrying their carpet bags to Kendal station to catch the Preston train, Flora had cried for hours, huddled in misery on her bed, and nothing Callum could say would cheer her.

'Who will care for us now, Callum? Where's me mammy? I want me mammy.'

The year was dying and Kate was still here. Occasionally they were allowed out into the garden for exercise, sometimes for as long as

314

thirty minutes at a time. The leaves were turning gold and crimson, purple heather ablaze on the hills beyond, rowan berries hanging like drops of blood from their fragile branches. Kate ached to be allowed to walk over the mountains as she had on that very first day almost a year ago, but it was not to be. Elvira had allowed her to go then because she wished to allay any suspicions Kate might have felt about where she'd been brought, quite certain she would return in time for the promised dinner. Now the staff knew that she, along with many another patient, would abscond given the slightest opportunity.

Kate had made no attempt to escape. She hadn't plucked up sufficient courage for that yet, not knowing the area well enough and aware that it was a long walk to the nearest village. But she did have a plan.

On their journey here she remembered passing a couple of farms, just down the road, and had it in mind that if she could smuggle a letter in to one of these, beg the farmer or his wife to post it for her, she might be able to circumvent whoever was blocking the correspondence between herself and her children. It was worth a try.

Peggy disagreed. 'She's giving you enough gip already. She watches you like a hawk, more than she does anyone else. If Elvira catches you outside these premises, even beyond the gate, you're done for. It'll be manacles and shackles for you after that.'

Kate laughed. 'Don't be ridiculous! She'd never dare. Sure and this isn't a prison.'

Peggy's eyes widened in disbelief at such casual

unconcern. 'Ye think not? Then why have I been here five years for the so-called crime of my lovely babies dying? Because they think I killed them and this is my punishment.'

Kate was instantly contrite. 'I'm sorry, I didn't mean to sound uncaring. Oh, but I must get a letter to me own children! I'm desperate, so I am. I haven't heard from them in months.'

Always touched by the plight of mothers with children, Peggy's eyes filled with tears. 'I'll take it for you, love. I've been here that long they pay little or no attention to what I do these days. Anyroad, the government pays Elvira to keep me locked up and where else do I have to go? I've no home, no husband or family, waiting for me outside. My parents are both dead, of grief I shouldn't wonder, and me husband – well, he gave up and ran off with someone else long since. Give the letter to me, I'll see it gets posted properly.'

'No, no, I wouldn't hear of it. You mustn't put yourself in danger for my sake, Peggy.' They argued for some time but despite Peggy's protests that she'd nothing to lose, that they'd never even notice she was gone, Kate was adamant. She would allow no risks to be taken on her behalf.

Kate stowed the letter away under her mattress and went to sleep, dreaming and planning how she might manage to break free of the staff and reach the nearest farm.

There was generally some game or other played during the exercise period. She'd slip away then, when everyone was occupied and the nurses engaged in having a quiet smoke.

But when the time for afternoon exercise came round the next day, Kate could find no sign of the letter anywhere. It had gone from beneath her mattress. Only then did she realise that Peggy too had vanished. She must have taken it and slipped out while the nurses were doing their chores after lunch.

Dear God, Kate could only hope and pray that neither Elvira nor her stalwart band of warders would miss her.

Her hopes were soon dashed. An hour or two later, a hullabaloo from outside alerted her, confirming her worst fears. Two of the nurses had Peggy grasped between them in an arm-lock, her body bent over and her head pushed forward.

'Peggy!' Kate dashed over to her instantly but, despite the awkwardness of her position, Peggy lifted her head with a sideways twist, her eyes blazing a silent warning. *Don't come near. Say nothing!* The nurses shouted for her to stand well clear and Kate was left helplessly standing by as a third nurse ran to help and Peggy was marched briskly away.

Kate didn't see her again for three days. All that time Peggy was kept in isolation in a padded cell with no light and no sustenance beyond a glass of water twice a day. All the other patients were made aware of her punishment and this knowledge subdued them to a mumbling silence, everyone fearful of saying or doing anything which might put them in a similar predicament.

When Peggy finally emerged, blinking in the pale wintry light of the hospital garden, she smiled weakly as Kate instantly ran to her. 'I did

317

it,' she said, her voice cracking against her dry throat. 'I bloody did it!'

Elvira, wise to the ways of her patients and Peggy's friendship with Kate, made a point of asking her staff where she'd been found. Wary of the reason for Lucy's sudden desire to visit and the likely loss of income resulting from Kate's removal, she decided that a visit to the nearby farms would be no bad idea.

The farmer's wife was easy to convince that a patient had run wild, and the letter to Callum duly handed over. Elvira took it back to her room and dropped it into the flames of her fire, then poured herself a whisky and seated herself comfortably to watch it burn.

Lucy was enjoying a late breakfast with Teddy in the new conservatory she'd had built when a letter from Elvira Crombie was brought to her in the morning's post. Ripping open the blue envelope she found that an appointment had been made for her to discuss Kate's future, as requested, on the following Sunday morning. A highly inconvenient time.

'Drat! I was planning to go to Chubby Jackson's do next weekend. Now I'm going to have to nip up to Scotland.' She glanced across at Teddy, slumped opposite her, sipping black coffee and looking very much the worse for wear. 'You wouldn't care to come with me, Teddy darling, would you?'

He gazed at her, bleary-eyed, across the marmalade. 'Scotland, old fruit? Always full of bloody midges.'

'Not in February, sweetie. If you don't come then I shall have to drive myself, all that way. I must go, you see, arrangements to make for my poor sick sister-in-law. It won't take long. You could drop me off, do some fishing or something, and we could meet up afterwards at a lovely hotel. Have the entire weekend all to ourselves. Blissful! Don't you think that would be too delightful?'

'Sounds damned boring to me,' said Teddy, and knocking the marmalade pot over as he got up from the table, lurched away, steadying himself against the door frame as he went out.

Amongst the post was another letter which she recognised as coming from the bank manager. Lucy quickly read it then ripped it to shreds.

'Drat! Drat! Drat! Damn men to hell.' She picked up the marmalade pot and flung it at the wall where it left a smear of orange all down the pristine white woodwork. 'No matter what, I can't *not* go to Scotland. I simply must get rid of that woman!' Lucy screamed, though there was no one left in the room to listen. No one, that is, but Callum and Flora who'd been about to enter from the hall but, changing their minds, headed for the kitchen instead.

It didn't matter how much he cuddled her, or urged her to be a brave girl, night after night Flora would sob as if her heart were broken.

Callum realised, in such moments, how very important Mrs Petty had been to her. Flora had adored the old cook who'd been like a surrogate mother to her, assuring the little girl that her own mammy would come home safe and well one day soon, and in the meantime, didn't she have dear old Mrs P to care for her? Now this last remaining buffer of protection and security had been taken from her by Lucy's vindictive nastiness. Finally, too exhausted to cry any more, Flora would fall asleep.

On this particular night, Callum sat on for some time, stroking his young sister's head, his mouth set in a grim line of determination, wondering what exactly had arrived in the morning's post to so upset his aunt. Time was surely running out. Their plan had to be put into effect soon. He could dally no longer.

He'd behaved like a fool, had allowed himself to be duped by a perfect stranger who'd robbed him of his week's wages, and now they'd lost Mrs P and Ida as well. He wished Bunty were here to help him, at least to talk things through with him, but she wasn't, and still no letter had come from her.

He was beginning to think that perhaps she really had finished with him after all. The thought was well-nigh unbearable. But in the meantime he had Flora to think about and care for. He needed to find his Mam and bring her home. Who knew what she was up to, what malicious scheme Lucy would come up with next? No doubt she'd try to dispatch Flora to some dreadful school, far worse than the one Bunty was attending, and Callum himself would be booted out to survive on his wits as best he may.

Things surely couldn't get any worse.

He wished he were years older, instead of only

seventeen, with a man's experience and strengths to call upon. He wished he were old enough to make his own way in the world, free to marry the girl he loved.

That evening, Lucy was having yet another of her dinner parties and he chose the early hours of the morning as the best time to start his search, mainly because by then her loutish friends were either in bed with each other, dead drunk, or both. Making certain that Flora was still sleeping peacefully, Callum crept downstairs.

Loud snoring emanated from the drawing room and a peep inside revealed the Bennet brothers sprawled senseless, one on Lucy's new sofa, the other on the Persian rug. Callum sincerely hoped that they would vomit on both.

Quietly turning the knob of the study door, he slipped inside. The catch made a loud click in the darkness as he eased it closed, making him nearly jump out of his skin. Callum could hear his own heart pounding loudly in his ears and then another sound, that of heavy breathing. Someone was in here. He pulled out his Ever Ready electric torch and flicked it on, shielding it with one hand so as not to wake whoever it was.

A man and a woman lay entwined together on the leather couch, slumped in a drunken stupor.

Fearful of waking them for all they appeared utterly senseless, Callum made his way over to the desk, walking silently on the balls of his feet. Keeping the torch carefully pointed down to the floor, he sat in the swivel Captain's chair and began systematically to go through the drawers in the desk.

They seemed to be stuffed with bills of every sort, from the butcher, the baker, the dressmaker and milliner, and no doubt the candlemaker too, since the place had been decorated out like a sultan's harem, or an Indian princess's palace. Callum's heart sank, knowing it would take him hours to go through this lot, item by item. He opened another drawer, fumbled about deep inside. Yet more bills. And then his hands closed upon a leather folder, tucked right at the back. Drawing it out, he opened it up and swiftly rifled through the contents.

Eureka! Here it was, not one but two envelopes, each with a Hawick postmark. One did indeed contain an invoice for his mother's care and, impatient now, he ripped open the second and looked inside. It was then that the young man on the couch decided to wake up.

# 32

Callum hit the man over the head with the end of his electric torch. He'd barely got out the words 'What's going on?' when without a moment's hesitation or thought, Callum struck. As the young man slid back into unconsciousness, Callum feared for a moment that he might have killed him, but a loud snore soon put an end to that worry.

Hopefully, he'd been so far gone in drink he wouldn't even remember what had happened, but the blow would do nothing for his hangover the next day.

Before any of Lucy's friends had risen from their drunken slumbers the following morning, Callum made a point of getting to the factory early. He waylaid Toby just as he was entering the manager's office. 'I've got it!' Callum was breathless with pedalling hard in his rush to get there, his face scarlet from the exertion, and Toby made him repeat what he'd said, to be sure he'd heard correctly.

'I said, I've got the address, the information we need. Not only that, I've found a letter from the woman who runs the place arranging for Lucy to visit on Sunday next. Here are the details. I've copied them out. What do you reckon?'

Toby snatched the paper from him and grinned from ear to ear as he quickly scanned it. 'Good lad, I knew you'd come up trumps.' The crease of a frown appeared above his nose as he examined the scribbled notes Callum had made. 'She pays quite a sum. Knowing Lucy as we do, she won't keep this up for much longer. We've got to move fast, try to get there before her. Problem is, I can't get away before the weekend either, too many meetings I'm afraid. We could leave first thing on Saturday, or late Friday night. What do think?'

'Normally I'd say Friday, because the sooner the better only I must take Flora with us.' Callum explained then about Mrs Petty's dismissal over the weekend, and Ida going with her. 'I can't leave Flora alone in the house with Lucy. Bunty is still in Switzerland, Georgie at school and Jack doesn't give a monkey's about anyone but himself. I don't trust any of them.'

'Point taken but...'

'I could say I was taking Flora out for the day, on a picnic or something. Lucy will no doubt be glad to be rid of us for a while. If we start at six, we could be in Scotland by nine, ten at the latest.'

Toby wasn't particularly happy about the arrangement but found he had no choice but to agree.

On the same evening Lucy had held her Indian dinner party and Callum had later plundered her belongings, Kate was forcibly given three, instead of two, of the dreaded sleeping pills. She was then taken to a room in the castle where she'd never set foot before. She'd passed it often enough, seen other patients taken inside, and wondered what lay beyond that door. The moment she walked through it, she wished her curiosity had not been satisfied. It looked for all the world like a torture chamber.

This room had no windows. It contained strange-looking chairs and leather couches fixed to the floor beside which stood huge cylinders with wires and rubber tubes attached, odd sorts of head gear, looking for all the world like the battery from Callum's electric torch.

Kate thought she might actually pass out from fear. She stood rooted to the spot, quite unable to move forward or backward, and found herself poked in the back by a nurse.

'Get on with it, we haven't all day. There's nothing to be scared of. This is a new experimental treatment we're engaged in. You're very fortunate to have been chosen as not everyone will be given the opportunity to take part in the trials. It's your chance to get better, all for your own good, so sit yourself down, girl. You'll just get a good shaking up, that's all. Rid your brain of the devils that drive it.'

Kate wanted to say that there were no devils in her brain but somehow her tongue seemed to have cleaved itself to the roof of her mouth.

They strapped her into a chair and buckled some metal plates with bits of wire attached to her head, which was feeling particularly vulnerable with her hair still kept so short. One of the nurses told her to clench her teeth on a length of rubber tube.

'To stop you biting your tongue. Now be a good girl and don't make a fuss. I have a report to write.'

Even had she been able, Kate could not have protested. She was powerless to move, the sick feeling so strong in her stomach she thought she might actually vomit over the nurse's hands. Miraculously, she did no such thing. Instead she began to shake. At first she thought this was because she was so terrified, and then realised that it felt as if she'd been picked up in the jaws of a giant dog and was being shaken to bits. She squeezed her eyes tight shut, watching the blue flashes crackling at the backs of her eyes, and prayed silently.

Dinner the following evening was a much quieter affair. Only the malingerers remained, those who, like the Bennet boys, preferred to drink

Lucy's whisky rather than their own. And Teddy, of course, who was far too idle to move more than was absolutely necessary. Everyone else had gone home after lunch so it was a simple meal for once.

Lucy had eaten every morsel of her chicken and mushroom pie, and the sorbet which followed it, and was just raising her glass to offer a toast to the new cook for an excellent meal when the pain struck. It cut in beneath her ribs, seeming to split her in two and making her cry out loud in anguish.

The glass dropped from her hand, broken shards splintering all over the floor. But she was not the only one to be struck down. The rest of the small gathering, including the Bennet boys, were likewise afflicted, many doubling up and moaning, others gasping in agony. Poor Teddy had gone quite green, the ash from his cigarette fluttering down on to the Persian rug where it made a nasty grey mark.

'I say, old thing. What was in that dratted pie?'

Lucy screamed at the frightened new maid, *'Fetch the cook. Bring her to me at once, do you hear?'*

The experiment the following day was to do with inducing a fever. Kate was injected with some unknown medication, then wrapped in blankets and strapped in a hospital bed which itself was set over a burning hot stove until she thought she might expire from the heat.

They gave her hot wine and water to drink, glass after glass of it, till the sweat poured out of her.

Apparently, fever was supposed to be the body's natural defence method for curing disease, in this case her supposed depression after the alleged suicide attempt, but since she didn't have one, the fever had to be artificially created. Kate was quite certain they would roast her alive.

Lucy writhed in her bed feeling certain she was about to expire. She'd vomited all morning, had never felt so ill in all her life. How was it possible to bear such stomach pains and still live?

The new cook, an inoffensive woman with a bright, cheery smile who went by the appropriate name of Mrs Daily, had been sacked, as of course had the two hapless maids although they had all denied responsibility.

It was perfectly clear to all concerned that the culprit was the 'mushrooms', if that indeed was what they were, which had been used in the chicken and mushroom pie. Mrs Daily insisted she hadn't been responsible for buying them, that apart from the chicken, which was fresh bought on the Monday morning, she'd used ingredients left ready in the pantry. How was she to know that they weren't what they purported to be and therefore unsafe?

'It was a miracle I wasn't killed!' Lucy screamed. 'And my guests too. We could all have died in our beds. Get out of my house this minute. *Get out!*'

Mrs Daily left gladly, as did the maids, making absolutely no protest, having already made up their minds that this was not a happy household and Lucy Tyson not a woman they could wish to work for in any case, let alone ever warm to.

Fortunately, Callum and Flora had not eaten the pie. Before she had made her departure, Mrs P had suggested that it might be best if they avoided mushrooms for a while, in case they disagreed with their young stomachs. She'd suggested that they may prefer, should mushrooms appear on the menu in the near future, to eat up the nice Cornish pasties she'd left for them instead.

'Not that the fungi will do any real harm, mind,' she'd told them. 'Much as I might relish the prospect of seeing the end of a certain person whose name we won't mention, I don't reckon I'd best take the risk. But they'll give this certain person an upset tum for a while. A salutary lesson, as ye might say. We'll call it rough justice, shall we, Flora love? Callum, me old mate? We'll call it justified retribution for past injuries inflicted.'

Lucy was kept to her bed for the rest of that week, the aunts running up and down stairs answering her every whim and demand, holding the bowl as she painfully vomited on a long-since empty stomach, time and time again.

Aunt Cissie was very much of the mind that taking Flora out for the day on Saturday would be an excellent notion. 'This is certainly no place for a child. We don't want dear Flora to catch whatever ails Lucy, now do we?'

Cissie did not believe the tale of bad mushrooms. Nothing grown in God's good earth could cause such an affliction, in her opinion.

'Nor can we tolerate a child under our feet all day,' Vera tartly added, 'when we have so much work to do. We shall have to start all over again with finding another cook and maid. Really, the servant question is becoming quite a problem. Such a nuisance!'

'I'll keep Flora out of your hair for the entire weekend if you like,' suggested Callum, delighted that fate had given their plan a helping hand by confining Lucy to her bed. 'I'll put her to bed tonight and tomorrow, from now on in fact. Don't give us another thought.'

'Splendid, but see that...' Vera's lecture was interrupted by yet more wails from Lucy's bedroom.

'Vera ... water, water, I must have water! And the bowl, quickly, quickly, oh...'

By Friday evening, Lucy had received a second letter from the bank manager, more urgent this time, which she slipped under her pillow. The two aunts were still run off their feet and Callum and Flora went to the kitchen to make sandwiches for their journey. Upstairs, they packed a small bag each, then Callum read Flora a story and gave her firm instructions to go straight to sleep, no extra reading under the bedclothes with her torch on this night.

Just before dawn he woke her and within minutes the pair of them were slipping out into an early morning mist, only the sound of an owl marking their passage through the garden, down to where Toby was waiting for them by the river.

# 33

Elvira was waiting in her study for the expected meeting with Lucy Tyson when she was informed by her secretary that a gentleman had called to see her. 'He says Mrs Tyson has been taken ill and cannot attend. He has come in her place.'

Elvira glowered. She disliked unexpected changes of plan, but nevertheless saw no alternative but to receive him. 'Well, don't stand there dithering. Show him in, woman.'

'Yes, Miss Crombie. Right away, Miss Crombie.'

The nervous secretary relieved Toby of his hat and coat and quickly ushered him into Elvira's inner sanctum.

Once the niceties had been exchanged, Toby wasted no time in stating his business. Callum and Flora he'd left safely behind in a local hotel. If his plan didn't work, he would ask that they at least be permitted to see their mother. Lucy's illness could not have been better timed, nicely falling in with their plan.

'Mrs Tyson, Mrs Lucy Tyson that is, has made alternative arrangements for her sister-in-law,' he politely explained. 'And she has requested that I escort Mrs Kate Tyson to this new hospital which is closer to her home. This is no reflection on the care she has received in your own esteemed establishment, Mrs Crombie, but it is difficult for the family, you understand, being unable to visit.'

'Miss – Miss Crombie.'

'I do beg your pardon.'

'I find that a family visit generally leaves patients upset and homesick, which does them no good at all. Patients confined for the good of their mental health have no need of visitors, who can cause more harm than good in my opinion, Mr Lynch. Bearing that in mind, I see no problem with the distance. Kate would be far better off staying where she is. She's settled in most comfortably, has even made a few friends.' Elvira Crombie stretched her lips into what might pass for a smile.

'I do understand your point of view,' Toby agreed, not believing a word of it. 'However, in this case there are peculiar circumstances which I am not at liberty to divulge. I am duty bound to carry out Mrs Tyson's orders.' He gave a helpless shrug, his expression impassive, appearing to indicate that he may not entirely agree with his employer's decision to move Kate, yet as a loyal servant was forced to comply with it.

Elvira glared at him, her eyes narrowed with suspicion. 'And what proof do I have that you are indeed her emissary in this transaction?'

Toby had thought of this and now handed over a letter, written in a fair imitation of Lucy's hand, instructing Elvira Crombie to release her sister-in-law to Toby Lynch, her business manager.

He was well aware that when Lucy discovered what had taken place, and whether or not they successfully managed to take Kate home, she would most certainly be given details of this visit and then there was a very real danger he would

331

be out of a job. It all depended on what condition Kate was in when he found her, whether she was able to stand up to Lucy at last, could hope to rescue him from his otherwise certain fate. Whatever the outcome, he was prepared to take the risk.

Elvira read the letter and harrumphed, very loudly. It sounded more like a snort of disbelief and Toby's heart sank. It wasn't going to work. He felt despair creeping over him. He'd risked everything but didn't care if he lost his job, so long as Kate was out of this dreadful place. Even a few casual glances around him on this short visit gave him the shivers. No matter what the cost, he had to get Kate out somehow. Smoothly he drew his wallet from his inside pocket.

'My employer is aware, naturally, of the inconvenience this change of plan will cause and has authorised me to compensate you for any loss incurred. She is perfectly willing to pay for her sister-in-law's stay until, say, the end of the year? That would have been a reasonable amount of time in which to expect recovery, would it not?'

He saw the woman's eyes gleam as they fixed themselves on the notes in his hand. 'Assuming any sort of recovery is possible,' she corrected him.

'Quite,' Toby agreed, his heart sinking still further. What had they done to Kate in this hell-hole? He began to count out notes. 'I assume cash is preferable to a cheque?'

The woman was almost dribbling with greed as she snatched the notes from him. 'Always far less

332

trouble. I dislike banks intensely.'

Toby attempted a sympathetic smile. 'You have my agreement there, ma'am.' Perhaps there was something in the way he said it, the twinkle in his eye or his cheeky grin, which appealed to Elvira. She smiled back at him.

'A sherry perhaps, while I instruct my nurses to have Kate dressed and prepared for the journey?'

'What a splendid thought. Just a quick one. I have no wish to incur any delay in getting her safely to her new establishment.' His heart lifted. Could it really be this simple to win her round?

'And where is that to be?' Elvira politely enquired, after murmuring a few hasty instructions to her secretary to have Kate prepared.

While she poured the sherry, Toby's mind raced. 'I am to deposit her with the family doctor. He is the one who has made the arrangements, naturally.'

'Indeed!' Now Elvira was frowning, her gimlet eyes once more alert and wary. 'And why did the doctor not come himself?'

'You know doctors, always too busy earning a crust. Better to send a minion like me.' Again Toby grinned at her but this time there was no smiling response.

'Hmm!'

A knock at the door and the dithering secretary appeared again. 'All is prepared, ma'am.'

'Thank you.'

Elvira turned back to Toby, surveying him with shrewd intensity. He tried to appear calm and collected, but the tension in him was strung out like a fine wire which would surely snap at any moment. Did she believe his story? Had he damaged it by not having the name of a possible hospital ready in his head? He rather feared that he might have done. He'd never forgive himself if this carelessness had lost him the chance of winning Kate's release.

'You have secure transport?' she asked, breaking into his thoughts.

At least they'd thought of that. 'Most certainly! A motor car with doors that lock. She will be perfectly secure. Do you think she will travel well?'

'We can give her something for the journey. We do this with all our patients on the happy day of their release, to make life easier for all concerned. She'll be perfectly tranquil. You'll have no problems with her.'

Elvira led him to the door and a small nub of hope was born in Toby. Was he indeed about to succeed? Everything seemed to be going very smoothly. He glanced down the dark, dingy corridor, trying not to appear anxious, wondering where Kate was. Would she appear at any moment, or was she waiting in the hall by the front door? It had taken very little time for them to get her ready.

Elvira said, 'There's just one thing. Perhaps I should telephone Mrs Tyson, or the doctor, to check that this new place is ready to receive her?'

Vera was changing Lucy's bed when the telephone rang, Lucy herself issuing instructions as she sat hunched in her armchair by the bedroom fire, so it was Cissie who answered the call, down in the hall.

'Who is that again? A Miss Crombie. And you wish to speak to Lucy? Oh, dear me, no, I'm afraid that is quite impossible. The poor woman is sick.'

Cissie listened in silence for some long moments and then said, 'Well bless me, this is wonderful news. I had no idea. Lucy clearly meant this as a lovely surprise for us all. Yes, of course, I shall personally speak to the doctor and check the arrangements are in hand. I'm sure that our dear Kate will be perfectly safe with Mr Lynch. Do give her my love and tell her we are quite ready to receive her home.'

Elvira put down the phone and smiled at Toby. It was not a reassuring sight. 'There seems to be a problem, Mr Lynch. The family were not only unprepared for Kate to be brought home, or moved to a new hospital, they were quite unaware you had even come to collect her. Now why do you think that is?'

Toby's mind was in turmoil. What to say to alleviate Elvira Crombie's suspicions? It came to him then that she might not actually have given orders for Kate to be got ready at all. For all he knew she could have given instructions for the exact opposite. What was it that the secretary had said? *All is prepared, ma'am.* Not 'the patient has been prepared', or more simply, 'Kate is ready.' Why hadn't he paid more attention to that? He'd been duped. Elvira Crombie had his money in her greedy palm, and still no Kate.

Nevertheless he felt he must continue with this charade. What choice did he have? What did a

335

few lies matter if it meant getting Kate out of this hell-hole? 'I don't know who you spoke to just now, but of course they were perfectly well aware that I was coming here. Didn't Mrs Tyson herself instruct me, and haven't I handed over to you already, in good faith, the compensation she felt due to you in lieu of anticipated fees? She will be furious if her wishes are flouted.'

He recognised the doubt creeping into the woman's eyes. She clearly had no wish to give up the money, but she'd lose more through Kate's removal. 'Her aunt most certainly knew nothing at all of any plan to have Kate moved.'

'Did you speak to Lucy?' Toby held his breath. If Elvira had spoken directly to her, then all was lost.

'Mrs Tyson herself was not available.'

'There you are. Didn't I say that she was ill?'

Elvira stiffened her spine, her gaze hard and unyielding. 'Nonetheless, whether she is ill or not, it was clear from my conversation with the aunt that no doctor, nor other family member, was aware you are even here. No other place has been secured for Kate. None at all. I believe this to be a fiction, a trick of your own devising. For all I know, you may be her lover trying to spirit her away, or a kidnapper who will demand a ransom for the poor woman's safe return. How do I know who you are? I have absolutely no proof of your identity, nor your good will.'

He was angry now, a huge wave of fury and frustration washing over him, and with it a sense of futility and humiliation. To come so near, and yet to fail. It was too much. Toby ached to protect

Kate, had loved her from the very first moment he'd set eyes on her yet he'd kept his distance.

When he'd first known her she'd been a woman alone, with a child, grieving for another who was lost to her. He'd never transgressed beyond the usual boundary between employer and employee. Later, he'd respected the fact that Kate loved another man, was happily married, and even after Eliot's untimely death had remained respectful, careful not to overstep the mark. Yet surely he could at least be her friend. She was certainly in dire need of one now.

'Where is she? Where's Kate? Has she been got ready for the journey? I insist you bring her to me at once, or you'll answer for the consequences.'

Elvira made no move to obey. She simply stood smiling slyly at him, eyes glacial, not at all the kind of smile to fill him with confidence that she would do as he asked. Then she put her hands together and began to clap, very slowly, chains and bracelets jangling and clanking in an ugly sound.

'Very good. An excellent performance, if I might say so. You should be in the theatre. Your talents are wasted as a factory manager, if that is indeed what you are. More likely a con-man. Sadly, I spend my life seeing through such performances put on by clever patients, their agile, twisted little minds devising all manner of schemes to get past me. But I am not so easily fooled. Kate is going nowhere. She is not leaving this building unless her sister-in-law, or some other appropriate family member, personally comes to escort her out of it. And you are not that person.'

'Indeed I am. She isn't staying here another minute.' Toby pushed past her, flung himself through the door and strode up the corridor in seconds.

'Kate!' he cried, and again in a louder voice, 'Kate, where are you? *Kate!*'

Elvira came charging after him, screaming at the top of her voice, the pounding of her heavy tread loud in his ears as she shouted for help from her nurses. 'Leave the building at once, Mr Lynch, or I shall be forced to have you escorted from it.'

'You are welcome to try.' He ignored her, and began to fling open doors.

'Don't you *dare* go in there!' She shook a ham-sized fist at him, bracelets rattling with fury as she galloped towards him, attempting to fling herself across one door to prevent him from opening it, just a second too late.

A bathroom full of miserable, naked creatures being scrubbed and evidently half-frozen to death judging by the chill that emanated from the room. Toby flung open another door, the power of the blistering heat that met him almost knocking him sideways. He saw a fretful woman encased in blankets, her wild eyes begging him to help her.

'What is this? Have I stumbled into hell? *Kate?*' But it was not Kate and he left the poor woman to her agony. He couldn't save everyone.

Elvira made a grab for Toby, clawing at him, frantically trying to drag him away, nurses homing in from all directions to prevent his incursion, pushing and shoving at him to make

338

him give up and leave.

But nothing would stop him now. Toby cast them all aside, fought them off with a strength that surprised himself, let alone them. He flung open yet another door and some instinct told him at once that he'd found her. Perhaps it was the colour of the near-shorn head of the woman who lay unmoving on something like a hospital trolley. She was as waxy pale as the white sheet that shrouded her and for one terrible instant he thought he was too late, that she was dead. But then she turned anguished eyes to his and he knew that he was right.

'Kate?'

Cracked lips barely parted in greeting. 'Oh, Toby,' she breathed. 'You've come for me at last. I knew you would.'

He went to her and as Kate tried to get up stopped her, gently stroking her cheek with the back of his hand. 'Kate, Kate, I...' His voice choked on a tide of emotion and he could say no more, not able to believe what he saw.

Yet she smiled up at him, weak and fragile though she undoubtedly was, her face gaunt, cheeks hollow, grey eyes no longer filled with the storm of a Lakeland sky or blazing with passion for life but dazed with shock and fear, great dark caverns of agony.

Toby could find no words. The sight of her shocked him to the core and all he could do was to gather her gently in his arms, burying his face in the crook of her shoulder as she clung to him, and he whispered her name over and over.

They tried to stop him but he brushed them

aside like flies. With only the single sheet to cover her nakedness and protect her from the bitter cold, Toby carried Kate from the castle, Elvira and her evil helpmates chasing after him, screaming abuse. He settled Kate in the back of the car still swathed in the sheet, climbed into the driving seat and swiftly drove away while patients stood in the yard and cheered.

# 34

Kate could not believe her good fortune. It seemed like a dream, a blissful, magical, wonderful dream. Here she was, in a Scottish hotel, her children beside her and Toby too, grinning in that lovely, cheery way of his, every now and then rubbing a hand through his tousled fair hair and saying things like: 'That was a close shave', and 'I can't believe I just did that'. His daring behaviour had been so at odds with his more usual, quiet style, that Kate found herself marvelling with him.

'Did you see Elvira's face as you marched out the door?'

'And everyone cheering? It was tremendous.'

'Oh, I wish I'd seen my friend Peggy. I never got the chance to say goodbye.'

'If she's a friend, she'll just be glad you got out.'

Kate fell silent, wishing there was some way she could help her friend, but there was none. The magistrates would decide poor Peggy's fate.

She could hear the wind in the trees outside the window, smell the fragrances of pine logs, hot chicken soup and shampoo. Kate felt certain these sounds and scents would forever signify freedom to her.

Flora had tenderly bathed her in hot, soapy water in a beautifully appointed bathroom, anointed her sores and blisters with arnica ointment, had ordered for her a supper of tasty chicken broth which she was now urging her to eat beside a lovely, blazing fire. If before Kate had been in hell, this must surely be heaven, with all the people she loved and needed around her.

'You lied,' she said, smiling across at Toby. He was sitting watching her eat fresh, crusty bread, as if he'd never seen anyone do such a thing before. 'Not only that, you forged Lucy's hand-writing.'

'If I hadn't, you'd still be there, locked up in that awful place.'

Kate gave a quiet sigh of resignation. 'I doubt I'd've been there for much longer.'

'You knew that Lucy intended to move you?'

Kate frowned, shaking her head slightly. 'I mean, I wouldn't have survived. You saved me from almost certain death, or else the onset of true madness.'

'I'm sure he did,' Callum agreed. 'I only wish we'd managed it sooner. We couldn't find where she'd taken you.'

'Didn't you get my letters?'

Blank looks from them all, a shake of the head from Callum, more tears from Flora. 'I missed you so much, Mammy! No one would tell me

341

where you were or when you were coming home. I thought you might be dead.'

'Aw, don't cry, me darlin'. Of course I'm not dead. Mammy's here now, safe and sound, and nothing terrible is ever going to happen to me again. Everything's going to be fine.'

Once the soup and buttery bread had been eaten, and Flora had finally succumbed to exhaustion and fallen asleep in her mother's arms, Toby and Callum revealed the full story of how they'd discovered Kate's whereabouts. Kate responded by telling them a little about her ordeal. The two men grew angry as she related her experiences, and she strove to reassure them.

'No, don't blame them too much. Some of the nurses weren't so bad. One, an Irish nurse, actually saved me from a beating one day. And I think many genuinely believed that what they were doing would have some beneficial effect. Maybe it does, in some cases. Who am I to judge?'

'But there was nothing wrong with you,' Callum insisted.

Toby nodded. 'Lucy was the one who lied, trapped you into going to that dreadful place. She lied to Callum and to Flora, to all of us, insisting you'd tried to kill yourself.'

'I guessed as much.'

'What are we to do about her?'

'Aye,' agreed Callum. 'That's the most important question. What the hell do we do about Madam Lucy?'

'Nothing.'

'*What?*' The two men spoke as one.

'There's nothing we can do. Once before we

342

tried going to the police and she made me out to be an hysterical idiot, out of my mind with grief. If I now accuse her of trying to lock me away, she'll only say it was for my own good, that she felt that I needed care and shelter, or some such tale. She can prove that I was indeed suffering from depression, though in fact I was coming out of it, starting to feel better and much more meself. When she asked me to join her for a weekend's jaunt, wasn't I looking forward to dressing up and having a good time? I even bought myself a new frock. But how can I prove any of that?'

Toby managed an ironic smile. 'She's a clever, manipulative woman, that's for sure.'

'So how can we refute her argument that she meant it only for the best? The fact that the castle turned out to be little better than a torture chamber, she'll claim to be no fault of hers.'

'I can't bear her to get away with it,' Toby growled, while Callum sank into his own gloomy thoughts.

Kate managed an ironic smile. 'She always has before.'

Kate thought she might have trouble sleeping, but she fell into a deep sleep almost the moment she lay down beside Flora. It wasn't a particularly restful night but one filled with confused dreams of Toby and Peggy, of being trapped in a room, something pressing down on her preventing her from getting out; of heat and cold and overwhelming fear, which brought her to a shuddering, sweating wakefulness some time around dawn.

How long would it be before she recovered from her ordeal? A lifetime perhaps.

And did she even wish to return to Tyson Lodge? Kate rather thought not. Toby was absolutely right, Lucy shouldn't be allowed to get away with this. But the prospect of confronting her with what she'd done made Kate feel sick to her stomach. It was too soon to be making decisions but a part of her longed simply to up sticks and leave, to go somewhere completely fresh and start again. She could take her share of the business, leave the house to Lucy, and move out. Find them a place of their own to live in.

Kate stroked her sleeping daughter's cheek, lay back down beside her, drinking in the beauty of her face, and finally fell into a peaceful sleep. She was safe, and with Flora again. What else mattered?

Kate was absolutely correct in her assessment of Lucy's reaction. When they arrived back at Tyson Lodge the next day, her sister-in-law was all sweet concern and heartfelt cries of amazement that Kate should be deemed fit and well enough to be sent home.

'How secretive and naughty of you, Callum, and you too, Toby, not to tell me what you were about! But of course I'm so pleased that Kate has made such a wonderful recovery. An unbelievable and delightful surprise! Wasn't I right to send you to such a marvellous place, dear sister-in-law, where you received the best possible care? Was I not, Aunts?'

'Indeed you were, Lucy dear,' Aunt Cissie

344

agreed. 'How very clever of you to discover such a marvellous place.'

'It was darling Teddy's idea. A friend of a friend recommended it to him.'

'Well, they've done a good job, and returned our own dear Kate to us as good as new.' Aunt Vera actually put her arms about Kate and gave her a little hug. Probably the first time she'd ever touched her in all the years they'd lived under the same roof.

'Almost,' Kate conceded. 'Though still a little frail around the edges.'

Vera suddenly seemed to grow aware of how thin she'd become and her smile faded a little, to be replaced by a frown of concern.

'Dear me, yes, indeed you are.'

'Don't look so worried, I'm fine.' No thanks to Lucy, Kate thought, fixing her with such a fierce gaze that she grew uncomfortable and looked away.

Cissie said, 'Of course you are, dear. Nothing wrong with you that a few good nights' sleep won't soon put right. Once we've got some home cooking inside you, and fattened you up, you'll be quite your old self again, will you not, dear?'

'I certainly intend to be,' Kate agreed, her arm about Flora as she again met Lucy's gaze unblinking.

'There we are then,' said Cissie. 'Clever, clever Lucy.'

Clever she may be, but Lucy seemed far from pleased to have her plans ruined, all her hopes and wishes set aside and her rival back in situ.

The atmosphere in the house was rigid with tension, as sharp as the hoar frost now settling on Kendal's meadows, as cold as the ice forming on the River Kent.

The two women barely exchanged a word, civil or otherwise. Even the aunts lost their will to keep the conversation going and would sit in watchful silence, mealtimes becoming unbearably tense.

Kate told herself not to care. She was free. Not feeling too well, admittedly, but longing to get back to work and start living again. A few more days' peace and rest and she would feel fit enough to face the factory. Only then would she begin to make decisions about her future.

But the good food Cissie had promised her did not come from Mrs Petty's kitchen, nor feature any of the dishes Kate had dreamed of while in the castle. No steak and kidney pie or Lancashire hot pot, but lamb, cooked rare in unusual sauces by a smart French chef. Kate was devastated to learn that Mrs Petty and Ida had gone. Somehow, the house didn't seem the same without them.

She was devastated too over what had been done to her garden: those precious trees that Eliot had planted, intending them for the next generation, for Callum. Now they were gone, all chopped down, their roots ripped from the rich, brown earth to make way for a new tennis court, the latest fad apparently. It was the final straw and Kate put her face in her hands and wept.

'Why did you do it?'

Lucy tossed her head, pretending not to

understand. 'I don't see any problem, a tennis court is far more beneficial to the property than a few extra trees, and much more fun.'

'You had no right to make decisions about my house without my permission!'

'You weren't here to ask, and a decision needed to be made. I was already running the house and the factory. Deciding where to put a tennis court was trivial by comparison.'

It was all too much for Kate. At last the tension between them broke and erupted into the most terrible row. They argued about trees, the loss of Callum's heritage, the danger of tennis balls hitting the summer house, when really it wasn't about that at all. It went so much deeper.

Lucy's calm finally slipped and she screamed at Kate, 'I can do as I please because you are of no account! I am in charge now.'

'Only because you stole my life away from me. Well, I want it back!'

Lucy turned away on a shrug of dismissal. 'I did no such thing. You were sick, out of your mind, probably still are. The castle was the best place for you.'

'*You* know, although you'll never admit it, that I wasn't out of my mind at all. The truth is that you wanted me *out of the way*, so that you could take over. You planned the whole thing, set me up to go with you on that weekend, knowing exactly where you were taking me and that I wouldn't be coming back. All those lies, all that trickery.'

Lucy pushed her face close to Kate's, spitting with fury. 'You got what you deserved. Serve you right for thrusting your way into Eliot's bed all those years ago. Fortunately he's dead and gone, and your power with him. The family doesn't have to tolerate you and your brats any longer. They were glad to see you go and certainly don't want you back.' And, laughing with bitter satisfaction, she walked away.

Kate remained where she was, desperately striving for control, fists clenched in furious frustration. It was like battering against a stone wall, nothing moved the woman, nothing could break that ice-cold certainty that Lucy could do exactly as she pleased with other people's lives. What on earth had she been up to while Kate had been away? That was the worry. She was soon to discover the answer to that particular question.

# 35

Kate found the letter on the hall table. It was addressed to Lucy, bearing a local postmark, but she knew who had sent it instantly. Hadn't she received enough formal little letters from the bank manager herself to recognise the typeface of his secretary's typewriter: the *e* for instance had a break on the left side, and the dot of the *i* always left a little hole. This letter was undoubtedly from the bank and although it carried Lucy's name on it – Mrs L. Tyson, Director – it was addressed to Tysons Shoe Industries. Unquestionably a business letter. Kate picked it up and slit open the envelope.

As she read it she could actually hear the blood singing in her ears. She felt herself go hot and cold as if she were back in that room, being induced into a fever.

Then she collected her coat and left the house before anyone saw her.

'What is this all about? Why does the bank manager want to see me so urgently?' She put the letter on to Toby's desk, watching carefully for any change of expression. There was none. He wasn't in the least bit surprised.

Wearily, he said, 'I was going to tell you today, on your first day back in the office. I didn't tell you before, Kate, because I couldn't bear to spoil your first nights of freedom by revealing the truth about what was happening here.' He smiled ruefully at her. 'I'm not keen to spoil your first day back at work with too much reality either, but it must be done. I informed the bank that you were home. Sadly, they must have sent someone round with this by hand.'

'Why the urgency?'

'Because our finances aren't good, I'm afraid.'

From the moment Kate had opened the letter, she'd felt sick with worry. She'd tried to prepare herself for possible bad news on her return: perhaps hearing that the new line of ladies' shoes had been a failure or not sold as well as expected, for instance. Or that there had been strikes and production had failed maybe. It seemed she was right to be concerned. 'What is it, Toby? Tell me what has gone wrong.'

He sank into his chair, running a hand through

349

his hair. 'God knows what she does with the money. I hate to gossip, Kate, but some of it must have been used to pay for that new Daimler.'

'Daimler?' Kate paled. 'We can't afford to pay for a...'

'I know.'

'Are you trying to tell me that Lucy has been on one of her spending sprees again? Oh, dear Lord, no. Not more trouble.'

She swayed on her feet and Toby leaped to her side, made her sit down and personally fetched her a cup of tea. Only when he was sure that she had drunk it, even though she refused the biscuit he brought with it, did he begin to explain, gently and tactfully, all that had gone on in her absence.

He described the way Lucy had interfered in the business all along the line, increasing her personal allowance and the household budget; how she'd hired more maids and the expensive French chef. 'Not only that but she's disposed of some of our best operatives, and replaced Sam Blenkinsop by putting Jack in charge of sales and marketing, yet he isn't bringing in the orders. Sam had the greater experience and did much better. *And* she insisted on making Jack a director.'

Fear gnawed at Kate. It was as if she'd failed, as if she'd let Eliot down by not properly protecting his bequest. She'd failed to protect his trees and, even more vital, his business. Kate had always believed that Tysons Industries would be safe in her hands, yet it had not been. And she didn't even yet know how bad the situation was. 'Surely the company can't be in too much danger? Our borrowings are low, our assets high.'

'Not any longer.' Toby's discomfiture increased as he outlined Lucy's visits to the bank manager, the loans she had taken out.

Kate felt as though someone had kicked her in the chest, robbing her of breath. 'How dare she? How could she do such a thing without my say so?'

Toby shook his head. 'You weren't in any position to stop her, Kate. I expect she convinced the bank manager you were gone for good, that she had power of attorney.'

'But what has she done with these loans? What has happened to all the money? How can we have reached such a state in less than twelve months?'

'We were just hanging on. With the post-war boom over and industry in a slump, we depended upon the new lines you'd set up for our survival. Unfortunately, when the orders started pouring in, I didn't have sufficient operatives to carry out the work. Lucy had sacked them. We got behind, customers became irritated and disillusioned and finally took their trade elsewhere. It's been a downward slope ever since and I've had to lay off more and more men because I don't have the work to give them.

'Even old established customers are bailing out and Jack's failed to stem the tide. He's been too busy enjoying himself, living for today, just like his mother. As for Lucy, she's not only been spending wildly on her own account, it turns out she has also been lending money to those nefarious friends of hers: darling Teddy and the Bennet boys, to mention but a few. Both I and the accountant tried to stop her, but she wouldn't listen. We've done our best to make cuts, reduce expenditure, but with the best will in the world money has been bleeding away faster than we can earn it.'

Kate glanced again at the letter, holding it in a hand trembling with shock. 'And now that I'm home, the bank manager expects me to put everything right?'

'I believe he may be growing rather impatient.'

There was a silence, Kate was the one to break it. 'I don't seem to be doing very well, do I? Eliot trusted me with his company and I seem to be losing it.'

'Not you, Kate. Dear, sweet Kate, it isn't your fault.'

She glanced up, surprised by the unexpected endearment, to find his eyes burning into hers. Something lurched deep inside her, some unexpected response which surprised her, Toby was ... Toby was her manager, an employee, the man she worked with. Nothing more. Or was that no longer true?

'Don't blame yourself. It's not for me to say who is to blame, but the fault does not lie with you, Kate, of that I am quite certain. I too feel guilty. I wanted to hand back to you a healthy, thriving business, not one on the verge of bankruptcy.'

'Bankruptcy? Surely not.' She looked at him more carefully then, saw the haunted expression in his eyes, the gauntness of his face. While she'd been battling with Elvira, he'd had Lucy to contend with. Battles of his own to fight. It couldn't have been easy.

She stretched out a hand to grasp his, and his fingers curled around hers. 'Toby, whatever happens I want you to know that no blame will be attached to you. I do not hold you responsible in any way for the state of the business or the behaviour of my sister-in-law. How could I when she is quite beyond control? Beyond the pale.'

They each managed a wry smile at that, despite the bleak reality they were facing.

He stroked her hand, his gaze fixed upon hers. 'I appreciate your faith in me more than I can say. It's been hell these last months, worrying about where you might be, when and how we could find you and bring you home. I can't tell you how relieved I am to see you back in this office.'

Kate gazed up into his darkly mysterious grey eyes and found it quite impossible to look away. 'Thank you for not giving up on me. There seemed to be very little I could do to get myself out of that place.'

Another silence, a little longer this time. 'Do you know what I'm thinking now?'

She shook her head.

'That I would like, very much, to kiss you. There, I've said it. Maybe I shouldn't have but I won't take it back. I must be drunk with the joy of having you home, it's quite gone to my head.' He gave a sheepish smile, and Kate chuckled.

'Perhaps, as my rescuer, you deserve a reward.' And she leaned forward to place a kiss full on his lips. The feel of his mouth moving against hers was extraordinary, catching her unawares with the emotion it unleashed. He gathered her face between his hands, holding her gently while he kissed her. Except that the kiss itself was not in the least little bit gentle. It held passion and power, urgency and desire, creating in her a need she didn't dare put a name to. Kate had quite forgotten how it felt to be so close to a man, to be needed. She wanted the feeling to go on for ever but he suddenly pulled away, turned abruptly from her.

It felt like a slap in the face.

He stood at the window, fists clenched, shoulders hunched, staring out at the river. 'I'm sorry, I don't know what came over me. That was unforgivable, a bad mistake.'

Kate's cheeks were flushed with embarrassment and she didn't know what to say, where to look, didn't know how to ease the awkwardness of the moment. To be kissed with such passion and then told it was a bad mistake seemed wrong somehow. Almost an insult. 'Is that all it was, a mistake?'

Toby turned to face her, his expression cool and distant, clearly back in control of his emotions. 'I believe so. You are my employer. We don't have that kind of relationship. I overstepped the mark in a moment of weakness. I apologise.'

'I thought perhaps it was because you wanted to welcome me home, that you couldn't help yourself?'

Something flickered in his gaze, but was gone again before she could properly read it. 'Then I should practise more self-control, show proper respect.'

Kate stared at him, trying to understand what lay behind his words, trying to decide what she felt. Was it his respect she wanted, or something quite different? 'You think that would be best, do you?'

'I do, in the circumstances. You have enough problems already.'

Kate looked away, rubbed a finger over the trace of a headache. He might be right about that. She straightened her spine. 'I'd better go and keep my appointment with the bank manager.'

Toby seemed to breathe a sigh of relief as if he'd got himself into a hole and she had just rescued him from it. 'Do you want me to come with you?'

Kate shook her head. 'No, better I deal with this on my own.'

'Yes, of course. Call me if you need me.'

Later that same day, Kate sat on the edge of her bed, too numb to cry, too stunned even to think properly. It was all over. Everything was lost. No use now ranting at Lucy, accusing her of greed and selfishness, of stupidly throwing away all their futures on a hedonistic splurge of high living.

Where was the point?

It was all far too late, and no one would suffer more than Lucy herself. She'd been determined, at any cost, to own the goose that laid the golden eggs, and her own insatiable greed, her appetite for spending, had killed it.

Kate had spent the afternoon closeted with the bank manager. It had been the most difficult and painful interview she had ever endured. The accountants were eventually called in. Toby too had come along, eager to do what he could to help despite his earlier reluctance to be involved.

For what seemed like hours they'd pored over the books, studying the figures, discussing, arguing, debating over what could be done.

No solution had been found.

Finally, and painfully, a meeting of the entire board had been called and the directors informed, with all due sorrow and regret, that Tysons Industries was no more. They were finished. The company had gone bankrupt.

# 36

Selling up was hard. Kate sat in the loft of the summer house for hour upon hour, remembering, saying her own private farewells. Most painful of all was the destruction of Eliot's garden following the loss of his precious trees, dug up for a tennis court that none of them would ever now play on. Strangely, she grieved more for the lost trees than for Tyson Lodge itself, this fine old Lakeland mansion. They'd come to symbolise not only Eliot's love for his son and family, but his hopes for the future, one now lost to them all.

This house, she decided, had brought her nothing but heartbreak, particularly in recent years, and she would take her leave of it without regret. She and Eliot had enjoyed a few happy years here, but in the main Kate had found more misery than happiness within its four walls.

For this reason she was determined to be resolute, to accept what fate had dealt her. Nevertheless, the day the bailiffs moved in was harder than she could ever have imagined. The reality of losing everything was utterly devastating. The family were allowed to keep their clothes and a few personal items, but not much else.

Vera remained hatchet-faced throughout the entire ordeal, watching men crawl all over Tyson Lodge, rifling through drawers for any valuables and then carrying them away; walking off with objects that she considered belonged to the family and should not be removed.

Not simply the new sofas, dining table and chairs that Lucy had bought, but other more precious items: pictures that had hung on the walls for decades; vases, oriental jars, various throws and cushions; an elephant's foot umbrella stand that used to stand in the hall; a china cabinet crammed with unrelated pieces of Wedgwood and Royal Doulton; several small Japanese tables; even a selection of silver photo frames still holding formal family portraits.

'Give that to me!' Aunt Vera roared at one of the bailiffs. 'Let me at least remove the photographs.'

'Begging yer pardon, ma'am.'

She pounced on another unfortunate soul. 'Put that statuette down this instant, young man. You'll break the head off if you carry it in such a careless fashion. And take your grubby little hands off those lace antimacassars, if you please. They were my grandmother's.'

Mortified, he apologised most profusely, was

discreet and respectful, calling her Miss Tyson as was only right and proper, but still he walked off with the object in question.

What hurt the aunts most was that each and every item would be sold at Kendal Auction Rooms, putting their humiliation on public display. Cissie's handkerchief was soon sopping wet with her constant tears.

Kate watched them both with increasing pity and sorrow. Poor Cissie. Poor Vera. They had hoped to end their days in peace and comfort, not in shame and bankruptcy.

For her own part, she watched the possessions go without a trace of regret. She'd quite liked the drawing room as it had been, with its faded, shabby blue sofas, the scratched walnut sideboard and rugs full of dog hairs. Its reincarnation, under Lucy's regime, had resembled nothing so much as a museum; a 'symphony of light and shade', was the way her sister-in-law had described it. All white and gold with elegant French sofas and pretty little tables whose legs looked thin enough to snap if anything heavier than a cup was set upon them. Very much Lucy's style.

Who, in Kendal, would pay good money for such items? Kate wondered. No doubt some of Lucy's friends might, and she would have the humiliation of spotting the pieces whenever she called on them, perhaps being obliged to take tea on her own sofa in Teddy's house, or to see her finest, long-stemmed champagne glasses acquired by the Bennet boys.

She would be mortified.

Jack had fled abroad in a furious sulk, determined to make his fortune in France or Italy. He'd refused even to speak to his mother since it all came out, having believed in her utterly: thinking the directorship would make him free to live the life of a gentleman without the necessity to work at all. There'd been a painful row between them, Jack accusing her of cheating even him, her own son.

Georgie was obliged to leave school early, giving up all hope of going to university, and he too would now be seeking employment.

The shame of what she'd done should, by rights, haunt Lucy for the rest of her life, yet you wouldn't think so to look at her. When Kate had last seen her, she was already making plans to find a housekeeper to look after the aunts, suggesting the two maiden ladies take in lodgers to provide themselves with an income.

Strangely, the worst moment came when the newly appointed French chef left in a huff after a furious row with one of the bailiffs who had attempted to deprive him of a fine set of steel knives.

It became almost farcical but this, more than anything, served to bring home to Lucy what she had lost and she threw the most stupendous tantrum, stamping her feet and lashing out at anyone who came near. Kate thought she would remember Lucy's furious screams to the end of her days.

Vera was so alarmed she called the doctor who attempted to calm Lucy at first with a few severe words, then a light sedative, and finally, when her hysterics threatened to get entirely out of control, with a sharp slap across her cheek.

That certainly did the trick, although Kate rather thought the result would be that Lucy would be finding herself a new doctor in future.

When it was all done and the house completely emptied, Kate handed the keys to the bailiffs and Toby drove the two maiden aunts, together with Lucy, to their old home in Heversham.

Cissie did her utmost to persuade Kate to come too but she declined to accompany them.

'I know our old house is old and shabby, has been unlived in for a long while and we shan't be able to afford servants. Lucy is already complaining about that. I know she is quite impossible but we must look after her, you see. She is family, and so are you, my dear. Are you sure you wouldn't be better off with us? You'd be most welcome.'

Kate kissed and hugged her close, tears threatening to fall. 'No, dear Cissie, haven't ye been like an aunt to me too over the years, and to my children? I can't imagine how I would have coped without you. You've come to be a very dear friend, but I must go me own way. We need a change, a new beginning, d'you see?'

Again Cissie wiped away a tear. 'I shall miss little Flora.'

'To be sure you will, her endless chatter if nothing else. We're going to stay with Millie in Manchester, till we can sort ourselves out. She's offered to have us, and I've accepted. I shall send you the address when we get settled, then we can write.'

Cissie dabbed at her eyes, blew her nose rather

loudly. 'That would be lovely. Oh dear, this is all most unpleasant. You will come and see us, won't you, my dear? We are still family, remember. Dear Eliot would want us to keep in touch.'

Kate promised that she would, and made her escape before Cissie started blubbing again.

Callum was more upset over not hearing from Bunty than at losing his job, for all it left him with no qualifications. Like all young men he believed he had plenty of time to earn new ones, believed absolutely in his own ability to make a good future for himself, but it was essential to him that Bunty be a part of that future.

He'd written her so many letters, put them in the letter box with his own hand since his mother's warning so that no one could intercept them, yet he'd never received a single reply.

Could she have moved to a different school? He'd begun to think that may be the case. Lucy had moved her, as she so loved to do as a means of maintaining control, and no doubt had in some way prevented Bunty from writing to him, or else forbidden her to do so. Her power was awesome and poor Bunty probably in no position to defy her.

Callum was quite certain that he was right, and fully prepared to be patient for as long as it took for Bunty to break free. He would be waiting for her when she did.

The company had been bought for a derisory sum by another shoe manufacturer from the south; one of Tysons' competitors. They'd agreed to keep on a skeleton workforce, including Toby,

361

although how long the arrangement would last was anyone's guess as they also intended to bring in men of their own. Kate put in a word for her son with the new management and they graciously agreed that he could continue but Callum refused, on the grounds that if his mother was no longer working in the factory, neither should he.

He also refused point blank to move to Manchester with them, insisting that he could find work in Kendal, that that was where he belonged.

'I'll be fine, don't worry about me. How would Bunty know where to find me, if I vanished into a huge city like Manchester? I must be here, in Kendal, when she comes home at the end of the year. We mean to be married then.'

Kate tried to be kind, tried to warn him that Bunty might have changed her mind about him and that was why she hadn't written, but Callum wouldn't have it.

'No, it'll be all right once she gets back to Kendal, I know it will. Lucy can't stop us getting married once Bunty comes of age.'

'But she isn't twenty-one for a couple of years yet. A lot can happen before then. She may well find someone else, and Lucy will almost certainly do everything in her power to prevent you from getting together, be under no illusions there, m'darlin'.'

Callum merely smiled, hugged his mother and sister, and promised that he would visit them regularly, and that she and Flora could likewise visit him in Kendal.

He was lodging with a friend Kate didn't entirely approve of, and by the time she left her son still hadn't found himself a job. But he was almost a grown man, so what could she do?

However difficult it was to see everything she and Eliot had once loved taken away to be sold, saying goodbye to friends at the factory, to Toby in particular, proved to be the hardest thing of all. He had become her best friend, the person she'd turned to with her troubles. The one who had rescued her from a place of torment. Kate couldn't think how she would manage without him.

'Sure and I can't say I'm sorry to see that house go,' she told him. 'But the thought of losing all we've worked for at the factory breaks me heart in two, so it does. It's unbearable. All that effort, all that labour and enterprise, all those marvellous ideas – gone, lost for ever.'

'It's all going to be very different.' Toby sighed in despair, wandering back and forth in the office, his lean, loose-limbed figure restless and unsettled. 'Not sure I fancy working here any more, not without you.'

'Don't be a daft eejit, you still have employment, have ye not? Who knows what the future might bring.'

'You aren't serious about going to live in Manchester, are you, Kate? You aren't even properly well yet.'

'I'm perfectly fit, so I am, making a good recovery thanks to you, but I do wish Callum would listen to me and stick to his apprenticeship. Unfortunately, his pride won't let him. He's refused to come with us, so he'll have no job and no home to call his own. What if something should happen to him?'

Toby smiled. 'I'll keep an eye out for him, you know I will. I might even be able to help find him employment, I know one or two independent shoemakers. It's not Callum that worries me, it's you.' His grey eyes looked so sad, so beseeching, that she almost reached out to him then, but stopped herself just in time.

'I'll be fine. I can't bear to stay and see everything...' She stopped, her voice breaking with emotion.

Toby waited for her to find the strength to go on, but, as so often happened, she seemed to have lost the thread of the conversation, her mind engaged elsewhere.

Kate rubbed her forehead with two fingers, trying to ease away the ache which constantly plagued her. She was thinking that the loss of all their property and the business – Eliot's bequest left in her keeping – meant she would now have nothing to pass on to their son. Callum would have no inheritance of any kind. It meant that all those sacrifices she'd made years ago on his behalf had been to no avail.

He was now unemployed, like many another, admittedly with some skills at his fingertips but no proper qualifications. Only one step removed from Poor House Lane.

Despite all her hard work and effort, all the battles she'd fought, she'd lost. Lucy had won and destroyed them all. It was little comfort to know that her sister-in-law had ruined her own life too, and that of her own sons. Kate wished she could have found the strength to fight harder, to hang on to the company at least. In her heart of hearts she felt that she'd let Eliot down, let Callum down, failed everyone, in fact, even the aunts.

She gave a small, tired sigh, tears sliding down her cheeks which she brushed quickly away. Self-pity only sent her hurtling back into that dark pit of depression, and the merciless hands of Elvira. Kate put back her shoulders and managed a smile. 'I shall miss you, Toby, you will ever remain my very best friend.'

'You know that I'd like us to be more than friends, don't you?'

Kate looked into his face, saw the anxiety there, the rawness of hope in those dark eyes and knew what it had cost him to reveal his feelings, particularly after that kiss he had so bitterly regretted. She dropped her gaze, not wishing to witness the pain she was about to cause him.

'It's too soon. As you said yourself, we don't have that kind of relationship and I don't think I'm ready for any further complications, not just yet.'

'I'd give you all the time in the world if only you'd stay?'

Kate shook her head, swallowed the lump of fear that seemed to be lodged in her throat. 'I do care for you, Toby, but I'm not sure in what way or even if it's enough. I'm too confused, too sore after all that has happened. I need a breathing space. Can you understand that?'

She was meeting his gaze now, begging him to see her point of view. 'I have to make a new begin-ning, a fresh start. If I don't know what to do with my own life, can't even trust myself to make sensible decisions or reliable judgements, I'd only be a liability, a danger even, to everyone around me. I need to find myself again, do you see?'

He nodded, struggled to smile, seemed to fight a small battle with himself and then reached out for her, pulling her roughly into his arms, holding her tight against his chest. 'God, I'll miss you, Kate. You don't know how much.'

This time the kiss carried with it all his emotions from the depth of his soul. Deeply passionate, there was no sign in it of any concern for a lack of respect or overstepping the line, but then they were no longer employer and employee. With Kate held tight in his arms it seemed as if he might never let her go, and as she clung to him with equal fervour, answering the need that was swelling and blooming inside her like a flower being brought to new life, she didn't want him to.

When he finally released her, as abruptly as he had pulled her to him, she kept her eyes closed for a second longer, until she felt the cold draught of her loss. She could change everything now, with just a few words. But Kate said nothing, and the silence strung out endlessly between them.

Toby rubbed his hands together then shoved them in his pockets, as if afraid they might develop a will of their own and snatch her to him again. 'If you need me for anything, you've only to say the word.'

Then he turned on his heel and strode away, shoulders hunched.

Kate put a trembling hand to her mouth and watched him go in tearful silence.

# 37

Kate never imagined that moving to Manchester would be easy. It might represent a new beginning but many of her problems she carried with her, perhaps would do so forever. Her first concern was for her children, wondering if she'd done the right thing; worrying about Callum who'd lost his apprenticeship and was unemployed; fretting over Flora, thinking she might miss her friends too much and find it hard to settle.

Flora was growing up and never complained, although Kate noticed she'd become very protective of her mother, and more than a little clingy.

Kate herself grew a little stronger each day, although she remained troubled by headaches. She also suffered strange lapses of memory and panic attacks, genuine ones this time, not the imaginary sort manufactured by Jack or Lucy. This troubled her, and she put the blame firmly on the treatment she'd received at Elvira's hands, on the experiments that had been carried out upon her.

But that was all in the past. It had taken no more than a few days for her to fall in love with this city. At first Manchester had seemed huge and noisy, used as Kate was to the comparatively gentle bustle of a market town. She'd felt disorientated, still unsure of herself. Yet every small decision taken, even what to cook for Flora's tea, represented a small step towards her ultimate independence.

Despite everything she'd been through – dealing with her grief in the aftermath of the accident, losing the baby, her incarceration at the asylum, the loss of the firm – for the first time since Eliot's death Kate felt a genuine belief that she could find happiness again. Thirty-four was surely still young enough to make a fresh start and she was more than ready to face the challenge. Being far removed from Kendal, and from her sister-in-law, was a huge relief, providing the breathing space she so desperately needed.

But at what cost?

Lucy did not feel herself young enough to start again, she felt old beyond her years, cheated and robbed of a brilliant future despite all her careful planning and scheming. They said forty was a turning point for women and it certainly had been for her. She'd been let down by everybody, surrounded by fools and idiots who hadn't the first idea how to run a business. Even her darling Jack had deserted her. Georgie too had insisted on bunking with one of his pals, refusing to live in a 'mausoleum', as he called it. And really, she couldn't blame him.

But here she was, stuck in this dreadful house with the mad aunts.

Lucy paced back and forth in her bedroom, the largest in the house but still inadequate so far as she was concerned, and felt like a trapped tiger in a cage. What could she do? It was a painful reality that if she'd failed to find herself a husband when she'd been comparatively wealthy and below forty, there was little hope now.

Returning to her desk, she screwed up the piece of paper she'd been writing on and tossed it aside, then picked up her pen and began again on her letter to Bunty. Still ignorant of what had befallen them, the girl had to be told that no further funds were available to pay for her life in Switzerland. It was proving to be an extremely difficult letter to write because what other future did Lucy have to offer her daughter?

No beautiful home, and worse still, no money.

Lucy had written to the headmistress, hoping for an introduction to some family of note who might take Bunty under their wing, but had as yet received no reply. Her last hope was that perhaps the girl herself knew of someone.

What else could she do? Teddy and the Bennet boys once loved to tease her, calling her their 'old fruit', and Lucy had tried to take it in good part, assuming it was meant kindly, that they were her true friends. Yet there was no sign of these people now. Despite her entertaining them with fashionable dinner parties and weekend affairs, subsidising them through sticky times when they'd been short of funds, not a single one of these so-called friends of hers had picked up the telephone and commiserated with her over her loss. Not one had called to see how she was, to offer a crumb of comfort or soft word of condolence. They'd cut her off completely.

No one had contacted her save for the loathsome Swainson, of course. He'd turned up again, like a bad penny, and Lucy had taken great satisfaction in telling him that the well had run dry. She hadn't hung around to hear his curses.

Now she felt dull and lifeless, used up and quite wrung out. Even her skin had become sallow, her hair dull, having lost its once glorious sheen, and her voluptuous figure which darling Charles had once admired so much was ballooning out of all proportion. But then, what else did she have to do with her days but eat? Lucy was bored out of her mind.

If she didn't watch out, she would be the one going mad, not Kate O'Connor.

What was the answer? She couldn't stay here, in this shabby old-fashioned Victorian villa, growing old with the maiden aunts. She needed, if not a husband, a benefactor of some sort. She certainly had no intention of seeking a post as companion or governess to earn a crust. Faded gentility did not suit Lucy Tyson.

She glared at the empty sheet of paper, and then the answer came to her, clear as day. If she was too old for marriage, her daughter, at just nineteen, was ripe for it. There was the solution staring her in the face. She must bring Bunty home and marry her off to someone very rich. Once sufficiently besotted and captivated, wedded and bedded, he'd make little protest if Bunty wanted her darling mama to move in too.

The perfect solution. They would both be comfortably placed for life.

Lucy drew out a fresh sheet of paper, gave up all thought of letter-writing for the moment, and began to draw up a list of likely candidates.

If it hadn't been for Millie, Kate thought that she might not have found the courage to go on. Millie opened up her home and her heart to her old friend, just as she had done all those years before in Poor House Lane, welcoming Kate back into her life without a moment's hesitation.

She looked much plumper than the thin, underfed scrap she'd once been, but remained the same cheerful soul within, taking life in her stride and letting nothing get her down, despite having lost three of her children to consumption.

'The hair's gone a bit grey though, love,' she admitted, 'thanks to that rapscallion brood of mine.'

Most of Millie's substantial brood had thankfully left home and gone their separate ways, except for Tommy, who at seventeen was still at home and unwed, and the youngest child, Sal, a year older than Flora, who'd recently started work at the department store where Millie too worked in the haberdashery department. The one in between these two, Maisie, had just got married at sixteen and produced a child of her own. Millie was revelling in having a baby to dangle on her knee again. It wasn't her first grandchild, and certainly wouldn't be her last.

'Aw, wait till you're a grandmother, Kate, won't you just love it?'

'Sure and I hope it won't happen quite yet. Flora is far too young, and Callum can't afford to think of marriage just yet, not till he finds himself a job and a decent place to live. Not that he has a young lady friend, so far as I know.'

'A lad doesn't tell his mam everything.'

'There's Bunty, Mammy,' Flora reminded her.

'Aw, wasn't she no more than a childhood crush? I think Bunty has found another beau, and Callum can't quite accept it.'

Flora's little face was very serious. 'I don't think so, Mammy. Bunty loves our Callum. And he loves her.'

Kate quickly changed the subject. 'So, when am I going to be meeting himself?' referring to Millie's new husband.

'Don't ask,' was the swift response. 'He walked out on me a year or two back, ran off with the new barmaid from the Crown. I haven't seen him since. Good riddance to bad rubbish. We manage well enough without him.'

'We're both widows then, in a way.'

'Aye, you could say so, lass, so yer right welcome to stay. We can keep each other company, a nice quiet life, eh?'

Nobody could accuse Millie of being short of company, or consider her life to be the least little bit quiet. There was a constant stream of visitors popping in at all hours of the day and night since her family had now expanded to include sons and daughters-in-law, as well as numerous grandchildren. And they all seemed to be in constant need of cups of tea, reassuring chats, and an endless outpouring of their problems.

'Eeh, it's like London Road station here, at times,' she laughed.

Kate soon began to feel the need for a quieter place, somewhere to call her own.

372

Bunty came home in a fever of excitement, taking this sudden show of interest from her mother as a display of affection and forgiveness. It was what she had longed for, to be forgiven her terrible sin and allowed home, though it came as a shock to discover where her mother was living, and why.

Lucy hugged her daughter and said how pleased she was to have her home at last. It was important, vital even, that she keep the girl sweet. All their futures depended on Bunty's compliance so she made quite a fuss of her, making her sit beside her on the sofa set at the foot of her bed where they might talk in private.

Bunty drank in the unexpected attention with delight, along with the heady aroma of her mother's scent, and thought that Lucy had grown much rounder, her cheeks and neck sagging just a little, showing her age, although not for a moment would she risk saying as much. She was devastated to learn what had occurred, could barely stop asking questions, wanting to hear all about the bankruptcy, viewing it as the disaster it undoubtedly was.

'Indeed it has been a severe blow,' Lucy admitted.

Bunty's main concern was for Callum, not for how it might affect her own future. 'How has he taken it? He must be so upset not to complete his apprenticeship. I know he loved working with shoes, wanted to make up for being disagreeable to Eliot by making his mother proud of him. He must be unemployed now, absolutely desolate. Oh, poor Callum.'

'Never mind about that boy, child, he will

survive as all these people do. He isn't used to the affluence you are accustomed to. He isn't a gentleman like Jack, so it will be less of a shock for him.'

'Even so...'

'We must think about you, my darling, and your future. See what a fine young woman you've grown into! We need to take you shopping, to buy you some new clothes.'

Bunty was shocked. 'Have we money for such things? I'm quite happy with what I've got, thank you all the same. Don't worry about me, Mama.'

She longed to continue talking about Callum, to say that she needed to see him, but couldn't quite pluck up the courage. Her mother was still talking, rabbiting on about some smart function they'd been invited to on Friday evening and how they must choose what they were to wear with great care, just as if how they looked was the most important thing in the world.

Lucy conceded that it might be wise to exercise a little restraint and curb her spending until their situation improved, which it most certainly would if she had her way. Her plans were already going well and she was really quite hopeful.

The darling girl had slimmed down and lost her puppy fat, and shot up an inch or two. Even her face was passing pretty, or attractive anyway. Her pale, once insipid complexion was now clear and smooth as porcelain, her young body firm and enticing, and her blue eyes sparkled with youth and vigour. Lucy foresaw no problems at all in arousing male interest in her daughter, she had one or two of her acquaintances nibbling at the bait already. But the enterprise must be carefully orchestrated so that it was the right kind of interest, from the right person. Lucy meant to extract a high price for her daughter.

'How very frugal of you, and so absolutely correct. I expect we could do a little refurbishment and retrimming here and there,' she assured Bunty. 'A touch of lace or a flower can make all the difference to a gown. Perhaps we could alter one of mine to fit you. It is absolutely vital that we maintain our standards and not look down-at-heel, don't you agree, dear? We need ... *you* need, because you are my darling girl and deserve the best ... to make a good impression.'

Because she was so relieved to be home, Bunty submitted herself to her mother's ministrations and endless grooming with as much patience as she could muster, not giving the slightest consideration to what might lie behind it. Even the aunts were called upon to help with alterations, and did so with great goodwill, as always.

Bunty's mind was entirely fixed on how she was going to manage to sneak away and see Callum. She had so much to tell him, so many explanations and apologies to make. She could only hope and pray that he still loved her enough to forgive her.

# 38

They stayed with Millie for several weeks until Kate found them a house to rent just off Deansgate: small, admittedly damp in places, but it was a place of their own. It boasted a living kitchen and front parlour, two decent bedrooms on the first floor, plus one in the loft with a sloping ceiling and a high dormer window, which Callum could use whenever he came to visit.

Flora, ever optimistic and missing her brother badly, said, 'Or if he changes his mind and comes to live with us properly, Mammy.'

The house was empty when they took it over, the previous incumbent leaving nothing but an old tin tea caddy that stood on the high mantelshelf. It had been the first thing Kate had reached for when they first saw the house, that and the small pencilled note beside it. The writer said that she hoped they'd be as happy in her old home as she had been, and the caddy never get empty. Inside were a few tea leaves, enough for a couple of pots of good strong Lancashire tea. This thoughtful gesture seemed to instil a sense of warmth into the house, new hope for the future, and it soon became their dearly loved home, albeit a very different one from Tyson Lodge.

The tea caddy reminded her of the aunts. Kate had loved to watch them serve tea, the ritual of it all: cakes on a tiered stand, toast in a silver rack, gentlemen's relish; trying to coax the methylated burner into life beneath the silver kettle, the warming of the pot, the straining and serving of Earl Grey or Indian, whatever their choice of the day, in the best Sèvres china. You were sorely in need of a cuppa by the time it was actually ready.

More often than not these days, she and Flora brewed their tea in a brown teapot Kate had picked up at the Iron Market, and they always drank the good strong variety out of thick white everyday crockery. Kate kept her favourite blue and white Willow Pattern displayed on the dresser which she only took down on a Sunday now, to mark the special day.

She'd found the dresser in a little second-hand shop on Oldham Street and was thrilled with it.

Kate and Flora had together cleaned the house, given the walls a fresh wash of distemper to keep back the bugs, scrubbed the floors and put down clean pegged rugs. They'd gone round the markets and second-hand shops, picking up odd pieces of furniture here and there which Kate had waxed and polished till they shone. They included a couple of beds, a large mahogany wardrobe, a few chairs and a table as well as the dresser.

To these she added her best Irish linen, a few clothes and other personal treasures they'd managed to bring with them from Kendal.

'Won't we be grand here?' Kate said, proudly viewing the result of their labours.

'I don't care where I live, Mammy, a pig sty would do so long as we're together.'

'Isn't that the truth, m'darlin? A pig sty once saved yer daddy's life, I'll have you know, so I'll not hear a word said against them. Even so, we've done a bit better than that, I'm glad to say.'

Kate felt content to settle here in Manchester, for a while at least. She was free from the asylum, and from Lucy. She had some savings, some of Eliot's legacy to her that she'd managed to keep out of the hands of the bailiffs, and surely she possessed sufficient skills to find herself a new job. Though she wouldn't rush into anything. She still needed a little more time to recover, and to adjust to her new surroundings. Flora was settling happily into the local council school, so all Kate had to do now was relax and see if Mother Fortune would smile on her again.

The dinner party on the Friday evening was every bit as dreadful as Bunty had anticipated. It comprised, to her eyes, mainly of old people, and certainly very silly ones who seemed intent on drinking and eating just as much as they possibly could. Their host, plump and with pink veins threaded through his cheeks, must have been older even than her mother. He had ginger hairs growing out of his ears and nostrils, and kept resting one hot, sweaty palm on her knee.

Bunty had been placed next to him and once, he actually chucked her under the chin and called her his sweetie-pie. She was forced to keep making excuses to leave the room.

At one point Lucy followed her, rapping on the bathroom door and demanding to know if there was a problem.

'Yes,' Bunty said, rushing out to confront her mother. 'I hate it here. These are your friends, not mine. I want to go home.'

'Nonsense! Where is the evidence of the etiquette and good manners I have so expensively procured for you? Evan Hayton is our host and you are behaving with dreadful rudeness towards him. Now get back in there and smile.'

After the meal there was dancing, and, to her absolute horror, Bunty found that Evan Hayton insisted on partnering her in the waltz and then the shimmy.

'Topping fun, what?' he kept saying while Bunty pressed back hard against his hot, sticky hand in order to keep as much space as possible between them. 'Care for a turn about the garden? Dashed hot in here.'

'No, thank you. I think I'll sit this next dance out.'

'Nonsense, this is tophole entertainment. Love it! Love it! Young thing like you must have barrels of energy, what?'

Why wasn't her mother content with simpler pleasures, such as tapestry work, embroidery, or sewing on buttons as other mothers did? Why did she insist on this foolish round of endless parties? Desperate to leave early, Bunty feigned a headache, thinking this would force Lucy to take her home. It turned out to be worst possible thing she could have done.

'Poor darling,' Lucy said, all soft concern. 'Why don't you slip upstairs and lie down for half an hour? Dear Evan won't mind.'

'Not a bit of it, old thing. You take her up and

let the little cherub rest.'

'*Mother!*'

But Lucy was not to be gainsaid. Gathering her daughter in a solicitous embrace, she led her gently up the stairs and into a spare bedroom where she quietly closed the door before turning upon Bunty, her face like stone.

'You are behaving like a silly, spoiled child. Embarrassingly so. Take half an hour's rest, if you must, but use it to consider your options. It's either the poorhouse for us, or you start to grow up and face reality. I want you to be nice to Evan. He owns three hotels and a large mansion on Lake Windermere.'

Bunty gasped. 'What is this? Are you trying to sell me off to the highest bidder?'

'I'm trying to make sure that we survive.' Lucy pushed her face up so close that Bunty's own was flecked with spittle.

'Play your cards right, girl, and he may well prove to be our salvation.'

She left Bunty reeling with shock. What was happening to her? She saw all too clearly now that she'd been duped. She'd hurried back home with hope high in her heart that her mother had relented and forgiven her, that she would agree to Bunty's seeing Callum at last. A futile dream when all the time Lucy had other plans in mind. Surely she didn't seriously expect her own daughter to marry this old codger?

Bunty was trying to work out if there was some way she could slip out of the house unseen and somehow get herself back to Heversham when the door creaked open.

'Coo-ee! Thought you might lack a bit of company.'

To her horror, Bunty recognised the unmistakable, plump figure of her host and her heart began to race. She curled herself up tight in a protective little ball. 'I'd prefer to be left alone for a bit, if you don't mind?'

'Not in need of a bit of a cuddle then?'

'Not at all. Of course not.' Bunty was appalled by the suggestion but he was already sitting on the edge of the bed, his fat, podgy hand stroking her hair, her cheek. She cringed back against the pillow. Why did she have to be cursed with such a mother? Why did Lucy have this need to control everything, to meddle in other people's lives?

'Poor little pipkin, I think a cuddle will make you feel so much better.' Then somehow his mouth was on her cheek, his tongue pushing against her ear, and his hand – dear God – his hand was squeezing her breast!

Gathering all her strength, Bunty shoved him away and almost fell off the bed, quickly scrambling to her feet and confronting him with outrage sharp in her tone. 'I can't believe you did that. What gives you the right to touch me in that way?'

The smile slid from his face and his expression soured to a puzzled scowl. 'Thought that was the whole idea. Headache just an excuse for us to be alone, don't you know.'

'I'd like to go home now.'

He looked annoyed rather than ashamed, disappointed rather than apologetic. 'Only having a bit of fun. No harm in that, eh?'

'There is every harm. Don't you realise that I'm only nineteen, and engaged to be married? Did my mother not mention that, by any chance?'

'Engaged, you say? Stuff and nonsense. You mean that Callum boy? Lucy explained how he was your childhood sweetheart once, but you're a big girl now, pipkin. Nineteen is perfectly old enough to taste the fruits of love, in the right hands, don't you know.'

Bunty felt sickened, thought she might actually vomit all over his patent leather shoes and spats. 'May I have my coat? At once, if you please.'

Somehow, Lucy managed to maintain both silence and dignity as they were escorted to their vehicle. Bunty did not expect either to last very long once they were alone.

Kate got into the habit of rising early every morning, happily pottering about the house, cleaning and sweeping, polishing and titivating, since at first there was a great deal to be done. Monday was washday, of course, ironing on Tuesdays. On Wednesdays she gave the bedrooms a good clean, tackled the brasses, and the shopping on a Thursday. On Fridays she would turn out the kitchen so that it was nice and clean for the weekend. But as time went by, these domestic chores began to pall. She'd done all that was needed to the little house and Kate grew bored.

She took to walking about the city, exploring the shops and markets, Deansgate, St Anne's Square, Oldham Street, taking a tram home again when she grew tired or confused. Kate knew she should start asking around for a job, but she kept putting it off a little longer, needing this time to recuperate. The headaches weren't quite so debilitating as before but Kate would still find herself standing in her own kitchen, wondering what she'd come in for, not even able to recall what day it was. There were times when she feared that Lucy might have succeeded in turning her mind.

One day she lost her way and found herself in a district that was quite unknown to her. She grew confused and muddled, wandering down byways and dark alleys by the canal, trying to find the right one to lead her home. It was far less salubrious than her own street and she soon regretted her mistake.

A youth suddenly shot out from an alleyway, snatched her bag and ran.

'Come here, you nasty little...' She got no further as another youth thumped her in the back, knocking her over and leaving her lying in the filthy gutter, gasping for breath. It was a lesson learned. A woman alone really couldn't afford to take chances.

The incident unnerved her for a while, knocked back her confidence and Kate didn't go out again for over a week. Millie was there to help though, bolstering her courage, as always.

'Aw, don't let it bother you. The little tykes were no doubt starving so yer money will be put to good use. But next time you go on the wander, don't carry a bag. Asking for it, that is. You need to keep your wits about you, Kate O'Connor. Carry nowt, walk fast, and always stay in the centre of the pavement. Look like you know where you're going, even if you don't. Only it would help if you got yerself a map and learned.'

Kate acted on Millie's wise advice and resolved not to allow the incident to spoil her efforts to rebuild her life. She spent hours reading in the public library, or would sometimes go to a picture house which she thoroughly enjoyed. Once she saw Lillian Gish in *Way down East*. Another time she went to the theatre to see *Richard II*, though didn't entirely understand it, and at the opera she didn't have the first idea what they were singing about but enjoyed the music.

She much preferred the Gaiety and loved to go there with Millie, Maisie, Sal and Flora. Afterwards, they'd eat fish and chips out of paper on their way home, singing at the tops of their voices as if they were all silly young girls and two of them not sensible mothers supposed to be setting a good example to their daughters.

Kate had her hair Marcel-waved at Kendal Milne, tried out all the free samples of face cream and scent, once treating herself to some Parma Violet perfume to go with the artificial violets she'd pinned on to the lapel of her old grey coat. Her hair was growing, forming a halo of red curls all about her head so that she didn't look quite the freak she had before, which was a relief. And if her cheeks had lost some of their country freshness, then at least they'd filled out a bit and were no longer quite so hollow and gaunt. She was beginning to feel almost human again.

What was more wonderful still, deep inside her

a flame had been rekindled; that core of energy Kate had once taken so much for granted had again started to burn within her. It spread its radiance outward, warming her, feeding her spirit with new hope.

Although she was having fun and enjoyed pottering about her cottage or exploring the city, her little nest egg was beginning to slip away at an alarming rate. Something must be done about that. Kate felt ready now to find a job, to take on the world and start living again.

'I'm getting to be as bad as Lucy. Spend, spend, spend. If I don't start work soon I'll end up in Queer Street,' she announced to Millie one day.

'What would you want to do?'

'Anything. I'm not proud.'

Millie frowned. 'You don't have no references, which could be a problem. You'll mebbe need to explain that you've been running your own business for the last few years.'

'Oh, no, I couldn't do that. Folk would think I was too grand to work for them, or that I was incompetent since I didn't manage to hold on to it.'

'That wasn't your fault.'

'No, but I can't go into all that happened, now can I? To be sure, I'd say, in me best Irish brogue, I've really spent most of the last twelve months in a lunatic asylum.'

Millie was thoughtful. 'I agree, that could make matters a good deal worse. You might just have to settle for summat a bit – well, below your status.'

Kate chuckled. 'And what status would a girl

from Poor House Lane have, I wonder?'

'That was a long time ago. You've had it easy for a while, chuck.'

'Easy, you say, with all that's happened to me?'

Millie had the grace to flush. 'What I mean is, there's plenty round here would give their eye-teeth for a job and be jealous of the fact that you've lived in a posh house, with servants at your beck and call. You must admit that some of the nobs' fancy ways have rubbed off on you.'

'So what if they have? I reckon I can still cut the mustard, as they say. I'm not looking to run the world, not just yet, but I hope I'm not too proud to do a hard day's work.'

Kate did indeed find herself a job, even without a reference, working on Campfield Market, no questions asked. She spent three days a week weighing biscuits there and her evenings minding her daughter, and she'd never been happier in her life.

# 39

Bunty went to see Toby at the factory and per-suaded him to pass a note to Callum. He wasn't too happy about becoming involved in her sub-terfuge. 'This business has naught to do with me, but nor do I owe Lucy any favours so I'll oblige, this once. Don't make a habit of it, though. You and Callum must work your own problems out.'

Bunty promised that she wouldn't ask him

again, and Toby agreed to have a reply for her by the following Monday. She waited with increasing anxiety all week, kicking her heels and drifting about the house in an agony of tension.

Lucy grew irritated with her and told her to snap out of it. 'What on earth is wrong with you, moping about?'

'I'm thinking of Callum, who else? I worry about him.'

'That boy's name, as I have made clear a dozen times, is not to be mentioned in this house. He is nowhere near good enough for you and you will never see or speak to him again.'

'That's for me to decide, not you, Mother.'

'I think not, madam.' Lucy decided it was time to come clean. She made no bones about what was expected of her daughter, calling Bunty to task for her display of bad behaviour the other night and coldly informing her that she was to be found a husband, a sugar daddy, a man with sufficient wealth to keep them both in comfort.

Bunty laughed as if her mother had said something highly amusing. 'You can't be serious?'

'Never more so. Unless you can think of some other way to restore our fortune we must follow the age-old path of marrying into it.'

Bunty was utterly flabbergasted and protested strongly, insisting that she loved Callum, that they had dreams and plans of their own; that she had no intention of marrying some old man she didn't care a bean for. All of which her mother dismissed with contempt.

'It is your duty to make a good marriage, and mine to find a suitable husband to care for and provide for you. Isn't that what every girl needs, what every mother must secure for a beloved daughter?'

'If I really were your beloved daughter, you'd let me marry the man I love.' Bunty glared at her mother, and Lucy glared back.

'Until you come of age, you have no say whatsoever, and don't think you can put off the evil moment for well-nigh two years. We need a solution to our predicament *now*, and you, my dear, are the means to provide it. If you don't care for Evan Hayton, we can look elsewhere, although I must warn you that young men are hard to come by these days, so you must be flexible with regards to age.'

'*I will not marry a man I don't love!*' Bunty felt as she was falling over a precipice and no one was lifting a finger to stop her.

Lucy's response was astonishingly, dangerously calm. 'You will do as I say. We cannot afford the luxury of sentimentality. Besides, love comes later, after marriage, when you get to know a person. And if he's no good in bed, then you can always take a lover, although generally I've found the mature male to be far more experienced than a raw youth in that respect.'

'I don't believe you. Aunt Cissie told me you'd hoped to marry a man years younger than yourself, someone called Teddy? But you were disappointed in love. I assume you had an affair with him though. Maybe with several others as well.'

Lucy slapped Bunty hard, leaving four red fingermarks across her cheek. 'How dare you! Teddy and I... Well, never mind. It's none of your business, madam! Have you any idea what I've been forced to endure because of that dreadful woman who stole, and then lost, our entire inheritance?'

Bunty put a hand to her burning cheek, nursing it, wondering if it was a sin against God, or nature, to hate one's mother as much as she did. 'But was it Kate who lost it, or you who wasted it with your spend, spend, spend?'

Although there were tears of pain and misery in her eyes, Bunty dared to challenge Lucy because she remained resolute that she would win through in the end. This wasn't some penny dreadful romance or an eighteenth century novel, so how could Lucy possibly force her into an arranged marriage?

Callum would meet her next Monday and be only too ready to help her escape Lucy's clutches. They would both get jobs, rent a cottage, and live happily together until she was old enough to marry without her mother's permission.

Bunty was more than willing to defy convention for the sake of love. Who would have her then, once she and Callum were openly living as man and wife, as she so longed to do? She would have put herself quite beyond the pale. She had already, in any case, by giving up her virginity and having his baby. Except that she hadn't had it. Lucy had deprived her even of that possibility.

The thought of Callum and herself living as man and wife together brought a rush of warmth to her heart, a beat of excitement to her breast, restoring hope to Bunty's bruised heart. Oh, how she loved him, how she needed him! There were admittedly a few minor issues to clear up first between them, explanations and apologies to make about her long silence, as well as the baby of course. Then they could fall into each other's arms and live happily ever after, no matter what her mother tried to do.

Lucy was still talking, still scolding her in a voice that had risen in cadence and volume by several notches. Bunty had thankfully missed most of it but refocused upon the part where Lucy was insisting she was simply behaving like any loving mother with her own daughter's best interests at heart, which must be the biggest lie she'd ever told.

'I'm sure you'll come to see that a good marriage is the best possible course for everyone, once you've had time to appreciate how very difficult life is, living here in Heversham with the mad aunts.'

'They are not mad, merely eccentric.' Bunty chuckled, her equilibrium quite restored by her private musing. 'I'm very fond of Aunt Vera and dear Aunt Cissie, as a matter of fact, and I'm sure they would be on my side. They even like and admire Callum.'

'Which proves what complete nincompoops they are. Don't be misled, girl, they haven't a bean between them and know that they are dependent entirely upon my munificence.'

Bunty gasped. This was something she had not considered or expected. Being told one was penniless was one thing, experiencing it in reality quite another. She tried one last desperate bid for independence. 'Well, they certainly wouldn't approve of my marrying some dirty old man. I shall throw myself on their mercy and beg their support.'

'You will not! You will do as you are told.'

Finding herself suddenly dangerously close to tears, Bunty stamped her foot in frustrated temper and cried out, 'And I won't go to any more of your awful dinner parties, so there!'

For which piece of defiance she was locked in her room for twenty-four hours on a diet of bread and water, to 'allow ample time to come to your senses', which of course Bunty was compelled to do, if she was to be free to meet Callum on Monday evening.

Kate was fascinated by Ingram's department store where Millie worked, and on her days off would frequently wander about it, investigating the various departments, always striving to avoid the floor-walker whose task it was to supervise customers and direct them to the right assistant to be served.

Inevitably, she was drawn to the shoe department where Kate would secretly study styles and designs, critically comparing them with her own, and watch ladies occasionally buy half a dozen pairs at a time, proving there was money in this city.

Generally speaking, though, she was unimpressed with Ingram's selection and often noticed women walking away without having made any purchase at all.

Nor had she found any decent shoe shops in the city centre. Little had changed since before the war with plenty of boot and shoe repairers, but few shops which actually sold quality, well-designed footwear for ladies. Ingram's, in her opinion, was missing an excellent opportunity to cash in on this situation. Not that it was any concern of hers.

The haberdashery counter where Millie worked was situated quite near to the main entrance. Kate would hover close by in the hope of catching her friend's eye for a quick chat, or give a nod and a wink to say she'd meet her across the road in the café for a meat pie or a quick cup of tea. If the boss was around, though, Millie would panic, flap her hand and urge Kate to go away.

Kate sympathised. It was hard work on the haberdashery counter, a constant stream of customers mostly buying small items and spending forever choosing exactly the right shade of cotton, width of elastic, the right size or shape of button. Everything had to be measured out, cut and rolled up, put in a little paper bag, and some complicated arithmetic carried out, such as three and a half yards of rick-rack braid at eightpence three-farthing a yard.

After that, the customer would hand over the money which was put into a little wooden ball that hung from a rail which ran at a slight incline down to the cash desk. Kate would watch, fascinated, as the ball was unscrewed, the money taken out, change put back in together with the receipt, and the little ball pinged on its way again back to the counter, rather like a Swiss cable car. It all seemed to take an inordinate amount of time, with the customer patiently waiting on a chair by the counter, or impatiently in some cases, for the whole process to be completed.

'What a lot of fuss and bother you have to go through over a simple transaction, why doesn't the customer simply take the money to the cash desk? That would be so much quicker,' Kate remarked when Millie was finally free to escape for her dinner break one day.

Millie was shocked. 'You can't expect a lady to collect her own change, and they'd never trust us shop assistants with money, so what else could you do?'

'Seems pretty old-fashioned to me,' Kate ventured. 'But then Ingram's has been going a long time.'

And then there were the mysterious contents of all those drawers behind Millie's counter.

'What on earth is in all of these little drawers and cubby-holes?' Kate asked one evening, when she'd called to meet her friend just before closing.

Millie laughed. 'Every possible thing you can imagine.'

'But what do they all mean? Look at this, for example. What on earth is a puggaree? Or this, labelled a fascinator?'

'Many of these items must have been here since the store opened back in the last century. I don't know what half of them are for either,' Millie confessed.

'Can I take a peep inside?'

Millie glanced around. 'All right, just a quick one.' She opened a drawer, and then another. 'There you are, garters galore, belts and bindings, laces and muslins, corset busks and shields...'

The pair of them were starting to giggle by this time, opening drawers with increasing reckless-ness, pulling items out to examine and identify.

'Look at this,' Kate shrieked. 'It's labelled Madapollam. What on earth is that? Why, it's nothing more than a piece of cotton cloth.'

'Made in India,' said a deep male voice from behind her. 'Would madam be interested in pur-chasing a length of it? Or have you sufficient samples of our products spread all over the counter for you to choose from already?'

Bunty spent Sunday lunch attempting to fend off the attentions of one Daniel Perry. He was younger than the last candidate by about five years, being somewhere in his early forties according to Lucy, and rake thin, which was at least an improvement. He was also apparently eager for marriage and in need of an heir to his property fortune. His land and other assets had been listed at great length, like an inventory, by Lucy; not that Bunty had either listened or cared. As usual, an inordinate amount of time had been devoted to choosing the right gown for her to wear.

'An air of simplicity and charm is essential, I feel. Virginal white perhaps,' Lucy had suggested.

'But I'm not.'

'Not what, dear?'

'A virgin, if you recall.'

Lucy flew to the bedroom door and slammed it shut. 'Never, never, *never* say such a thing. That – unfortunate – incident has been dealt with and you must forget it ever happened. So far as anyone is aware, and certainly any gentleman to whom you are introduced, you are as pure as the driven snow. Is that quite clear?'

Bunty hid a smile. 'If you say so, Mama.'

Now she ate her roast beef in silence, offering only the occasional, perfunctory smile, going through the motions to satisfy her mother, but making no effort to charm or win him over.

Mr Daniel Perry was the third suitor in one short week to be paraded before her and Bunty was already bored by the whole stupid enterprise. Lucy absolutely refused to give up this crazy notion of finding her a husband, and Bunty was beginning to feel as if she'd got caught up in a very bad French farce.

Her nerves were a wreck in any case, a sensation of sick anticipation deep in her stomach. Tomorrow was Monday, the day she would finally see Callum again after all these long months apart. She ached to have his arms around her, his mouth on hers. Would the moment never come?

The day dragged endlessly on, and as her mother nudged and prodded her to speak and smile, Bunty kept her mind firmly focussed on that glorious reunion. Tomorrow they would be together at last. Would he sweep her into his arms? Would he have missed her as much as she had missed him? Would they make love there and then, in the sweet-smelling grass at their trysting place on the fells?

Oh, Callum, will tomorrow never come?

# 40

So anxious was Bunty about the coming reunion that she arrived a good two hours early. She paced to and fro, agonising over what she would say to him, imagining what he might say to her, how he would look, what he would think of her. Would he notice that she had changed, grown into a young woman?

The minutes ticked slowly by. She counted ants tramping back and forth about some invisible business of their own, studied a dung beetle as if it were the most fascinating creature in the world. And as time seemed to slow and falter, the sensation of sickness increased accordingly, her confidence evaporating as the appointed hour arrived and Callum did not.

What if Toby hadn't passed on the note? What if Callum simply wasn't interested in her any more? How would she live if he no longer loved her, no longer wanted her? If he didn't even come.

And then suddenly there he was, hurrying up the hill towards her, his face bright, his eyes riveted upon her face, and when he pulled her into his arms and kissed her, Bunty thought she might swoon with joy, or explode from sheer ecstasy.

The kiss went on and on, each reluctant to end the embrace. Callum studied every inch of her face, kissed every part of it over and over, stroked her hair, nibbled her fingertips, even tweaked her nose, and laughed and hugged her from the joy of being together at last.

It was some moments before they finally sat, settling themselves beneath the inadequate shelter of a silver birch, still holding tight to each other. The sky was overcast, a chill breeze stirring the clouds, though they didn't notice. A golden autumn day was turning into a chill dusk but neither of them cared.

So overcome by emotion were they that both were now struck by a shy silence. They simply sat on a cushion of bracken, speechless with happiness, gripping each other's hands and gazing deeply into each other's eyes. Bunty swayed a little towards him, wanting him to kiss her again, but then a leaf floated gently down, landing on top of his head, and she was overcome by a fit of giggles. The spell was broken.

'Will you marry me?' Callum said, and she put back her head and laughed joyously.

'You wouldn't believe how many times I've evaded that question in this one week alone.' She told him then, very briefly, about her mother's latest scheme. 'It's all rather like some daft Victorian melodrama. She thinks she can avoid the dire prospect of certain poverty by marrying me off to the highest bidder, would you believe?'

'I'm afraid I'd believe anything of your mother. She kept you from writing to me, didn't she?'

'I did write, at first. Every single week. But since I never got any reply I assumed she was intercepting our letters, and then – then something happened. I was moved to another school, and I was afraid to write after that. She said she'd hurt you, have you sacked or something, if I did.' Bunty swallowed. She hadn't meant to reach this point of her story quite so quickly, and she was filled with a sudden gush of fear. She prayed he wouldn't notice. 'I decided there was nothing for it but to wait till I was free, which I now am. Isn't it wonderful?'

His gaze was fixed on her brightly smiling face. 'You've changed. Grown up. Have I?'

She shook her head, laughing delightedly. 'No, you look just the same. You will always be the boy I love, even when you are very old.'

Callum grinned. 'We could have been married already if it hadn't been for blasted Lucy and her conniving ways. Not that we'd've had much money. No doubt have been living on a dry crust in Poor House Lane.'

'That would have been a million times better than what I did have to endure when...' She stopped, and a blush of hot crimson seeped into her cheeks.

'Than what? What is it, Bunty? What happened to make her move you to another school? What are you not telling me?'

She half turned from him, dropping her gaze so that she wouldn't see the condemnation in his eyes. 'There's something you need to know. It isn't easy for me to say it, so I'll do it quickly, get it over with.' She took a deep, steadying breath then blurted it out, forgetting all the careful phrases she had practised.

'I found I was having a baby after ... after that

time we were together in the summer house. I was expelled from school and Mother made me have an abortion. There, that's it. It was an awful, terrible time, but it happened and then I was packed off to another finishing school, to learn deportment, study French as if...'

Callum interrupted. 'You had *what?*'

She glanced sideways at him, saw how the skin had tightened around his flared nostrils, how his jaw clenched. He'd dropped her hands and was gazing at her in stunned disbelief.

'I didn't want to have it taken away. I know it's against the law to kill a child, and very dangerous for the mother, but I'd no choice. My mother met me in London, marched me off to some doctor she knew in Harley Street. It was all over in hours.'

'You didn't tell me. You never said a word. Why didn't you say that you were having a baby?'

'How could I? None of my letters got through.'

'You could have tried harder, sent a letter to Toby or to the aunts. This was important, Bunty. You should have told me! You'd no right, no right whatsoever just to do away with it – the baby – *my* baby. An innocent *child!*' He moved away from her, gazing at her in open horror. 'How could you allow it to happen?'

Bunty felt the small kernel of fear inside her start to grow bigger. 'But I've just told you, I didn't have any choice.'

'There's always a choice. It's your body. You could have refused.'

Bunty thought of how upset she'd felt at the time, how vulnerable and scared she'd been at the prospect of bearing and bringing up a child on her own. She wanted to tell him all of this, to explain how alone she'd felt, how young and confused and miserable. But she only said, 'Mother wouldn't have allowed us to marry, even then, baby or no baby. She made that very clear. I would have been shamed, ruined.'

'So you were thinking of yourself, not the child?'

'*No!* I didn't mean it like that.'

'Sounds like it to me.'

'*Callum!*'

She saw, to her dismay, that his eyes were suspiciously bright, and very angry. Then he got to his feet and walked away from her, his voice a muffled murmur so that she didn't quite catch what he said, something about trust and true love, and needing time to think.

Bunty called after him but he didn't stop walking. He just kept right on going till he was out of sight. Then she put her hands to her face and found it wet with tears.

Bunty couldn't believe his reaction. How could Callum be so cruel? Why didn't he understand that she'd had no control over what had happened to her? She tried to see him again, to reiterate how helpless she'd felt, but Toby refused to pass on any more of her notes.

'I'm sorry but I told you, once only. I can't put right whatever has gone wrong between you. And whatever it is, it has affected Callum badly. He's taken to going to the Rifle Man's every night now, instead of just Fridays. He's drinking far too much and that's not good, Bunty, not good at all. He's getting in with the wrong crowd.'

'Then help me to speak to him.'

Toby considered for a moment, then shook his head. 'If I do that, he might cut me off too and where would that leave him? No, I promised Kate ... promised his mother I'd watch out for him. I have to stay on his side. I'm sorry, love.'

Since she couldn't follow him to the pub and her mother never allowed her out at night, Bunty hung around the factory, hopeful of catching a glimpse of Callum. She was supposed to be taking an afternoon stroll and didn't dare stay long, fearful as she was of alerting her mother's suspicions. When a week of such loitering brought no results, she tried chatting with one or two of his friends who revealed that he didn't even work at Tysons any more.

Why hadn't Toby told her that much, at least?

His mates, however, did give her the address of his lodgings and she boldly paid a call and knocked on the door. A scruffy-looking young man answered, his unshaven face darkly unwelcoming. 'What d'you want?'

'Is Callum in? I need to speak to him. Tell him it's me – Bunty.'

The young man turned and shouted back over his shoulder. 'Theer's a lass here to see thee. Bunty, she sez her name is.'

Silence, then a mumbled response came from within.

'He don't want to know,' said the scruffy young man, and slammed the door shut in her face.

Bunty was mortified. How could he be so rude?

She hammered on the door again. This time it remained shut and in the end she was driven to admit defeat and go home.

After that, life slipped from farce into nightmare. Lucy's plans seemed to be intensifying, her determination to find Bunty a husband growing stronger by the day. Every week there were parties, dinners, social occasions, lined up for her to attend, comprised mainly of men before whom she was paraded, like a brood mare. More dresses were refurbished, her hair restyled, the aunts chivvied into long hours of sewing since money was tight.

Lucy would study her chosen candidate's attributes, age and assets as if she were studying form in order to place a bet on a horse in the Grand National. Should she choose the favourite or the outsider? Bunty was given lengthy instructions on how to behave, how to capture the interest of this businessman or that financier.

'This is like a bad joke,' she complained. 'You'll make us both into a laughing stock.'

'I'll make us very rich.'

Sickened by the whole performance, Bunty soon came to realise that there was nothing even vaguely amusing about the situation in which she found herself. She became deeply troubled and increasingly desperate, seeing no hope of escape.

Today she intended writing Callum yet another letter which she would put through the letterbox where he appeared to be lodged. Over the last several weeks she'd sent three already. Or was it four? Time made no sense to her now for there had been no response. Nothing but a long, terrible silence, stretching on and on.

She walked and walked, needing time alone to think. This letter was her last hope, so she must choose her words with care. She walked for miles, right out of town, following the river till it narrowed through the villages of Natland and Sedgwick.

Now she sat on the wooded bank, the water rushing and tumbling beneath an outcrop of moss-coated limestone, curving through a copse of slender birch and sycamore, onward to the estuary at Arnside and into the sea. Further along the bank she could see an angler casting his line, and upstream of him stood a watchful heron. Which would catch its prey first? she wondered.

That's what she was, helpless prey, exactly like the poor fish.

That summer when they'd first met she'd believed their love would endure forever, she and Callum used to pick anemones and sweet violets here. He'd taught her how to tickle trout, described how they buried themselves in the river gravel when the freezing weather came.

Today there was already that nip in the air that betokened the onset of winter, and Bunty shivered. Where had the summer gone? What a waste that it should slip away unnoticed, the year passing by so quickly. If only there were some-where she could hide, like the trout, before she too was caught in the freezing trap her mother had set; hooked by one of those dreadful old codgers fishing for a pretty young wife.

She recalled with a sad smile the jolly picnics

403

she and Callum had once enjoyed; that first one by Lake Windermere, going off to eat their sandwiches alone, sharing a first kiss. How wonderful life had been then, so full of promise and excited anticipation.

A damselfly settled on a reed and Bunty chewed on her pencil and worried, mesmerised by its dazzling blue beauty. What could she say to touch his heart? What magic words would bring him rushing back to her? How to make him see that she was as helpless a pawn in her mother's cruel games as he was, as poor Kate had been.

She began to write, pouring her heart on to the page as tears welled in her eyes and slipped down her pale cheeks. This was no hasty note begging for a meeting, for one more chance to explain, this was a cry from the depth of her soul.

When the task was complete, and it took many failed attempts before she was satisfied, Bunty walked slowly home again, following the course of the river as far as she was able. Then, slipping through town, she dropped the letter through the letterbox of the still firmly closed door.

Now all she could do was wait, and pray.

She did not have to wait long this time. His silence was at last ended. The reply was delivered by hand the very next day, sent via a young boy, and its message was stark.

Callum bluntly wrote that he'd thought about it long and hard, but had decided that he couldn't ever see her again. He'd always believed her to be a better person than Lucy, but now he saw that he was wrong. She was exactly the same, every bit as selfish and ruthless as her mother, doing as she pleased without any consideration for other people's feelings, or any moral sense of what was right or wrong. It concluded with a chilling message:

*Please don't try to contact me again. I shall throw any more letters away unopened. Your family have ruined my mother's health and all our lives. It's over between us. I see no possible way for us to be happy.*
  *Callum*

Bunty tore the letter into shreds then rushed to her room where she sobbed on her bed for hours.

When her mother tapped on her door that evening and reminded her that they were expected for dinner at the Wilsons' by eight, Bunty rose dry-eyed and obediently began to get ready. She knew when she was beaten, and if she couldn't have Callum, what did it matter who she married?

# 41

Two years on, Kate did not regret her decision to move to Manchester. She was more than content with her little cottage. She always had preferred the cosiness of the old nursery, or the small parlour, to the grandeur of what she'd now come to think of as Heartbreak House. She felt well rid of it, was determined to look on the positive side and believe things had turned out well for her.

She might miss seeing the aunts toasting their toes before the fire of an evening, Vera's spectacles sliding down her nose and Cissie snoring gently in perfect rhythm with her spaniels but she did not miss the stately rooms of Tyson Lodge. Not in the slightest.

Kate hadn't abandoned the aunts entirely and would often visit them. She and Flora would take the train up to Kendal on a Saturday morning and take lunch with them at The County, thereby avoiding Lucy's presence, and pressing a little money into their protesting hands whenever she could afford to. She would also visit Callum, of course, and call on Toby who, without fail, would always urge her to stay. Kate would smilingly assure him that she was very happy in Manchester, thank you very much.

'What, working on a market stall?' he would say. 'That's not good enough for you, not for the Kate O'Connor who built up her own business from scratch and saved Tysons Shoes, the first time it was in trouble at least. You're worth more than that.'

'All the more reason for me to keep learning and working, so that I can better myself and get back to where I was. I shall find my own way, Toby, have faith.'

Everything changed the day she met Theo Ingram.

Kate still cringed with embarrassment, remembering that day. He'd been typically stuffy and pompous, looking down his elegant nose at her and at the mess spread all over Millie's counter, making her feel like a daft schoolgirl caught at some prank with her chums.

'I take it, from the expression of guilt on your face,' he said, in that rich, vibrant voice of his, 'that you are not actually a customer but a time-wasting friend of my assistant here.' He turned to her friend. 'Put everything back where you found it, collect your wages and go.'

Kate gasped. 'You can't sack her for what I did! That's not fair. We were just having a laugh, so we were.'

'Then you can take your amusement at someone else's expense, not mine. Life is never fair, I've found, but I expect loyalty from my staff, not levity.' He began to walk away but one glance at Millie's white, shocked face galvanised Kate into action, and she ran after this stranger who must be Theodore Ingram, the owner of the department store.

'She has a family to feed, a roof to keep over her head! You'd risk all of that because we were having a bit of a joke? I'd never treat people so callously. What sort of man are you? What sort of an employer?'

Millie was at her side, urging her to hush. 'Never mind, Kate. It were me own fault.'

Kate rounded on her. 'No, it wasn't, Millie. It was mine. I asked you to open all those damn drawers, which should have been sorted out years ago considering their old-fashioned contents. Pre-war the lot of it, if not Victorian.'

'You know all about drapery, do you?' the man acidly enquired.

'Not a thing.' Kate straightened her spine and

confronted Theo Ingram, grey eyes blazing as they hadn't done in months. 'But I know a badly run business when I see one. Like your shoe department, for instance, which was surely created when Noah was building his Ark and hasn't been changed since. I'd say a bit of a flood might do it a whole lot of good. No wonder so many women walk away having bought nothing.' She wagged an admonishing finger at him. 'And don't tell me I know nothing about shoes either, because...' She stopped.

Kate longed to tell him that she used to run Tysons Industries, the best shoe manufacturers in the north, but that would be treading on difficult territory. She had no wish for him to associate her with the woman who had failed to save her husband's business. He would be aware that the company had gone bump, perhaps even that Tyson's widow had been incarcerated in a mad house for a while. It wouldn't do. She'd no wish to spoil her chances of a fresh start.

'I just know, that's all,' she finished, rather lamely. 'I worked in a shoe shop once.'

'So you think you know more about shoes than me?'

'I'm certain I do.'

There was a silence, long and pained. In it Kate found ample opportunity to reflect on her own error of judgement. She'd fallen into the trap of losing her temper as she'd used to do so often in the past, sounding just as dreadful as him. Millie was whimpering at her side, clearly wanting the ground to open under her feet, while Theo Ingram allowed his arrogant gaze to sweep over

Kate from top to toe.

Finally he spoke. 'In my office. Both of you. *Now*, if you please.'

She'd been forced to eat humble pie, of course. Kate felt duty bound to apologise for her rudeness because of course she'd been entirely in the wrong. In the first place by tipping out the contents of the shop's display drawers all over the drapery counter, and secondly by insulting both Mr Ingram and his business. A worse catalogue of disaster it would be hard to imagine, and poor Millie was the one being punished. Didn't Kate owe her friend more than that, after all she'd done for her?

She tried not to think about how good it had felt to have the blood surging through her veins again, to feel fire and energy licking her spirit back into life.

Theo Ingram stood listening to her explanation and garbled apology in complete silence, his tall, broad-shouldered frame rigid with disapproval. The worst of it was that he was exceptionally good-looking, and not in the least little bit old, for all his apparent pomposity. He couldn't be a day over thirty-five, his hair dark and neatly cropped in a fashionable cut, his pin-stripe suit typically businesslike since he was on duty but nevertheless of the finest quality worsted. He wore a grey silk cravat, elegantly knotted, and shoes of the finest leather. More important still, it was clear from the expression on his handsome face that he was unmoved by Kate's halting apology, making no effort to ease her embarrassment. Standing rigid before her he could well have been carved out of stone; a beautiful Greek statue.

Kate stuttered to a halt, gathered the last of her pride. 'I can see that I'm wasting me time. Perhaps you're a man with no heart, as well as no soul.'

She sensed Millie flinch, heard her quick indrawn breath, and realised that she'd done it again. She'd entirely ruined her long-drawn out apology by tacking an insult on to the end.

Kate risked a glance up at Mr Ingram's face and caught a glimmer of something she couldn't quite believe. In anyone else she might have called it amusement, but it vanished as quickly as it had appeared, and she realised she'd been mistaken.

And then he caught her completely off guard, as he had on many occasions since, by bluntly and without warning offering her a job. 'If you think my shoe department is in such dire straits, then perhaps you should come and put it right. The drapery I shall leave in the fair hands of Millie here. Perhaps she is in a more fitting position to decide whether a pudger–'

'A puggaree,' offered Millie.

He actually smiled at her then. 'Pray what is that exactly? It looks simply like a length of rather moth-eaten muslin to me.'

Millie cleared her throat. 'It was used in India to form a turban or to wrap around a hat, sir.'

'Ah, a leftover from our colonial days. Then you may have a point, Miss, er, um – I'm afraid you haven't given me your name yet? And I do like to know all my employees personally.'

'Kate. It's Kate–' and then before Millie had the chance to cut in, she added '–O'Connor.'

'Well then, Kate O'Connor, will you accept my offer or are you not in the market for a job?'

There was only the slightest pause before she answered. 'I'll take it and gladly,' Kate said. 'Thanking you kindly, sir.' My Lord, she thought, I sound like a humble skivvy now. She bit her lip, to damp down this newfound fire in case it seared her tongue and made her say something that would spoil everything yet again.

That was more than a year ago now and Kate had worked for Theo Ingram ever since, loving every minute of it, although he was not an easy man to please. He was the most picky employer imaginable. The most disagreeable, independent, pig-headed, domineering man she'd ever met. He was the sort of person, in Kate's opinion, who knew the answer to everything and the value of nothing. He was always absolutely convinced that he was right. Perhaps that was why she liked him, because he reminded her of Eliot.

But only a little. Theo Ingram possessed a single-minded ruthlessness in business which Eliot had never possessed, but he lacked her husband's charm, his sweet nature, his caring thoughtfulness and Eliot's natural artistic flair.

'Retailing,' Kate would tell him, 'is all about flair. You don't just put things in drawers or stack them in piles and hope they will sell. You have to display them, make them look enticing. Set the product in an environment which will give the customer some idea of what it will look like in her own home, or, in the case of shoes, on her own feet.'

'Is this your way of telling me that you need new display stands, Kate?'

'Yes,' Kate agreed. 'I wouldn't give house room to that boxed in staircase you use to line the shoes upon in your window. Just shows how penny-pinching this store is. Or those dreadful chairs you expect women to sit on while they're trying on shoes. And not a single mirror in the place! It's time Ingram's Department Store started treating its customers with proper respect.'

He'd glared at her and walked away, but a week or two later a huge carton had been delivered to the shoe department, containing all manner of display units and shoe trees, even posters and show cards. Kate had been triumphant.

Later came new chairs for the department which set the shop girls in a lather of excitement, and even two mirrors which could be set on the green linoleum at just the right angle to flatter a lady's feet. Kate would have liked a new carpet too but settled for a strip upon which a customer could walk about, to check the comfort of the shoe and admire herself in the mirrors while she did so.

In a matter of weeks Kate had transformed the department. As well as new window and in-store displays, she brought in stools so that a lady could rest her foot while the correct fitting was established. Using her knowledge learned at Tysons, Kate trained all the staff in the art of fitting, showed them how to judge pressure on the toes within the shoe, and the correct amount of space behind the heel.

'You don't just sell anything and hope it will do. A customer will not return for a second pair if the first crippled her every time she wore them.'

Thanks to the Jazz Age, shorter skirts, and crazes like the Charleston, a dance that demanded footwear with a low heel, closed toe and excellent fit, shoes had become a popular fashion item.

'Mass production and the development of affordable synthetic fabrics have made shoes much more affordable,' Kate would tell her staff. 'But just because the girl in the street can now afford to enjoy the pleasure of pretty footwear, doesn't mean we no longer need bother to give good service. We treat everyone like a lady here, right? Housemaid or dowager duchess, they're all valued customers. Understand?'

'Yes, Miss O'Connor,' they would obediently chorus, and go about their business.

Goodness, Kate would think. I'm turning into a dragon.

Theo Ingram grudgingly praised her achievements, even went so far as to admit that sales had improved considerably since she had taken over the management of the department. But he didn't always care to hear her criticise what he'd bought to put in it. Kate never hesitated to tell him if she thought he'd made a mistake.

'These are cheap and nasty, the result of shoddy production. They'll fall apart after a month's wear.'

'You're an expert on shoe making as well as retailing, are you?'

'I am so.'

'How come, hmm? How is it that you apparently know so much about shoes?'

Kate was silent. She really must learn to hold her tongue. The last thing she wanted was to have Theo Ingram poking his nose into every corner of her private affairs. She shrugged her shoulders, apologised for her bluntness and sweetly begged leave to return to work.

'Diplomacy doesn't suit you,' he called after her. Yet despite her continued rudeness and defiance towards him, he made no move to sack her. Probably because he also wanted to be more than her employer, which gave Kate much pause for thought and many sleepless nights.

# 42

Theo asked if he might take her out for a meal one evening. Kate refused. He invited her to accompany him to the theatre to see the visiting Royal Ballet Company perform *Swan Lake*. Kate declined and said that she had seen it already with her friend Millie. Of course this wasn't strictly true. They'd seen a humorous version of *The Nutcracker* performed in a pantomime at the Princes Theatre, which had been great fun but with nothing the least royal about it.

He asked her to the cinema, perhaps thinking this would be more in her line, and she refused even that.

Millie asked her how she felt about him but

Kate wouldn't answer. How could she admit that she did secretly find him attractive and would love to go out with him, but that it didn't seem right?

'It's far too soon for me even to look at another man after losing Eliot,' she protested.

Her friend made short work of that argument. 'Rubbish! Are you planning on turning into a nun?'

Remembering Toby's reservations about the inadvisability of relationships between employer and employee, it occurred to Kate that using that as an excuse seemed as good a reason as any. Which would surely be the safest way, in the long run.

Theo asked her out to dinner and again she refused.

'Kate, why are you being so obstinate? Don't you like me?'

'I don't know you.'

'Nor will you ever if you refuse to come out with me.'

'You're my boss. I don't approve of fraternising at work.'

'Then perhaps I should sack you. Would you come out with me then, if I was no longer your employer?'

'Of course not, not if you'd sacked me. That would be unjust.'

'Kate, I despair, I really do.'

And then everything changed yet again.

Now that Flora had reached fourteen she declared that she hated mathematics and boring geography and was keen to leave school and get a job so that she could be a proper grown up and make a contribution to their modest income. Kate wanted her to remain a child and urged her to stay on at school for as long as possible.

'Why don't you take your school certificate?'

'Did you, Mammy?'

'No, course I didn't.'

'Well then, neither will I,' as if that was as good a reason as any.

'Indeed, when did I ever have the chance, half-starved orphan that I was? I wanted you to grow up to be a fine lady and do as ye please, and now look at us, back in the sewers.'

Flora hugged her mother close. 'Don't exaggerate. We're not in the sewers, we're fine.' Flora was too much her mother's child to suffer from any airs and graces. She was happy to be herself, whatever that might turn out to be. And happiness, it seemed, did not involve her taking examinations. 'I might start me own business one day, as you did. Don't you miss it, Mammy? Wouldn't you rather have a shop of your own?'

Kate looked at her daughter. 'A shop of me own, ye say? Aw, now, wouldn't that be grand? But not possible, m'darlin'.'

'Why isn't it possible? Why couldn't we open one together, mother and daughter? Wouldn't that be fun?'

'It would indeed, but where would we find the money?' Even as she said this, Kate was thinking, we do have some savings left, although maybe not enough, when Flora said the words for her.

'I thought you had some savings left?'

'I'm keeping that for me old age, so I am. Your daddy wouldn't want me begging for a crust when I become decrepit.'

Flora smiled at her mother's humour but persisted. 'Wouldn't it be better to make that money work for you and make more? And you're a long way from decrepit, Mammy, nowhere near forty yet, are you?'

''Course I'm not,' Kate responded tartly.

'Well then? Are you going to spend the rest of your life working for Mr Grumpy Ingram?'

'Now you sound like Toby.'

The following Saturday, Toby himself came to visit, as he often did. Kate told him how pleased she was to see him, as indeed she always was. After that, she brewed a pot of tea and asked him point blank: 'What would you say to my opening a shop of me own?'

He looked at her for a moment. 'I'd say, about bloody time!'

And that's how it all began.

O'Connor's Shoe Shop was planned that day on the kitchen table, with Flora excitedly joining in and Toby offering to put money in too, which caused some initial discord between them.

'Before you say no, let me make it clear I want only to be a sleeping partner.' A sheepish smile and then he added, 'Of the business variety, that is, since I've all but given up hope of the other kind.'

'Stop up yer ears, Flora,' Kate said, but she was smiling. 'That's not very flattering for a woman to hear, is it, that you've all but given up hope? I would've thought I was worth more patience and effort than that. Someday I might feel entirely different. Who knows?'

His head jerked up and his dark eyes twinkled. 'Don't tease and plague me, Kate Tyson, with your maybes and somedays. Just take the money before I come to my senses, and be thankful I still care enough about you to risk my hard earned cash.'

'Oh, I'm more than grateful, Toby Lynch. I depend upon you still as me best friend, so I do.' And they looked into each other's eyes and smiled.

They agreed to find premises to rent right in the heart of the city and worked out how they'd fit them out, Flora having some surprisingly good ideas about colour and style. They discussed what they would stock and which supplier they would use, sadly not Tysons, as that would be too painful. Last, but by no means least, they agreed to work for peanuts until it was successful.

'Which it certainly will be, if you're in the driving seat, Kate.'

'I'll do my best, for sure,' was all she could say, her heart full of emotion, flattered by their faith in her. 'Aw, make a fresh pot of tea, Flora, we need to celebrate. At least this time we won't have Madam Lucy sticking her oar in.'

Lucy was more than fully occupied dealing with her sulky daughter. Surprisingly though, for all Bunty's lack of sparkle and irritating habit of bursting into tears at the slightest provocation, she meekly acquiesced to whatever Lucy asked of her, albeit with ill grace, attending any number of

418

social functions without argument.

She even allowed Timothy Tiffin to walk her out alone by the lake one Sunday afternoon, with Lucy acting as chaperone, of course, although not with any degree of diligence. She'd managed to drop out of the walk for a whole half-hour when she got a stone in her shoe. The girl had returned quite flushed about the cheeks but had made no complaint. Later, she'd sat on Timothy's knee and let him feed her chocolate drops. It was really most encouraging.

Lucy couldn't quite understand what had brought about this sudden change in her behaviour but was relieved not to have to endure any more hysterics or endless arguments. But since there was still no engagement in sight, she judged it time to lead her daughter a little further along the path of dalliance. More drastic measures were clearly called for.

'I have no wish to know what naughty Timmy has been up to, but if he wants to go any further,' Lucy instructed her daughter, 'that's perfectly all right, above the waist, shall we say? Anything lower down demands an engagement ring first. Those are the rules. Is that clear?'

She'd thought the girl might throw a fit but Bunty only stared at her in obstinate silence, her blue eyes giving away nothing of her feelings on the matter.

'You must smile a good deal, and listen. Being a good listener is so important. There is nothing a man likes more than to talk about himself. It makes him feel that he is the centre of the universe.' Lucy glanced across at her silent daughter, curled on the window seat, chewing her nails.

'And do stop that filthy habit! You must appear elegant at all times, and utterly charming. Remember, it does no harm to flirt a little, and to flatter him. It's vital that you make a man feel good. And should he take a few liberties, then do not squeal in a silly feminine way, or protest, but rather use his interest to make him want you more. Only when he's panting for you will he suggest marriage. What else do we have to offer except our bodies? Are you listening to me? Do you understand how important it is to please?'

'Yes, Mother.'

'Good. He may ask you to stroke his cock. Don't grimace or show the slightest distaste because really it isn't unpleasant at all.' Lucy went on to describe yet more liberties which could be allowed, under the right conditions, as Bunty listened with increasing horror and disgust.

Lucy believed she had succeeded, that progress was being made. But after a second encounter with Timothy Tiffin her daughter's silence extended for three long days and nights. Quite intolerable. When asked what had occurred to send her into this unnatural decline, the girl refused to speak, remaining mute even at meal times and only pecking at her food. Something obviously wasn't quite right.

The aunts became concerned and poked their noses in, wanting to know if Bunty was quite happy about all of these arrangements, if she minded being paraded at tea parties and social events as a prospective spouse.

Irritated by their interference, Lucy longed to snap that she didn't care a jot whether the girl minded or not, but was anxious not to alienate them. The last thing she wanted was for Bunty to get the impression she had only to turn to the aunts and she could escape her duty. They'd made other comments, been somewhat obstructive at times, so it was essential that Lucy should calm their fears and win them round to her way of thinking.

She decided to appeal to their snobbish side, which, for all their high moral tone, was very much a part of their nature.

'If things had been different, darling Bunty might well have been presented at Court, enjoyed a year of being brought out with any number of parties and dances provided for her. Since that can't now happen we must make the best of things, must we not?'

'Oh, indeed,' Vera agreed.

Cissie said in wistful tones, 'We were never allowed to be brought out either. It might have made such a difference.'

'Papa held a dance for us once,' Vera snapped. 'And that young man marked himself for every dance on your card.'

'Yes,' Cissie agreed with a sigh. 'He took me cycling the following Sunday afternoon. Cyril Peckham was his name, I recall. He took rather a shine to me did Cyril, but Papa did not approve. His family were in ironmongery, and strong Methodists, not quite the thing, so I wasn't allowed to see him any more. At the time I thought it so cruel. I was heartbroken, being just a young girl, but I had no choice but to obey. Papa was most insistent. Cyril married Barbara Johnstone instead. So sad.'

Vera patted her sister's hand in a rare demonstration of affection after this unexpected baring of her soul.

'There you are then,' said Lucy, well pleased. 'We must not allow darling Bunty to suffer a similar fate, and with so few young men left after the war, we must give her every opportunity to meet new people.'

'Indeed we must,' Vera agreed. 'I thought I might embroider a pretty silk stole to match the blue velvet.'

'Oh, how delightful,' Cissie agreed. 'And I shall make a little Dorothy bag to match.'

'What sweeties you both are,' said Lucy, quite certain she'd have no further trouble with the aunts, and since Bunty too was behaving with a much greater maturity, sulky silence or no, she expected success in her little scheme to follow shortly.

Kate wasted no time in looking for premises and quickly discovered that they couldn't afford city-centre rents. Undeterred, she spread her search wider and found a suitable empty shop on Stretford Road. This was one of the major shopping thoroughfares of Manchester, boasting tailors and dress shops, grocers and furniture emporiums, and of course Paulden's, another famous local department store which drew shoppers from far and wide. It might be off-centre and not quite the most glamorous area of the city but shoppers came here in droves, handy as it was to Oxford

Road, and Kate thought it would make an ideal location for their first shop.

She had already decided that there would be another. This was but the beginning. Kate saw no reason why she and Flora shouldn't own a whole chain of shoe shops right across Manchester. But to have any chance of achieving that, they must get the first one absolutely right. An advertising campaign would be essential, posters giving the bus number that people would need to take to reach them, a small map to pin-point their location perhaps, and most certainly a picture of the shop or one of their most stylish products.

Toby was in the process of making arrangements for her to visit the warehouses of a couple of suppliers to start placing orders for her initial stock. The idea filled her with excitement and trepidation as Kate hoped to persuade them to make up some of her own designs eventually. For now, she must simply choose the best she could. It was so important to get it right.

Flora, meanwhile, had left school and the misery of mathematics and geography lessons behind her and was busily choosing the right colour paint for the Art Deco style she favoured.

'Not too classy, we don't want to put folk off. But it should be light and airy, with modern clean lines. I thought blue and grey with perhaps a touch of silver here and there, to brighten it. What do you think, Mammy?'

'I think it all sounds wonderful,' Kate said, and left her to it as she clearly knew what she was about.

'Now all I have to do is tell Theo Ingram that

I'm leaving.'

Flora looked at her mother with sympathy. 'He isn't going to like it.'

'You're right. He isn't.'

'Don't let him bully you into staying.'

'As if I would!'

Flora was entirely wrong. Kate began with an apology, saying how sorry she was to let him down but that she was handing in her notice. 'I'll be leaving at the end of the week, if that's convenient?'

She expected Theo to bark that it was not at all convenient, but not for the first time he caught her entirely off balance by seeming not the least bit concerned.

'Excellent news! I can't tell you how pleased I am to hear that.'

Kate was dumbfounded. 'You certainly know how to make a person feel wanted.'

'Don't fish for compliments, you are fully aware that you are wanted, Kate. Has someone made you a better offer? Who?'

'N-Nobody.' Why did he always unnerve her? His glittering gaze and cynical manner seemed to imply that he'd known all along what she was about to say, what she was about to do with her life, just as if he had personally planned it. 'At least, I'm setting up on me own. That is, me and Flora, we're opening a little shop of us own on Stretford Road, so we are.'

Ingram looked momentarily startled and then gave a soft chuckle. 'So you're setting up in competition? How very enterprising of you.'

Kate gave a half-smile, thinking maybe she'd surprised him after all. 'Competition is a strong word. That would be stretching it a bit, I reckon. I shouldn't think your customers will even know that we're there.' They would if she had any say in the matter, but it didn't seem polite to say so.

'It's a brave, if not foolhardy, thing to do. Some might even say reprehensible, use me to gain the necessary skills and confidence and then set up a shoe store of your own in opposition.'

Kate stiffened. 'Hold on, I told you from the start I knew about shoes.'

'But you never said how?'

'I explained that too. I used to work in a shoe shop – well, a shoe factory as a matter of fact.'

'Which factory? Where? Come on, Kate, stop being coy. Where and how did you acquire these skills, if not from my store?'

She felt cornered, not wishing to answer. 'It was further north. You've probably never heard of it. Anyway, what has that to do with the price of fish? I'm leaving and, as I say, I'm sorry to let you down but there it is. I like to be me own boss. Just like you.' And again she cast him a sideways smile, longing to escape and have done with this difficult interview. It would be so much easier if Theo didn't have this charisma about him, if he were ugly instead of so attractive. If she didn't fancy the pants off him.

'Oh, I understand perfectly, but that isn't the *real* reason you're leaving. I understand perfectly why you're doing that. Indeed, I half expected it.'

'You did?' Now she felt bemused. Had he thought of something that she hadn't? Could he truly read her mind?

He took her gently by the shoulders, 'You've decided to take down this foolish barrier you've erected between us, because we're employer and employee. Quite frankly, I'm delighted. On Friday you can leave my employ, and on Saturday I'm taking you out to dinner to celebrate the start of a new dimension in our friendship. And I won't take no for an answer.'

Kate realised that she'd set her own trap and now sprung it.

# 43

She had meant to go up to Kendal to see Callum come the weekend. Instead, Kate put on her glad rags and prepared to be wined and dined by Theo Ingram. Was it a mistake? She rather thought it might be or why did she feel so nervous, so uncomfortable? And yet, deep down, dangerously excited.

He took her to the Midland Hotel, all rather formal and stiff, where they ate potted shrimps, lentil soup and a fancy dish called Chicken *Fermière*. Kate would have preferred to go to a smaller café for a nice bit of haddock but Theo Ingram was a man accustomed to getting his own way and it clearly never occurred to him to ask her what she wanted to eat. He even looked offended when he had the waitress bring her a slice of lemon sponge and she declined to eat it.

'What is wrong with it?'

Kate giggled. 'Nothing, but I really couldn't eat another thing.'

'Well, I've ordered it now, so eat what you can.'

'No, thank you. I'm sorry, but you should have asked me before you ordered it.'

Clearly irritated, he spooned it into his own dish and ate both puddings. Kate watched him in amusement.

She did agree to have coffee which they took in the lounge, a rather grand room reminiscent of a bygone age.

'I think you like playing hard to get,' he said, about to spoon sugar into her coffee until Kate stopped him.

'I don't take sugar, thank you, and I like my coffee black.'

'Good gracious!' He lit up a cigar, not asking if she minded. Kate said nothing, probably because she rather enjoyed the scent of a good cigar, confining her attention to his earlier remark.

'I'm not playing anything, certainly not hard to get, just trying to earn an honest living and look after me daughter.'

'We could have done this months ago, enjoyed any number of dinners together, if you hadn't been so stubborn. Although now you're leaving the store it will certainly make matters much easier between us. Less gossip among the other staff.'

Kate looked at him and blinked, saying nothing. The arrogant assumption of the man was breathtaking. Why didn't she tell him so?

'So, what gave you the notion to open a shoe

shop? Generally speaking, women don't have the first idea how to run a business. They don't normally possess either the intelligence or the education. I'm sure you'll do your best, you and your daughter, since you've got spunk if nothing else, although I doubt your little shop will last the year.'

Kate was reeling, struck almost speechless by his casual dismissal of her abilities, not quite knowing which criticism to tackle first. She took a swallow of her coffee, almost scalding her mouth. Setting down her cup with a clatter, she caught his eye. Could he, very possibly, be teasing her? She decided to play safe and not take offence at his remarks. Besides, she hated to be put on the defensive. Smiling, she said, 'We've every faith we can make a success of it.' And then before he had the chance to interrogate her further, she asked him a question.

'How did you get into business then? Did you inherit the store from your family or start it yourself?'

The rest of the evening Theo Ingram did what he liked to do best, talk about himself, and Kate found herself listening with interest. He was the eldest of four, apparently his three younger siblings all girls, and once his father died, had readily taken control of the business at just eighteen. 'None of my sisters could possibly have coped,' he explained, rather dismissively Kate thought, though she made no comment.

For all he was young to be in such a position, it never troubled him, probably because there didn't seem to be any shortage of funds. Theo had had a much more privileged and easy route to success even than Eliot, who had also been left a business by his father although with no money to capitalise it. Consequently, he'd been forced to drag Tysons Shoes out of debt and difficulties more than once.

Yet despite Theo Ingram's rather high opinion of himself, his somewhat bossy, over-controlling manner and arrogant assumption that he knew best, he was an engaging raconteur, an amusing and companionable dinner partner, and Kate found herself relaxing in his company. Aware of the admiration in his eyes, she felt like a woman again for the first time in years.

He swung the conversation back to her, complimenting her on the ribbed silk gown she was wearing. 'That is a most delicate shade of pink, and a beautiful fabric. Not at all the sort of frock one would expect a shop girl to wear. You're a woman of mystery, Kate O'Connor. And those shoes ... very stylish. Of the latest design too. May I examine one?'

Kate abruptly stood up, feeling flustered. She'd made a bad mistake dressing herself up like this, out of pure vanity, and Tysons' name would be inscribed on the sock-lining of her shoe. 'I don't think that would be quite appropriate. Thank you for a lovely evening. I'd like to be getting off home now. I've left Flora with a neighbour.'

He insisted on escorting her, hailing a taxi cab for the short journey. Kate asked the driver to drop her at the end of her street.

'I'll walk you along to your door.'

'There's no need.'

'There's every need. This is not the best of areas, not at all in keeping with your expensive gown.'

Flushing bright pink, Kate said nothing as Theo paid off the taxi and then, taking her arm, led her into the shadowy darkness. They passed a reeling drunk spewing his guts into the gutter, a couple canoodling under a lamp post.

'It's not usually like this. It's generally a quiet neighbourhood. Flora and I feel perfectly safe living here.' But Kate saw it all through Theo's eyes tonight, knew she sounded unconvincing and hated herself for feeling embarrassed.

'Let me find you somewhere better.'

'I don't want anywhere better. I mean, I'm sure that once our little shop is successful, we'll be moving out of this street. We can manage, so we can.'

He regarded her steadily for a moment. 'You are a remarkable woman, Kate O'Connor, if remarkably stubborn, and I'd really like to get to know you better.'

Kate reached her front door with a sigh of relief. 'Here we are. Thank you kindly for a lovely evening.' She held out her hand in a polite gesture of farewell, and he just looked at it.

'Aren't you going to ask me in?'

'To be sure I'm not. Aren't I a respectable m–' Kate stopped, confused. Even after all this time, it was so easy to make that slip of the tongue. 'Sorry, I've not been widowed very long,' she said, by way of explanation, although this was far from true. Eliot had been dead nearly three years.

'I understand. You need looking after, that much is quite clear, but I've no wish to alarm you by rushing things.' Smiling sympathetically, Theo took the key from her hand and unlocked the door. Still Kate blocked the way, making it very clear that she meant what she said, slip or no slip. He nodded, raising his hands in mock surrender. 'Next time, perhaps.' Then, pulling her gently into his arms, he kissed her. She could taste the cigar on his tongue, the wine they'd drunk, and, despite herself, was stirred by the kiss, even if there was something cool and impersonal about it. But then, they were still little more than strangers.

When he'd gone she locked the door and skipped quickly up the stairs to bed, her heart pounding. What was she doing? Playing with fire, that's what.

Kate spent every day after that working to get the new shop ready for opening, Flora beside her. Toby came over to Manchester ever more frequently to check on progress and offer what assistance he could. He would always ask her what she'd been up to since he last saw her, but for some reason she made no mention of having been taken out to dinner by her ex-boss so that it came as a surprise when he challenged her about it.

They were cleaning out what was to be the stock room, breaking up old boxes, stripping torn paper from the walls. 'You're being courted by the great Ingram himself, I understand?'

'Who's been gossiping about me? Flora, I suppose.'

431

'She happened to mention he'd taken you out. Moving up in the world, eh?'

'It was only dinner.'

'Careful, you don't want him taking too much of a personal interest.'

Kate bridled. 'And why not, may I ask?'

'He's your boss.'

'Not any more.'

'He might start being nosy and asking questions, which you're best avoiding in the circumstances. We don't want any bad publicity at this stage.'

'Aw, so you're regretting involving yourself with a loony now, are ye, in case it gives you a bad name too, mebbe?'

'Don't be daft, Kate. I was thinking of the shop. I thought you wanted to be careful what folk learned about you, and he's clearly the nosey type. His sort usually like to know everything about any likely rival, to help them damage the competition, so be careful, that's all I'm saying. If Ingram thinks you have a dark secret, he'll winkle it out of you.'

She was irritated now, her independent streak coming strongly to the fore. 'I think it's up to me what I tell him, or who I go out with for that matter.'

Toby ripped up a battered cardboard box and stamped on it hard to flatten it, just as if he'd like to be doing that to Ingram. He'd tried telling Kate before how he felt about her, but it hadn't helped, so what else could he do now but bite his tongue and hope for the best? 'I only want you to be happy.'

Kate stifled a sigh. 'I know.' She decided to change the subject to safer ground. 'Why don't you bring Callum next time? Sure and it's weeks since I visited Kendal, and aren't I feeling guilty because I haven't seen him lately.'

Toby had said very little about whatever had gone awry over the arrangements Callum had made to stay with his mate except that he was now lodging with Toby, and had been for over a year. Whenever Kate had visited, she'd been happy to see that the pair of them seemed to get along well, for which she was grateful. She liked the idea of an older man keeping an eye on her over-sensitive son.

Now Toby said, 'I'm a bit worried about Callum, truth be told. His drinking isn't getting any less, that's for sure, and he can be a touch quarrelsome when in his cups. It's hard sometimes to keep a proper eye on him.'

Kate put both hands to her mouth. 'Is it because he feels I've deserted him? Jesus, Mary and Joseph! I've abandoned my own boy.'

Over pie and peas at the Crown, Flora having joined them for a bite to eat, all they could talk about was Callum. He was a great worry to Kate, but at least Toby understood so she had the relief of expressing her feelings. They were like family, the three of them, sharing their concerns over a loved one. Dear Toby, she took him so much for granted. What would she do without him?

'He's been behaving badly ever since it all fell through between Bunty and him,' Toby was explaining now.

'Aw, didn't I warn him that it would? He wrote

433

to say she was back home, but that they weren't together. I didn't like to ask why.'

Toby shook his head. 'He still isn't saying. Won't talk about it, won't even mention her name. I know they met up once, because they used me as go-between. Maybe they had a row, I'm not sure. After that, he once gave me a letter which I passed on to her by the office lad, but there's been no contact since, or not so far as I know.'

Flora looked solemn. 'I asked him what had gone so badly wrong, and he nearly snapped my head off.'

'It would be a good idea, Kate, if happen you could pop up to Kendal some time soon and have a word with the lad. He's not himself, not at all.'

'I will, I will. I'll come soon. Next week if I can,' Kate agreed.

Toby stayed for the rest of that day and in the evening took her to the pictures before he had to catch his train, as he often did.

He washed and shaved in Kate's back kitchen, put on a clean shirt and made some attempt to tame his wild hair. He really looked quite smart. Kate put on a new blue two-piece, linking arms with them as they walked along Oxford Street, feeling very content with life.

Their friendship became increasingly close as they worked together on the shop, and Kate found that she enjoyed Toby's company. She also accepted the odd invitation from Theo Ingram, and would find herself making comparisons, which wasn't really fair considering they were poles apart in income and education, not to mention class.

But Toby was certainly a hard worker. He didn't mind what task Kate gave him to do. He was happy to tackle the dirty, messy jobs, or to sit and worry over finances with her. He happily knocked down a wall in the little shop to open it up and make it bigger, although he let her deal with the landlord and sweetly persuade him to agree to the changes they wished to make to the premises.

'You're prettier than me,' Toby joked.

And always at the end of a day's work, they would enjoy a fish supper, or a film, or else the three of them would simply sit by Kate's fireside and talk endlessly, making plans for the future of the business. It was all so exciting.

She still hadn't found time to see Callum and guilt was gnawing at her. 'I've been that busy, so I have. Will I write him a letter to explain?'

Toby frowned, looking unconvinced. 'Something's eating him, that's for sure. Got absolutely plastered the other night. His drinking does seem to be getting worse.'

'Lucy isn't creating more problems for him, I hope?'

'Thankfully, she has other things on her mind right now. Haven't you heard? Rumour has it there's a wedding in the wind. She's apparently found herself a rich husband, a Ralph Powney, who must be a good few years younger.'

Kate gaped. 'I've heard nothing of any wedding, nor received any invitation.'

'I believe it's to be a quiet ceremony, with no fuss.'

'Praise the Lord,' Kate said to Flora, and they both laughed. 'At least this means she'll be out of my hair for good now.'

In this, as so often in the past where Lucy was concerned, both rumour, and Kate, were quite wrong.

# 44

'Are you going to open this door or must I call for help to break it down?'

Bunty sat curled on her bed with her hands over her ears, refusing to listen to her mother's shrieks. She felt numb, stunned by events. Could this really be happening to her? A week ago she'd still been free, congratulating herself on her increasing skill at evading her mother's schemes. Now disaster loomed and she really didn't know how it had come about. She was over twenty-one, for heavens' sake, so why did she still have no control over her own life?

In the two years since Callum had turned his back on her, she'd gone through the motions of obediently doing exactly as Lucy demanded, not caring one way or the other what kind of future she had, since it didn't include Callum.

Lucy hammered on the door again. 'Our appointment at the dressmaker is in half an hour precisely and *you will be there if I have to drag you by the hair!* A bride cannot be married without a wedding gown.'

But she could apparently be married without her consent, Bunty thought gloomily. She could barely recall even being asked, let alone agreeing. Why did she even bother to make this last stand? Where was the point? She was lost, doomed, no doubt had been from the start.

Bunty had eaten more roast beef dinners and cucumber sandwiches, drunk more cups of tea and glasses of champagne, than were really quite good for her, yet hadn't cared one iota. She'd been on a social treadmill, going through the motions of politeness, filling the endless days.

Some of it had been quite amusing, like the dressing up and going to the theatre, or sailing on the lake in private steam yachts, being bought delicious little presents and made to feel special. All of this had served to take her mind off her misery over Callum.

But much of it had been decidedly unpleasant. Having to let old men paw and pat her, for instance, like that Timothy Tiffin creature who'd touched her where he shouldn't. She'd success-fully managed to dampen *his* ardour though.

At one especially dreadful musical soiree she'd got really rather tiddly which had resulted in the unfortunate, if rather hilarious, incident in the garden.

The aunts' tiny house at Heversham was far too small for such an event, not that Lucy would allow this small detail to stand in the way of her ambition. Nevertheless, the effect of all those people crowding into the small front parlour had been stifling and Bunty had escaped briefly for a breath of fresh air.

Timothy Tiffin, he of the fat wandering fingers, caught her nursing a sore head beneath the rose arbour. Bunty had been wishing that boredom and near suffocation hadn't tempted her to accept a third glass of champagne when a pair of large, clammy hands had reached around her and firmly planted themselves upon her breasts. He always had been fascinated by her bosom.

She'd screamed and there'd been a most unseemly tussle with 'naughty Timmy' trying to push his hands up her skirt and Bunty kicking his shins for all she was worth. He very nearly succeeded in having his wicked way with her as she'd been prostrate on the paving stones when, fortunately, she'd been saved by one of Aunt Cissie's spaniels. Jess had heard her yells and come bounding out to join in the fun. She wasn't the sort of dog to attack an intruder, unfortunately, being rather soppy with a very wet lick, but had certainly put Timothy off his stroke by jumping excitedly all over him.

'Dratted animal,' he grumbled, taking an unsteady kick at the poor dog. Then he'd adjusted his tie and lurched off in search of more liquid comfort.

It was all really rather shaming, and, to Bunty's distorted sense of black humour, absolutely hilarious. She'd sat on the arbour wall and laughed till her sides ached, and had treated the dog to chocolates and extra biscuits ever since.

Most suitors had not been quite so adventurous, nor so difficult to repel. Somehow or other, despite all Lucy's conniving and machinations, Bunty had successfully managed to remain largely, if not entirely, untouched and unfettered, and certainly fended off all offers.

It had been surprisingly easy. All she had to do was veer from sulky black moods to mute defiance, the predictable result being that most of Lucy's candidates had taken one look and fled. The last thing they wanted to saddle themselves with was a difficult, petulant child bride.

But then along had come Ralph Powney.

He wasn't like the others. Ralph Powney not only had more money, power and influence than all the rest put together, owning a large estate in Yorkshire as well as another in the Lakes, he had a persistence and strength of will which put even Lucy's machinations in the shade.

Which was why Bunty had this morning shut herself in her bedroom, making a desperate last stand, rather like a condemned prisoner refusing to eat his last meal.

The hammering had reached an impossible pitch and Bunty could hear the two aunts remonstrating with Lucy, demanding to know what on earth was going on.

Tears rolling down her cheeks, Bunty slid from the bed and made her way over to the window to stare out on a huddle of cottages. The whole of Heversham would be alerted if her mother carried on in this fashion. What on earth could she do?

If only she could get to Kendal, find Callum and talk to him one more time; explain how desperate her situation was. Surely he wouldn't turn his back on her again. The question was, how to get out of the house?

Dashing the tears from her eyes, Bunty considered the drop from her bedroom window. An overhanging branch from a nearby beech tree looked temptingly close. Seconds later, she'd climbed out on to the sill and was making a perilous leap into the leafy arms of the old tree. A glorious sense of freedom soared through her veins as she clung to its knobbly trunk. It felt even more wonderful when her feet touched solid earth. Then she was off, running along the lane towards the main road where she hailed a lift on a milk cart. She'd beat her mother yet, see if she didn't.

The shop had been painted and fitted out as smartly as they could manage on their limited budget. It was not quite so large or grand as Ingram's shoe department, but they would make up for that by offering a more personal level of service.

Kate had visited several shoe manufacturers and stocked the shop with the very latest, up-to-the-minute styles that any flapper, or woman about town, would be only too delighted to wear. Children too had not been forgotten, and she'd bought a range of children's wear in various sizes and fittings. Kate was most particular about the fittings. Not everyone's foot was the same shape, particularly children's. They were specialists and must behave as such.

She instigated a system of stock control and trained Flora in how to use it so that slow-moving stock could be identified and marked down in an end-of-year sale, while popular lines could quickly be replaced.

This was the way, Kate knew, to ensure maximum profit for minimum investment.

They inserted a large advertisement in the *Manchester Guardian* for the first day of October, the date they planned to open, in good time for Christmas; put up posters in neighbouring shops; handed leaflets out to shoppers in the street. Yet still there seemed to be a great deal left to be done. The specially printed paper bags hadn't yet arrived, nor had much of the stock, and Kate and Flora were on pins every day watching for deliveries.

Kate had sent invitations for the opening party to a few friends and neighbours, to Millie and her family, Callum of course, new business acquaintances, fellow shopkeepers, plus a sprinkling of local reporters who she hoped would write a little piece about the shop in their newspaper.

She'd received acceptances from all of them, except her own son.

It had been agreed that Toby would arrive a couple of days before the event in order to help with final preparations and assist on their first day of trading. She hoped he would bring Callum with him but that was still a week or two away. In the meantime, Kate had decided it was long past time she went up to Kendal and spoke to Callum herself.

'I need to talk to the daft eejit about whatever problem is driving him to the demon drink. Will you stay with Millie while I go?' she asked Flora.

Flora hugged her mother. 'Go and tell him we need him here, working with us.' And so it was agreed.

Bunty discovered almost at once that she had made a futile, empty gesture. Long before the rickety milk cart had travelled the six or seven miles to Kendal, Ralph Powney had been informed of her escape, had easily waylaid the slow-moving vehicle and driven her home again in his fast Ford motor car.

Where would she have gone in any case? Callum would have refused to see her, as he had once before when she'd called. Why had she fooled herself into thinking otherwise?

The last time she'd knocked on the battered old door, that scruffy friend of his had told her Callum had moved and he'd no idea where to. Bunty hadn't believed him, but since she had very little freedom to scour the streets of Kendal, what else could she do but cling to the hope that she might run across him by chance one day? Unfortunately, she never had, and never dared risk another letter.

Callum seemed to have meant it when he'd said he wanted no more contact between them.

Even so, in her heart she knew that he still loved her, for all he'd set his mind against her – and for such a silly reason. All because he believed she'd willingly agreed to the abortion.

As a consequence, Bunty was left to deal with Ralph Powney on her own.

From the first moment he'd set eyes on her, he'd resolved to have her. It had been at a

Christmas function where everyone was in fancy dress. Bunty had been dressed as Fairy Crystal, her mother's idea and quite inappropriate since the handkerchief hemline of the short skirt revealed far too much of what Bunty considered to be her worst asset, her rather chunky ankles.

Ralph Powney, however, thought otherwise. He was clearly enchanted and, unlike Evan Whatshisname – fat suitor number one – or naughty Timmy, he made no attempt to force himself upon her. Nor, as many others before him had done, did he run a mile when Bunty resorted to her usual trick of rudeness by telling him that the Prince of Darkness would have been a more suitable disguise for him rather than Good King Wenceslas.

Ralph had been amused, had congratulated her on her wit, and thereafter he was present at every party she attended, quietly observing her, giving the lop-sided leer that was the closest he ever came to a smile.

He seemed to take great pleasure in provoking her into ever more outrageous remarks. When once he asked her to dance, Bunty said she'd rather cut off all her hair and enter a nunnery. Powney said it could be arranged but then he'd have to become a monk so that he could still see her.

Another day, when he invited her to accompany him to a recital, Bunty remarked that she hated music.

'So do I. Clearly we are the perfect match.'

'I think you're ugly,' she bluntly responded when he complimented her on her appearance.

'Splendid! Beauty and the Beast. What a pair we'll make.'

Now it seemed that they were indeed to be a pair. Without her even realising his intentions, Ralph Powney had approached Lucy and asked for her consent. When her mother had told her of this, for one wild moment Bunty had hoped he meant to marry Lucy herself, as they were certainly much more of an age, but her mother's sharp rejoinder to this suggestion brought her quickly to her senses.

'I know that you will come to love me, my sweet, once we are man and wife, even if you don't quite yet,' Powney informed Bunty now with calm assurance as he handed her over to her mother's far from tender care. 'So do please stop fighting me.'

Lucy, fearful that her carefully laid plans could fall apart at the last moment, thanked him profusely. 'I have been out of my mind with worry, every since the silly girl ran away.' As if it had been a day rather than an hour that Bunty had been missing. 'She is little more than a child, after all, so I do hope that you'll make allowances for her foolishness?'

'Indeed, but now is the time for her to grow up. Very soon, she will have the responsibilities of being my wife and helpmate. And lover,' he said, deliberately allowing his gaze to rove over Bunty's firm young flesh.

'Quite so. Quite so,' Lucy agreed. 'You can safely leave her in my hands. I shall make sure that she understands how fortunate she is.'

'This silly performance,' Lucy forcibly informed her recalcitrant daughter the moment they were alone, 'very nearly cost us everything. Fortunately, since Ralph is so captivated by your charms, he wants no further delay. You are to be wed within the month. Please try to remember how very privileged you are to have received such an offer, considering our situation and your own shameful, past history, secret though it must remain. He is an excellent catch, so do not even consider being as difficult as this ever again. Do I make myself clear?'

'He hasn't even bothered to ask me himself,' Bunty said, struggling to retain her composure. 'I'm twenty-one years of age. Don't I have any say?'

Lucy sighed heavily. 'We've been through all of this a million times and my patience is quite exhausted. How you have managed to hold them all off so long I cannot imagine, but there will be no further delays. Ralph Powney has offered a marriage settlement which will see us all in comfort for the rest of our lives, so the deed will be done. The aunts and I are depending upon you. You will marry him before the month is out, whether you like it or not.'

Bunty once again sat in her bedroom and wept with fury and despair, swamped in a black suffocating blanket of depression. No matter how nasty she'd been to him, Ralph Powney had resisted all her schemes. He was not put off by her rudeness, her sulks, or even her defiance. What could she possibly do or say to make him withdraw his offer?

445

She chewed on her nails and thought for quite some time. More than ever she sympathised with Kate's efforts to fight off Lucy's machinations in the past. No wonder the pair had been at daggers drawn half the time. How could one loathe one's own mother so much? It was obscene, and yet she did. Bunty hated her because Lucy was utterly out of control, obsessed with her own needs, with money and boring security. She crushed dreams, destroyed hopes and desires, took a person's life and twisted it to suit herself.

She'd done it to Kate, apparently, and to Callum too. Strong as they both were, they'd been unable to confound her, so what could Bunty hope to do, a mere girl?

And then it came to her. The perfect solution, or the last desperate throw of the dice, depending on how you viewed it. It would most certainly be a lie, and a risky one at that, but desperate straits called for desperate measures. Bunty realised, in that moment, that she must take the chance. What alternative did she have?

# 45

Flora opted not to come with her to Kendal but to stay on in Manchester to work on the shop, which was a relief in a way. It would give Kate the opportunity to talk to Callum alone. The instant she set eyes on him, the first time she had seen him in months, Kate saw at once how her son had changed.

He looked gaunt, his face sickly and pale, jaw set tight upon some suppressed anger. His once laughing blue-grey eyes were hooded and unfocused, never quite meeting her gaze.

'Aw, what is it, me darling, what is eating you up inside? Don't ye look dreadful, poor boy? Haven't I been worrying meself sick over you? Toby tells me that your boss is threatening to sack you because you keep turning up late for work, or not at all. This won't do, Callum, it won't do at all. You need to finish your apprenticeship and qualify.'

'Don't fuss, Mother. And don't pretend you give a monkey's what's wrong with me. You're fine and dandy in Manchester, so why should you care?'

'Of course I care. Aren't you my fine boy? Don't I love the bones of ye? Did you not get me invitation to the opening? I hope you'll be coming to see what yer mammy and sister have been up to ... even join us in the business once you've qualified. Now wouldn't that be grand?'

'I know what you've been up to. Flora's told me all about your fancy man.'

Kate jerked as if she'd been struck. 'Fancy man? What are you talking about?'

'Flora's told me how you have a new man in your life, how he's been wining and dining you. No wonder you've never been near Kendal in months.'

Kate was appalled that he should think such a thing. ''Tisn't so! That's not the way of it at all. I've been out with Theo Ingram once or twice but there's nothing in it. Anyway, just recently, with us being so busy getting the new shop ready for opening an' all, didn't I tell him to stay away? That's what's kept me tied up in Manchester, me new shop, not Ingram. Though, I must say, if I should wish to go out with a fella again, I don't believe I need ask your permission first.'

'Then don't come pretending to care about me, or start poking your nose into my life. I'll do as I please.'

'What is it? What's upset you so badly? Is it that Bunty creature?'

He turned on her then, eyes alight with fire and fury. 'Don't call her that.'

'I – I'm sorry. I didn't mean...'

'Aye, you did. You want to say that you told me so, that you knew it wouldn't work out, that she was only playing games with me. Well, I hope you're satisfied because you were obviously right. She's getting married. How about that? She got over me pretty damned quick, didn't she?'

'But I thought it was Lucy getting married?' Kate tried to put her arms about her son but he thrust her away, the distress in his face breaking her heart. 'Aw, don't I know how you must be hurting, but drowning yer sorrows in drink isn't the answer. Won't it only ruin yer health, and yer life?'

He shouted at her then. 'What do you bloody care? You have your fine new business and yer fancy man, so can afford to leave me high and dry. Leave me alone, I tell you. Leave me alone!'

Upon which note he strode away, leaving Kate filled with confusion and shame. She'd tried to make things better for her son and only succeeded in making matters worse.

It was true what she'd told Callum, that for the last few weeks Kate had managed to avoid going out with Theo Ingram, yet he always seemed to be around. Sometimes she would laugh at his audacity. 'Not you again,' she would say. 'Don't you ever give up?'

'No. I want to see you, Kate. I mean to win you over.'

'Wear me down, more like. Will ye behave, ye daft eejit?' She had to hand it to him for persistence. Nevertheless Kate refused to accept any more of his invitations, claiming she was far too busy getting ready for her opening, but then he caught her unawares again.

She came home from the shop one night to find him talking to Flora in the street. He was leaning close to hear what she had to say and they both laughed, as if sharing a joke. Kate rushed up, annoyed that Theo should speak to her daughter without her permission, although really she couldn't have said why it should matter. Hadn't she made it plain to Callum that she was perfectly entitled to have a man friend, if she'd a mind? Yet what was it they were talking about with such earnestness?

'Why are you here?' she bluntly demanded. 'I told you I was too busy to go out with you at present.'

His dark eyebrows rose in mild surprise at Kate's tone, then he gave Flora's shoulder a little squeeze. 'We were just getting acquainted, were we not? Admittedly I was asking her where you were and if I could waylay you and carry you off on my white charger, but your charming daughter said you had no head for heights.' Again they both laughed in unison and Kate felt suddenly rather foolish. She smiled, in a vague attempt to prove that she really did have a sense of humour, even if she was too tired at the moment to exercise it.

She felt obliged, in the circumstances, to invite him in for a cup of tea although managed to keep the visit short and to send Theo on his way with vague promises for the future. Whether they would come true or not, and whether she would wish to spend her time with him if she did have some to spare, Kate couldn't quite decide.

'Usually women are queuing up for me to take them out. You, dear Kate, are proving to be a particular challenge.'

'I'm pleased to hear it. Never let it be said that I'm easy.'

Theo leaned close, brushing his lips against her ear. 'Nevertheless, you'll succumb to my charm in the end, just like all the rest.'

'He's nice,' Flora said, after he'd left. 'He has a lively sense of humour, and he doesn't look too bad either. You could do worse, Mammy.'

'Worse in what respect?' Kate had disliked his parting remark, had felt an instinctive need to deny she would do any such thing. Succumb to his charms indeed. Her traitorous flesh, however, said otherwise. 'Sure and I don't know what you mean.'

'You aren't going to spend the rest of your life

all alone, are you? I know Callum was disapproving of the friendship, but what does he know? You do as you please, I don't mind.'

'Well, thank you kindly for your permission, miss. Do I look so desperate that I need a man to look after me? Indeed, I think not.' And Kate shushed a laughing Flora and packed her off to bed, her own cheeks bright crimson. If only she could decide how she felt about Theo. One minute she ached to fall into his arms, the next she couldn't bear him near her. It was all most odd.

Ralph Powney was staring at her as if she'd gone quite mad. For the last few weeks Bunty had been the soul of discretion. She'd endured endless dress fittings, shown interest in her bridesmaids and the wedding breakfast, even discussed which hymns were to be sung by the choir. She'd helped write scores of invitations, and agreed which of their various cousins would act as ushers.

When events had reached a point of what felt like complete chaos, and even the well-organised Lucy was tearing her hair, Bunty chose to make her move. She suddenly insisted that Ralph be called, as she had something of great importance to tell him.

'You aren't going to call it off, not again. I won't allow it.'

'I need to speak with him. Now!'

Lucy had railed and wept, raged and stormed, insisting Bunty tell her first what this was all about, but she absolutely refused. In the end she'd been forced to comply with her daughter's request.

Now Bunty was sitting on the aunts' threadbare sofa in the front parlour, the aunts themselves huddled in the back living room with her mother, no doubt itching to know what was going on. Bunty wouldn't put it past any of them to listen at the door.

She got to her feet. 'Shall we take a turn about the garden, or perhaps down the lane? This is a very private and personal matter, just between ourselves.'

Reluctantly, although he was every bit as curious as they to hear what she had to say, Powney agreed.

Bunty had wondered how to broach the subject, how to begin, but remembering how a previous blunt approach had devastated Callum, opted for the same method. 'I am sure my mother has explained that I am not entirely innocent but I feel I should make things quite clear between us before it is too late for you to change your mind. I want you to know that I have enjoyed the attentions of a lover.'

He stopped dead, looking most satisfactorily shocked, which clearly told Bunty that, true to her word, Lucy had said nothing at all about her past indiscretions. How wonderful to have upset her mother's plans at last! In the silence which followed she heard the unmistakable call of a wood pigeon and Bunty thought how much more appropriate a cuckoo would have been, in the circumstances. Which errant thought almost made her laugh out loud, except that she managed to control herself just in time. Hysteria would not help her now.

She caught the fresh tang of newly cut grass from a neighbour's garden, perhaps the last mowing before the autumn rains came. The sappy scent of it somehow filled her with new strength, reminding her that the chill days ahead would soon pass, spring would come again and she was still young and full of vigour, with all her life before her. She didn't have to be bullied, not by this man, nor by her mother.

And it would seem that she had, at last, silenced him. Ralph Powney was glaring at her, mute with fury.

Bunty blithely continued with her tale, her gaze kept modestly downward, hands clasped as if in anxiety. 'My mother did not approve of our relationship and she insisted I stop seeing him. However, I have to tell you now that I did not obey her. We have not only continued to see each other regularly but have been intimate.' It was only a slight adjustment of the truth, after all. They had been lovers, and would be still if Bunty had her way. She felt no compunction about lying to her unwelcome suitor.

'Now I must confess to you that I carry his child. So, you see, it is quite impossible for me to marry you. It would be most unfair, even to please my mother. I am already compromised.'

She lifted her eyes briefly to his, ready to meet cold fury, incandescent rage. Even physical abuse would not have been unexpected. Bunty would gladly have endured the odd slap if she was then left free as the sweet blackberry brambles frolicking over the autumn hedgerows. She was shocked instead to find that Ralph's mouth was curling

453

into that supercilious smile of his.

'Your mother prepared me for this moment. She said you might well come up with some fanciful yarn about having relinquished your virginity for love, and that I was not to believe a word of it.'

Bunty's heart gave a little jump. She'd played her trump card and still she'd lost. 'But it's true ... it's true.'

Ralph Powney shook his head, looking happier than she'd ever seen him. 'I think not.'

Anger raged through her then like a forest fire, hot and swift. 'It happened, I tell you. He got me pregnant and my mother made me have an abortion!'

Now Ralph actually laughed out loud. 'If you are going to lie, my sweet, at least get your story straight. Either you are pregnant with his child, or you have had an abortion. You cannot have it both ways.'

Too late, Bunty saw her mistake. By being unable to lie convincingly and now resorting to the truth on a burst of anger, her story had lost credibility entirely. 'But it's true, it's true, I swear it! I was still a schoolgirl, had to be moved to a new school to avoid a scandal.'

He looked at her askance, one eyebrow raised in disbelief. 'And now you're pregnant again? You are having a *second* child?'

'Y-yes, I am.' Oh, Lord, she'd messed everything up. Much as she might rant and swear that she was guilty of this shameful act, Bunty knew her fiancé did not believe a word of it. He was laughing uproariously, as if she had said something hugely amusing. He sobered up eventually and kissed her gently on the brow.

'I realise you are nervous of matrimony but fear not, my sweet, you will enjoy intimacy with me, I promise you.'

'No, that's not the problem at all. I really am in love with someone else and could well be carrying his child.'

'Hush!' Once again he gave that lop-sided leer which sent shivers down Bunty's spine, his tone condescending, as if speaking to a child. 'If this tale is true, and I must say that you do not appear *enceinte*, then I am prepared to take the chance you are mistaken. If you are indeed carrying this man's child, then I will accept it and bring it up as my own. I cannot say fairer than that. I shall be the perfect gentleman, behave like a man of honour. You have no need to fret, my lovely, I will not see you disgraced.'

Lucy couldn't believe her own ears. After all her hard work, all the effort she'd put into launching her daughter over these last months to have her try to undo it all with a streak of perverse rebellion on the day before the wedding was too much to bear. Yet here was Ralph Powney telling her exactly that.

'I cannot imagine what possessed her to make up such lies.' Lucy gave a trill of uneasy laughter. 'Saucy madam! I should think it is but wedding night nerves.' Could it be true? she thought wildly. Had the stupid girl indeed been seeing Callum secretly and got herself pregnant again?

'My sentiments entirely. I said as much.'

'Did you indeed?' Lucy stifled a sigh of relief. Perhaps the situation could be saved after all, yet rage roared in her like a furnace. She must damp it down, try to appear calm, even though she was beset by fools and idiots at every turn, even though her own daughter seemed hell-bent on ruining her own future, all their futures. She wouldn't tolerate it, not for a moment longer. 'I'll speak with her, give her something to calm her nerves.'

'I would recommend that you do.' Ralph half turned away, and then on a more casual note remarked, 'Of course, I am assuming that it is indeed a lie, that there isn't a single grain of truth in what she says?'

'Of course not. How could there be?'

'Only she did change her story halfway through, which rather gave the impression that it started out as a lie and ended up as gospel truth, if you catch my drift? Something about an abortion?'

Lucy went white. What had the girl told him? 'My daughter, sir, is as pure as a young girl ought to be on the eve of matrimony, as you will discover for yourself on your wedding night.'

His eyes narrowed. 'Except that it will be too late by then, will it not?'

'I believe what you really mean is that will be entirely the right time to discover that she is indeed a virgin,' gently scolded Lucy. 'Isn't that the way of it? That you, as her bridegroom, have that pleasure to look forward to?'

'Of course,' he said darkly. 'That is exactly what I meant.'

After he had gone, Lucy picked up a porcelain vase which stood on a marble pedestal and flung

it in the hearth, smashing it into a dozen pieces.
'Drat! Drat! Drat! I'll kill her ... I'll *kill* her for
this!'

# 46

'Yes, I told him that I was pregnant! *And* that it
was Callum's child. *And* that I don't want to
marry him. And, no, I don't care if we have to live
on porridge oats for the rest of our lives, *I will not
marry Ralph Powney!* I've changed my mind.'

'You most certainly *will* marry him. All the
arrangements are made. You cannot back down
now. *I will not allow it!*'

The raised voices, and the sound of the stinging
slap which followed, rang through the little house
in Heversham, rousing the two aunts from their
afternoon slumbers and bringing them bolt
upright in their wing chairs before, shamefaced,
they crept to the parlour door to listen closely to
every word.

'You lied! How dare you try to ruin everything
by lying.'

'Of course I lied. I love Callum, and always will.
Can't you understand that one simple fact,
Mother? If I can't have him, I shall have no one.'

Cissie whispered, 'Did she say that she was
pregnant, Vera?'

'Hush! She said that she lied.'

'Callum left me because of you, because *you*
forced me to have that abortion and he believes I

wanted it too. He was eager to marry me, would have welcomed the baby, *our* baby, but you killed it, Mother. *You killed it!* But I've had enough. I won't obey you any more. I'm twenty-one and I mean to live my own life in future, whatever that might be, and do exactly as I please! If it means I must lie in order to achieve that, so be it.'

Lucy was incandescent with rage. 'You can't possibly mean to persist with this stupid tale? I've encouraged Powney in the belief that you're merely suffering pre-nuptial nerves. It won't work, I tell you. He means to have you.'

'And I am certain that he will not. I shall shout it in church tomorrow, if necessary. Tell the whole world. You cannot make me marry that man, and I'll do anything, *anything*, to make sure that I don't. *I want Callum!*'

Again a ringing slap, more screams and raging, the slam of a door and the sound of a key turning in the lock. Then silence, ominous and deep.

The two aunts exchanged shocked glances. Never had they heard such heartbreak and despair in a girl's voice and their maiden hearts were deeply touched. 'Something must be done,' said Vera, usually the more unemotional of the two.

'Indeed, and we must be the ones to do it. Poor dear Bunty is to be wed to this man in just a few hours.'

'Time,' Vera agreed, 'is of the essence.'

Theo Ingram had called again the following evening, and the one after that. Kate had shooed him away but this Friday lunchtime, here he was again, waiting outside the shop for her to lock up, insisting on walking her home. It was then that Kate lost her temper. Perhaps she was tired, overwrought with nerves over the opening next week, but somehow Theo seemed to be hovering around every corner and she really didn't care for it.

She stopped dead in the street and shouted at him. 'I thought I asked you to leave me alone? You're starting to get on me nerves, so ye are.'

He looked startled. 'But I care for you, Kate. I want to be sure that you're all right, that you do well. Look, I've been thinking... This area is no good, and the shop is far too small, it won't work. I know you've done your best but really, it isn't good enough for you.'

Kate gasped. 'Haven't ye the cheek of the devil himself? I think that's for me to decide, don't you? We open Saturday week, for heaven's sake. I'll make it work, so I will.'

'I could lend you money, if that's the problem. Then you could find somewhere bigger and better in the centre of the city. Better still, Ingram's could supply you with stock. We could go into partnership. Wouldn't that be best? You'd have your independence but security too. Let's go and eat somewhere. We can at least talk about it.'

Kate stormed away, shouting back to him over her shoulder, 'I don't want yer flamin' money, or your security, or your awful old-fashioned stock! I'll succeed on me own, see if I don't.'

'You need me, Kate.'

'I don't need anyone, ta very much.'

He hurried after her, caught her by the arms and gave her a little shake. 'You do. You need a

459

man in your life. You need someone to take care of you, to get you out of that pig sty you call home.'

Twin spots of colour burned on her cheeks and she pushed him furiously away. 'I've a soft spot for pig sties, if you want to know. But whatever you might think of my house, it's home to me and I like it. Really, I think it would be best if we didn't see quite so much of each other in future. I've told you, I've enough on me plate at present with the opening of my new shop next week. Besides, you're wrong, I'm not in the market for a new fella in me life. I was happily married once ... twice as a matter of fact, but I was only a lass first time and the poor lad drownded in the River Kent. Anyway, I haven't yet found anyone fit to replace either one of them.'

Theo's eyes were regarding her with a strange intensity. 'You've just told me more in these five seconds than you have in all the time I've known you.'

Kate flounced away from him. 'I've just told you, as my friend Millie would say, to sling yer hook.'

'You've hardly given me a chance, Kate.' Then his voice dropped, his dark eyes softened and he caught her to him again, and no matter how she wriggled, this time he wasn't letting go. 'I'm sorry if I offended you. I get a bit carried away, want to put everything right for you. You're lovely, do you know that? I can't resist you, can't stop thinking about you, can't keep my hands off you. I need you, Kate.'

His kiss this time shook her to the core, it was

long and deep and drove her to respond whether she wanted to or not. Oh, but she did want to. When it came to it, she wanted to very much, so much that she did agree to have a meat pie and a glass of sherry with him at the Crown, and then invited him back to her house.

She'd never meant it to go this far. They were sitting on the settle in the front parlour and his hands were under her blouse caressing her bare skin, teasing her breasts, kissing and loving her as she remembered Eliot had once used to do. She really should be getting back to the shop, un-packing more of the newly delivered stock ready for the opening, but excitement was mounting in her. A desire to be loved, to be needed, was growing with a frightening speed and intensity.

His hand was on her knee, smoothing her thigh, the pressure and promise of his touch sending waves of emotion shooting through her. She felt like a silly young girl again, not a twice-widowed wife and mother. But then that was half the trouble, she was still young, still needing the love of a man. Dear Lord, help me, Kate thought. I'm putty in his hands.

She could hear him moan her name. He captured her face between his hands, kissed her till her mouth was bruised and rosy with his kisses.

'Can't we go upstairs? We're two adults, after all. You know that I love you. I want you, Kate. I want you very much.'

In that moment, Kate realised it was what she wanted too. She led him upstairs to her bedroom, let him lay her down on the bed, responding despite her better judgement to the ecstasy of being slowly undressed, of being made love to by a strong man. His kisses thrilled her, his touch set her senses alight. She felt powerless to resist. Yet at the last moment she was overcome by a strange shyness, a sudden reluctance to proceed. 'It's been so long, I'm not sure I remember how...'

'Too long, my sweet. Let me show you, lead you into...'

When the hammering began on the door, she didn't know whether to weep with disappointment or relief.

Toby stood grinning down at her. 'I thought for a moment that you weren't in. I know I wasn't supposed to arrive until next Thursday but thought I'd pop over this week as well, so we could get things finalised.' He suddenly noticed that she was in her dressing gown, and it barely four in the afternoon. 'Oh, I'm sorry, have I come at a bad time? Were you going out?'

Kate would have asked him to leave at that point, would have explained that, yes, she was indeed going out, anything to be rid of him. But the stair door behind her opened and Theo's voice called out to her as he put his head around it, 'What's keeping you, Kate? It's lonely up here by myself.'

Kate thought she might never forget the look of shock on Toby's face. He was clearly appalled to have found them thus, and hugely embarrassed. So was Kate. She wanted to say that nothing had actually happened with Theo but since that was only because Toby had interrupted them by knocking at the door, there didn't seem much point. It would be viewed as little more than a pathetic attempt to restore her damaged honour.

Toby glared at Theo Ingram as if he'd like to kill him, there and then, on the spot. He advanced upon him, seeming to swell with fury, going red in the face and demanding to know what the hell he was doing in Kate's house.

Theo gave his usual arrogant grin and chuckled. 'I should think that much is obvious.'

Kate grabbed Toby by the arm. 'Leave it, Toby. It isn't like you think. It was a mistake, there's nothing between us and...'

But Toby wasn't listening. Again he was addressing what he deemed to be an intruder, a defiler of her virtue. 'I know about men like you, taking advantage of a single woman, seducing anything in a skirt!'

'Not at all. I was invited. And she doesn't have a skirt on in case you haven't noticed.'

Toby took a swing, a powerful punch that landed full on Theo's jaw and sent him sprawling to the floor. He flung himself upon the prostrate man, dragged him to his feet by his shirt collar, then knocked him down again.

Kate was beside herself with dismay. This was terrible. 'Stop it, Toby! Stop it, stop it, for God's sake. You'll kill him!'

'I sincerely hope so.'

Theo staggered, seemed to collect himself as he found his balance sufficiently to fight back, but it was very much a one-sided contest. Within minutes Toby again had him pinned to the ground,

463

pummelling the life out of him, giving no mercy. Theo was very nearly unconscious before Kate managed to drag Toby off.

'Stop it, I say! You must *stop* this minute before you really do kill him.'

She got through at last and Toby backed off, dusting his hands as though relishing a job well done. He didn't even glance at Kate as he turned to go, narrow shoulders hunched, and somehow the very sight of him, the bitterness of his disappointment, filled her with unexpected shame and a deep sense of despair.

'Toby,' she called after him, but he didn't stop or turn around. He just kept right on walking.

'Is he your lover?' This was the first question Theo asked when he finally recovered sufficiently to speak. Kate had bathed his wounds, which were in fact little more than a few cuts and bruises, but she could see that he was deeply, dangerously angry.

'No, of course he isn't.'

'Your previous boss then?' His tone was bitingly cold and hard.

'No, quite the opposite. I mean... Look, will you please leave too? Go home and rest and you'll be fine. There's no real damage done, though you might have a black eye in the morning. And I think it would be best if we didn't see each other again, not for a while anyway, and not like this. This is all too embarrassing for words, I need time to think.'

'You do care for him. Or you did once. I can see it in your face.' He struggled to get to his feet.

Kate made no attempt to help him. 'Look, whatever there was between the two of you, it's over. I'm the man for you now, Kate, not that vicious lout.'

'Toby isn't vicious, nor does he usually go in for punch-ups. He meant well, I know he did. He's over-protective of me, that's all. We've known each other a long time.'

'No matter how long you've known him, or what you've enjoyed in the past, it's over. Understand? Haven't I made it plain enough how I feel about you? You belong to me now. He has no rights over you at all. Forget him.' Theo was pulling her to him again, stroking her hips, her waist, running his hands over her back, tugging at the cord on her dressing gown. 'Let's go back upstairs, carry on where we left off.'

'What are you saying? Stop it! I don't belong to anyone. Please stop that.' Kate had forcibly to remove his hands, tried to push him towards the door, yet still he resisted.

'You're surely not throwing me out?'

'I am so.'

'Don't you realise what you are doing by refusing me?' he snarled. 'I was considering asking you to be my wife. You'll never get as good an offer again, not a woman such as yourself with no breeding. Although since you were willing enough to allow me into your bed, perhaps it's just as well that I didn't propose. Was this chap calling round for a taste of your favours too?'

'*Get out!* Go on, go home. I don't ever want you to call at my house again!'

He took it badly, very badly indeed. He scorned

and scoffed, ridiculed and insulted Kate, obstinately refusing to believe that she could resist him. Theo Ingram was not a man to accept defeat easily and his arrogance was such that he couldn't seem to take in the fact that he was the one being told to leave. His success with women in the past, usually beneath him in status, of course, and therefore grateful for his attentions, meant that the reverse was generally the case. Love 'em and leave 'em, that had been his byword. Now he was caught in the net of this woman's charms and couldn't believe she was actually throwing him out.

Pride was all he had left. 'All right, don't fret, I'm going. Just as well. I don't really care for other men's leavings.'

Kate was crying by this time, tears rolling down her cheeks as shame and a new self-knowledge bit into her. Not a pleasant experience. It was true what he said, it had been easy for him to persuade her. Her great desire to love and be loved, and to trust in people, had been her undoing, as so often in the past. Was she turning into a woman of easy virtue? God forbid. Yet this man was manipulative and controlling, wanting to take over her life, and she wasn't having that, not at any price.

'Find some other woman who appreciates your magnanimous offer more than I do. It's over.'

'You can't really mean that. You'll have changed your mind by morning. Women always do.'

'I *do* mean it. Believe me, I do. Don't ever call here again.' And she slammed the door shut in his face.

From Aunt Vera's expression you would not have guessed that she was on an errand of mercy. 'Such a nice young man,' she'd remarked to her sister as the pair of them bowled along in the ancient pony and trap to Kendal, past Levens Hall with its beautiful topiary gardens and the ancient walls of Sizergh, feeling a trace of regret that the Tysons had lost their own family seat, albeit a much more modest one.

The fresh, country breeze brought an unaccustomed pinkness to Vera's usually sallow complexion and now, faced with the young man in question, the excitement of their small adventure made her cheeks appear as if she were wearing rouge, although her expression was as stern as ever. Sterner perhaps, due to the condition he was in.

They had found him not at the factory, nor at his friend's house, nor even at Toby's where they'd learned he was apparently lodging now, but in the Rifle Man's Arms, and very much the worse for wear.

He'd resisted their polite request to accompany them quietly outside; had turned argumentative when Vera suggested that he might, just possibly, have taken a glass or two too many of that strong ale and should set aside the tankard in his hand without finishing it.

He had refused, most vociferously.

In the event, they were forced to take charge of the situation, Vera taking a firm hold of his collar and the seat of his pants, frog-marching him down to the river where, without further ado, she flung him into the cold, muddy water and gave him a good ducking.

'Oh, Vera, what a shocking thing to do,' Cissie said, when she'd left him sprawling in the mud.

'Yes,' agreed her sister with some satisfaction. 'Wasn't it?'

# 47

Callum floundered about in the shallows, shocked to find in his drunken stupor that he was suddenly, and comprehensively, soaked to the skin. 'What the bleeding hell...?'

'Don't use profanities in front of us, Callum Tyson. Cissie and I remember you as a child, the dearest, sweetest child imaginable, so you can stop this posturing, this maudlin self-pity, and start to think of someone other than yourself for a change.'

'I don't give a sh—'

'*Callum!*'

Something in Vera's tone brought him to his senses and he crawled from the filthy river to lie prone on the bank, and gave himself up to a sound scolding. He knew when he was beaten. Hadn't he suffered the sharp end of Aunt Vera's tongue more times than he cared to remember?

But as she began to talk, the words that came streaming out of her mouth with the sharpness of knitting needles were not at all what he expected to hear. She wasn't ranting at him, ticking him off for being bad, or not too much anyway. Instead

Vera was telling him about Bunty, and how utterly miserable she was, and how she was being dragooned into marriage. 'She is being forced to go through with this farcical alliance while declaring, nay, shouting to high heaven, her undying love for you.'

Cissie put in, 'If it wasn't so tragic, it would really be quite romantic.'

Callum wiped the water from his face with the flat of one hand, sat up, and focused sharply on Vera's face. He'd never sobered up so quickly, but then he'd never seen the aunts so distressed.

'We cannot go on defending Lucy, not in these circumstances. Perhaps we have made too many allowances for her in the past, for the sake of family pride, but certainly we cannot continue in this fashion to the detriment of poor, dear Bunty's happiness. Something must be done, and quickly. She despises this man, this Ralph Powney, to such an extent that she is actually prepared to lie, to ruin her own reputation. She must either submit herself to a marriage she does not want, or cast herself out as a pariah from society by declaring herself pregnant with your child.'

'What? But I haven't seen her in months. How can she be?'

Cissie said, 'Exactly,' as if she understood perfectly about such things.

Vera stoutly continued, ignoring the interruption. 'Bunty has, in fact, admitted to her mother that she lied, that she is not carrying your child, but swears she'll repeat the tale tomorrow anyway, in church, as a just cause and impediment why the marriage cannot go ahead. Shout

469

it out loud if necessary. And how can it be proved otherwise, that she is still a maid?'

'I'm afraid she's not that,' Callum ruefully admitted, and the two maiden ladies exchanged a significant glance. Vera hunkered down beside him, while Cissie settled herself comfortably on a stone. As Vera talked, her sister plucked strands of duckweed out of his hair.

'If what you tell us is true, Callum, then is it also true about the abortion? You can be honest and open with us. I assure you we will not fall into a decline.'

Callum took a breath, put a stop to Cissie's grooming and set about putting his side of the story. 'Bunty claimed that her mother forced her to get rid of the baby. I blamed her. That's why I left her, said I didn't want to see her ever again, because I thought she'd willingly agreed to kill my child.'

Cissie clucked her tongue in sympathy. 'It is shocking, I agree: a violation against God. I can understand how hurt you must have been, that she didn't feel able to tell you.'

'But has it occurred to you,' Vera chipped in, 'that she might have tried to tell you, and failed? Or at least have badly wanted to. Lucy was determined, at all costs, to keep you two love birds apart. It would surely not have been beyond her to destroy your letters, Bunty's too.'

'Oh, she must have done, I agree.' And now Callum looked shamefaced. 'I accused Bunty of not trying hard enough to get a letter to me.'

'Yet you couldn't get one to her?'

He shook his head, looking increasingly hang-dog. 'No, and apparently Lucy threatened to have me sacked, or horsewhipped, if Bunty *did* try to contact me.'

Vera made a sound that was quite indescribable. 'Then if the poor girl did indeed fall pregnant with your child, and lose it in that despicable manner, then we know – we all of us know – that poor, darling Bunty would never willingly choose such a terrible thing to happen to her unborn infant.'

Callum was staring at the muddy ground in abject misery. Why hadn't he seen that for himself, instead of being blinded by rage and remorse? And because of his selfishness, in thinking only of himself and of what he'd lost, he'd very nearly lost Bunty too. 'Yes, I can see that now. I was too hasty. I condemned Bunty for something she had no control over, when she was perfectly innocent. I should have stopped to think.'

Again he wiped a hand over his face. This time Vera suspected he was sweeping away tears. Very kindly and quietly she said, 'You have watched your mother pull herself up by her boot straps more than once, have you not?' Taking his silence for assent, she continued in a more robust tone, 'Then you must do the same. You must consider carefully, Callum, what is to be done about all of this.'

Cissie eagerly added for good measure, 'Bunty needs your help, dear boy. Do you still love her, that is the question?'

The power of their combined gaze, the way they each seemed to be holding the same breath, brought his head up with a jerk. 'Of course I still

471

love her. Love isn't something you can switch off, like an electric light bulb.'

Vera sat back on her heels with a gusty sigh of satisfaction. Cissie clapped her hands with joy. 'Exactly what I hoped to hear.'

'We will need to be move quickly,' Vera reminded him. 'There is little time to be lost. Bunty is at this very moment locked in her room, and tomorrow at noon she is to be wed.'

There was little hope of releasing her from a locked room, not with Lucy keeping a tight hold of the key. Once Bunty reached the church, the deed would be practically done and Callum didn't dare leave it so late. What if something went wrong and he didn't get there in time? The aunts agreed. Their best chance to execute a rescue was during the mayhem of dressing and preparation beforehand.

'Guests will be arriving and everyone will be milling around. That must be our most likely opportunity.'

Vera elected to snatch a moment to whisper a word about their plan in Bunty's ear, tell her she must find some excuse to take a stroll in the garden, where Callum would be waiting. The pony and trap, they decided, was far too slow a means of transport and so Callum was instructed to borrow a motor car. No easy task. Not even Toby was rich enough to own one of those.

This proved to be a major stumbling block and, in the end, the only solution Callum could come up with was to use Lucy's own car. Cissie promised to 'borrow' the keys which Lucy kept on her dressing table.

In the event, Cissie's courage failed her at the last moment, but she did succeed in keeping Lucy satisfactorily occupied with meaningless chatter that irritated her beyond endurance, trapping her in the hall behind a barrier of noisy spaniels all jumping about excitedly waving their muddy paws while Vera stole swiftly upstairs and lifted the key from the little china tray.

Lucy was going nearly demented. 'Cissie, I really don't have time to stand here and listen to your stupid concerns about leaving your damned dogs for an hour or two! Lock them in the cellar for all I care, but stop them from barking and jumping up at me, for God's sake.'

'Oh, indeed, I'm so sorry, Lucy.' And getting a signal from Vera, who had by this time slipped out unnoticed into the garden, keys in pocket, Cissie whistled for her dogs and fled.

Callum secreted himself in the hawthorn hedge where he sat shivering on this cold October morning for what seemed like hours. The sky was overcast, a fine drizzle starting, and he was racked with nerves. Where was she? When would she step out into this small, untidy garden? What if she was prevented from doing so, for some reason? What if Vera didn't get hold of the keys? What if the car wouldn't start? Engines could be so temperamental.

And then Vera suddenly and silently emerged from the undergrowth, her head swathed in a scarf, and thrust out her hand.

'The key,' she whispered hoarsely as she handed

it over, then vanished back into the undergrowth, offering no further advice or information. Nothing but a huge wink.

Callum was impressed by the aunts' efficiency, but still in an agony over Bunty's continued absence. Where was she, for God's sake?

Unbeknown to him, Lucy and Bunty were engaged in another ding-dong war of words, this time over shoes of all things. Lucy was insisting that Bunty wear blue satin, to match the ribbons on the gown, while Bunty had got caught up in the argument and was insisting on cream suede.

Vera shot her a furious glance which spoke volumes, a what-does-it-matter-what-colour-the-shoes-are-since-you-aren't-going-to-go-through-with-this-wedding? sort of look.

'Right, have it your way then,' Bunty said, in a fret. 'Blue it is. I really don't care one way or the other, and you're getting me so upset, I can't think. I shall be in tears any minute and then my face will be all blotchy and look horrid for my own wedding.'

'Don't you dare to cry, not when I've hired a most expensive photographer,' came her mother's swift rejoinder.

'I'm going out into the garden then, for a breath of fresh air.'

Lucy glanced out of the window. 'It's starting to rain. You'll get your hair wet.'

'I don't *care!* I just need space to breathe. I feel quite light-headed. And sick. Pregnancy has that effect on people, you know. Do you want me to vomit all down my wedding gown?'

'Bunty, stop this. Behave!' Lucy had to confess

474

that the stupid girl did not look at all well, fever-bright cheeks set in her ashen face. 'You should be getting dressed. Put on your gown this minute, and I'll bring you a glass of something to soothe you.'

'But then I'll get mud on it when I walk around the garden, and I insist upon having some air or I shall pass out! There are too many people in this tiny house, too much noise. I need five minutes, that's all. Five minutes of clear, fresh Lakeland air, then I'm all yours.' So saying, she marched out of the door, chin held high.

'Daughters!' Lucy cried. 'They really are the very devil.' She was about to go after her when Vera suddenly remembered an urgent problem in the kitchen concerning the canapes that Lucy had lovingly prepared herself.

The wedding breakfast was to be held at the County Hotel later in the day, but early guests would be regaled with drinks and appropriate titbits before the ceremony began, to stave off any possible hunger and put everyone in a celebratory mood.

'I think one of the spaniels ate a plateful.'

'What? Drat those dogs. I'll have the damned things put down.' Lucy rushed off to the kitchen, very possibly to carry out her threat.

'Poor Cissie,' Vera muttered to herself, as she heard Lucy call out her name. 'Never mind, all in a good cause.'

Vera could see very little out of the window as it was by this time raining quite hard. Nothing but a blur of colour and movement that seemed to merge into one down by the hedge and remain there for a frighteningly long time. 'Oh, do hurry, please.' She sent up a silent, hasty prayer that the pair would not linger in their embrace, but make haste to get away as safely and swiftly as they could. They couldn't hear her anxious muttering, of course, yet she felt compelled to continue, 'Bunty, Callum, I beg you. Run, run!'

Listening intently, Vera thought she detected the sound of a car engine starting up and smiled secretly to herself. Then, wiping the hint of a tear from her eye, she set off in pursuit of Lucy, and to offer her support to Cissie in her hour of need.

The day of the grand opening had finally arrived, and Kate still hadn't seen Toby. He hadn't come near, not to help with the final preparations, nor this morning on the day itself. Callum hadn't turned up either. The sky was clear and sunny after what had been a miserably damp week, so at least the weather was improving.

'The sun may be shining but it looks like we'll be on our own,' Kate sadly remarked to Flora. 'Let's hope the good weather encourages a few shoppers at least.'

She glanced across at her silent daughter, apparently engrossed in the morning newspaper, which was unusual in itself, but then she noticed that the girl's face had gone all pinched and white. Flora, young as she was, tried a brave smile. 'I reckon that's the least of our worries, Mammy. Have you seen this?'

'What is it?'

'I think this is all my fault. Oh, Lord, it must be.'

'All what is your fault? What are you talking about?' Kate took the paper from her. The headline blazed out at her and Kate recoiled in shock.

*Mad Woman Opens Shoe Shop.*

She had to sit down since her knees had given way. The article went on to describe how Kate Tyson, widow of Eliot Tyson, former proprietor of Tysons Industries, a well known shoe manufacturer situated in the beautiful Lake District, had spent almost a year in an asylum.

Following the death of her husband in a tragic road traffic accident and the bankruptcy of his business, Mrs Tyson appears now to have left Kendal behind her and is turning her attention to Manchester's needs. She has opened a new shoe shop on Stretford Road. But is Manchester ready to buy its shoes from a known lunatic? Can she be trusted to serve the ladies of our fine city with calm and decorum, or will they be subjected to all manner of abuse and hysterics?

The article continued in the same vein, but Kate could read no more.

It was crystal clear what had happened. It didn't need her sobbing daughter to explain or apologise for how she'd inadvertently let slip a few facts in their short, telling conversations; sufficient for Theo Ingram to discover Kate's true identity and take his revenge by exposing her colourful past.

'To hell with him,' Kate said, hugging Flora close. 'To hell with the lot of 'em. Let's get going, we have a shop to open.'

Kate had little hope of any custom at all that day following that piece of shocking news. She was more hurt and disappointed that Toby had apparently let her down, and wouldn't be there to offer his support when she most needed it. Callum too was noticeable by his absence. Not even a good luck card to wish her well. What was wrong with them all?

Not a single customer walked through the door of the shop all morning. Kate did think at one time that she caught a glimpse of Theo Ingram hovering about outside, but when she went out to check there was no sign of him.

'Just as well, I'd've pulverised the nasty, interfering bugger.' The little celebratory party was due to start at one o'clock but Kate was certain by this time that no one would turn up, neither customers nor her new business associates. Besides, it was raining now. She set out a few sandwiches and glasses of sherry, but didn't expect any takers.

She was proved entirely wrong. At one o'clock precisely it was as if someone had fired a starting pistol. People simply poured in: neighbours and local shopkeepers, business associates, reporters from other local newspapers, no doubt all anxious for an even juicier story, and customers by the score. They came, Kate decided, out of curiosity.

'Perhaps they've never seen an escaped lunatic before,' she whispered to Flora. But her daughter was far too busy serving a plump lady with a pair of stylish dancing shoes.

'May I try on those with the button bar?' said a polite voice at her side.

'Of course, madam.'

'I rather like those pink silk evening slippers with the pretty design on the heel,' said another.

'Do you have any brown lace-ups in my size? My feet are quite tiny.'

And so it continued for the entire afternoon. Kate and Flora were rushed off their feet. People may have come to gawp, to drink Kate's sherry and see what someone who had spent almost a year in an asylum looked like, but they stayed to buy.

Attracted by the display of smart, stylishly designed shoes, the gossiping ladies simply couldn't resist and spent a great deal of money. And as she served them and took their cash, Kate found the odd moment to answer questions put by curious reporters, even promised one a proper interview later.

There didn't seem any point in secrecy any more. 'Besides, all publicity is good publicity. Isn't that what they say?'

Flora gave a little giggle, not really having time for much else.

And then, to Kate's utter joy, Toby strode in. Something kicked inside her chest, reminding her how very much she had wanted him to come. Wearing a dark suit and tie with a pristine white shirt, he looked so good, every inch the successful businessman, even if his shock of fair hair was as untidy as ever. 'Excuse me,' she said to her current customer. 'I must just say hello to someone. Try these while I'm gone. The bow will suit your

479

slender foot. I won't be a moment. Toby!'

She ran to him, wanting him to sweep her up into his arms and hug her, to say that he forgave her for her little indiscretion, that they were still friends. Kate realised, in that instant, she wanted them to be much more than that, and perhaps she'd spoiled her chances and it was too late. She wanted him to congratulate her on having a shop crowded with customers, her small opening party having turned into a resounding success. But he wasn't even smiling.

When she finally reached him, pushing her way through the crowd, he grabbed her by the hands and said, 'You must come. Bunty didn't get married after all. She ran off with Callum. Now he's been arrested for abduction, stealing a car, and murder!'

# 48

It was awful. Absolutely terrible. Kate couldn't take in what he was telling her. Apparently, Callum and Bunty had eloped a mere hour or two before she was due to marry another man. And no wonder, since Ralph Powney was old enough to be her father. Kate might have rejoiced at her son's determination to win the girl he loved, except that Lucy, being Lucy, had not been prepared to leave it at that.

She'd called the police, insisted they give chase. As they travelled back to Kendal together by express train, Toby went on to explain: 'The police refused at first to get involved, saying that since the girl was of age and Callum twenty, it was no concern of theirs. But then Lucy accused him of stealing her car.'

'I'm sure he only borrowed it,' Kate scoffed.

'Exactly what the police said, so she gave them her soulful look ... you know the one, it neatly disguises the depth of her fury. She told them that it wasn't the first time he'd borrowed her motor, that he'd taken it once before and used it to kill his own father.'

Kate gasped, 'She's lying! Surely the police didn't fall for it?'

'Hook, line and sinker. She explained, with heartbreaking accuracy how much Callum had hated Eliot; how he'd resented the fact that he was adopted, and how Eliot had not given him any proper role in the business except to put him to work as an apprentice. She made no mention, of course, of her own part in their relationship, of how she'd abducted Callum as a child and left him in the Union workhouse. So, yes, they believed every word. To be fair, I don't think they had any choice. They set off in pursuit and the young pair were apprehended long before they reached the border.'

'Callum didn't kill Eliot. He wouldn't – couldn't – do such a dreadful thing. He's innocent. This is all one of Lucy's tricks.'

'I agree. You understand that. I understand that. But will anyone else?'

'Then we have to find who was driving her car that night. We have to find who did kill Eliot.'

Kate was permitted a short visit with her son, who was still being held in Kendal police station while a statement was taken, questions asked and the matter properly investigated. The cogs of justice had been set in motion and nothing could be done to stop them. They had little more than twenty-four hours' grace in which to prove his innocence before he was transferred to Lancaster or Carlisle on remand. The thought of her son being taken to prison, put in amongst thieves and genuine murderers, filled Kate with horror. He looked gaunt, his face grey with fatigue and worry. That he might be tried and possibly found guilty of murder was more than she could bear to contemplate right now.

'I'll be hanged by the neck until dead,' Callum said, his young, frightened eyes wide with terror.

'Don't say such a thing. Don't even think it. We'll have you out of here in the shake of a lamb's tail, so we will. Trust us, Callum, it'll be fine. We'll have you released in no time.'

'I don't seem to have much choice. Who else can I trust?'

His mother spoke with brisk authority. 'You asked lots of questions at the time, about the accident. Tell us briefly what you found out. Who did you see? What exactly did you discover?'

Callum told them again about how he'd discovered an old woman, called Edith who claimed to have seen a black car parked at the end of her street on numerous occasions, including the day in question. 'Her neighbour agreed but was unable, or unwilling, to tell us anything about the driver.

Then Edith disappeared, vanished off the face of the earth, her whole family doing a moonlight flit.'

'Now I wonder who persuaded them to do that,' said Kate sourly.

They were allowed twenty minutes, nowhere near enough, and then Kate and Toby were ushered out of the police station and Callum was locked back in his cell.

Kate and Toby sat in a corner of the Rifle Man's and had a long and agonising discussion over what needed to be done. It seemed that any differences between them had faded into insignificance against this more serious issue. Nevertheless, Kate felt the need to say something. She couldn't bear the thought of Toby thinking badly of her.

'I'm sorry about Ingram. You were right, he was a slimy toad. I nearly made a bad mistake.'

'This isn't the time to be worrying about that,' Toby said, rather sharply, making her feel more foolish than ever.

'What are we going to do about this? I can't think, can you?'

The police failed at the time to find Edith, or any other witness to the accident, found no evidence of any kind, so how could they possibly hope to succeed now?

'They didn't even check Lucy's car until it was too late, until after she'd had the crumpled wing smoothed out and the broken headlamp fixed.'

Toby looked across at Kate, considering these remarks with a thoughtful frown. 'Who did that for her? Which garage would she use to repair the car?'

Kate gave a bitter little laugh. 'She would never risk using a local garage. She'd go somewhere she wasn't known, unless...' A thought occurred to her. 'There is one person she might have asked for help. I'm trying to remember if Callum said something about that, but I reckon it would be worth having a wee word with our old friend Ned Swainson.'

Swainson was not particularly pleased to see them. They'd had trouble finding him, trawling the streets of Kendal half that Sunday morning, since his living quarters were now little more than a filthy shack, a tumbledown shed made from bits of packing cases and cardboard, situated quite close to what had once been Poor House Lane, the place where his reign of terror had begun.

The Cock and Dolphin, where Millie's husband Clem used to warm his heart, was still there, as were the glebe lands of the church opposite and the wooded grounds of Abbot Hall beyond, but the narrow yard that had been Poor House Lane was now no more. The workhouse which had given it its name had long since been demolished, along with the stinking cottages it had harboured. A new world was dawning, where such horrors would no longer be tolerated.

Kate tried to find some pity in her heart for Swainson, still stuck firmly in the past, but it was a struggle. She remembered only too well how he had abused Tysons' women workers, had reduced her own friend Millie to a thin shadow of her former self. Even to this day she refused to talk about it. There had been no hope of escape from his clutches, not if the women wanted to hold on to their jobs and carry on bringing in money to feed their starving families.

Some of the younger ones, fearful of telling their husbands what he did to them since it might cost them their marriage as well as their jobs, had found running away or even suicide their only means of escape.

Kate had been the first to stand up to him, and he'd hated her for that, had been hell-bent on a path of revenge ever since, even to the extent of destroying her, if he could. She'd never seen her brother Dermot since the day Swainson beat him to a pulp, near drowned him and drove him out of town back to Ireland. Oh, and didn't she miss him sorely? When this was over, wouldn't she take the ferry to Ireland and see him again?

What part this evil man had played in Lucy's schemes, Kate didn't care to contemplate. He'd kept a finger pressed hard down on the pulse of her life for far too long. It was long past time to lop it off.

Toby put a hand on her arm, silently urging her to remain in the doorway and not venture into this hovel. Kate had no intention of doing so. The stink of it was making her feel giddy from here. Perhaps Swainson himself was adding to the offensive odour. He certainly didn't appear to have enjoyed a good wash in a long while, and most of the food he'd recently eaten seemed to have left its mark on his black stuff trousers and that so-familiar checked waistcoat.

Now he regarded her with bloodshot eyes, a tell-tale bottle of whisky clutched tightly in his hand. 'What the hell brings you here, turning up like a bad penny?'

'And the top of the morning to you too,' Kate said, in her cheeriest, most Irish brogue. 'You haven't forgotten who I am then?'

'Wish I could. You lost me the best job I've ever had, ruined me life you did.'

'I reckon we're about even there, or you might be a bit ahead, but we're about to change all of that. We're here to help you make reparation for your sins, as ye might say. Won't it stand ye in good stead when you come face to face with St Peter at them pearly gates?'

A grunt was Swainson's only response.

'No, thank you, I'll not sit down if it's all the same to you,' continued Kate, eyeing the wooden crates and boxes that made up his furniture as if he'd offered her a velvet divan to sit upon. 'It'll not take more'n a minute to state our business. You know Mr Lynch here, manager of Tysons Shoes, now operating under new ownership?'

Another grunt, which might have been an acknowledgement.

'What we have to say to you is with regard to that terrible accident which befell my lovely husband. You do remember Eliot, of course you do. Well, my son...' At this point Kate faltered, emotion suddenly choking her, but only for a moment. Straightening her spine, she went on, 'Without going into too much detail, the fact of the matter is that my son has been arrested for his murder. The police have been informed that it was Callum driving the car that night. Now you and I both know that was not the case. He is innocent in all of this. We are both aware who the guilty party is, but we also know how difficult it is to prove. The police have tried to discover the culprit, and failed once already.'

'That accident were nowt to do wi' me. Don't try and pin this one on me.'

Despite Toby's warning, Kate did now step into the shack. She'd endured worse places in the past. She wanted to look this man in the eye. 'What we're needing, you see, is some way to get my lad out of jail. You'll appreciate that I'm not too bothered how I achieve that.'

Kate saw panic register in his mean little eyes. 'I've told you, I did nowt.'

She smiled at him then, and the brilliant warmth of it, false though it might be at this juncture, stunned him. His hand had begun to shake and he set down the whisky bottle, fished a dock-end out of his waistcoat and began to search for matches.

Kate waited until he had the cigarette alight and had stuck it in the corner of his mouth before she quietly remarked, 'That's the biggest porky I ever heard. I'm no fool, Swainson, and realise you must have been the one to get the car mended. Did you take it somewhere it wouldn't be recognised, so it could be made good as new? And I expect...'

He interrupted her, 'I don't need no garage. I can fix such things meself. I'm good wi' me hands, I'll have thee know.' He held them up, as if to prove his point. They were stained with nicotine, black with dirt, criss-crossed with scars and horn-hard.

A small silence followed, long enough for

Swainson to appreciate how pride in his own ability had tripped him up. 'Of course you are,' Kate agreed, her voice soft and encouraging. If getting his help meant flattering the bastard, she'd do it, so she would.

'You were used by Lucy, same as we all were. You were every bit as much her victim as I was, as Callum is now. Isn't that the truth? Although I dare say she paid you for that little service.'

'Not enough! Nowhere near enough, not for the risks I took for the bloody woman. Then when she'd got rid of you, packed you off to the mad-house and got herself nicely settled at Tyson Lodge, she dropped me like a hot potato. Had to squeeze every last penny out of her I could, but she still didn't pay me what was due.'

'Of course she didn't. This is Lucy we're talking about. Why would she, when she needs every last penny for herself?' Kate stepped closer, aware of a quick, indrawn breath from Toby behind her, who was clearly concerned for her safety. Kate folded her arms, smiled again and tried not to breathe in too deeply. 'It must have been harder still for you when the factory went bankrupt. I hope you aren't expecting any more money from her, because you'll never get it. Even if she succeeds in marrying poor Bunty off to some rich suitor, no money will come in your direction, you can be sure of that.'

'Why the bleedin' hell do you think I'm living in this midden? This is all her fault, the nasty piece of shite.'

'So you would not be against getting your own back? Settling a few old scores for her ill treatment of you?'

The silence this time was heavy with tension, Swainson's eyes narrowed against a thin curl of smoke threading up into his greasy hair from the cigarette butt clenched between his thin lips.

'Well? Wouldn't you like to see her suffer for a change?'

He removed the cigarette and tossed it to the dirt floor where it smouldered dangerously for a moment before he finally pressed his booted foot on it. 'I'd like to string her up meself.'

The police came for her shortly before breakfast on Monday morning. Lucy was irritated to be so disturbed when she was about to sit down to grapefruit and kippers. A cup of fragrant coffee had already been poured for her.

'Constable Brown, Sergeant, this is remarkably early for you. Whatever it is, it will have to wait,' she imperiously informed them. 'I could call into the station later today, if there are matters still to be discussed.'

'We'd rather you came with us now,' said the sergeant. 'I'm sure you'll be happy to assist us with our investigations.'

'I shall finish my breakfast first,' Lucy snapped.

'No, Mrs Tyson, I think not. There are a few important questions we'd like answering. And time, as they say, is of the essence.'

'Oh, very well,' Lucy said. 'I shall be heartily glad when this whole business is over and done with.' Turning to the aunts, who were wide-eyed with curiosity, she instructed them to keep Bunty within doors. 'And do keep my kippers warm.

I'm sure this won't take long.'

In that surmise she was to be bitterly disappointed. Once at the station, the police calmly informed her that they'd spent the previous afternoon being presented with fresh evidence which had thrown new light on to the entire sequence of events. 'Your friend Ned Swainson has been singing like a canary, probably desperate to save his own neck.'

Shock registered on Lucy's face, in a slackening of the muscles around her mouth, a snap of the neck as her chin jerked upward. 'There must be some mistake. Swainson is no friend of mine.'

'So he informs us. Nevertheless, he has been most helpful with our enquiries, describing certain tasks he carried out for you. Something to do with several dead rats. Do you recall anything of the sort?'

'Absolute nonsense! There were only two, in point of fact, not several. Swainson always did love to exaggerate.'

'Ah, so you do remember? You and he are indeed acquainted.'

Lucy had begun to shake. 'No, of course we aren't. I am simply referring to an unfortunate infestation which upset my sister-in-law, who was out of her mind with grief already. Whatever else he may have told you is a lie ... *a lie*, I say! He has done nothing but make a nuisance of himself. I should have made an official complaint.'

'Indeed. A nuisance in what way, might I ask?'

Lucy's lip curled. 'Insinuating himself into my life, pestering me.'

'It isn't true then that you were offering him

favours in lieu of cash for these certain matters he carried out for you?'

Her face bleached of all colour. 'How dare he suggest such a thing? We had no dealings of any kind.'

The sergeant held up his note pad. 'Then let us check his evidence, see if we can jog your memory. Item one, repairing of a damaged car wing and headlamp following the fatality on Aynam Road. Item two, disposal of a witness to said accident. Item three – now this one I find particularly distasteful – placing a small amount of rat poison in a child's milk drink. Flora is, I believe, the girl's name. That could have turned very nasty indeed, don't you agree? One grain too much and...' The sergeant shook his head, clicked his tongue and grimaced.

Panic gripped Lucy, fogged her thoughts. 'It was him, not me. He's the guilty party. It was all Swainson's idea. He drove the car, not me.'

'Ah, so you are now saying that the driver was not Callum O'Connor, after all, but Swainson?'

'Yes! No!' Lucy could no longer think straight. Fear and panic had muddled her thought processes. Which man to blame? Her desire to condemn both, and save herself, created total confusion. The questions fired at her over the next half-hour distracted and infuriated her all the more.

Yet the sergeant relentlessly continued, in his calm, matter-of-fact manner. 'To sum up, we believe you were the driver of that vehicle. It was you who drove the car that day. *You* who deliberately knocked down your brother-in-law in order

491

to inherit as much of Tysons Industries as you could get your greedy hands on. To this end, you also attempted to frighten your sister-in-law by leaving rats about the place and making her child ill, then by implying that she was mad and having her incarcerated in an asylum for a period of almost a year.'

'She is *not* my sister-in-law! Kate O'Connor is a dirty little whore from Poor House Lane.' Lucy was on her feet, shrieking and screeching her fury at the sergeant. 'Eliot had no right to marry her, no *right* to bring her into our house and deprive my children of their rightful inheritance in favour of that brat of hers. I'm *glad that I killed him*, do you hear? *Glad!* He deserved to die for betraying us.'

As the silence lengthened in the room, only then did it dawn on Lucy to what she'd confessed, and she let out a horrified wail.

She didn't hear the words of the charge, never felt the handcuffs as they were clicked on to her plump wrists, she was far too intent on screaming out her innocence to the high heavens. Sadly, no one was listening to her, since her undoubted guilt would take her to the gallows where she would be hanged by the neck until dead.

'I can hardly believe it, but it's all over at last,' Kate said, on a sigh of relief.

She and Toby had collected Callum from the police station cells and taken him home to Heversham where there'd been a touching reunion between him and Bunty. Now they were in the garden, enjoying a breath of welcome fresh air after all the trauma.

'All over and done with, at last, except for that dreadful Elvira Crombie of course. I mean to have her defrocked, charged with assault, removed from her post, whatever one does to dragons of her ilk who take pleasure in hurting the innocent. You'll help me, Toby, won't you?'

'It will be my pleasure.'

There was a small silence. 'And after we've slain the dragon, what then? You've no other little project in mind?'

'Only a wedding, mebbe,' Kate said, watching the young couple stroll off together into the evening dusk, a soft smile on her lips. 'Sure, and I adore weddings. We'll have a really good do. Irish jigs, the lot. Don't those two love birds deserve the very best after all they've been through?'

Toby slid an arm about her waist to pull her close. 'I don't suppose you'd consider making it an even more special event, by turning it into a double wedding?'

She lifted her face to his, eyes bright with love. 'You know, I never thought you'd ask.'

'And what have you to say, now that I have?'

Kate regarded him in silence for a moment, then remembering his own reaction when she'd told him about the shoe shop she planned to open, said, 'About bloody time.'

The publishers hope that this book has given you enjoyable reading. Large Print Books are especially designed to be as easy to see and hold as possible. If you wish a complete list of our books please ask at your local library or write directly to:

**Magna Large Print Books**
Magna House, Long Preston,
Skipton, North Yorkshire.
BD23 4ND